★★★ SONS OF ★★★
VALOR II
VIOLENCE OF ACTION

Books by Brian Andrews and Jeffrey Wilson
Sons of Valor Series
Sons of Valor
Sons of Valor II: Violence of Action

Tier One Series
Tier One
War Shadows
Crusader One
American Operator
Red Specter
Collateral

Tier One Origins Novellas
Scars: John Dempsey

Books by Alex Ryan
Nick Foley Thriller Series
Beijing Red
Hong Kong Black

Other Titles by Brian Andrews
The Calypso Directive
The Infiltration Game
Reset

Other Titles by Jeffrey Wilson
The Traiteur's Ring
The Donors
Fade to Black
War Torn

ANDREWS & WILSON

★★★ **SONS OF** ★★★

VALOR II

VIOLENCE OF ACTION

**BLACK
STONE**
PUBLISHING

Printed in the United States of America

First edition: 2022
ISBN 978-1-0940-9353-6
Fiction / Action & Adventure

Version 1

CIP data for this book is available
from the Library of Congress

Blackstone Publishing
31 Mistletoe Rd.
Ashland, OR 97520

www.BlackstonePublishing.com

For Bonnie & Peggy
For making us who we are

NOTE TO THE READER

We've provided a glossary in the back of this book to define the acronyms, military lingo, and abbreviations used herein.

PROLOGUE

WOMEN AND CHILDREN'S HOSPITAL

RAMADI, IRAQ

SEPTEMBER 2006

Zain al-Masri leaned into the padded cheek riser fixed to the buttstock of his suppressed Dragunov sniper rifle. Closing his nondominant eye, he sighted through the Russian-made PSO-1 optical sight and scanned the streets of Ramadi from his rooftop hide on the Women and Children's Hospital. It was the perfect location to engage the infidels because it was one of the few places in the city that was off-limits to drone strikes. Oh, how the Americans loved raining hellfire down from above—dealing death from UCAVs circling so high they were all but invisible to the naked eye.

But not here, not today . . .

Targeting a civilian hospital—even one housing jihadis—was something even the unapologetically brazen Americans would not dare do. The optics simply would not permit it, even if the collateral damage was minimal. Which meant Zain could fire with relative impunity from the rooftop without fear of being targeted by air-to-ground missiles from above or RPGs from below. But today's mission was not entirely without risk. The Navy SEALs were deployed in Ramadi and conducting daily raids, and Zain felt positive he was on their kill list.

"I have a Humvee," his spotter, Ahmed, said beside him. "To the west, fifteen degrees south of where you're looking."

Zain didn't say anything, just shifted his scan to that location and saw the American Humvee stopped in the middle of an intersection, parked at an angle with armed, uniformed personnel milling about. Using the slope-shaped stadiametric rangefinder in the bottom left corner of his sight, he picked a target—an American Marine—at six hundred meters. Whoever designed this scope was both a pragmatist and a genius, because the simple little reticle tool took all the complicated calculus out of ranging. Just line up the target's head with the bottom of the slope line and then multiply the corresponding number by one hundred meters and you had the range.

He turned the elevation turret two clicks clockwise to compensate for bullet drop. Next, he placed the targeting chevron dead center on the gunnery sergeant's helmet. Senior enlisted personnel were his target of choice. They were the soldiers with the most combat and leadership experience, which was why his boss, Abu Musab al-Zarqawi, paid bonuses for killing E-7 personnel and above. If he executed this shot successfully, it would be Zain's seventh kill and his third bonus. But for him, it wasn't about the money.

With every kill he logged, the name Juba—a celebrated Iraqi sniper who moved like a ghost about the city, murdering American soldiers at will—gained power and esteem. In reality, Juba was fiction. He was not a gifted, lone-wolf sniper as al-Qaeda's propaganda machine suggested, but rather the combined effort of three jihadi snipers all working for al-Zarqawi. With six kills under his belt, twice as many as his brothers, Zain was the undisputed star of the trio. Many of the younger fighters had even taken to calling him by the Juba legend, a practice Zain did not discourage.

What is Juba without me? he thought, applying tension to the trigger. *Someday the truth will be known that I, Zain al-Masri, am the one and true Lion of Ramadi.*

The Dragunov burped and he watched the gunnery sergeant's head snap back violently as the 7N1 variant 7.62×54 mm round punched a hole through the man's helmet. The American warrior dropped like the sack of shit that he was. Zain scanned left, looking for a second target as the Marines scrambled for cover. He worked quickly, sending a bullet whistling into the back of another Marine, striking him between the shoulder blades. The man pitched forward and writhed in agony a few seconds before going still. Zain swept his targeting reticle right, around the front of the Humvee, looking for a third target crouching at the bumper . . . but all the Marines had retreated to the opposite side of the vehicle now. He reversed his scan, dragging his chevron over the passenger side windows.

Finding no new targets inside, anger flared in his chest.

Damn it, I should have been able to get three, he thought, silently chastising himself as he finished his sweep.

"Pull back," Ahmed said. "It's been five seconds."

With a grudging exhale, Zain heeded his spotter's advice and dropped below the half-meter-tall concrete ledge that surrounded the rooftop. He rolled onto his back and, clutching his Dragunov to his chest, stared up at the cloudless blue sky.

"You got two," Ahmed said, grinning from where he lay propped up on his elbows, clutching a pair of binoculars.

Zain didn't reply.

"Was one of them an officer?"

"Gunnery sergeant," Zain answered, his voice all business.

"You're going to get another bonus!" the young man said, making no attempt to contain his enthusiasm.

"You can have it, Ahmed," he said.

"Are you serious?"

Zain nodded. "Yes. You have been a loyal and skilled spotter. We are a team, and as my brother in arms, you should share the reward. I am generous to those who are loyal."

"Thank you, Juba," Ahmed said reverently. "I will follow you anywhere."

Zain turned to look at him—a boy not older than fourteen whose right cheek was marred by a crescent-shaped scar stretching from eye socket to jaw. Seeing the adoration in Ahmed's eyes, epiphany struck. Teamwork, purpose, reward, and recognition . . . these were the keys to building a truly motivated and powerful army. Al-Zarqawi understood this, but the al-Qaeda leader's brutality and sadistic nature undermined most of his efforts. Too many in their ranks feared for their own survival, worried more about losing their lives to the whims of his temper than to the Americans in battle.

Vicious zealots made terrible generals.

Someday, I will lead an Army of Allah. Like Saladin, I will be a noble general . . . a warrior tactician who leads from the front with a gleaming sword instead of from the rear by pointing a rifle at the backs of my soldiers.

"I accept your pledge, but in order to serve me," Zain said, seeing his own destiny clearly for the first time, "I must first teach you how to kill . . . how to kill as I do."

PART I

"No man is worth his salt who is not ready at all times to risk his body, to risk his well-being, to risk his life, in a great cause."

–Theodore Roosevelt

CHAPTER 1

MH-60M HELICOPTER DESIGNATED HAMMER ONE
OVER THE SUROBI DISTRICT
KABUL PROVINCE
AFGHANISTAN
PRESENT DAY
0121 LOCAL TIME

The Special Operations helicopter beat a methodical rhythm across the night sky as it cruised toward the drop zone. For Lieutenant Commander Keith "Chunk" Redman, who was riding in the cargo hold with his team of Tier One Navy SEALs, it was a rhythm steeped in irony. Sometimes, the melodic thrum was a potent lullaby, soothing him into a drowsy stupor. Other times, it was a battle drum, summoning his inner warrior.

It is definitely vector-based, he thought with a smile.

On infil the rhythm stoked his fire.

On exfil . . . sleepy time.

He glanced at his LCPO, Senior Chief Riker, the toughest and luckiest damn SEAL he'd ever had the privilege of serving with. He often joked that Riker's momma must have dipped his naked, redneck baby ass in the River Styx because the dude has walked away from every engagement without injury—like a modern-day Achilles. Chunk had lost track of how many times Riker had been blown up, shot at, or nearly drowned. Further cementing his golden reputation, Riker had been the only one to walk away without a scratch or broken bone from their helo crash in Pakistan while pursuing Hamza al-Saud and a band of al Qadar terrorists on the very first deployment of the newly reconstituted Tier One SEAL Team. God only knew how many times the senior chief had saved Chunk's life over the years, both while they were operating with the white side teams and now at the Tier One. Riker probably had no idea either, because in the teams it wasn't about keeping score or IOUs. In the brotherhood, they always had each other's backs.

Riker looked up while tightening the Velcro straps on his tactical gloves, perhaps feeling his brother and commander's eyes on him. Channeling Ron Burgundy, the senior chief lowered his chin, raised an eyebrow, and said, "Do you know who I am?"

"No, I can't say that I do," Chunk said, playing along.

Riker flashed him a cheesy smile. "I don't know how to put this, but . . . I'm kind of a big deal."

Somehow, this bit between them never got old. "Really?" Chunk said.

"People know me . . ."

"Well, I'm very happy for you," he said, trying not to break character and laugh.

"Listen, can I start over?" Riker said, getting serious.

"Sure."

The SEAL leaned in and squinted at Chunk. "I wanna say something. I'm gonna put it out there. And if you like, you can take it. If you don't, send it right back . . . I wanna be on you."

At this, they both busted up laughing. Was it childish and ridiculous? Yes, it was, but everyone on the team had

Anchorman memorized. Chunk and Riker could have kept it going all the way to the LZ, but one of their teammates interrupted them.

"Dude, Chunk, have you looked outside with the new NVGs?" Trip flipped up his night-vision goggles and swiveled to face Chunk. "It's frigging unbelievable. This tech is a game changer, bro—it's like daytime viz. You gotta take a look."

Chunk looked out the open starboard slider door at the darkened mountain range to the north. The infils were painfully long now, since the US had abandoned Afghanistan, and more dangerous. But he supposed that was part of the job. Adapt and overcome. Afghanistan still harbored terrorists and it was still his job to capture or kill them. He tipped his NVGs down over his eyes and watched the landscape transform from night to day. Gone was the typical greenish-gray monochrome with the high-contrast ghosting and pixelated graininess he was used to. In its place, these new NVGs used special optics and an advanced processor to render a high-definition, full-color view of the battle space. If that wasn't badass enough, both the visible and infrared spectrums were also processed, to aid in discerning friend from foe.

Chunk turned back to look inside the Blackhawk, scanning down the row of his fellow Gold Squadron operators. "Be the night" was a favorite team expression not because SEALs liked operating in the dark, but because of the supreme tactical advantage of operating under conditions where they could see the enemy but the enemy couldn't see them. Now, with this new rig, Chunk and his boys gained the ability to see color details that were lost to them with traditional NVGs, further upping their game. He looked at Trip.

"And bonus," he said. "I can see that chunk of bacon stuck in your teeth that I totally would have missed otherwise."

Before Trip could clap back at him, the Blackhawk pilot jumped in.

"Thor, Hammer—five mikes out," the Army captain said over the comms channel.

"Roger, Hammer," Chunk replied. Then he switched channels and relayed the message to analyst Whitney Watts and Petty Officer Michelle Yi, who were manning the Tactical Operations Center at their new JSOC FOB in Tajikistan. "Asgard, Thor—five mikes."

"Thor, Asgard—check," Watts replied. He could practically hear the cringe in her voice at the Marvel-inspired call signs selected by Jamey Edwards—the team's comedian and comic book expert in residence.

"Any changes at the target compound?" Chunk asked.

"Negative. Still looking very sleepy. We have good eyes with Munin in orbit at twenty-five thousand feet." The mythological Nordic raven was the call sign for the Reaper drone circling above them.

"Check," he said.

Beside him, Saw, the team's sniper, lifted the silver cross he wore on a chain around his neck and pressed it to his lips before disappearing it back inside his shirt. Chunk watched the man's mouth move in silent prayer, and he was pretty sure he read the names of Saw's wife, Ellie, and his son and daughter on his lips. Across the aisle, Riker ran his hands over his kit, checking his gear by feel and seemingly finding everything in place. Chunk followed suit, checking his own loadout, while Trip bounced his heel up and down against the deck in anticipation.

"Sixty seconds, Thor," the pilot said.

"Check." Chunk scooted to the edge of the canvas bench seat next to one of two massive green bags that held a three-by-three-foot block of coiled rope with one end clipped to an overhead stanchion just inside the door. "All right, fellas, just like we briefed. This is a quick in and out. We're not here to take crows or collect intel. We know who these assholes are already. Our only objective is to get our man out of this Taliban hornet's nest before he has a very bad day."

"Hooyah, let's get some," Riker said and slid into position to act as rope master and direct traffic.

Chunk felt the Blackhawk flare into a static hover.

"Hammer is Bifrost," the helo pilot reported, calling the drop zone waypoint. Chunk pictured the Army captain rolling his eyes as he said it.

Riker shoved the starboard-side rope bag—aided by a kick from Chunk—out the side of the helo. Chunk immediately slid off the bench and into a seated position on the deck, his legs dangling in the air as the bag tumbled toward the ground twenty-five feet below. He grabbed the rope with both gloved hands, twisted them inward to tighten his grip, and pinned the line between the arches of his right and left boots. Then, with a scoot of his ass, he dropped out the door and into the night.

Controlling his rate of descent with pressure and friction, Chunk landed on the hard-packed, dusty earth mere seconds later. He quickly stepped clear of the rope and moved left, bringing his rifle up to scan for threats. Behind him and three meters to his right, SEALs touched down with alternating precision and synchronicity on the port and starboard ropes in the middle of a swirling cloud of dust thrown up by the Blackhawk's rotor wash. When the last member of the eight-man strike force had landed, the Blackhawk dropped the ropes and bugged out—heading south, where it would loiter until exfil.

One by one, his seven teammates called, "Clear."

Chunk checked the compass on his Suunto wristwatch,

then chopped a hand north. The terrorist compound sat two miles away in the Surobi valley, located south of the Kabul River, which was dammed a few miles east. That's where the intel geeks believed that an American serviceman, PFC Louis Gonzalez, was being held. Al-Qaeda were using Gonzalez as a bargaining chip to broker the release of ten al-Qaeda fighters held in a detention center in Jordan by the US government. Three of the terrorists were particularly dangerous fighters who had been rounded up by US Special Operations Forces over the last three months before the fall of Kabul and whose release was simply nonnegotiable. The Taliban, who now ran the country, were predictably no help. And so, it was time for the Tier One SEALs to do what they did best: recover the hostage and kill some bad guys to make them think twice before grabbing another American.

In Chunk's mind, tonight's mission was a mixed bag.

On the plus side, Watts had a high degree of confidence that Gonzalez was alive. Proof of life was three days old, but that didn't worry Chunk. The terrorists wanted their jihadi brothers back and would keep Gonzalez alive as long as necessary to achieve that goal. Tonight Gold Squadron wouldn't be hitting a dry hole—of that much he was certain.

In the minus column sat precedent. When you've been at war with somebody for twenty years, you learn a thing or two or a hundred about the other side. America and the Taliban, who no doubt aided al-Qaeda despite their public rhetoric, understood each other intimately—motives, tactics, and policy. Both sides continued to run their rhetoric engines at redline, pumping out clouds of verbal exhaust, but the leadership on both sides saw through the smog of war. The Taliban and their al-Qaeda friends knew Special Warfare was coming for Gonzalez . . . maybe not when, maybe not how, but they knew, and that made tonight's mission all the more dangerous. Chunk didn't have to remind his guys of this fact. They understood it, and the underlying tension in their movements was proof.

The drop zone was in the middle of a dry riverbed, a snowmelt-fed tributary that dumped into the Kabul River. It snaked along the foot of a five-mile-long, low mountain ridgeline on the east side of the valley that ran directly past the target compound. Chunk's team moved silently, in two modified arrowhead formations, up either side of the dry riverbed. All the ass-grabbing and verbal bullshitting ceased the instant boots hit the ground and every SEAL became a stone-cold professional warrior. They advanced north, each man scanning his sector, communicating only with hand signals. Twenty minutes passed in a blur of total concentration before Chunk held up a closed fist. Each of the SEALs took a knee and scanned for threats in their respective sectors.

"Asgard, Thor is Zephyr," Chunk said softly into the boom mike at the corner of his mouth.

"Show you at Zephyr, Thor One," came the reply from the TOC, Watts's voice cool and professional. As a former analyst from NCTC with no field experience, she'd come a long way in an incredibly short time at the Tier One. Coordinating mission packages from a TOC and interfacing directly with operators was a far cry from writing briefs at a desk inside the Beltway. "No new intel to report."

"Check."

With no change in the tactical picture, Chunk split the team at waypoint Zephyr as planned—sending Bravo element northeast to take the high route in the mountains while his Alpha element doglegged northwest across the farmland in the valley. Both approaches afforded cover, albeit by means of wildly different terrain. Chunk's element had waist-high crop cover in the fields and a stand of trees directly west of the compound. Way better than the highland element, led by Lieutenant Spence, who would be forced to hike to a secondary ridgeline to the east to have any cover on the final approach.

While Alpha crossed the riverbed and hit the compound from the west side, Bravo would take the crest and assault from the tactically superior high ground on the east. Prior to kicking things off, the team sniper, Saw, would peel off from Bravo and provide overwatch from a hilltop three hundred feet southeast of the compound—a position that gave him the necessary height and angles to fire over the perimeter wall at each of the five different buildings that made up the complex.

Ten minutes later, as they moved swiftly through the brush, Chunk whispered into his boom mike, "Asgard, Thor One—sitrep?"

"One, Asgard—I count fifteen thermal signatures in and around the compound. Two roving watches walking the perimeter outside the wall, maintaining one-hundred-and-eighty-degree offset and moving counterclockwise. Building One, south and outside the main compound wall, has two signatures—likely the patrol shack with relief watch—both horizontal, presenting as sleeping. Five signatures in Building Two, the target. Four are seated around a table, and one presents horizontal—presumably, this is the package. Building Three, just north, has five signatures. We're not exactly sure what's going on in there, but they appear to be awake."

"Copy. What about the fifteenth signature?" Chunk said, doing the math in his head. "That was only fourteen."

"Number fifteen is inside what looks like a bathroom and, um, he appears to be . . ."

"Appears to be what, Asgard?"

"Masturbating," she said.

Chunk shook his head. "Wonderful, thanks for sharing."

"You asked."

Chunk picked up the pace, leading his four-man element of Riker, Antman, and Trip in a lopsided diamond formation across the field toward the grove of trees that would be their final staging point. Quickstepping in a tactical crouch on this final hundred-meter stretch, his thighs protested with that old familiar burn—the CrossFit equivalent of doing lunges in the gym until your legs give out. Upon reaching the grove, the fire team spread out and pressed up to the tree line, each man sighting over his rifle at the compound.

"Alpha is Ragnarök," Chunk said, really hating these call signs as he reported that his element was in position.

"Copy," Watts said in his ear. "Bravo is still half a click out."

This news did not surprise Chunk, as Spence's team had to make a double ascent, traversing not one but two ridgelines. He pictured the satellite imagery of the region in his mind and tried to imagine the most likely position of the four SEALs still making their grueling infil.

"Bravo is over the second ridge, heading north," Spence said in between heavy breaths. "Ten mikes from calling Ragnarök."

Chunk double-clicked his acknowledgment and shifted in his kneeling stance, grateful that Spence had volunteered for the highland approach.

Nothing to do now but wait . . .

As he scanned the compound, he had to remind himself that he was still viewing the world through NVGs. The full-color photo-realism almost made him forget this was a middle-of-the-night operation. His teammates must have been experiencing the same feeling because Chunk noticed them actually smiling as they scanned over their rifles. Certain camouflage elements that an enemy might use were difficult if not impossible to detect in monochrome night vision. Digital cammie uniforms and camouflage netting were perfect examples—the human eye could parse them in daylight, but they disappeared into the background under low-light monochromic amplification. That wasn't an issue with these X27 NVGs.

After what felt like ten minutes burned, Chunk checked his watch and confirmed his internal clock was still properly calibrated. A moment later Spence radioed in.

"Bravo is Ragnarök," Spence called from two ridgelines over. "Eight is climbing to his perch."

"Check," Chunk replied. He'd keep them in position until Saw was settled in as overwatch.

"Asgard, this is Eight," Saw whispered a minute later. "Do you hold me on thermal?"

Chunk picked up the tension immediately and felt his jaw tighten. *Now what?*

"Roger, Eight," Watts came back. "We see you climbing all by your lonesome to the top of the bowl-shaped rock."

"I think I see something," he said. "Are you detecting a secondary thermal up here with me?"

"Hold, One . . ." Watts said.

"That's a negative, Eight," said a new voice on the line, belonging to Petty Officer Yi. "What do you see?"

"I think there's a sniper up here. It looks like the Talies built an earth-covered sniper nest up here, blocking thermals from above with camo webbing draped over the open sides. Alpha, continue to hold—the second you step out of that tree line, he's gonna cut you down."

"Copy all," Chunk said, turning to look at Riker, who gave him a "looks like we dodged a bullet" thumbs-up.

"Eight, Five—are you going to try to take him yourself?" Spence asked, the exact question on Chunk's mind. "Or do you want a wingman?"

"My goal is to take this dude with stealth, without waking up the neighborhood," Saw said. "So, I could definitely use a second."

"Roger that," Spence said. "Sending Six up to join your party."

"Typical," Edwards chimed in with his trademark ill-timed comic relief. "Always looking to get me capped since I'm better with the ladies than you."

"Check," Saw came back. "Holding for Six."

This new development got the wheels in Chunk's mind spinning. If it was true that this compound was protected by a dedicated sniper using thermal blocking and camouflage to protect his nest against drone surveillance, then it meant the terrorists were ready and waiting for this rescue attempt. It also meant the Taliban were providing direct support to the al-Qaeda terrorists, who wouldn't have access to the stolen technology without them. The sniper could even be Taliban himself. What other tricks did the enemy have up their sleeve? Watts's last sitrep seemed to indicate that twelve of the fifteen thermals in the compound were awake. Why else would they all be up unless they were expecting to boogie?

"Asgard, One—did you catch all of that?" he said into his mike.

"Roger, One, we heard it," Watts said. "We've asked the drone pilot to drop to a lower altitude and circle west to see if we can get a better angle to analyze the sniper nest."

"Any vehicles driving around in the area we need to know about?"

"Negative."

Chunk switched his radio from VOX to PTT so he no longer broadcast to the group and turned to Riker, who was on a knee beside him, scanning his sector over his rifle. "If they're covering the western approach, then that means they understand our tactics. They know this grove is perfect staging cover."

"Yeah, so their sniper cuts us down in no-man's-land when we cross that dry riverbed. That's a hundred and fifty feet of wide-open nothing we gotta traverse."

"And what if the sniper isn't their only defense? What if they've got IEDs buried along the riverbank or just outside the perimeter wall?"

Riker nodded. "There've been five roadside IED explosions in Surobi over the past month. Which means we've got an active maker in town. It's certainly possible."

Chunk lowered his rifle and hung it from its sling while he retrieved a compact tablet computer from his left thigh cargo pocket. He flipped up his NVGs and powered on the tablet with the lowest illumination setting. It revealed a bird's-eye view satellite topography of the compound and surrounding area.

"We're here," he said, pointing to the middle of the trees. "Bravo element is here," he added, pointing to a position east of the compound. He traced his index finger over the riverbed, which formed a one-hundred-and-sixty-degree arc around the compound. "That oxbow is probably eight hundred feet from east to west. It's big, but not too big to load up with IEDs . . . Maybe we shouldn't cross here."

Riker scratched at his beard. "I wouldn't want to cross up there to the north, in case they have a QRF staged or a second sniper in one of those huts on the west side of the river. That would put us in a crossfire."

"Agreed. Which leaves only one choice, which is to back-track south and cross here," Chunk said, pointing at the screen. "We hump it over this first ridge and assault from the south and reposition Bravo element fifty yards farther north. We swap primaries. They hit Building Three, we hit Building Two."

"I like it, but what about Building One? I know it's only two guys, but I don't want to get shot in the back trying to breach Building Two if those dudes wake up."

Chunk tapped one of several grenades fixed to the front of his kit. "We hit it en route."

"We'll lose our stealth," Riker said.

"Yeah, I think we're gonna lose our stealth when Saw and Edwards try to take the sniper."

"Ye of little faith . . ."

"Just sayin'."

"It's a good plan, boss. Let's do it."

Chunk switched his radio back to VOX and said, "Eight and Six, hold on taking that sniper. Alpha is going to reposition first."

A double click in his ear, presumably from Saw, served as a stealthy acknowledgment.

With hand signals, Chunk motioned for his element to follow him as he backpedaled deeper into the grove and then retraced their tracks south. As he did, he gave a quick recap of the revised plan to Spence, as well as Watts and Yi back in the TOC. Nobody challenged his logic, and their exfil bird had plenty of fuel to absorb the slip in the timeline. Once they cleared the grove, Chunk picked up the pace, traversing the field in a hard run. He directed his formation an extra hundred yards south before crossing the dried-up riverbed, just to be safe. Then he led his team up and over the four-hundred-foot incline of the first ridgeline, before vectoring north.

Chunk felt his breath come in long but fast, deep pulls of cool night air. He signaled his teammates with a closed fist and a sweep of his hand to take cover behind a rocky outcropping forty yards from Building One—the sentry hut and southernmost structure of the compound.

"Eight, One—you in position to take that sniper nest?" he said into his boom mike.

A double click in his ear served as confirmation.

"Asgard, sitrep?" Chunk said to Watts.

"The two roving sentries are at the nine o'clock and one o'clock positions, walking the perimeter. You should be able to see the south sentry any minute. No change to personnel activity inside the compound. You're still the night," Watts said. In the short time she'd been with the unit, she'd already picked up the operational lingo and cadence of an operator. Most importantly, however, she'd learned when *not* to talk. The days of her babbling to fill the void were, blessedly, only an annoying memory.

"Check," he said and brought his suppressed SOPMOD M4 up. He steadied it on top of the boulder he was crouching behind and sighted up the valley, waiting for the roving sentry to walk into view. Then, an idea came to him. "Eight, One—stand by. I'm going to take Sentry One and that will be your signal. It should give you a moment of confusion to capitalize on when you take your tango out."

A double click came back from Saw.

Chunk moved his index finger inside the guard and applied tension to the trigger. With his left hand, he switched on his target designator and watched it appear in full color on his X27 night-vision goggles, a green laser streaking across the valley. And that's when all hell broke loose.

A second green targeting laser materialized, streaming west from the rocks above but quickly swiveling toward Chunk's position. A decade of operational experience, combined with finely honed operator reflexes, took over and Chunk dropped into a crouch behind the boulder. A heartbeat later a sniper round whistled past overheard and slammed into the rocks behind him.

"Oh shit," Riker said, looking at him. "That dude was fast."

Chunk glanced up and saw the enemy sniper's infrared beam, green in the world of NVGs, sweeping overhead for a target. "Yeah, and that asshole is wearing NVGs because he saw my fucking IR."

Two suppressed rounds, fired sequentially, echoed from the ridgeline . . . followed a moment later by a third.

"One, Eight—enemy sniper is neutralized. Repeat, enemy sniper is KIA. I'm taking his roost," Saw reported.

"Roger," Chunk said. "Bravo team, reposition north to breach Building Three."

"Check," said Spence in his ear.

"Thor, Asgard," Watts said, her voice tense. "You're blown. The fighters inside are scrambling and repositioning to defensive positions."

"Shit," Chunk growled through clenched teeth, his mind churning through the most likely scenarios of how things would play out. Breaching an alert and actively defended compound was a much different operation than assaulting with the element of surprise. The officer in him wanted to abort the op; the SEAL inside said, *No friggin' way.*

"Eight is Odin," Saw said, announcing to everyone that he was set as overwatch and ready to go to work.

"This op is blown, boss," Riker said, his back still pressed to the boulder, shoulder to shoulder with Chunk. "What do you want to do?"

"Odin, you're cleared to engage," Chunk said, giving Riker his answer.

"Check," Saw said, and Chunk immediately heard the burp of his suppressed sniper rifle going to work. "South sentry's down."

"Dude, there's a lot of Tali-supported al-Qaeda in this city. In ten minutes this place could be swarming with fighters. And I'm not talking a QRF, Chunk. I'm talking about a whole army of assholes here on top of us," Riker said.

His LCPO's warning resonated with Chunk, because of all the SEALs in Gold Squadron, Riker had the highest risk tolerance.

"So what are you saying? We just leave Gonzalez here?"

"Either that or we escalate really fast."

"Building One is clear. Two tangos down," Saw reported, his voice cold iron; he was in the zone now. "Only the north sentry remains, and I don't have eyes on him."

"Five, One—change of plans," Chunk said, his voice ripe with frustration. "Alpha and Bravo are hitting Building Two. Repeat, Alpha and Bravo elements hit Building Two."

"What about Building Three?" Spence came back.

"Asgard, Thor—we need you to put a Hellfire in Building Three," Chunk said into his boom mike, answering Spence's question for everyone.

"Thor, Asgard—say again?" Watts came back, her voice suggesting she'd heard him perfectly but disagreed with the order.

"You heard me, Asgard," he said. "I wanna put a Hellfire in Building Three. We don't have time to screw around."

"One, Five—Bravo team is clear for the strike. Ready to assault Building Two on your mark," Spence reported.

"But what if the package is in Building Three?" Watts protested. "Don't you want to put eyes on before you—"

"I guarantee you the package is not playing cards with his

captors. All the imagery data strongly indicates Gonzalez is in Building Two," Chunk said, cutting her off. "In less than ten minutes these hills are going to be swarming with Taliban. We have one and only one shot at this. Do it now."

"Roger, Thor," she said, her voice going flat. "Issuing the kill order to Raven's Nest."

"Copy, and when you're done, get Hammer heading our way. Exfil in seven minutes." Chunk glanced at Riker, popped to his feet, and chopped a hand forward toward the compound. "Let's go get our man."

CHAPTER 2

AL-QAEDA COMPOUND

SUROBI DISTRICT

KABUL PROVINCE

AFGHANISTAN

0242 LOCAL TIME

Chunk's breath came in pants as he surged his team forward. Upon reaching the corner of the sentry shack, he stopped and glanced around the corner to the south wall of the compound.

It's now or never, Raven, he thought, tightening his grip on his rifle.

"Thor, this is Raven's Nest," the drone pilot said on the comms circuit, reading his mind. "I see y'all on thermal. Be advised you are danger close to the target."

"Copy, Raven's Nest. Understand danger close. This is Thor One—you are cleared hot," Chunk said.

"Roger, Thor. Missile away."

Chunk looked up and watched a streak of orange carve a line across the night sky. Instead of whiting out, his NVGs rapidly compensated for the new light source and processed the imagery. To Chunk, the Hellfire missile looked like it would have during the day—the rooster tail of flame, bright but far from blinding. He watched it streak all the way to the target, turning his head just before impact. The explosion shook the ground and sent a rumble through the mountain canyon that was certain to be heard for miles. A fireball belched skyward as chunks of wood, rock, and earth rained down in a forty-meter radius around the smoking hole that had once been a building with five enemy shooters inside.

"Target destroyed," the drone pilot reported. "Scanning for survivors . . ."

"Five, One—go," Chunk ordered, directing Bravo team to hit Building Two from the east while his element entered the compound from the south.

Legs pumping and boots crunching rock underfoot, Chunk led his three teammates across the open gap between the sentry shack and the earthen perimeter wall.

"Mother, threat assessment?" Chunk said, dropping the annoying Asgard handle for the one he preferred. As Watts spoke, he imagined the bird's-eye heat map imagery she stared at on a wide-screen monitor in the TOC.

"Four KIA in Building Three. One figure is crawling from the wreckage, but he looks to be in a bad way. The north sentry squirted when the Hellfire hit. He's running down the ridgeline northwest, heading for civilization. Three of the four shooters in Building Two have taken defensive positions at the south, east, and west walls. The fourth is holding a gun to another person's head—presumably the package."

"Odin, how are your lines on Building Two?" Chunk asked.

"I have a good line on the east window and the south courtyard inside the wall," Saw said.

"Bravo is holding on the east wall outside the perimeter," Spence reported. "No gate on this side."

Chunk's mind churned like a tactical computer, reworking the breach strategy. The original plan had his element entering the compound via the west wall, where imagery indicated the only perimeter gate was located. But he didn't dare risk going in that way, having convinced himself the west approach was booby-trapped with IEDs. This unusually stout earth-and-stone perimeter wall was too thick for the breacher charges they carried to blow holes in, which meant they'd have to go over the top and face enemy fire from the window shooters.

A suppressed sniper round from the east echoed over the air.

"Fifth tango from Building Three is dead," Saw reported.

"Check," Chunk said and then added, "Bravo, sweep north around the corner. Maybe that Hellfire knocked down the wall on the north side."

"Bravo," Spence came back, signaling acknowledgment.

"Thor, we have a problem," Watts announced. "Two trucks just pulled up to the cluster of houses on the northwest side of the riverbed. Looks like QRF fighters."

"See, I told you that spot was trouble," Riker said, running his tongue between his teeth and his bottom lip where he normally packed a dip.

"How many heat signatures?" Chunk asked.

"Eleven," Watts said. "And one of the trucks looks like it has a technical in the back."

"Shit," Chunk said.

"One, Five—north wall is intact," Spence reported. "But there's a pile of rubble up against it now, so climbing over is going to be easier."

"Bravo, toss smoke over the wall to feint entry, but reposition to the northwest corner and cover down the mountain.

Let's not make it easy for that Tali QRF to get that technical into position."

A double click in his ear served as acknowledgment and Chunk yanked a smoke grenade from the front of his kit. He pulled the pin and tossed it over the wall into the courtyard. Riker, Trip, and Antman did the same and four sequential pops followed as the grenades lit off. A few seconds later, billowing tendrils of dusty-gray smoke began to creep up into view above the wall as the courtyard filled with a tactical haze.

"I got this," Riker said to Chunk, nodding at the top of the wall, conveying his intention to be first over and lead the charge.

"Of course you do," Chunk said.

"Odin, One—Alpha is going over. Give 'em something to think about."

"Check," Saw came back as Trip and Antman clasped hands to form a foot sling and boosted Riker over the seven-foot-tall wall.

Covering fire from Saw's sniper rifle punched loud, ringing holes in the building's corrugated metal roof as Chunk got boosted onto the top of the wall next. Glass shattered and AK-47 gunfire cracked nearby as he flung himself over. He landed hard and off balance, but he rolled out of the fall and up into a kneeling firing stance, sighting at where he guesstimated the south-side window was located. Even their new badass night vision couldn't see through smoke, however, and Chunk didn't have a target.

"Oh, fuck you," he heard Riker growl somewhere ahead, followed by the familiar sound of a double tap from Riker's Sig P229, which Chunk imagined his LCPO fired through the window at close range.

A heavy thud to Chunk's left announced the landing of

Antman or Trip—probably Trip since Antman could scale walls and defy gravity like, well, an ant.

"Thor, Hammer," the Blackhawk pilot's voice said in his ear. "Hammer is eight mikes out."

The prompt got Chunk thinking. The Taliban sniper had seen his IR designator earlier, so he had to assume there could be more than one set of NVGs in the bad guys' hands. They'd left millions of dollars worth of tech in the country during the chaotic withdrawal and it was naive to think the Taliban hadn't shared the bounty with their al-Qaeda friends. Normally, he might consider popping strobes now, but in this case, he couldn't risk making themselves easier targets.

"Copy Hammer, LZ is at the southeast edge of the compound. Be advised, enemy QRF is approaching from the north. Will need a little bird to snatch up Odin when we're clear. Odin and assault team will strobe on your arrival, but not before."

"Roger, Thor," the pilot acknowledged.

Chunk felt a hand on his shoulder and turned to find Trip beside him. "You ready, boss?"

Antman materialized in the haze an instant later.

"You two with me. We're breaching the front door," Chunk said and took off in a tactical crouch toward the west side of the building.

"Second sentry down, One," Saw called in his ear.

Six bad guys left . . . but another dozen just a few minutes out. We need to be gone before then.

A burst of fire that his brain identified as coming from an AK-47 echoed to his left, from the side of Building Two. Two cracks of 5.56 rounds answered and Trip said, "Tango down."

Chunk sprinted through the haze toward the building entrance, where he found Riker pressed against the wall. Chunk fell in on the opposite side of the door in a mirror-image posture and they locked eyes. Riker summoned that famous dumbass grin of his and everything suddenly felt right as rain. Chunk nodded and held up three fingers, ready to count down the breach.

"Bravo, if you have any targets at the north window, shoot them on my call," Chunk said into his boom mike.

Spence answered with a double click.

"Dead guy by the shitter," Saw announced, reporting another enemy KIA.

That leaves three bad guys in here with our package and two others still at large in the compound, Chunk thought, updating his mental count.

"Let's do this," Riker prompted.

Chunk nodded and counted down with his fingers. On reaching one, Riker positioned himself in front of the door to breach.

"Now, Bravo," Chunk called.

Riker kicked a booted foot against the door at the same time gunfire erupted from the inside. Splinters of wood and sawdust exploded around Riker in a cloud as tracers ripped through the wood slab in a scattershot pattern. Chunk's heart told him to rush to his friend—who he assumed was riddled with bullets—but his officer's mind held him back. The first rule in combat was to kill the enemy and remove the threat before rendering aid. With gritted teeth, Chunk tossed a flash-bang through the gap into the building. Like lightning and thunder in a bottle, the grenade detonated a second later, and he barreled through the door. He moved and cleared left while Trip followed behind, clearing right. A target popped up from behind an overturned table. Chunk put a red dot on the bearded face and squeezed twice; the Pashtun-style cap blew off the man's head, full of bone and blood, and the fighter fell.

Chunk swiveled right, sighting across the room to where a gray blanket hung in a doorway.

He was just about to surge forward when an unexpected and irate voice behind him shouted, "You did not just try and shoot me through the door, motherfuckers."

Consecutive three-round bursts from Riker's SOPMOD M4 flared in Chunk's peripheral vision as Redneck Achilles rushed up the middle and took out a fighter charging from the other room.

"Dude, are you okay?" Chunk asked with a quick and disbelieving sideways glance.

"Five by," Riker replied with a pissed-off grin.

How the hell does he do it?

They took either side of the doorway as Trip and Antman checked the three dead terrorists on the floor before setting up defensive positions to cover the windows and doorway behind them. Chunk repeated the same three-fingered countdown, then together they moved through the blanket-covered opening to the back room where he predicted Gonzalez was being held. Chunk moved left and Riker right, keeping low. A bullet tore a chunk of stucco from the wall just above Chunk's head as he entered the room. At reflex speed, he sighted on the head of a terrorist fighter, who was standing beside a serviceman dressed in Marine Corps BDUs. Chunk was about to order the man to release the hostage and put down his weapon, when a crack from Riker's weapon from beside him ended the negotiation and the fighter pitched backward and slid down the wall, leaving a trail of blood and gore in his wake.

"Don't shoot," the American Marine shouted, his arms flying up over his head. "I'm American."

"We got ya, son," Chunk said. "We're here to take you home. Tell us your name."

"Private First Class Louis M. Gonzalez," the young Marine replied, his voice loud but cracking.

"Where'd you go to high school, PFC Gonzalez?" Chunk asked as Riker checked the terrorist dead behind the young man.

"Uh . . . ummm . . . Rosa Christa High School."

"Your first car?"

The young Marine seemed to relax, memories of his training now kicking in.

"Same as now," he said and lowered his arms. "Nissan 370Z. Got it right out of basic. I love that fuckin' car."

Riker nodded and moved to check the Marine for injury while Chunk made the call.

"Asgard, Thor One—Thor is Valhalla."

"Roger, One. Understand you are Valhalla," Watts said, her voice tense but clearly relieved to hear the checkpoint call indicating they had recovered Gonzalez. "Thor, be advised the enemy trucks will be at the north end of the compound in under two mikes. ETA for Hammer One at the LZ is three mikes."

"Roger, Asgard. Stand by." Chunk approached the Marine as he continued talking. "Alpha and Bravo, Thor One—fall in south of the target building. Dust-off in three mikes."

The QRF with heavy machine guns—probably American weapons—made Hammer's approach risky as hell, and he always assumed that terrorist fighters had RPGs. American forces had lost far too many brothers to RPG fire on approaching helicopters and he wasn't about to repeat that mistake. The safest option was to shift the LZ, but that would depend on their package.

"What's your status, Gonzalez? Can you move? Are you hurt?" he asked.

"They beat the shit out of me, and I think my left collar

bone is broken or dislocated, but I'll sprint all the way back to the States if that's what it takes."

Chunk nodded and called Watts. "We're assembling behind Building Two, Mother," he said, deciding never to say *Asgard* again. "Merge on channel three." Chunk flipped a small switch and then spun the dial on his MBITR radio on the front of his kit, merging channels one and three. "Hammer, Thor One . . ."

"Hammer, go," the pilot said.

"Hammer, be advised you have a QRF of enemy fighters arriving at the north side of the compound. Recommend you redirect your approach or we move the LZ east, clear of fire."

"Hammer One, roger that. Asgard already advised. I'll be approaching the LZ from the south for pickup. Hammer Three, if you could lay some fire in front, we should be good to go without relocating."

"Oh yeah," the MH-6 pilot replied, delight in his voice. "Hammer Three is in and hot in one mike. Clearing the path for you, Hammer One."

Chunk moved PFC Gonzalez behind the building and then pressed against the corner in time to see the headlights of two trucks tearing up the dirt road from the north. Before they even slowed down, the gunner in the lead truck fired what looked to be an American-made M240 machine gun. Cement and wood exploded into the air and fell like rain behind them.

"We gotta move," Chunk shouted and chopped a hand back the way they'd entered. He surged forward, with Gonzalez following behind and Riker bringing up the rear. Chunk ripped the blanket down as he passed through the doorway into the neighboring room where Trip and Antman were ready and waiting. Their four-man team, plus the rescued Marine, charged out of the target building toward the rally point where Spence's Bravo were waiting.

"Hammer Three is in and hot," came the MH-6 pilot's call not a moment too late.

An instant later, the night sky lit up as a half dozen 70 mm Hydra 70 rockets found their targets. Chunk could hear the screams of men on fire as the MH-6 little bird streaked past overhead.

"Thor, Hammer One—thirty seconds," the Blackhawk pilot radioed in.

"Move, Thor," Chunk called. He fired a few bursts at the wall of flames where the trucks had been, in case someone might still be there to take a potshot at his back, then led the team at a full sprint south, toward the LZ.

"Hammer Three in and hot," the MH-6 pilot called again, and this time Chunk heard the long belch of the M134 Minigun strafing across what was left of the al-Qaeda QRF.

Then he was at the wall, hauling his stocky frame over and clearing left, just as the sound of the MH-60 Blackhawk's rotors reached his ears.

"Odin, Hammer Three—stand by for pickup," the MH-6 pilot called.

"Hooyah," Saw replied from his overwatch position three hundred meters away. "Thanks for a great show, brother."

While the little bird banked and swept around to pick up Saw, the rest of the team—seven SEALs and the rescued Marine, PFC Gonzalez—crowded into the Blackhawk. Seconds later the burning compound disappeared below and behind them, as the Blackhawk pilot maneuvered at high speed along the twisting ravine. After putting distance between them and the compound, the pilot popped up to altitude, pressing Chunk and his SEAL brothers into the deck with the high G maneuver, before slipping over the ridgeline and disappearing into the night.

"Hammer Three has Odin. We're clear," the attack helo pilot said, confirming Saw's exfil.

Chunk exhaled with relief and checked in with Watts in the TOC. Then he dropped his NVGs into place and looked Riker up and down for crimson stains. He spied a bullet hole on the outside thigh of his teammate's unmarked BDU pants, but no blood to speak of.

He shook his head.

Talk about one charmed son of a bitch.

"I swear, Chunk, if we ever use these dumbass Marvel call signs again, I'm quitting the team," Riker grumbled.

"We never will, I promise," Chunk said with a laugh.

"You guys suck," Edwards said in his ear. "Those were the most epic call signs ever."

"Sorry, bro, we disagree. Your call sign picking privileges are permanently revoked," Spence said in their headsets.

As the banter continued, Chunk leaned against the rear bulkhead of the open port-side doorway and dangled a leg out into the wind, smiling. His team was gelling like never before. Even with all the twists and surprises, they had executed a flawless rescue op of an American hostage held deep in Taliban country. They had arrived. Gold Squadron was the most badass, covert Special Operations team in the world, and he had the privilege of leading them.

He didn't have a crystal ball.

He had no idea what the world was going to throw at them next.

But whatever it was, Chunk wasn't worried . . . because they were ready.

CHAPTER 3

Chunk watched with an overwhelming sense of satisfaction as a team of Navy corpsmen and CIA case officers led the young Marine away. He smiled as PFC Gonzalez refused the rolling stretcher and instead limped beside the medical team, looking over his shoulder and shooting Chunk a grin and thumbs-up. Chunk nodded in reply. There might be an operator inside that skinny young Marine just waiting to emerge. Either this experience would drive the kid home to small-town USA to tell tales into old age about the time the SEALs rescued him, or Chunk would run into Gonzalez three years later and thirty pounds heavier after the kid became a Marine Raider.

"Tough kid," Saw said from beside him, reading his mind.

Chunk nodded.

"It was a good op, boss," the SEAL sniper added, clapping him on the back.

"Nice shootin', bro," Chunk said and pressed a wad of snuff into his lower lip. He handed the can to Riker, who had come up beside him, and the SEAL snapped the can to pack the tobacco before loading up his own lipper.

"Good call going in despite our stealth getting blown by that sniper," Riker said, then dribbled brown spit onto the rocky ground between them. "Sorry I was sounding like a pussy out there."

Chunk waved his hand and his two teammates followed him off the flight line toward the white pickup trucks where the rest of the fire team was waiting.

"The day you don't give me your honest, no bullshit assessment is the day we're all screwed," he said to Riker. "I need my senior NCOs, especially you, to tell me anything on your mind."

"Roger that," Riker said. "Glad we got the kid instead of bugging out."

"Hooyah," he said, his voice neutral. It was big boy rules in the Tier One. Chunk owned his decisions and this one had worked out, but he also recognized that if the timeline had shifted by even a few minutes, it might not have.

He piled into the rear bed of the second pickup truck and nodded at Watts in the driver's seat through the back window. He tucked in beside Riker and Saw as Spence hopped up front with a victory smile still lingering on his face. Chunk got it. Rescue missions—especially with zero organic or collateral injuries—were special.

The pickup truck weaved around the short line of CH-47 helicopters and then hung a right, leaving the flight line and turning onto a narrow road that ended in a small compound surrounded by a low wall, its height extended an additional eight feet with a heavy-duty fence topped by concertina wire.

They stopped at the JSOC compound entrance while Watts punched an access code into a box beside the gate. The box beeped and the gate rattled on its track as it slid open.

Watts glanced over her shoulder and gave Chunk a smile and nod, then pulled into the unassuming little compound that served as the FOB for their activities in the region. It was a far cry from the base within a base at Jalalabad Airport, operational for nearly two decades, but it did the job. If the war on terror was winding down in Afghanistan, there was little evidence of it in their world. The loss of support for the mission after the drawdown of other military units in Afghanistan that served as medical, logistical, and QRF support was painfully obvious and dangerous.

That's the job.

"How much time before we load up for breakfast?" Trip asked, gesturing with a thumb at the ribbon of pink now forming a ragged halo over the mountains to the east.

"KBR opens in two hours," Antman said, referring to the contract chow hall supporting the CIA operations at the small base, "and I intend to be first in line at the omelet station."

"Plenty of time for a workout," Trip said, lifting his rifle sling over his head, dropping it into a more relaxed carry on his right shoulder. "Let's change and meet in the gym and then get in a quick five miles."

"On it," Antman replied, pulling loose the Velcro cummerbund of his tactical kit.

The "gym" where they trained looked like little more than an oversize garage, but it had a full complement of free and machine weights, pull-up bars, and aerobic machines like rowers, treadmills, and stair climbers. SEALs trained like professional athletes. At the Tier One, maintaining supreme levels of fitness was the rule, not the exception.

Chunk also felt a run calling but knew it would have to wait until after the post-op debrief. He led the way to the TOC, a stucco building situated across from three rows of white shower trailers. The first trailer had a hand-drawn caricature of an ape on the door. The second featured a caveman. The third trailer, however, had a pinup model airbrushed on the door, of a caliber worthy to serve as nose art on a World War II B-24. This trailer was reserved for the women on the team.

Watts, who was holding the heavy door of the TOC open, caught him glancing at the voluptuous door art.

"What?" he said, unabashed. "*That* was here when we arrived."

"Sure," she retorted.

"This used to be a Delta compound. You know how those guys are."

"You're all the same, near as I can tell," she said, sucking in her abdomen to allow the three kitted-up SEALs to pass through. "And why am I holding the door for you anyway?"

"Because we're gentlemen," Riker said with a grin.

"No, you're not . . ."

Chunk and his guys stripped off their rifles and kits, setting them against the wall, and sat down across from where Yi was typing on a computer at a long, rough-cut wooden table. The wide-open room was a workspace with a half dozen similarly crude one-person desks strewn about, each with a closed laptop. The only thing breaking up the unstained wood decor was memorabilia nailed to almost every wall from the JSOC Army unit previously running this TOC, much of it brought along from the abandoned TOCs on the other side of the border, he imagined. Pictures without frames—helicopter pilots, Delta operators in blue jeans and Hawaiian shirts kitted up and grinning—adorned the walls beside captured ISIS and Taliban flags, a pair of crossed Arabian swords, worn-looking AK-47s, and even two RPGs. The wall in the back had a truck steering wheel affixed to it, but no one working here now knew its story—a metaphor for the never-ending war on terror. Chunk reminded himself that the JSOC operators who first occupied the TOC where much of this originated were all retired now. By comparison, Trip, who was in the prime of his career, had been only seven years old when 9/11 happened.

They debriefed the op as a group, an exercise that often felt superfluous but was a long-standing military practice to make sure all facts were straight and agreed upon before the data package was submitted to the command and archived. Many a lesson learned were born in debriefs, but most of the time for Chunk it was as much fun as banging his head against the wall.

". . . looked to me like the QRF trucks came out of this location," he said, a finger dropping onto a long, low building on a satellite imagery printout.

"Yep," Watts confirmed. "Passing that on to OGA as well, as they have assets in the area. As you know, we're still searching for a bomb maker released from prison after the Taliban takeover, though he might be in the stack of bodies you left behind."

"Let's hope so," Chunk said.

"Or maybe he was in Building Three where you dropped the Hellfire," she said, glancing at him then quickly back at her computer screen.

"What?" he said, eyebrows up, wondering if she'd meant that to be a jab.

"What, what?" she said, looking up, her face all innocence.

"You have something you want to discuss, Watts?"

She shrugged.

"You don't think it was the right call to drop the Hellfire on Building Three, do you?"

"Well, obviously it was," she said, the angsty tone of a few months ago absent in her voice today. "Gonzalez is in the clinic and you guys are all here safe and sound. Big boy rules, isn't that what you like to say?"

"But you wouldn't have made that call."

She laughed. "Thank God it wasn't my call to make, because it worked out."

"Right," he agreed, folding his arms over his chest. "It worked out."

"This time," she added under her breath and turned back to Yi's computer wearing the slightest hint of a grin.

"Un-uh," he said, shooting her a sharp look. "You don't get to do that."

She met his gaze, eyebrows up again. "I don't get to do what?"

"Make comments under your breath. If you have something to say, Heels, then spit it out," he said using the nickname he'd christened her with just months ago, when she reported to her first day on the job wearing high heels and a pantsuit.

Instead of getting defensive, she simply sighed. "I was just messing with you. All kidding aside, Chunk, everyone knows I'm more risk averse than you—maybe than everyone in the command—but that's part of the system, right? We all get input, but it's not a democracy. You're the boss, and I trust your judgment."

"Your job is to give me your unfiltered opinion. Seems like in this case you're reluctant because my call turned out to be right."

She flashed him a genuine smile. "My unfiltered opinion is that I wouldn't have made the call. Okay . . . are we good?"

Chunk relaxed his shoulders and nodded. "We're good."

Yi's computer chimed with a notification, ending the discussion. The petty officer tapped a key and spun it around for Chunk to see. On the screen the serious face of Captain Bowman, current Chief Service Officer of the Tier One SEALs, stared back at him.

"Well done, Lieutenant Commander Redman," his boss said. "A perfectly executed JSOC rescue mission."

"Thank you, sir," Chunk said, uncomfortable with the praise in front of everyone. "They threw us a few curveballs, but we got it done."

"There're always curveballs, Chunk. Success is determined by how we handle them. Results matter. You made the right call." Across from him, Chunk was aware that Watts was looking at her hands.

"It was a team effort, sir. Our intel team here in the TOC gave us the data and input we needed in real time to allow us to execute the mission despite the dynamic conditions," he said, throwing in a nod to Watts as a subtle peace offering.

"All right, enough patting ourselves on the back," Bowman said. "Let's move on. What else do you have for me?"

Chunk grinned. Bowman was the best boss he'd ever had, and he loved the crusty SEAL officer's no BS leadership approach.

They ran through a few minor housekeeping updates regarding previous ops, but there wasn't much to tell.

"All right, where are we with tracking down Hamza al-Saud's lieutenants? Watts, give me an update on your progress piecing together the remnants of the al Qadar network?" Bowman said.

The question was a good one but also happened to poke at Watts's most tender spot. It had been over three months since Gold Squadron had neutralized al Qadar's combat drone program and captured the terrorist organization's leader, Hamza al-Saud. Thanks to Watts's tenacity and smarts, they'd been able to find and thwart al-Saud's drone operation, but not before one of the drones launched a pair of missiles at Kandahar Air Base resulting in millions of dollars of damage and loss of American lives. In the time since, however, precious little progress had been made prosecuting the "ones that got away." The abandonment of Afghanistan made it harder, of course. She'd also had trouble figuring out how the upstart terror group had managed to source Chinese Pterodactyl UAVs, ground control units, and HJ-10 air-to-ground missiles. Besides being a clever tactician, it seemed that al-Saud was also quite skilled at the financial and logistics side of procuring arms. Watts had complained to Chunk on more than one occasion, saying, "How am I supposed to follow the money when there's no money to follow?" A part of Chunk was empathetic to her situation and wished he could be of some help, but the spooky shit just wasn't his wheelhouse.

He turned to look at her as she fielded the question.

"Not much new to report, sir," Watts said. "We're still working with OGA and leveraging the connections you made for us at NSA to monitor SIGINT for communications and any signs of reconstitution. We even have the Group Ten folks in theater squeezing their assets in Pakistan for information, but so far nothing earth-shattering. What we can say with confidence is we see no evidence whatsoever of non-nation-state combat drone activity in theater after the one we destroyed outside of Kandahar."

Chunk saw something flicker across her face. She'd been different since the Kandahar attack. They'd lost people. She'd seen things that couldn't be unseen, and that affected a person's psyche.

"So, we think that Pterodactyl drone was the only one in al Qadar's arsenal?" Bowman pressed.

"Well." Watts hesitated and looked at Yi who shrugged. "That's what everyone seems to think, sir. The mobile GCUs they used have all been destroyed. The Mingora airport, where they were conducting nighttime sorties, has been monitored twenty-four seven since the incident. CENTCOM has dedicated resources to monitoring all Ku-band transmitters in the region and the PakSat-1R—the satellite al Qadar hacked into to conduct the Kandahar attack—is on SPACECOM's watch list. In addition, Kandahar has implemented new airspace deconfliction and identification protocols to address the vulnerabilities al Qadar exploited the first time around. So unless they've somehow gotten their hands on a next-generation stealth UCAV, I'm ninety-nine percent sure they're not operational. That said, there are still puzzle pieces about al Qadar's operation that we've yet to put together."

"I take it from your tone, Ms. Watts, that you're not quite ready to put this to bed?"

She seemed to gather her thoughts a moment.

"Sir, my instinct tells me there's more to this story. The operation that al-Saud conducted was far more sophisticated and tech-savvy than anything we've encountered before. It would be a mistake to assume that a man who was so successful operating undetected under our noses—sourcing and deploying advanced Chinese military hardware—did not have a succession plan in place. Yes, we eliminated a significant number of his rank-and-file members, but where are the engineers? Where are the black hat hackers and drone technicians? It's impossible to pull off what he did with goatherds and illiterate jihadists who have no cyber and technical skills whatsoever. Honestly, sir, I feel it would be a huge mistake to assume we had dismantled the al Qadar network simply because we captured al-Saud and a handful of his operators. And, with the terrorist organizations emboldened by the Afghanistan withdrawal, recruiting would be easier than ever."

"Okay, okay, I get it," Bowman said. "Just so you know, CIA considers this a closed operation, though they are ready to assist if something new comes to light. For the record, I agree with you. So, keep beating the bushes and find us who is running al Qadar in al-Saud's stead. When you do, we run the standard Tier One playbook against them—capture/kill missions, one after the other—until we chase it up the chain to their leadership or wipe them all off the face of the earth. But before that can happen, I gotta have targets, Watts."

"Understood, sir," she said and smiled over at Yi who gave her a subtle fist bump under the table. They were becoming an unstoppable team, those two, and Chunk was glad they were part of Gold.

"In the meantime, I'm sure we'll find some Tier One level tasking for you guys in the next twenty-four to forty-eight hours," Bowman added.

It wasn't like a few years ago, when the JSOC units conducted raids nearly every single night of deployment, sometimes more than one a night. But there were plenty of threats still to prosecute. After the ambush that had wiped out their Tier One SEAL Team predecessors in Yemen a few years ago, higher authorities seemed far more cautious about not overtasking the JSOC teams. But there was still plenty of work to do, mission packages that would never be reported on CNN. Most of the military didn't yet know that the Tier One SEAL Team had been reconstituted and that sat just fine with Chunk and his teammates. Quiet professionals needed secrecy to do their best work.

"Rest the team and be ready for the next op, Chunk,"

Bowman said, "but assist Watts and Yi with whatever they need, including running low-level ISR."

"Yes, sir," Chunk said.

Bowman disappeared from the screen without so much as a goodbye, piss off, or job well done.

Chunk looked at Watts, who was unconsciously tracing the trefoil knot tattoo on her wrist with her index finger.

Her comments to Bowman about missing puzzle pieces and the disconnect between the level of sophistication of al Qadar's operation and the level of sophistication of the dudes they'd captured suddenly resonated with him.

"Is Hamza al-Saud still being held at the CIA black site across town?" he asked. Like JSOC, the CIA and other elements of the US intelligence community had been forced to move their counterterror operations across the borders of Afghanistan, mostly to the various other "'stans"—Tajikistan, Uzbekistan, Turkmenistan, and even Pakistan.

"Yeah," Yi answered. "Buried in black right here in lovely Tajikistan."

"Wanna take a ride?" he said, shifting his gaze to Watts.

"For what?" she asked. "CIA and the task force guys have been hammering at him for months. That well has run dry."

"Maybe," he agreed with a shrug. "But what else have we got going on? Let's grab breakfast with the guys and then head over, you and me, and shake that tree one more time."

"Yeah, if you want," she said, but her tone suggested she felt the field trip to be a waste of time.

"I want," he said with a devilish grin as a new and fresh theory started to gel in his mind.

CHAPTER 4

Diba Nadar stepped out of the modest redbrick house and onto Cambridge Road feeling self-conscious and insecure without her headscarf. Qasim had instructed her not to wear a hijab after their wedding in London three months ago. At first, she'd felt liberated by the sudden and surprising edict from her husband, but that feeling vanished the first time she had gone outside without it. In that moment, with the invisible eyes of all her neighbors boring into her, she'd promptly turned around and walked straight back inside.

She hadn't even made it past the front stoop.

Qasim, for his part, had laughed at her, which had only amplified her guilt and embarrassment.

"Why must I give up my hijab?" she'd asked him, in a moment of frustration before an outing to the grocery shop.

"Because in this country, the hijab makes you look like an

outsider. I want us to assimilate—to blend in. Do you under-stand?" he'd replied.

"But there are so many Muslim women here who wear their hijabs. In this country, it is okay to wear it. British people are accepting of different religions and customs."

"Not all of them."

"Yes, but those people hate me because of the color of my skin, and the way I look, and the way I talk. Even without the hijab they will stare and judge me. There is nothing I can do to please those kinds of people except leave this country."

He'd nodded at this, conceding the point.

"All I'm saying is that I *am* a Muslim woman and I am not ashamed of it. The hijab represents both my faith and heritage. I'm surprised it does not please you."

"I thought you would be happy with this freedom, Diba," he'd said, staring at her with incredulity. "Would you prefer to return to wearing a burqa?"

"No," she'd snapped, heat rising in her chest.

She hated the burqa. With her entire body and face covered, she felt subjugated and suffocated—her only view of the world a three-inch square fabric grill.

"You see," he'd said with a victorious smile. "You've already changed."

"The burqa and the hijab are night and day."

"Maybe so, but the matter is not open for discussion. While we are living here, you will dress and act in the Western style. I forbid you to wear an abaya, hijab, or a veil of any kind unless we are attending a mosque. End of discussion."

So, there it was. The decision had never been about her empowerment. It had never been about choice or personal liberty. It was about appearances. It was about deception . . . like everything else in their new British life together.

She walked east, keeping to the sidewalk, all the way to High Street. At the intersection, she turned south onto the main shopping and dining avenue in town. Qasim had informed her he would be working late this evening and so not to count on him for dinner. The idea of eating leftovers and dining alone in their flat sounded dreadful, so she'd decided to go for a walk and get takeout from Nando's—her favorite. She'd already decided what she would order: Quarter Peri-Peri Chicken with Spicy Rice and Macho Peas. Nando's South African style cuisine was no substitute for authentic Afghan cooking, but she did love the spices and quality of the ingredients. Also, she never felt out of place inside as the patronage was ethnically diverse. East Asians, South Asians, Africans, and Arabs all frequented Nando's along with white Briton locals. The atmosphere inside was always warm and inviting, and she'd even developed a quasi friendship with one of the Korean female cashiers—Soo Jin.

The thought of seeing Soo Jin today brought a smile to her face.

It was only a ten-minute walk to Nando's, and that was if she took her time which she liked to do—peering in the windows of the shops, cafés, and restaurants along High Street. There was nothing analogous to the hamlet's quaint little main street in Afghanistan, and having never traveled before moving to England, she was still quite in awe of her newly adopted hometown. On this one street, she could buy practically anything—every type of food, every type of beverage, every type of good or service. There was an optical store, a pharmacy, a bank, a hair salon, a hardware store, clothing boutiques, car repair, computer repair, a law firm, and a real estate service . . . Qasim had to explain all of these businesses to her as she'd never seen any of them before.

Moving from her village in Afghanistan to London was a rebirth.

I was a baby before, sheltered and naive. I knew nothing of the world.

She glanced down at the handbag bouncing against her left hip and felt the pull of disobedience. Inside she'd stuffed her favorite headscarf—silky soft and dyed a deep purple, so dark it was almost black. With a mischievous curl of her lips, she retrieved it from her purse and paused in front of a shop window to look at her barely recognizable reflection. Already feeling better, she fixed the hijab around her head and neck. With a cleansing exhale, she turned on a heel and walked the final block to the restaurant.

She pulled the door open to Nando's and was greeted by a savory olfactory kiss—roasted chicken, tangy spices, and grill smoke. Her mouth instantly watered in anticipation. She'd intentionally timed her arrival before the dinner rush, so the normally robust queue of patrons waiting to order barely stretched to the corner. Behind the register, Soo Jin was working. Diba watched her friend greet the next pair of patrons and take their order. When Soo Jin smiled, Diba smiled, mirroring her friend subconsciously. And then as if an invisible connection between them was activated, Soo Jin turned and looked in her direction. The Korean girl's face lit up and she gave Diba an animated wave.

"Hi, Diba, how are you?" Soo Jin asked when it was Diba's turn to order. Soo Jin was a native English speaker, born in New Malden, and spoke with a rapid-fire Londoner's accent. But when she spoke to Diba, she slowed it down and enunciated her words more clearly, which Diba appreciated very much.

"I very well," Diba said.

"Shall I key in your regular order?" Soo Jin asked.

Diba nodded. "Two portions, one for my husband, one for me."

"Would you like it to go?"

"Yes, please," she said and, seeing nobody in line behind her, took the opportunity to loiter at the register, practice her English, and talk with her friend for several minutes.

Learning English was difficult, but with nothing else to do all day while Qasim worked, she'd thrown herself into the task. Recently, she'd had her first dream in English. When she told Qasim about it, he'd congratulated her and explained that this represented a big milestone, because it meant her mind actively tried to process and internalize the vocabulary and structure of the language. Since then, she'd decided he was right because the words were coming a little easier to her over the last few weeks. She'd also asked him to speak to her in English in their flat, which he did most of the time until his frustration with her got the better of him.

With her order filled and packed, Diba bid Soo Jin goodbye and left the restaurant. She turned right and walked to a nearby park bench located on the north side of the roundabout. She took a seat facing south, with the fading afternoon sun shining down on her. This was her favorite spot in New Malden. It was a simple place, where the pedestrian and car traffic converged and diverged, converged and diverged, all day long. The roundabout reminded her of a beating heart, circulating cars and people like life-sustaining blood. She liked watching the activity, without feeling trapped in the hustle and bustle herself. She'd only been to central London on a few occasions with Qasim, and it was too much commotion and noise for her. She didn't like feeling crammed and bumping into people. She didn't like anyone touching her except for Qasim.

But she did like feeling part of a community.

She unpacked the Nando's bag, opened her to-go container, and leisurely ate her dinner on her lap, not rushing, chewing slowly to enjoy and savor both the food and the moment. And when she was finished, she tossed her trash in a nearby public rubbish bin and walked home the back way via Kingston and Cleveland Roads respectively. Before turning onto Cambridge, she removed her hijab and stuffed it in her handbag, just in case her husband surprised her by deviating from the schedule he'd given her earlier—something he did unexpectedly from time to time. Today, however, he was true to his word and did not return home until after nine p.m.

She greeted him at the door.

"I'm famished," he said in English, after giving her a hello kiss. "Do you have dinner ready?"

"Yes. A minute to warm for you," she said, hoping he'd be pleased.

"It smells like peri-peri chicken," he called from the living room when she pulled the steaming food container from the microwave. "Did you get Nando's?"

"Yes," she said as she transferred all the food to a wide bowl. She walked from the kitchen to the living room and handed it to him.

"Have you already eaten?" he asked, accepting the bowl and silverware.

"Yes," she said and took a seat beside him.

He nodded and devoured his dinner wordlessly in less than five minutes. As she watched him, she thought about their past three months together in London. Initially, during the days leading up to their wedding day, he had been sullen, impatient, and quick-tempered—almost cruel to her. But the night he'd taken her virginity, something changed in him. She'd cried and confessed her true and innermost worries and feelings, and instead of punishing her, he'd listened and taken them to heart. After that night, things between them had gotten better and better. They talked many times a day, and he often tried to make her laugh. He seemed happier lately. His confidence had bloomed and he'd received a big promotion at work.

They never discussed the Americans, his best friend Eshan's death, or the events in Mingora—events about which she still did not know the details. She'd not seen Asadi Bijan—the man who had paid for their wedding and all the travel expenses for her family to fly from Afghanistan to London and back— since their reception. Despite Bijan's sophisticated charm, wit, and good humor, she knew who and what that man was—a dangerous and wanted terrorist. She didn't know what Qasim owed this man or what he had pledged in fealty, but on their wedding night, she had begged Qasim to cut ties with the organization and live a simple and honest life.

"I will try, Diba," he had said, after embracing her as her first and only lover. "For you."

They had not spoken of it since—with her not daring to bring it up, while hoping for the day he'd confirm he'd kept his promise. But deep down, in the darkest corner of her heart, she knew the truth. Qasim had *not* tried to get out. He'd not done anything at all. He was simply biding his time until Bijan returned. This was why she was not allowed to wear her hijab. This was why Qasim so adamantly demanded she assimilate, blend in, and not draw attention to their presence in New Malden.

"What are you thinking about?" he asked, with food in his mouth.

"Nothing," she said with a polite smile. "How is your day?"

"The correct way is to say, 'How *was* your day?'" he said. "*Is* is the present tense. *Was* is the past tense."

"But this day still happens?" she said, cocking an eyebrow at him.

"That's true," her husband said with a kind smile, "but your question concerns my workday which is over now that I am home. So, the correct question is to ask, 'How was your day?' Do you understand?"

She nodded and looked down at her lap. "I understand."

He smiled at her. "You're making good progress, Diba."

"You think so?"

"Oh, yes," he said. "Very good progress."

She looked at him and met his gaze. "I am trying hard for you."

At this, he reached out and caressed her cheek.

She saw a carnal fire burning in his eyes; his lust for her glowed like an aura around him.

"Do you want to take me here?" she asked, switching to her native tongue while coyly undoing the top button on her blouse. "Do you want to take me now?"

"Yes," he said, quickly undressing himself and then her. They made passionate love on the sofa, both getting lost in the moment and very much enjoying themselves. When he finished, he propped himself up on his elbows and gazed down at her. "You are so beautiful."

Demure to the core, she blushed and looked away.

But what he said next took her by surprise.

His eyes scanned lustfully and unashamedly across her body, and she felt both modesty and arousal again at his gaze. She really did love this man, despite the uncertainty of her new life. "Maybe I should change my mind," he said, running his eyes over her nakedness, "and have you wear the burqa here after all . . ."

"What?" she said, the word a gasp in her throat. "Why?"

"Because this beautiful body belongs to me," he said, shifting his minacious gaze from her breasts to meet her eyes. "No other man should have the privilege to look upon any single part of you."

This candid admission sent a chill down her spine. Moments like this were proof of a growing duplicity inside Qasim. She was beginning to wonder if their time in the West was *accelerating*, not reversing, his transformation into . . . into . . . She couldn't even bring herself to say the word. She'd tried so hard to get him to let go of his anger and regret and see the good in this new life they were making together in England. On the outside he almost had her fooled into thinking she'd succeeded. But on the inside, hate festered, and she feared what would happen if it consumed him. If he embraced revenge with the same passion that he embraced her, what would become of their partnership? Would she go from being a wife to a slave? Was her fate to become the property of a terrorist—a woman damned for the rest of her days to live a life of fear, subservience, and punishment?

I cannot permit that to happen.

I will not permit it to happen.

Looking at her husband now, it was clear that this honeymoon period they'd been living was nothing more than the calm before the storm. Qasim was just biding time until the terrorist prince returned. And when he did, Diba was certain Asadi Bijan would come like a hurricane—leaving nothing but pain and devastation in his wake.

CHAPTER 5

Chunk couldn't help himself as he scanned up and down the corridor for threats.

Objectively, he and Watts were perfectly safe, but that didn't matter. That was the unnerving thing about black sites, they were so good at being what they were that he never really felt comfortable inside one. Everyone was in a NOC, being disingenuously genuine. The site itself, like this operational marble and talc factory, was living a double life too—on the one hand producing actual salable products while on the other hand housing some of the world's most dangerous terrorist criminals. The irony of him disliking the duplicity of black sites was not lost on him, as he himself was visiting this installation under a NOC. Even during intelligence-gathering trips to partner facilities like this one, he had a mandate to protect his unit's anonymity.

Isn't that always the way of it, he thought. *It's okay when I do it, but not okay when other people do.*

"This way," their CIA escort said, turning left and leading them down the hall. Moments later he stopped in front of an elevator. Once inside, he inserted a key card from a lanyard around his neck into a security reader slot and pressed an unlabeled button at the bottom. It turned from red to green and the elevator began to quickly descend, traveling much farther than the twelve-foot distance between a single floor.

"I'm Ralph, by the way. Ralph Mitchell," the spook said, now that they were in the elevator. "You're with one of the task forces?"

"Something like that," Chunk said.

"Any trouble finding us?"

"Nah," he said. "Easy day. You guys got GRS here with you?"

The man laughed. "Most definitely, my friend. GRS is a team of six, but we have organic operators from Ground Branch as well—another half dozen guys in garrison here for other operations, but an important part of our security. We try to keep a low profile. So far, the NOC is holding up, but you can never be too careful. Plenty of bad guys, even up here in Taji."

"Tricky business, NOCs," Chunk said, his mind flashing back to the night in Mingora when their DIA contact in a NOC got blown up on a rooftop.

The elevator stopped and the doors swished open, then Mitchell led them into a dark room that for some reason reminded Chunk of the prison block scene from *Star Wars*: a large circular desk with laptops and multiple TV screens and two long dark corridors leading away from the desk.

"Holy shit, is that Whitney fucking Watts?" a male voice said.

"Danny?" Watts said, lighting up. "Oh my God, what are you doing here?"

Chunk watched as she gave the tall Black man a warm hug. The guy was dressed in black jeans and a 5.11 tactical plaid and wore a GLOCK 19 in a holster on his right hip.

"This is Danny Lannon," she said, turning to look at Chunk. "Danny was with me at the Farm although we were in different tracks. We had to do the final exam drill together and it was a hot mess."

"Chunk," he said and stuck out his hand. There were some tactical advantages to using a nickname.

"Team guy?" Lannon said, clamping down with his own large weathered hand.

"Yeah," Chunk said. "You former Army?"

"Marine."

"Gotcha."

Lannon turned to Watts.

"So, you're hanging out with some spooky task force now? How the hell did that happen? I thought you were at NCTC after . . . you know."

"I was," she said, keeping it vague, "now, I'm doing something else."

"Something related to the mumbler we got in lockbox three, I assume?"

"The mumbler?" she echoed, cocking an eyebrow.

"Yeah," Lannon said, and gestured for them to follow him over to the circular desk where a female case officer looked them up and down and scowled.

Lannon gestured with a finger at the center screen, where a camera streamed imagery of Hamza al-Saud. The man sat cross-legged on the floor, hands in his lap, and stared without blinking like a wax statue—except no statue could exude the absolute hatred in those eyes.

"Some other 'task force' brought us this dude. He was

involved in the attack on Kandahar, apparently, though the information given to us was sketchy, as usual. What we know is his name is Hamza and he led a new, upstart terror organization called al Qadar. Did you guys get the full brief?"

"Actually—" Watts started to say, but Chunk cut her off.

"We were fully read in by the task force guys on this one. And yeah, we get it. Sucks to be in charge of extracting information without much background. Sorry they did that to you, bro. We're all supposed to be on the same team."

"Yeah, well, the deep dark task forces keep shit close to the vest, but I guess that's for their own survival. Anyway, if you got all the gouge from the brief you're all up to date, 'cause the mumbler doesn't say much. Every session he just closes his eyes and mumbles scripture from the Quran, no matter what techniques we use. Enhanced interrogation is useless because he clams up completely under duress. Dude's like a bear trap. Definitely a true believer. Sorry to be the broker of bad news but looks like you came all the way here for nothing."

"Not nothing," Chunk said and gave the man his charming we're-all-just-bros-here smile. "We're here to take a crack at him."

Lannon looked irked. "Is that true, Whit?"

"Yeah, Danny. Sorry."

"You know the shit we do here is actually pretty complicated and highly scientific, right? We don't just beat the dude with a rolled-up phone book until he cries and confesses. Every single interaction, conversation, and intervention builds on the last. You jump in the middle of that and we get to start all over. This is, like, PhD level psychology program stuff. The dog collar shit doesn't fly around here."

"We know, Danny, and we're not here to take charge or burn down your house. But it sounds like you don't think things are going anywhere. You said it yourself, he's a bear trap, so it's not like we can mess anything up, right? And if we do happen to shake something loose, all the better for everyone."

Lannon bristled. "Well, I doubt that. But I can't let you in without authorization, Whitney."

"I have it here," she said and handed him a letter giving them unfettered access to the detainee and ordering that the CIA staff abide by all their requests. The letter was signed by the DNI.

"Damn, girl. Who did you say you were working for these days?"

"I could tell you but then I'd have to . . ."

"Yeah, yeah. Spare me the bullshit. I'll still have to confirm."

"The exact same letter was sent to your admin on the high side," Chunk said.

Lannon looked over at the woman manning the terminal beside him and nodded. She tapped her keyboard to open their comms server. She scanned for and found the letter, and Chunk could practically see her blood boiling beneath the skin.

"It's here, but this is bullshit, Danny," the woman said, spinning in her chair to look up at Chunk with venom in her eyes. "You gonna take al-Saud with you when you go? I can see by the look on your faces the answer to that question is no. So, what's the plan—after you're done fucking up our program, we get to clean up the mess and start over? Is that how this friggin' works?"

"Guys, I get it," Chunk said, "I do, but I'm just following orders."

"Fine," Lannon said but he folded his arms across his chest. "But Whitney, you of all people, I would think would get how messed up this is."

"Sorry, Danny," she said and reached to touch his arm but

pulled back before making contact. Chunk wondered suddenly if they had been more than colleagues for a time. "I really am, but it is what it is."

"Fine. It's not like I can say no," Lannon said, pouting.

Watts glanced at Chunk and he nodded.

"Um, our next ask is really gonna piss you off . . ." she added with a sigh. "We need cameras and mics off while we're in there."

"Oh, come on!" the woman at the desk barked, popping to her feet. "What the hell, guys? You jack our program and then we don't even get the benefit of any intel you might actually collect? What was all that 'on the same team' bullshit, Mister Navy Frogman?" Her hands were on her hips now, her muscled arms making the two sleeves of tats jump in the strange light, her right hand just forward of her pistol, a Sig Sauer P229 he noticed.

"Look, we'll share one hundred percent of whatever we uncover, I promise you that, but it has to be off-camera," Chunk said.

"Then why do you need the cameras and sound off?" Lannon asked.

"Because we may be required to discuss details that are classified TS/SCI. Come on, Danny, you know you can trust me," Watts said, with pleading eyes to the man Chunk now suspected might be a former lover.

Lannon stared at her for a long hard moment then, with a snort, said to his colleague, "Jen, shut down eyes and ears in interrogation room one."

"I'd rather do this in al-Saud's cell," Chunk said. "Is that possible?"

Lannon turned on him with more ire than he expected. "Well, your little fucking courtesy card from the DNI says anything's possible. No weapons in the room, so you can leave your shit here at the desk, and I'll take you down. Jen, shut down cell three."

"Danny, we can't just—"

"Shut it down."

Jen glared at Chunk, mumbled something, and then flopped in her seat and shut off the camera and mike in the cell where al-Saud continued to stare like a statue at them until the image disappeared.

Chunk slipped an arm out from his jacket and pulled the Sig MPX Copperhead over his head and placed it on the edge of the round workstation, then pulled his Sig P226 from the holster on his hip and set it beside the machine pistol. Watts set her more compact Sig P365 beside his weapons.

"This way," Lannon grumbled, and they followed him down the long dark corridor to the right, angling away from the identical hallway going off at a forty-five-degree angle, completing the *Star Wars* look. Now all they needed was a Wookie, but they'd left Riker outside in the pickup truck. The corridor had six detention cells on each side of the hall, which meant a dozen possible detainees for this block, but he doubted they were all occupied. Chunk wondered just how many terrorist prisoners had been disappeared down this dark bunny hole in Tajikistan over the years.

They stopped at the middle room on the left, a windowless black door in the black wall, and Lannon pressed his hand onto a biometric reader beside the door.

"If he attacks you, do *not* do some frogman judo shit and kill the guy. *That* would be an ass load of paperwork for me. And don't"—Lannon paused and looked over at Watts—"let him touch her."

She gave Lannon a tight smile back and then looked at

Chunk with an expression he'd only seen once before, when he was teaching her to shoot on the range at MacDill . . . unconditional trust.

He looked from Watts to Lannon. "You have my word."

The CIA man tapped in his access code, the lock clicked, and the door slid open. Chunk stepped through the gap into the dank and foul-smelling room—the source of the stench apparently the toilet in the corner.

"The smell ain't because of us withholding sanitation privileges," Lannon said, somewhat defensively from behind. "This asshole just refuses to flush."

The terrorist remained seated, his expression a mask, but his eyes bored into Chunk with both recognition and rage.

"*Shoma* . . ." Hamza al-Saud growled.

"We'll take it from here, brother," Chunk said with a backward glance at Lannon.

"Yep," was all Lannon said and then the door slammed shut with a loud click of the magnetic lock.

Chunk advanced on the terrorist, towering over the seated figure. After a few seconds, al-Saud stood, slowly and fluidly, so that they were face-to-face.

"*Shoma*," the man said again. *You* . . .

Chunk didn't flinch, just crossed his arms. "So you remember me." He returned the man's gaze with hatred of his own. "That's right, I'm the guy that took down your operation and captured your jihadi ass."

Al-Saud said nothing.

"I know you speak English," Chunk said, walking in a tight circle around the man. He wanted to send a clear message about who was predator and who was prey in this scenario. "We have signals intercepts of you talking on your mobile phone before the raid. So, you can drop the charade anytime."

The terrorist prince rattled off a defiant statement in Pashto. Chunk, who was by no means fluent in the dialect, translated it to something of the effect, "I am Allah's servant. Whatever you do to me, he will revisit on your head a thousandfold." But as he continued to circle the terrorist, something clicked and he realized that *shoma* was a Dari word, not Pashto . . .

Interesting, he thought, *that his first raw reaction when he saw me was in the native Afghan Dari but then after collecting himself he switched to a Pashtun dialect . . . Why? Is Pashto the dialect he's "supposed" to be speaking? Something weird is going on here.*

"See," he said, turning to Watts with a triumphant grin. "I told you. This guy isn't Hamza al-Saud. Al-Saud is fluent in English, and this guy doesn't understand a word I'm saying."

She arched an eyebrow, clearly confused by this non sequitur but prepared to go along for the ride anyway.

"I understand everything you are saying," the terrorist said in heavily accented English, crossing his arms over his green cotton shirt. "Allah wills that I do not engage with the Great Satan. I may have been pulled from the physical battlefield, but the spiritual war with the enemy of my God rages on. It does not matter where you keep this body. No matter the prison, I will witness your final destruction."

"Oh look, you found your tongue," Chunk said, smiling for real this time. He was no professional interrogator, but he was starting to have fun and realized he'd already learned something they didn't know before, possibly something of great importance. "Sit down, Hamza. My colleague has some questions for you."

Al-Saud did not move.

Chunk balled his fists and got in the terrorist's face.

"The cameras are off, Hamza. What happens in the next

fifteen minutes is off the record. Let's say I break your jaw into a hundred pieces. Nobody will blame me, because I'm just going to tell them that you tripped and hit your face on the toilet over there. Do you really want to eat all your meals from a straw for the next six months?"

Al-Saud looked at him, seemingly testing the validity of the threat.

"Dude, I'm an operator, not an interrogator. You killed my friends. I want to hurt you. I wanna hurt you real bad . . . but I would like to be able to understand you and that's a lot harder when you're missing all your teeth."

"Please sit down, Mr. al-Saud," Watts said, speaking for the first time. "My colleague is an angry man. Please just do as he says."

The jihadist looked at her, then after some internal calculus, slowly lowered himself onto the Army-style cot.

"Thank you. Let's start with your base of operations in Mingora where you orchestrated the drone attacks on US forces in Afghanistan," she began, using a classic interrogation technique: begin with easy things, facts that the detainee accepted his captors already knew. Lead the prisoner on a little journey, get him complacent, and maybe something new would slip out.

"You raided our operations center at the hangar at the Saidu Sharif Airport in Mingora. You murdered my men there, what else is there to say?" Hatred and anger flared in the man's eyes as he said the words.

Watts nodded, unfazed. "I want to know more about the site. I want to know more about how you were able to pirate a signal from the Pakistani satellite and—"

"We want to know about the other site. The safe house in Kanju," Chunk interrupted her. He was in total improv mode, but a voice whispered in his ear that there was something here. Something important worth digging for. "Don't pretend you don't know what I'm talking about. I led the assault myself. Before we hit the warehouse and killed your friends, we hit your secret safe house. Your business guy was there. He was still wearing his suit. He went for a gun, but he was no warrior and I shot him in the face."

Al-Saud broke eye contact and picked a spot on the far wall to stare at, which Chunk took as a cue to keep probing.

"We know all about him, the money laundering, the fundraising . . . but I want to know more about others there that night. We have their DNA samples, but we don't know their names. Can you help me, or do we let our CIA friends take you on another journey of stress positions and let you pretend to be a fish again? Seems stupid to go through all that pain for a couple names. We already have their DNA . . ."

"I will tell you nothing of the brave men who served Allah at my side. I will not disgrace their sacrifice by mentioning even their names in your presence. And I will not betray my mission. Your CIA friends have surely told you this already," the terrorist said, raising his chin in pride. "You can break my face or murder me as you have my brothers, but it matters not. I will go to paradise, while you burn forever in the fires of hell."

Gotcha, you sneaky sonuvabitch.

"We're done here," Chunk said, turning to Watts with a disappointed grimace. "We'll have the CIA guys run a program on him for two weeks and come back . . . see if he's more cooperative then."

"What?" Watts said, now unable to act her way through her shock. "Are you kidding me?"

"Nope," he said, pounding the door twice. He turned back to the prisoner. "You may think you're invincible, Hamza, but you're not. Everyone talks. I mean everyone." He heard the door click open behind him but kept his eyes locked on the terrorist. "Ahmed Farouq cried like a baby and told us everything. So did Khalid Sheikh Mohammed. You think you've won because you didn't talk after listening to some rock and roll and having some water splashed on your face? You've only seen the tip of the enhanced interrogation iceberg. You're in the level one program—level one of five. Faruq Ahmed broke at two. KSM, who was trained in AQ resistance tactics, broke at level three."

Chunk turned his back on al-Saud to face Lannon who was now standing in the door with his hands on his hips and a confused look on his face.

"We're taking this guy up to level two, bro," he said with a wink at the CIA officer as he walked out of the cell. "I'll sign the paperwork on the way out."

Watts followed him out and Lannon shut the cell door behind her.

"What in the hell just happened?" she said, stopping him by the arm.

"Yeah, seriously. You know we're not gonna torture this asshole, right?" Lannon said.

Chunk pulled a tin of Kodiak from his cargo pants pocket. "I know that, but he doesn't. And even if you could, it wouldn't matter anyway, because he can't tell us anything we don't already know."

"And why is that?" Lannon asked.

"Because that shithead is not Hamza al-Saud," Chunk said, turning to Watts with a grin.

"Chunk, are you out of your mind? What are you talking about?"

"You lost me too," Lannon said. "JSOC processed him as Hamza al-Saud in the first place, if I'm not mistaken."

"Hear me out," Chunk said, setting off down the corridor and waving them to follow. "Something has bothered me about this guy for a while, but I could never quite put my finger on it until today when everything clicked into place. When he first saw me, he spoke in Dari."

"So what?" Watts said, striding to catch up to him.

"Why Dari?" Chunk said.

"Because he's Afghan?"

Chunk nodded. "Exactly. *This* guy is Afghan."

"I still don't follow," she said.

"Our signals intercepts of Hamza al-Saud were him speaking Pashto and Arabic . . . this guy messed up. He slipped out of character for a second, and I busted his ass."

"Hold on a second," Lannon pressed. "These groups in Pakistan and the border region of Afghanistan mix it up when it comes to jihad. It's only the peace-loving ones who stick to their tribes."

Chunk stopped and thrust a finger back at al-Saud's cell. "That guy is no Arab. Arabs don't slip into Dari. He's Afghan."

"No, no, don't go there," Lannon said, shaking his head. "We've always assumed al-Saud was a legend this guy created. He probably picked a Saudi surname for branding purposes. Al Qadar was born in Pakistan, not the Peninsula. Let's not confuse the matter with Monday morning quarterbacking."

"We've all been operating off of a lot of assumptions," Chunk said, "But what just happened back there was real and I think it's a red flag. And there's more . . ."

"Like what?"

"You said this guy has been a complete nothing in interrogation, right?"

"That's right," Lannon said. "He just mumbles scripture."

"But when we engaged him on Mingora, he easily

confirmed the locations at Saidu Sharif Airport and the safe house in Kanju. Why would he do that?"

"Because you told me you didn't think he was Hamza al-Saud," Watts said, slowly nodding. "He was worried we thought we had the wrong guy, so he talked enough to validate his legend."

"That's right, and another thing," Chunk continued. "When I pivoted to the safe house in Kanju where we whacked those guys ahead of the hit on the hangar, his reaction was totally inconsistent. When we brought up the hangar, he was filled with rage and pain—those were men he knew and maybe his brothers in arms. But when I brought up the dudes in the safe house, his reaction was more clinical. He steeled himself and stared straight ahead at the wall."

"It might have been new information to him," Watts said.

Chunk nodded. "Exactly, or if not, I bet he didn't know those guys like the real Hamza would have."

"And the real Hamza definitely knew about the hit in Kanju, because it was the hit on the safe house that sparked the evacuation of the hangar."

"Exactly," Chunk said, while Lannon looked back and forth between them like he was watching a tennis match.

"Wait a minute," Lannon said, getting up to speed. "If the guy in the cell isn't Hamza al-Saud, then who the hell is he?"

"A decoy," Chunk said, saying the crazy part out loud. "We grabbed him off the X where intel said he was, he confessed to being al-Saud, and so we assumed we'd nabbed the right guy." He looked over at Watts and flashed her a big smile.

"Confirmation bias," she said and chuckled.

"Confirmation bias," he echoed, remembering the conversation they'd had on the topic during the Beech 1900 exfil out of Mingora.

Lannon swiveled his head back and forth between them as they savored their inside joke, perhaps even feeling a little jealous. "So now what the hell are we supposed to do with this guy?"

"Prove Chunk's theory right or wrong. At least now you have goals and fuck for your program. If something new shakes loose, call me directly." Watts handed him a card with nothing but her name and the number for the sat phone she shared with Yi. "Thanks, Danny. I really appreciate your help."

"You really got sucked through the bunny hole this time, didn't you Watts?" Lannon smiled and squeezed her arm. "I always knew you weren't the type to just sit at a desk and crunch data. Knew it when I saw how you tackled the problem in the final exam at the Farm."

"Yeah, well, I'm still just crunching data—only doing it for a different group that happens to be fire at getting things done."

"Well, good for you."

Chunk led them down the hall and away from the awkward memory lane conversation. They retrieved their weapons while Jen glared at them from her workstation.

"Thanks again, bro," Chunk said, extending his hand to Lannon.

"Like I had a choice," the CIA man said, gripping it with a frown.

"Yeah, well, sorry to piss in your lemonade today, but we really do appreciate the access. We made serious progress because of it."

"Then it was all worthwhile. Sometimes it's easy to forget we're on the same team," Lannon said, then gestured to the elevator. "I'll escort you out."

Chunk nodded but glanced back at the monitor one last time, where the man he'd dubbed "Fake Hamza" in his mind was staring at the camera, unblinking, just as he had been when they'd arrived.

Look at me getting my spook on, he thought as he finally had a chance to pack a fresh dip. *I broke your jihadi ass and I didn't even have to throw a punch to do it.*

CHAPTER 6

Qasim Nadar hummed "Shape of You" as he walked down Cambridge Road fantasizing about dancing naked with Diba in the living room. He despised Ed Sheeran but he heard the damn song everywhere all the time, and tonight it had buried itself deep in his brain and he couldn't get it out.

I'm in love with the shape of you.

We push and pull like a magnet do . . .

He laughed and shook his head at the lyrics but instead of fighting, he just went with it—his humming morphing into outright singing and the rhythm finding its way into his stride. He never did this sort of thing, but today he just felt like . . . like getting his groove on. After happily cavorting his way down the block, he slid theatrically to a stop at the iron gate in front of the courtyard. He trotted his way to the front door, retrieved his keys from his pocket, and undid the lock.

Then, with a wide Cheshire grin plastered across his face, he opened the front door and announced, "Diba, I'm home and I feel like dan—"

The word caught in his throat and he promptly choked on his own saliva at the sight of the unexpected visitor sitting in the living room with his wife. Both Diba and the houseguest looked up and met his gaze, chameleon smiles on their faces. In Diba's eyes he saw terror, and in Hamza al-Saud's he glimpsed bemusement.

"Don't stop on account of me—you feel like what, Qasim?" the terrorist prince asked, getting to his feet to greet him.

"That I . . . I . . . feel like dinner," he stammered.

"Oh, I could have sworn you were about to say you feel like *dancing*," Hamza said, testing and prodding in his signature fashion.

The wheels in Qasim's mind were churning but, like automobile tires spinning in the mud, couldn't gain traction. What was Hamza doing here? Why hadn't he called first? In the three months since the wedding, he'd not heard a peep from the man, and now here he was—making a house call out of the blue? Qasim was so caught off guard he couldn't even remember Hamza's new legend . . .

Damn it, why can't I remember? What is wrong with me? I can't call him Hamza.

"Qasim, you remember Mr. Bijan, from our wedding?" Diba said, rising from her seat on the sofa.

Thank God for you, Diba, he thought and forced a pleasant smile onto his face. *Asadi Bijan, that's Hamza's legend now.*

"It is good to see you, brother," he managed to say, thankful his voice didn't crack.

"You too," the terrorist said and stepped up to give Qasim a back-slapping hug.

After the embrace, Qasim took a seat on the sofa next to Diba, while Hamza settled into one of the two club chairs opposite the coffee table.

"Diba has been filling me in on all the news from the last several months. It sounds like everything has been going well. I understand you are enjoying your new position at British Aero?"

"Yes," Qasim said. "I'm now the Program Director for Design Avionics and Software Integration."

"Congratulations," Hamza said. "A well-deserved promotion."

"Thank you."

For the next thirty minutes, two conversations took place simultaneously. The pointless one between the three of them as they sipped tea and talked about benign, safe, and pleasant topics, and the heated, conflicted one unfolding silently in Qasim's head. On the one hand, the terrorist's arrival stirred feelings of dread and foreboding. The past three months had lulled Qasim into a false sense of security and normalcy. He'd slipped back into his old life and very much enjoyed his newfound respect at work and lovemaking with Diba. He'd even begun to consider the possibility that Hamza would never contact him again—a fantasy he, at times at least, embraced passionately. The communication blackout had been absolute, and he'd wondered if the terrorist prince had been killed or captured by the Americans, releasing Qasim from the growing sense of indentured servitude. At other times, memories of Eshan, his sister, and his father would fill his heart to bursting with rage and hate. At such times, he longed for Hamza's return with a zealous craving so that he could exact revenge on their murderers. But, as the weeks had grown into months and he'd fallen into the routine of this life with Diba, such feelings had been coming less frequently.

The events in Mingora—his recruitment into al Qadar, configuring the Pterodactyl drone, and piloting the attack on the American base in Afghanistan—felt like something that had happened a lifetime ago. No, not a lifetime ago . . . They felt like memories that belonged to someone else. It wasn't him who'd done those things. It wasn't him who'd pledged his fealty to the terrorist sitting in his living room. And yet it had been him. He had done those things. His subconscious refused to play games of self-deception. Even now, months later, he would wake in the middle of the night, bolt upright, gasping for air after pulling the trigger on the flight control stick to launch the Chinese-made HJ-10 air-to-ground missiles at the Kandahar Air Base in his dreams.

I'm a murderer, he reminded himself, and he felt ashamed.

But then, as if in counterpoint, his subconscious sparked a different part of his mind—a video clip he'd watched of his lifelong best friend's murder.

Three men asleep in a safe house, one man on each sofa and a third on the floor. Then the door on the opposite wall is blown off its hinges. Something arcs into the room and a brilliant flash of light washes out the picture. After a second, the feed refreshes and three American operators, dressed in tactical gear and wielding assault rifles, enter with extreme prejudice. The three men who had been sleeping jump to their feet. Two of them scramble for AK-47s, while the third man—Eshan— reaches for a pistol. The Americans open fire. Eshan is shot in the chest and looks down, almost in surprise. Then the back of his head explodes . . .

"Qasim?" Diba said, snapping him from his fugue.

"Yes," he said, blinking twice.

"Mr. Bijan asked you a question," she said, with that nervous look in her eyes.

"I'm sorry," he said turning to Hamza. "I tuned out there for a moment."

Hamza flashed Qasim his trademark easygoing smile. "I said while Diba makes dinner, how about you and I take a walk?"

"Yes, it's a very nice night for a walk," he said and, resisting the urge to look at Diba, got to his feet.

I don't need her permission, nor do I want to see the wounded expression on her face that will distract me during the critical encounter to come.

Turning his back on her, he left the flat to walk with Hamza down Cambridge Road.

"Your wife is even more beautiful than the last time I saw her, and that was on your wedding day when a bride glows most vibrant of all," Hamza said. "You are a lucky man."

Qasim nodded, feeling both possessive and gratified at hearing another man speak about his wife in such a suggestive way. "Your unexpected visit today caught us both by surprise, but please do not read anything more into it."

The terrorist laughed. "Be honest, Qasim. You were beginning to think I'd forgotten about you . . . that maybe I had forgotten our mutual commitments?"

Qasim shook his head. "No, never."

"It is natural for a man to become seduced by this life of excess and moral depravity. The West is full of forbidden fruit. Once tasted it is impossible not to savor the sweetness. I am no different. We are both educated, worldly, introspective men. I understand how difficult it is to lead a double life—like a two-headed dragon, one life is always trying to devour the other."

Hamza's metaphor perfectly captured his quandary; it was as if the man had a window into his very soul.

"Yes, it feels that way," Qasim said, finally being honest. "What do you do when you feel like you are beginning to lose your way?"

"I remind myself of what they have taken from me,"

Hamza replied, his demeanor that of the cold and calculating mastermind Qasim had first met in the hangar in Mingora. "I remind myself of what I have lost and what I have still yet to gain. Have you forgotten what they have taken from you? Do you need me to remind you?" Qasim shook his head, but the terrorist sage continued anyway. "Your father . . . your sister, Saida . . . your best friend, Eshan . . . everyone you loved— murdered and stolen from you."

Qasim clenched his jaw and his hands balled into fists. "I have not forgotten. Not a day goes by that I don't tear the stitches from the scars to let the blood run fresh."

"Do you feel like dancing now, my friend?"

"No," he said, the warrior inside fully reawakened.

"I have been busy these last few months, busier than you might expect," the terrorist said, the heels of his black leather wing tip shoes clicking on the sidewalk as they walked nowhere with purpose, "recruiting talent, raising funds, negotiating with suppliers, plotting strategy, and planning operations."

Qasim nodded, suddenly very curious for details and yearning to be read into al Qadar's plans.

"I have a new general in our ranks—a warrior who has been fighting the Americans for nearly twenty years, a legend who has slipped their nets more times than I can count. Maybe you have heard of him—the Lion of Ramadi?"

Qasim turned to look at Hamza. "I thought he was only a myth."

"No, but he would have the world believe as much."

"Will I get to meet him?"

"Do you want to?"

"Yes."

"Good, because he wants to meet you," Hamza said with

a smile. "I've told him many stories about you. The two of you are the future of al Qadar. You are the yin and yang of the organization; it is time that you start working together."

Meaning what, Qasim thought, his insecurities getting the better of him, *that we are opposites? That he is strong and violent, and I am weak and cerebral?*

He forced his expression to remain neutral. "I will be attending the International Defense Global Exhibition in the UAE next month. British Aero is an exhibitor. If you both can travel to Dubai, we could meet then."

Hamza smiled. "Yes. Yes, that would be perfect—both the location and the timing. I will make the arrangements. In the meantime, be watching the news this week. The Lion of Ramadi and I have something noteworthy planned."

Qasim's stomach suddenly felt heavy. "Will you tell me what it is?"

The terrorist pursed his lips with indecision. "Wouldn't you prefer to be surprised?"

"But what if I can help?"

"I don't think so. This is a boots-on-the-ground operation against a Navy SEAL squadron in Iraq—like the ones who killed our brothers in Pakistan. It is a mission of vengeance, but no drones are involved. Regrettably, there is nothing you can contribute."

Qasim put a hand on Hamza's arm, stopping the terrorist in his tracks. "I have been conflicted these past three months, it's true, but it's not because I lost my faith in you, our cause, or Allah. I've realized something important about our adversary and our mission."

"And what is that?" Hamza said, turning to face him.

"We can never forget that we are engaged in asymmetric warfare. We must exploit as many American vulnerabilities as possible in every engagement to achieve disproportionate effects."

"Go on . . ." Hamza said, curiosity bright in his eyes.

"The British are always in my headspace—their music, their ideology, their propaganda. They make me paranoid, anxious, and stoke feelings of guilt. We need to do the same to our adversaries."

"You're talking about PsyOps?"

"Yes. This is what made the Lion of Ramadi so powerful—and a legend. He got into the American's headspace. They were afraid of him. Just the threat of his presence impacted their operations and tactics."

"I agree, which is one of the reasons I recruited him into al Qadar. So, tell me, brother, what is it that you propose?"

Qasim laid out his plan, praying to Allah as he did that he would be able to deliver on it, while Hamza listened without interruption. When finished, he said, "What do you think?"

"I think al Qadar is only just beginning to see what you bring to the table," Hamza said, clutching Qasim by the arms. "We don't have much time, but you have the green light. The present operation in Iraq is already in motion, but I'll provide you with all the intelligence I can on the target and the timing. If your instincts are correct, your plan will amplify the impact tenfold of what we are trying to accomplish. Allah has clearly brought us together for a great purpose."

Qasim felt himself beaming like a schoolboy. He couldn't help it. The charismatic terrorist prince had that effect on him. Perhaps their partnership was Allah's way of bringing out his gifts and providing a path to fulfill his purpose.

"You will need black hat assistance to execute the plan you suggest," Hamza said. "Do you remember how to access our dark web email client?"

"Of course. I check it regularly despite having never received a communication from you."

Hamza smiled. "The fewer fingerprints we leave in cyberspace the better. Use great care, Qasim. The Americans have eyes and ears everywhere, even in the underground and darkest of places."

Qasim nodded. "I'll be a ghost."

"You will also need a secure workspace," Hamza said, stroking his neatly trimmed beard while turning to walk. Qasim fell in beside him.

"I agree," Qasim said. "The British counterterrorism units are robust these days and watch all of us with ties back home. With the promotion, I'm respected at the office, but they've never really accepted me as one of them. We must assume there are eyes on me at all times—perhaps even ears in my home."

"I agree," Hamza replied. "We have secure sites in East London, and I will contact you in the next twenty-four hours with more information. And, I have someone watching over you—for your protection as well as the safety of your lovely wife."

"Watching over us?" Qasim said, fighting to keep the distaste from his voice. To think that Hamza had been spying on him without his knowledge angered him.

"Do not worry, Qasim. They are trusted and well-vetted brothers who respect your privacy. But it is imperative that we identify and monitor any British surveillance assets assigned to you."

Qasim nodded, but this knowledge made him even more uncomfortable. "Very well. I thank you, brother."

"With that, I think our business is finished for tonight," Hamza said. "I'm keeping you from your lovely wife."

"Aren't you going to stay for dinner?"

"No. I dropped by unannounced because she needed a reminder of her place in the world, but I make her very nervous. There is nothing more to be gained by tormenting poor Diba with my presence. I have other business to attend to, so I will leave you to each other tonight. Please give Diba my apologies," the terrorist said and stuck out his hand. "*Ma' al-salāmah.*"

Qasim shook it. "*Fī amān Allāh.*"

They parted ways and Qasim walked the several blocks back to his flat lost in thought. For months, he'd been dreading this moment—the moment when Hamza returned to pop the bubble of his fairy-tale life—but now that the needle had done its work, Qasim was surprised to realize that he felt better. All of the pent-up anxiety and uncertainty he'd been carrying inside was gone. He was a soldier of Allah, and it was time he reembraced his calling. On that cue, a snippet of his conversation with Hamza replayed in his mind.

"*What do you do when you feel like you are beginning to lose your way?*"

"*I remind myself of what they have taken from me. I remind myself of what I have lost and what I have still yet to gain. Have you forgotten what they have taken from you?*"

In answer, flashbulb images of his father, Saida, and Eshan—each of them smiling lovingly at him—paraded past his mind's eye.

"They took everything from me," he muttered, harnessing all his hate and rage. "I must never forget that."

When he reached the tiny courtyard in front of his place, he paused and looked in the front window of the living room which, at just the right angle, offered a straight view into the kitchen where Diba was cooking. She was not a particularly good cook when he married her, but over the past three months, she had immersed herself in YouTube culinary vlogs and become quite skilled at making a handful of dishes. He wondered what she had decided to make for tonight and whether she would be upset when he told her that their impromptu guest had put her to work for nothing. She was a good wife . . .

With a pitying exhale, he went inside.

Upon hearing the door shut, Diba turned and greeted him with a brave-faced smile. Her gaze flitted about, however, and when she saw that he was alone she said in their native tongue, "Did Mr. Bijan change his mind? Will he not be dining with us?"

Qasim shook his head. "He apologizes, but something came up and he was called away."

On hearing the news her shoulders sagged with what he could only imagine was relief. "In that case, we'll have plenty of food for leftovers."

He kissed her on the cheek, careful not to lean against her apron which was dusted with flour and dotted with orange spots. "What did you make?"

"Chicken korma, chana balti, and rice," she said. "But it is not quite ready. Ten minutes."

"Okay, I'm going to go change my clothes and then we can eat." The look on her face told him she had a question poised on the tip of her tongue but was deciding whether to ask him or not. He decided to answer it for her. "Don't worry," he said, turning to leave for the bedroom. "Nothing has changed."

"Does that mean you are working with him or not?" she asked, surprising him.

He paused in the doorway but kept his back to her. "It means nothing has changed."

"You promised me you would try to get out," she said, finding her courage. "Did you try?"

He hesitated for a long moment and then, to both their surprise, he told her the truth. "No . . . nor do I intend to. This is my life now. Our life. It's time you accepted that."

CHAPTER 7

Zain al-Masri, the Lion of Ramadi some still called him, pressed his cheek against the riser on the buttstock of the Russian-made Chukavin sniper rifle. Using the Rayan Roshd Afzar RU120G thermal-night vision rifle scope, he scanned the street below, dragging his targeting reticle to the entrance of the small house with the large walled-in front yard. All was quiet, but that would change soon. The microearbud in his left ear was silent, his spotters with nothing to report. But the SEALs were coming any minute now . . .

Because they always come.

He wondered if the American Special Warfare Operators had any idea how predictable they had become. For Zain, who had been in the business of hunting and killing Americans for twenty years, their arrival was as predictable as the rising and setting of the sun. Even the time of the hit, sometime between two and three a.m., was so predictable that he had not settled into his sniper roost on the fifteenth floor of this building until just forty minutes ago. He'd chosen this position quite intentionally, as it offered sufficient height but also a defensive advantage because there were no good countersniper lines to his perch from the other buildings in the area. But he scanned the homes, parks, and buildings out of an abundance of caution anyway—looking for anyone or anything out of place.

The target house that the SEALs would be striking sat just over a thousand yards away, well within range of his sniper rifle. He switched to higher magnification and then from IR to thermal on the scope, immediately dialing in on the warm-colored signature of the lone sentry pacing in the yard. The poor fool didn't know he was merely bait for a bigger-picture operation and that he would die tonight in service to the cause.

Inshallah, such is the way of things.

He switched the scope back to ambient light and scanned across this road, where the eastern suburb of Duhok looked eerily similar to where he'd grown up. Poor, dirty, low-rise buildings clustered around dirt-covered parks where during the day, kids would kick soccer balls and at night hide behind locked doors. Neighborhoods like this were where he'd spent his time the past twenty years. Neighborhoods like this were the recruitment grounds for tomorrow's Lion of Ramadi.

That's how it had happened to him . . .

The young Zain al-Masri had once dreamed of being a soccer star—of representing his country in the Olympics. There'd been no high-rises in Zain al-Masri's childhood Iraq. No city buses, coffee shops, and fancy hotels. These were the types of Western conveniences that led to corruption and the inevitable fall of Iraq to the infidels. After the fall, he'd given up his dream of soccer and joined the tiger cub military training cadre, established by Iranian proxies. His natural marksmanship skills had earned him a spot in a sniper program led by an old Russian who made Zain lethal. Killing the infidels had become his sport. Were there an Olympics for such things, he would be a legendary gold medalist.

"Juba," said Ahmed's soft whisper in his ear.

"Yes," he whispered back, amazed at the crystal-clear quality of Ahmed's voice. Were the thirty-five-year-old man Zain still thought of as a boy beside him, Ahmed's voice would not have sounded any clearer. The new tools provided to him by his current benefactor—a younger new generation jihadi— were taking the fight to a level never achievable before.

"The Americans are coming. Two vehicles driving east on Highway 2 from Simele. They will make the turn in five minutes onto Tenahi from the circle."

"Very good, Ahmed," he said. He had considered having his protégé and former spotter in the apartment with him, but in the end, he needed his trusted brother positioned in a second kill zone. "You are in position?"

"Of course, Juba," came the reply.

In addition to Ahmed, he had a third sniper working with him tonight. A female shooter who—if he was honest with himself—might one day eclipse his own abilities. Ahmed was good, but Nurbika was gifted.

Five minutes until the Americans are on target.

He rolled his neck and let his thoughts drift a moment to the passionate, charismatic young man who had recruited him into al Qadar ranks. Initially, Zain had resisted, not wanting to make the same mistake he always did of falling in with an impassioned zealot who later turned out to be nothing but a power-hungry sadist. But Hamza al-Saud, in addition to being tech-savvy and financially solvent, understood that the old ways were no longer effective. Killing innocents, women, children, and civilians had done nothing but turn the world against Islam. It had steeled the resolve of the infidels, and it resulted in the deaths of hundreds more Muslims than infidels in the end.

Insanity.

He thought of the Butcher, Abu Musab al-Zarqawi, the al-Qaeda cell leader in Ramadi when Zain had first risen to fame as one of the trio of snipers behind the Juba legend. Even then, as a young man, he knew that sadistic and barbaric psychopath, killing children with a power drill in the public square as their parents watched, had done more to hurt the cause of jihad than the American invaders had. The average person, no matter what their religion or beliefs, first and foremost wanted peace and security for themselves and their families. When the Butcher became more of a threat than the infidels, the people had turned to the Americans as saviors— liberators of the Iraqi people from the jihadist murdering their neighbors.

And so, Ramadi had been lost.

These lessons had followed him the next fifteen years, and now he'd finally met a leader with the cool intellect to bring the war to the enemy instead of his Muslim brothers. And when the only blood that ran through Iraqi streets was American blood, the tired and complacent Americans would finally lose their stomach for war. Only when that happened would their SEALs and soldiers be called home for good.

What Hamza al-Saud did after that was history unwritten. If it was up to al-Masri, the leader of al Qadar would carry the jihad across the sea to the American shores. So long as the infidels were out of his homeland, he didn't much care what happened to them. After twenty years, he too was growing weary of war. But violence and death were the price of peace, as it had been since the time of the Prophet, and Allah still had work for him to do.

"They are turning now onto Tenahi," Ahmed reported.

Zain scanned to the left and watched through his scope as the two strange-looking vehicles turned north, lights out, moving swiftly. Like overgrown, bulky Humvees the Americans had once used, these new generation Joint Light Tactical Vehicles or JLTVs pushed north, gunners up and manning the fifty-caliber machine guns on top. Killing the gunners would be so easy as they approached the westbound turn into the neighborhood, but doing so would reveal his position and not have the desired psychological effect. So, he tracked them, his targeting reticle bouncing on the head of the lead gunner as they entered the neighborhood.

The trucks, rolling with lights out, approached the corner of the walled compound. They would dismount here, split into two teams, and then cross the wall from two points, kill the sentry quietly, and then attack from the front and back using explosives to breach the doors. They would execute the hit in less than five minutes, leaving the bodies of the dead behind and hauling hooded HVTs back to their vehicles.

So predictable.

Through the scope, he checked the streamer he'd tied on a fence rail in the park a block north, validating the wind direction and speed. He calculated in his head, and then clicked the top knob on the scope twice to compensate. He had already doped in his elevation. For a moment, he wished he were on the fifty-caliber AMR, but the slower bolt action would limit what he could accomplish, despite the dramatic effect the large-caliber round had when striking targets.

No, he reassured himself, *the magazine-fed Chukavin is the right choice tonight.*

The vehicles stopped, one canted left and the other right. He placed his reticle, with the glowing up arrow, onto the center of the rear door of the vehicle. The door opened and a fully kitted-up SEAL exited, moving left. He let the man drift out of his gunsight. The second SEAL turned right as he exited, sighting over his short barrel, suppressor-mounted assault rifle. Zain led the second SEAL, the tip of the aiming arrow and the surrounding reticle at the level of the man's temple but a few degrees in front of his face. He squeezed tension into the trigger, exhaled, and held his breath, moving his rifle just millimeters to the left to hold the sight in front of the man's face. When the third SEAL emerged, he finished the trigger pull.

Zain held the sight steady while the .338 Lapua Magnum round traveled the nearly one thousand meters. His vision had cleared from the suppressed muzzle flash just in time to see the SEAL's head snap right and the gore spray from the other side of his head. The two other SEALs already out of the JLTV moved rapidly and instinctively around the vehicle, finding cover, so he placed his sight on the operator who'd just emerged from the door and squeezed again. A second and a half later, his second target collapsed backward into the cabin of the vehicle. Someone pulled the door shut from the inside, as another SEAL grabbed his first victim and dragged him toward the lead vehicle and into cover. Zain searched for another target and let out a frustrated *tsk* at not finding one. A moment later both armored vehicles bugged out, accelerating west and then turning left onto the first side street.

"They turned exactly where you said they would, Juba," Ahmed said with admiration.

Zain watched through the sight, the tops of the vehicles

visible behind the low buildings from his perch, and he smiled. He switched out of night vision to protect his eyes.

NOW Ahmed!

Twin explosions lit up the darkness as the lead vehicle rolled across the perfectly placed and perfectly detonated IEDs.

Charges detonated, his newest team member and secondary sniper on tonight's op could go to work. With their vehicles disabled, the SEALs would set up security around them and await pickup by their QRF or seek cover in a nearby house. He might even have an angle for another shot of his own—three kills instead of two . . .

But the vehicles didn't stop.

They didn't even slow.

After rocking up on the two right wheels, the lead vehicle landed back on the ground, swerved, and accelerated west with the second vehicle in tow.

Damn . . .

"They were not stopped, Juba," a tense, female voice growled in his ear.

"I see," he said, seething himself. "Exfil the area carefully. The Americans will have drones and satellites looking for anything unusual. We will meet at the rendezvous."

He was already disassembling the Chukavin into its carry bag as he talked. Two dead American SEALs were better than none, but he'd hoped to wipe out at least half of the assault team. Jaw clenched, he picked up the two spent shell casings with a gloved hand and slung the bag strap over his shoulder.

No matter, he told himself in consolation. *My new benefactor promised continuous intelligence and whatever resources necessary to win the war.*

For him and his team—a new trio of snipers resurrecting the Juba legend—tonight's operation was only the beginning.

CHAPTER 8

TOP SECRET JOINT SPECIAL OPERATIONS

TASK FORCE COMPOUND

THIRTY-FIVE MILES NORTH OF THE AFGHANISTAN BORDER

QURGHONTEPPA, TAJIKISTAN

0315 LOCAL TIME

Chunk reread the same paragraph in *Nemesis Games* for the umpteenth time. After not registering a word of it yet again, he tossed the book aside with a disgruntled sigh and climbed out of his rack.

This is why I don't read, he told himself. *Too many damn distractions.*

As he was alone in the room, the only person distracting him was himself. He had his OCD SEAL brain to thank for ruining pretty much every attempt to relax and take his mind off work. Especially when downrange, he was always thinking about the next op.

Or the last op.

Or the one before that.

Or the one way before that.

Tonight, however, he was thinking about Fake Hamza.

No matter how hard he tried, he just couldn't get that fucker out of his head.

Dressed in a faded Bonefrog Coffee T-shirt and a pair of workout shorts, he slipped his sockless feet into his maritime boots and, without bothering to tie them, walked out of his bunk room to find Watts. Deployed SEALs were vampires—working nights and sleeping during the day—so even though they hadn't had an op tonight, everyone was up. Laces flapping, he shuffled down the hall toward the intel shop's "suite"—a windowless room only big enough for a couple of workstations and a four-top table. En route, he peeked in the break room where the boys were hanging out and found them dipping, bullshitting, and watching *Anchorman* for what had to be the fifth time in two weeks.

"Chunk, dude, you gonna join us?" Riker called, somehow sensing him without even turning to look at the doorway.

Damn if that frogman doesn't have eyes in the back of his head, Chunk thought with a laugh. *How does he do that?*

"No dude, I've gotta run something by Watts. You guys seen her?"

"Haven't seen her, bro," Trip said with a bad-boy grin, while lifting his left leg to blast a truly impressive fart. "She's totally afraid to come in here."

"Afraid . . . or repulsed?" Chunk said, noting that practically every flat surface in the room was occupied by a spit cup. "I'm thinking the latter. Seriously, y'all need to clean up those frigging spitters sometime, cuz that's just nasty."

Trip gave Chunk a two-finger salute and turned back to the TV.

Shaking his head, Chunk walked over to the next door on the right, rapped twice with his knuckles, and turned the doorknob. He opened the door twelve inches and looked inside to find Yi hunched over a laptop at the table.

"You seen Watts?" he asked.

"Have you tried her Batcave?" Yi said.

"Nope."

"Try there. Otherwise, I can't help you. The girl doesn't work out, and she only hits the canteen like once a day. I think she might actually be cold-blooded."

"Ouch," Chunk said with a chuckle.

"No, not cold-hearted," Yi came back. "*Cold-blooded*, you know literally, like a reptile."

"Maybe you're on to something. Next time I find her curled up around a space heater or basking on a hot rock, I'll be sure to let you know."

They both laughed at this and he shut the door. With imagery of the latter scenario percolating in his mind, he turned around and headed back down the hall to the women's bunk room which could accommodate four but was presently occupied by only Watts and Yi. He rapped on the door twice and heard something that sounded remotely like, "Come in," from inside. He turned the knob and pushed the door open a crack.

"Watts, you decent?" he said.

"If you're asking if I'm dressed, yes," she said. "Otherwise, the answer is no."

This comment earned her a genuine laugh from him, and he pushed the door open the rest of the way and stepped inside. The sight greeting him took him by surprise.

"What the hell?" he said, his voice trailing off as he stared at the opposite wall in the dimly lit room, which was plastered with photographs, print pages, hand-scrawled Post-it notes of every color, push pins with string connectors, and a poster-size map of the Kashmir region.

"Have you not been in here before?" she said, looking up at him from where she was sitting at a small wooden desk.

"Not since the day we checked in. Looks like you've been busy."

"Yeah, especially after our meeting with Hamza . . ."

"Fake Hamza," he corrected.

"Right—Fake Hamza." She gestured at her wall. "You like?"

He stepped closer to inspect her handy work. *She's like a dog with a bone*, he thought looking at a cluster of photographs of the dead terrorists they'd whacked in Mingora three months ago. *Won't let it go . . .*

"I know you're dying to say it, so go ahead," she said with a slight defensive edge to her voice. "Call me OCD . . . it wouldn't be the first time I've heard it."

He turned to face her, ready with a quip, but did a double take and instead said, "Since when do you wear glasses?"

"Since whenever my contacts are bothering me."

"Hmm," he said, wondering how many times he'd seen Watts in glasses before and simply not noticed.

"Hmm, what?"

"Hmm, am I really *that* unobservant?"

"Like most men, you're selectively unobservant," she said with a hint of a smile. "Which is the worst kind."

"Well, that sucks," he said, looking for something to sit on and finding nothing suitable. He turned back to the wall. "Yi calls this your Batcave. Now I understand why."

"I told her she could be my Alfred, but she didn't think that was very funny."

Chunk's eyes focused on Mingora and a pinned picture of a man with a ruined face. The photo had a yellow sticky next to it with a large red question mark. "You wanna read me in on what you're doing here."

"Sure," she said, pressing to her feet and joining him at

the wall. "It's pretty simple, actually, I'm just trying to piece together the al Qadar network before and after the drone strike in Kandahar. Like I told Bowman, I'm convinced they're still out there—reformulating and rebuilding after the losses we dealt them—and if you're right about Fake Hamza then they may already be far more operational and capable than we think."

"And this dude?" Chunk said, tapping the photo with the question mark.

"You mean the one you guys shot in the face and doesn't ping on facial rec?"

"Yeah," Chunk said. "That's the guy I mentioned yesterday. He was in the safe house we hit in Mingora before you retasked us to the hangar."

"That's right," she said. "I haven't figured out who he is, but something tells me he matters. He wasn't dressed like the other fighters you killed. He was wearing slacks and a dress shirt. My gut tells me his stop over at the safe house was unexpected or possibly out of necessity that night. Maybe Hamza felt the noose tightening and knew we were closing in on him. Maybe this guy was supposed to meet with Hamza at the safe house and Hamza aborted or postponed. Maybe we hit the house before that could happen and screwed it up. I don't know . . . but what I do know is that I definitely want to figure out who the hell this guy is and what his ties to al Qadar were."

Chunk nodded. "Yeah, good idea. I had the same idea about that guy, I guess. Must have been why it came to me when we were talking to Fake Hamza. This guy always seemed out of place. You don't think he was the real Hamza, do you?"

"I don't know," she said and leaned in, looking closer, as if that might help. "Thanks again for shooting him in the face by the way. Veeeeery helpful."

"Wasn't me. You can thank Riker for that."

She shook her head with feigned condemnation. "Why am I not surprised?"

Chunk was about to ask her a question when his phone buzzed with a notification. He retrieved it from his pocket and looked at the screen. The message was from a SEAL buddy at Group Four and it included a hyperlink:

> Chunk, just heard about Team 2
> Bravo platoon. Social media is on
> fire. Word is they got ambushed
> on an op in Iraq and took
> casualties. Not sure what you're
> hearing over there, but lemme
> know.

"What the fuck?" Chunk said through a breath, staring at the screen.

"What happened?" Watts asked.

He showed her his phone. "You know anything about this?"

"No," she said. A heartbeat later, both their mobiles buzzed simultaneously—a message from Bowman summoning them to the TOC. "But it looks like we're about to find out."

They jogged out of Watts's Batcave and headed to the TOC where Yi was already pulling up a video chat window with Bowman at the Tier One compound in Tampa. Spence, Riker, and Saw joined them a moment later and Bowman got straight to business.

"There's been an incident in Iraq," he said in a tone suggesting he was still wrestling with tamping down his anger at the news. "SEAL Team Two was ambushed during an operation and has taken casualties. The details are still trickling in, but initial reporting indicates one KIA and one critically wounded."

"Ambushed by who?" Chunk asked, sitting on the corner of the plywood table closest to the screen.

"From what I understand, the tangos had a sniper in position and IEDs prestaged," Bowman said.

Chunk felt a swell of something like heartburn in his chest and swiveled to look at Riker and then at Spence. "Sound familiar?"

"What the hell, man?" Riker said, shaking his head.

"Just like what we encountered on the Thor op," Spence said. "I hope we're not looking at a new terrorist playbook, with different groups sharing best practices and the like."

"Good God, I hope not," Chunk said and then looked back at Bowman. "Any indication we suffered an intelligence leak or telegraphed the op somehow?"

The CSO shook his head. "Details are spotty. I've told you everything I know. I just wanted to give you a heads-up before you heard it from someone else."

"Do you know who we lost?" Riker asked.

"Senior Chief Chris Johnson," Bowman said.

The name hit Chunk like a punch to the gut and he completely zoned out for the next thirty seconds. Somebody gave his shoulder a squeeze and he looked up to see Riker standing there.

"Wasn't CJ in your BUD/S class?"

"Yeah," Chunk said.

"I'm so sorry, bro," Riker said with a dutiful frown.

"Anyway," Bowman continued, "I wanted you to hear from me first. We'll be monitoring the situation and will update you when we can." And with that, he was gone.

A man of very few words.

Everyone cleared out of the TOC except for Watts, to Chunk's surprise. She didn't say anything, however, just sat quietly in her seat while he wrangled with the bad news.

"I remember this one time, during Hell Week, CJ was my swim buddy on this two-mile swim." The words poured out unbidden. "The water was so freakin' cold that day, and that's saying something because the water is always cold in Coronado. We hit that last half mile and all my muscles just started locking up . . ."

"You mean you got a cramp?"

"No, it was almost like trying to run an engine without oil—things just started seizing up cylinder by cylinder. First the calves, then my quads, then my arms and my chest. I remember telling him that my body was locked and I wasn't gonna make it."

"What did he do? Give you a pep talk?"

"Hell no," Chunk said through a laugh. "He grabbed me under the armpit and started towing my frozen ass. He said he wasn't going to repeat the swim because his buddy couldn't make it, all the while making fun of Texas and dissing me for being a redneck—insults the likes of which I'd never heard before. It was like being rescued by Deadpool or some shit."

She nodded but stayed quiet and let him continue.

"You know how I am about Texas. You can diss on me 'til the cows come home and I don't care, but if you rip on Texas—them's fightin' words."

"So, I'm guessing it worked. He got your blood boiling and you finished the swim?" she said.

Chunk shook his head and snorted. "That's how I usually tell the story," he said, the memory so real he could taste the briny water and feel an actual chill. "But, the truth is he towed my frozen redneck ass all the way to the beach."

A big fat grin spread across her face. "I love it. That's a great story."

Chunk pulled out his mobile phone, cued up the message from his buddy at Group Four, and then clicked on the web link which pulled up a memorial Facebook post written about the event. Dozens of pages and persons connected to the NSW community had been tagged.

In his peripheral vision, he saw Watts get to her feet. "Well, I'll leave you to it . . . I'm sorry you lost a friend, Chunk."

"Thanks, Heels," he said.

The nickname probably earned him an eye roll, but he didn't see it because he was looking at the social media post.

"When you're ready, come find me and we can finish our discussion about Fake Hamza and my wall of terror," she said and headed off toward the hall.

"Sure . . ." But then an unexpected thought struck him, and he stopped her. "Hey, hold up a second."

"Yeah?" she said, turning.

"Take a look at this Facebook post." He scooted off the table and walked to meet her halfway. "Does anything strike you as odd about it?"

Taking the mobile phone from his outstretched hand, she said, "Umm, not at first glance . . . but it's certainly gained a lot of traction, if that's what you're talking about."

"No, although in our business that's problematic in and of itself. I was talking about the time stamp."

She glanced up at the big digital operations clock on the wall then back at his phone. "It posted forty minutes ago."

"Yeah, don't you find that a little odd? I mean we just found out about this. Whoever did this posted it practically in real time."

"Yeaaaah . . ." she said drawing out the word. "Maybe it was someone at Two?"

"I don't think so. Look at how it's formatted. It's written like a retrospective—you know, like the kind of post you see on tragic anniversaries or Memorial Day," he said.

"Never forget the brave men of SEAL Team Two who sacrificed their lives . . ." she began and then read the rest of entry in a murmur. "Hmm, it is a little odd. Whose page is this . . . Have you heard of VetsForFreedom4ever?"

"No, but I don't do Facebook. I mean, you know the rules. We can't risk social media at the Tier One," he said. "It's discouraged and monitored closely even on the white side, but here it's verboten."

"Yeah," she said absently, her mind apparently already working on the problem. "Why don't you forward that to me. I'll do a little digging."

She handed the phone back and gave him a tight smile.

"Thanks, Whit," he said.

She cocked an eyebrow at him.

"What?"

"You've never called me that before."

"Heels?"

"No, you called me Whit."

"Oh, sorry, I didn't even realize."

A victorious grin spread across her face. "No need to apologize. I'll take it as a compliment . . . or at least an upgrade from Heels."

As he watched her leave, Yi's comment from earlier popped into his head, and he thought: *Watts, cold-blooded? Nah, definitely not . . .*

CHAPTER 9

Whitney left Chunk in the TOC to grapple with his thoughts and his grief and went to task Yi with researching VetsForFreedom4ever.

"Definitely seems shady," Yi said, her tone conveying she sensed something new and potentially nefarious to investigate. "I'm on it."

"Thanks, Michelle. I'll be in the Batcave if you need me," she said and walked out.

Back inside her bunk room, she walked up to her al Qadar case wall and looked at the picture of the terrorist with the ruined face. The man's maxilla—the bone that served as the framework for the center of the face from the bottom of the eyes down to and including the upper jaw—had been completely shattered by the bullet. The middle of the face had imploded, and the left eye had been dislodged from the socket.

In the beginning, just looking at the gruesome visage turned her stomach. But having forced herself to look at the horror show of an image countless times, she'd eventually become numb to its grotesqueries. *Was* numb *even the right word?* She wasn't sure anymore . . . it was as if her mind had sterilized it of its humanity. On some visceral level, she'd disassociated the thing in the image from being a person who'd been subjected to profound violence and turned it into a puzzle to be solved.

He was not a man—just a knot, tangled and frayed and in need of reconstruction.

Had they recovered the body, she imagined a coroner could have done quite a bit to reconstruct the face, but that wasn't how these ops worked. The unit had been operating in Mingora under NOC, without the knowledge or permission of the Pakistani government at the time. The hit on the safe house had been an eight-minute evolution; it was capture/kill, then exfil. Chunk's guys had snapped a single picture of the dead man's face and taken a DNA sample, but the latter had been contaminated, leaving her only this single image to work with. And because of the damage, critical identifying features that facial recognition algorithms relied upon for computational analysis—like the shape of the nose and mouth and distances between key features—were badly compromised.

"If only I had an eyewitness and one of those police sketch artists who can draw a face just from a description," she lamented, shaking her head. Then it hit her. "Wait a minute, I do have an eyewitness."

Suddenly energized, she marched out of the bunk room to the break room across the hall where the guys were bullshitting and watching a movie. She didn't bother knocking on the door, just walked in.

"Heels!" several of the SEALs shouted in unison, flashing her wide, tobacco-stained smiles.

"You here to watch *Wedding Crashers* with us?" Riker said from the sofa. Then, scooting left and pushing Saw right to make some room, he added, "I got a spot for you right here."

"As fun as that sounds," she said, laying the sarcasm on shamelessly thick, "I was wondering if you could help me with something else?"

"Me?" Riker said, his eyebrows going up.

"Yeah, you."

"Some super Secret Squirrel shit that only I can pull off?"

"Something like that," she said.

He slapped his knee and popped to his feet. "Well, boys, guess you're gonna have to Wedding Crash without me. Apparently, the spooky lady here requires the services of a real man."

"I'm pretty sure that comment qualifies as offensive," Georgie quipped. "Come to think of it, Senior, I don't remember you attending the sensitivity training we had before this deployment."

"That's very sweet of you, Georgie," she said with a wry grin as she turned toward the door. "But everything about this unit is offensive. I'm pretty sure we're well past sensitivity training."

She led Riker to her bunk room and opened the door.

"*Whoa*," he said throwing both hands up and stopping at the door. "I was just bullshitting around, Watts. You know I can't come in there."

"Oh my God, Riker, it's not the girls' high school locker room," she said, laughing, and jerked him inside by the sleeve of his T-shirt. She led him over to her wall of murder and mayhem and stood, hands on hips, waiting for his reaction which did not disappoint.

"Whoa," he said, his eyes going wide. "This is some serious CSI shit you got going on here, Heels . . . So this is what spooks do in the dark?"

"Yeah, pretty much," she said and then reached out and tapped the picture of the man with the ruined face. "Do you remember this guy?"

Riker squinted at the image. "Can't say that I do. Probably because there's not much left of that face to remember."

"You shot him during the safe house op in Mingora. The hit before the warehouse op where you got blown up," she said. "Ring any bells?"

"Oh yeah," he said, scratching the scruff on his neck. "I remember now, but um, sorry, Heels, I didn't shoot that fucker."

She screwed up her face at him. "Yes, you did."

"No, I didn't."

"That's not what Chunk said."

"Well, Chunk's wrong. Who is *he* to say who I did or didn't shoot?" Riker said with theatrical indignation. Then, slamming his index finger on a different picture, he said. "I shot this dude. Edwards shot the asshole with no face."

"Edwards, huh?" she said, staring at him. "You're sure?"

"Yeah," he said. "Want me to get him for you?"

"If you wouldn't mind."

"Sure, be right back," he said and disappeared.

Through the open door, she heard laughing and lewd mudslinging echoing from the Team room about Riker "not being able to get the job done," and even more laughter and hazing when he told them she was ready for Edwards now.

Oh my God, she thought and felt her cheeks going red. *Why did I take this job again?*

A moment later Riker returned with Edwards in tow and they were both grinning.

"I heard that. It's not funny," she said, trying to put on a mad face but laughing instead.

"I mean, it's kinda funny," Edwards said, chuckling until Riker elbowed him. "Sorry, what can I do for you, Heels?"

"Do you see that dude missing half his face?" Riker said, beating her to the punch. "He was in that safe house in Mingora we ran a capture/kill on before that horrible warehouse op."

"You mean the one where we were looking for the drone and the CONEX box blew up?" Edwards said.

"Yeah, that's the one."

Edwards took a couple steps closer and looked at the picture. "Yeah, I remember. What about it?"

"I think this guy might be important, but for obvious reasons, I can't get viable returns from the facial rec database on this image. So, I was kinda hoping you could help me try to reconstruct what his face might have looked like," she said.

"I can try, but Watts, you know that was over three months ago. I remember shooting him, but we're talking milliseconds of visual contact and I was on NODs."

"NODs?" she asked.

"NVGs," he came back. "You know, night vision."

"I knew it was kind of a long shot, but I had to ask," she said, deflating.

"Hold on," Riker said, jumping back into the fray. "Edwards, dude, I've seen your comics. You could totally sketch this guy. Besides, I thought you had a photographic memory or some shit."

"They're not comics; they're graphic novels," Edwards came back, his voice totally defensive. "And it's called eidetic memory."

"Wait, what?" she said. "You're an artist?"

"Yeah, he's a badass artist," Riker said. "You should see the stuff he draws, it's incredible."

"Okay, perfect, because that's exactly what I was wanting to try. You know how the police have sketch artists who can draw a suspect from an eyewitness description? I want to do that with this guy," she said.

"I guess I could try," Edwards said. "I can kinda picture that guy. Give me a few minutes."

"Great! You can take the photo with you if you need to," she said.

"Nah, I got all I need right here," he said, tapping his temple with an index finger.

A few minutes after Riker and Edwards left, Yi returned to the bunk room carrying a notebook computer.

"Hey, Michelle," she said. "Any luck?"

A strange grimace washed over Yi's face. "Yeah, and it gets even weirder."

"Go on . . ."

"The page, VetsForFreedom4ever, was created yesterday," Yi said.

"What?" Whitney said, confused.

"I know, I told you it's strange, but it gets worse—the post went live *while* the op was in progress. I queried the N2 shop over at Group Two about the operational timeline, and the time stamp on this post corresponds with the middle of the engagement."

Whitney stared at Yi, speechless as her mind worked through the implications.

"I know what you're going to ask next," Yi said, "and the answer is yes, I put in a priority request with NSA to backdoor this account and they got me in with administrator privileges.

The post was written five hours in advance and scheduled to go live at the time of the event."

"Hold on, are you saying whoever posted this knew in advance this was going to happen?" she said, a lump forming in her throat.

"I can't confirm that, obviously, but it sure looks that way."

"And you said the page was created yesterday?"

Yi nodded.

"Do they have any other posts?" Whitney asked.

"Nope, just this one," Yi said, "but whoever is running the page certainly did their homework. They tagged dozens of legitimate, veteran-run and special warfare related groups, former operators and active duty personnel who maintain pages, as well as wives and relatives of SEALs who have a social media presence."

"What's the MO here?" she said and combed her fingers through her espresso-brown hair, working it into a stubby ponytail. "Did you try to trace the contact details? I mean, who's running this group?"

"Yeah, I tried, but you know how it is," Yi said. "Anybody can create a Facebook page with fake information. None of the contact info in the admin settings appears to be legit."

"Can NSA do a deep trace or whatever they call it?"

"I asked that question. They can't do anything retrospectively. But with Facebook's cyber department's cooperation, they can monitor the account and run a trace if and when the user logs in again or tries to draft another post."

Whitney pursed her lips, contemplating next steps. "Okay, let's make that happen. I should probably brief Chunk and Commander Day first and then we can loop Bowman in. I'm sure NSA is gonna ask for authorization to do this next step."

"They already said as much."

She nodded and absently rubbed the three-lobed trefoil

knot tattoo on her wrist. "I haven't studied the post. Did they call out Chris Johnson by name as killed in action?"

"No," Yi said. "It was vague, just mentioned casualties, but it did include a group picture of a number of the guys in the unit. I found that picture posted on another page nine months ago, so either they grabbed it there or maybe this user is connected to that page somehow."

"God, I hate social media . . ."

A knock behind them grabbed her attention and she turned to find Chunk standing there, his stocky, stout frame taking up almost the entire doorway. Whitney greeted him and updated him on everything she and Yi had just discussed; when she was finished, he didn't say anything for a moment. Instead, he ran his tongue between his teeth and lower lip and then pulled out a tin of Copenhagen wintergreen snuff.

"I don't know," he said, packing the tobacco. "It feels like a taunt to me."

This comment surprised her but also instantly resonated, him having succinctly put into words the nebulous feeling she couldn't articulate. "Expand on that," she said.

This time she had to wait on Chunk's answer until he was done stuffing his lower lip with tobacco. "Memorial posts happen on anniversaries of tragedies. Statements of condolence happen only after an official public announcement by the command or Department of the Navy. This post is neither. Sure, the language sounds properly crafted, but it lacks sincerity given that the page has no history in the community. To me, it feels like these assholes are just using the post to communicate or even celebrate that they killed some frogmen."

"He's right," Yi said. "It totally feels like a taunt."

"PsyOps," Whitney mumbled.

He nodded. "During the Iraq War, we dropped leaflets

showing Abu Musab al-Zarqawi in a cage with a caption in Arabic that said, This Is Your Future. The purpose of the campaign was to get inside his head and the heads of his followers."

"And was it effective?" Yi asked.

"I mean, we got him, but it's impossible to say for sure what role the PsyOps campaign had," Chunk said. "For as long as there's been warfare, there's been PsyOps. Alexander the Great used it. Genghis Khan used it. The British and the Americans ran competing messaging campaigns during the Revolutionary War, and both the Axis and Allied powers had broad programs during World War II. If it wasn't effective, we wouldn't do it." He rolled his thick neck and something flared in his eyes for a moment and then disappeared. "Not sure I'm ready for the terrorists to be using it against us, but in any case, it won't work."

"Why's that?" Whitney asked.

He stared at her, his eyes still full of something but his tone even and measured.

"Because the SEAL Teams are a powerful, emotionless, killing machine. This changes nothing for us, other than giving us a trail to follow."

"Well, it changes things in my book," she said. "I think we're looking at a much more sophisticated, premeditated counteroffensive in Iraq than it appeared at first blush. I think we need to brief Bowman."

Chunk nodded. "Agreed, but he's going to want a trail before he puts us on a hunt. So develop this a little more and then grab me."

The face he showed her now was the face she imagined terrorists saw when the SEAL officer bore down on them from behind his SOPMOD M4—focused, lethal, and unflappable.

She nodded. "Okay, boss."

As Chunk slipped out, Riker and Edwards returned, with Edwards cradling a sketchbook under his arm.

"Back so soon?" she said.

"I work fast," Edwards said with a cool-guy grin. "Are you ready?"

"Just show her," Riker said, exasperated. "It's not like you found some long-lost Picasso or some shit."

Edwards shot Riker a dirty look and then opened his sketch pad to reveal a scene straight out of a graphic novel. The perspective mirrored that of a first-person shooter video game—looking over a rifle at three terrorists in a darkened room seconds after the breach. Forty percent of the sketch was portrayed through the rifle's holographic sight, with the targeting reticle centered on the face of what she assumed was the man with the ruined features.

"What do you think?" he asked.

"Um, well, first of all, let me just say that the level of detail is incredible," she said, couching her response. "I feel like I'm right there with you that night."

"You don't like it?" Edwards said, his tone more verdict than question.

"No, that's not it at all," she came back. "It's just that . . ."

"Dude, this totally doesn't help her," Riker said, laughing. "You literally drew her a comic. She wanted a witness sketch, remember? Like the kind the cops use."

"First, I don't draw comics," Edwards snapped. Then, tapping a smaller inset panel in the upper right corner of the page, he added, "And second, the dude is right here. That's what he looked like before I shot him. See his expression?"

Whitney shifted her gaze to the second panel which was a close-up of a wide-eyed Arab man in a collared shirt, looking straight on in terror. Edwards had even taken the liberty of giving him a thought bubble that read: *Oh shit, the Navy SEALs are here. I'm going to die!*

It took every ounce of willpower for her to keep a straight face and not to chuckle. She considered her words carefully because he was already getting defensive and Riker's ribbing certainly wasn't helping matters.

"Well, the thing is, Jamey, while this is very good—I mean incredible work, just like what you'd find in a top graphic novel—I can't use this in the facial recognition database," she said.

"Why not? That's what the dude looked like," he said, tapping the inset panel again for emphasis.

"Because it's caricature. Everything's exaggerated, like a movie. Look how chiseled his cheekbones are and his eyes are super dramatic."

Edwards nodded. "Yeah, yeah . . . I see what you're saying. Well, uh, maybe I can try to do just his face like a police sketch."

"That would be awesome," she said with a grateful smile. "Try to imagine what he might look like in his passport photo—a straight-on view with a focus on accurate proportions. The facial rec algos rely on the shapes of key features and the relative distances between them. Any exaggerated features for effect will impact the search and lead to erroneous results."

"Got it," he said and flipped his sketchbook closed. "This will probably take me a lot longer because that's not how I normally draw. But I'll give it a try . . . for you, Heels."

"Why thank you, sir," she said with a bow of her head.

"Never call me *sir*," he said heading for the door. "I work for a living."

"Ahh, that one never gets old," Riker added with a chuckle

and followed the SEAL sketch artist out, leaving her and Yi alone.

"You think he'll come back with something that works?" Yi asked still grinning at the whole incident.

"I don't know," she said, suddenly and inexplicably feeling optimistic, "but what I do know is that whenever I write any of these guys off about anything, they always find a way to surprise me."

CHAPTER 10

TASK UNIT COMMANDER QUARTERS

TOP SECRET JOINT SPECIAL OPERATIONS

TASK FORCE COMPOUND

THIRTY-FIVE MILES NORTH OF THE AFGHANISTAN BORDER

QURGHONTEPPA, TAJIKISTAN

0055 LOCAL TIME

Chunk couldn't sit still so he paced, a predator with an intense call to violence of action, but no prey on which to focus. Sharing the story about CJ and the swim in BUD/S with Watts had brought everything back to Chunk about his lost friend and fellow frogman. While never on the same team, they were both East Coast operators and had spent countless hours socially together for a decade. Images flashed through his mind of great times with the boys in Virginia Beach and on a variety of liberty calls around the globe. CJ had been at some, but he represented them all. He had been the lease holder on the first Chicks Beach town house Chunk had lived in on his first tour with Team Four—sharing the rent with a rotation of a half dozen other SEALs from various Group Two teams as they deployed on different schedules. But whenever they were both in town, CJ had always been there for him and vice versa. Five years ago, Chunk had stood beside CJ at his wedding. Three years ago, he had been the first one outside the family to hold CJ's new daughter Mariah. He remembered how he'd locked eyes with his brother SEAL in that moment, all the joy and contentment communicated in a blink.

Mariah was walking and talking now.

And old enough to process that her dad is gone.

Little Trace, CJ's son, was only seven months old, and would never even remember his father. But Mariah . . .

"Son of a bitch," Chunk growled, both anger and frustration driving the words and the tears that followed. He sat on the edge of the bed and held his face in his rough, weathered hands, trying to slow his breathing and control of himself.

He would need to call Bethany. He hated that the years had taught him that the best time to call was less than twenty-four hours but more than twelve. Too soon and the widow was still numb; too late, she'd begun to feel isolated and alone. He set an alarm on his watch for ten hours from now.

Who pursues a life where knowing such a thing is second nature?

A mental picture of Bethany holding Trace as she sobbed, her daughter crying beside her, confused, as the Group Two chaplain did his level best to comfort them after breaking the news. He forced the imagery away and focused like a laser beam on what he could control—bringing a reckoning to those responsible. They hadn't just targeted Americans; they'd targeted the SEALs specifically.

Echoes of Operation Crusader . . .

Watts would figure this out—that's what she did. Chunk had worked beside intelligence experts from the Navy, the Army, CIA, NSA, and a ton of organizations that didn't even exist—like the amazing Ian Baldwin and the Signals Team at

Task Force Ember, whose direct-action unit was led by Chunk's spooky former SEAL friend John Dempsey. But Watts had something different. She had insight and intuition the likes of which he'd ever seen before. As much as he liked to tease her about being "a dog with a bone," the trite expression didn't even scratch the surface of her tenacity. She was a meticulous craftsman, a driven investigator, hunched over her lighted magnifying glass, teasing apart each impossible, matted knot of information one strand at a time. The trefoil knot tattoo on her wrist embodied and defined her—a metaphor he'd come to understand having watched her unravel the al Qadar combat drone plot.

And she would unravel this new knot as well.

A knock on his door snapped him back to the present. He pressed to his feet and pulled the door open to find Saw standing in the hallway. "Since when do you knock?" he said, forcing a grin . . . trying to be the rock-solid leader his guys expected and needed.

"You good, Chunk?" Saw asked. "You wanna talk about it?"

He sighed, opened the door the rest of the way, and gestured for Saw to come in. Talking about feelings was not something SEALs usually did. Why was Saw doing this to him? Then it dawned on him—Saw wasn't here for Chunk . . .

"I'm five by, bro," Chunk said as Saw plopped down into the chair in front of the plywood desk holding Chunk's laptop. "CJ was one of the best operators I've ever known, and I'll never stop missing him. But he died doing something he loved and believed in. He answered the call. He loved being an operator . . ."

Saw nodded, and Chunk took a long, slow breath and sat on the edge of his bunk, elbows on knees.

"You know his kid—the little boy?" Saw said.

"Trace," Chunk said gently.

"Yeah, Trace. He's only seven months old, bro. He'll never know his dad as anything but a picture and a folded flag on the mantel. And little Mariah . . . This one hits pretty close to home." Saw let out a shaking breath, staring at his feet. "You know, I'd follow you and this team anywhere. I'm not afraid of dying. If I give my last full measure and it stops one of these insane jihadi assholes, if it prevents one attack, if it saves just one American life, then bro, I'm all good. But Keith, I just . . ."

Saw using his real name felt both odd and poignant for him, and he let the silence simmer between them for a moment, even though he knew what was coming next.

"You know Maggie is just two, right?" Saw continued when he was ready.

"Yeah. She's gorgeous too—takes after her mom, thank God."

Saw continued as if he'd barely heard. "Connor is four. He'll be five in another few months. The deployments are getting harder for him. He's a tough little man, but if I didn't come home . . ."

Saw looked away.

Before their screening to the Tier One, Chunk knew Saw had been thinking about retiring from the teams to be with his family, to be a *real* dad. But when JSOC and the Navy stood the Tier One back up and every frogman's ultimate dream was presented to him, Saw had tabled those thoughts. Chunk imagined the decision had been preceded by a long, difficult conversation with Saw's wife, Ellie—a strong, capable, and independent woman and perfect Navy wife. She was loving, supportive, put others before herself, and yet still tough as nails. She ran their household just like she ran half marathons—tirelessly and undaunted. The woman was something special, and every time Chunk interacted with her, a tiny unacknowledged part of him envied what Saw had found.

Saw turned back to him, eyes almost pleading for guidance or direction or something. Chunk had none of those things to offer, so instead he said, "I don't have what you have, Saw. I think I might have chosen the path I did so I wouldn't have to face the choice you're facing now. But, if I was in your boots, I think that knowing they're safe—back home in Florida and far away from the evil we prosecute every day over here—would give me solace. And knowing that we *keep* that evil at bay by doing what we do, it makes the separation and commitment to the job an easier pill to swallow."

Saw held his gaze for a long moment, then pressed to his feet.

"Look, I'm sorry for laying all that on you, man. I'm just babbling. This conversation was supposed to be about CJ, not me. He was a badass SEAL. It just makes you think, you know?"

"I hear you." Chunk clapped Saw on the shoulder. "And I know the burden that you and the other married guys carry on your back is heavier than mine. But I also want you to know that your presence on this team—as an operator, a leader, and a brother—shapes who we are. I know it might sound trite, but for this unit the age-old adage 'the whole is greater than the sum of its parts' is especially true. You make a difference here, Saw. I couldn't do this without you."

"Hey, now, I'm not here for an ego rub," Saw said with a forced laugh. "I'm just making sure you're okay, 'cause I know you and CJ were tight."

Chunk clapped the frogman on the shoulders and nodded. "Thanks, bro, for checking on me."

Saw gave him a fist bump and walked out.

Chunk paced back and forth a moment, then his mind went back to the problem at hand—getting Bowman to give the nod for Gold to head to Iraq and hunt down and destroy whoever was responsible for the sniper ambush. A thought suddenly occurred to him, and he went to find Watts.

"Chunk?" she said, looking up with concern as he barged into her room. "Everything okay?"

"The target package," he said.

"What target package?" she echoed, confused.

"Sorry," Chunk said, taking a long, slow breath. "The target package that SEAL Team Two was moving on when they got hit. What do we know about it?"

She leaned over and pulled up a page on her laptop. "Looks like the HVT was a bomb maker . . . thought to be part of the ISIS network in Duhok, where roadside bombings have been spiking."

"No, no," he said pulling at his face. "I know that. I want to know if the intel was good. Was the bomb maker on the X?"

She looked confused. "Well, I'm not sure. They got ambushed before the breach. I imagine the bad guys at the compound squirted once the gunfire started. Look, I know there's probably a need to make sense of things, to make the sacrifice seem worth it . . ."

"Damn it, Heels, it's not about that." Chunk leaned his hands on the desk. "Whoever ambushed Team Two would have to have known when the SEALs were coming and where they were going. I can see the 'when' leaking if ISIS had some local snitches working at the FOB or spotters watching for the team to head out in their vehicles all kitted up. But to know the 'where' means the bad guys would also have to know the mission objective. That's TS/SCI level information that even the most trusted local assets and terps wouldn't have access to. The target package wasn't leaked . . ."

"It was predicted," she said, finishing his thought.

"Bingo. Because over the last twenty years of fighting this never-ending war on terrorism, we've become predictable. Someone fighting against us on the other side long enough would find our rhythm. Shit, it wouldn't even be that hard."

"I'll look into it," she said, the gentleness in her voice out of place and annoying. "But whether we find a bomb maker living there or not doesn't really answer the other question you're asking."

He blew air through pursed lips. "What if it was a setup from the beginning?"

"PsyOps," she said, her face losing its color.

He nodded. "What if they manufactured the intelligence Team Two used to plan the raid?"

"It wouldn't be that difficult if they were familiar with our procedures and methods," she said and laid it out. "Leak the bomb maker's location to our local assets in Duhok, let the HUMINT percolate in the network for a day, give Team Two another day to validate the intel and plan the hit, and the next night set an ambush."

"So fucking easy," he said, and all they could do was stare at each other for a long moment.

"What now?" she said at last.

"We've gotta find the asshole pulling the strings and take him out," he said, heading again for the door. "Because if we're right, then this is gonna happen again, and probably soon." He realized that he didn't have time to build a case. He needed to loop Bowman in immediately on what they were thinking and where this trail of intel was taking them. He turned and stomped toward the door.

"Where are you going?" she called after him.

"To the S2 shop to call Bowman," he said, pausing at the

threshold and talking over his shoulder. "Tier One problems call for Tier One solutions. Gold is going to personally take out these assholes before they kill any more frogmen."

"What about al Qadar? Chunk, if we're right about Fake Hamza, and al Qadar is still operational, then we have another problem. And if they still have drones—"

He turned to her.

"I agree completely," he said, cutting her off. "But we're the fucking Tier One. We can prosecute two urgent targets at once. Put Yi to work and exploit all the spooky channels so we can try to track down the real Hamza and penetrate what remains of his network. I'll take a fire team to Erbil to start working this new problem. If Yi uncovers actionable intelligence on al Qadar while we're hunting in Iraq, Spence will execute on it with the team we leave here in Taj. I'll take Riker, Saw, Georgie, and Trip with me. We can walk and chew bubblegum—or, in our case, walk and pack a dip."

"What about me?" she asked.

Despite knowing her talents would be better utilized here, the selfish part of him won the day. "Pack a bag, because you're coming with us to Erbil to help me hunt down the assholes who killed CJ."

CHAPTER 11

Chunk gripped the proffered hand of the SEAL officer walking up to greet him. "Hope you don't mind us popping in to play in your sandbox for a bit?"

"Hell no. It's a party, didn't you hear?" Lieutenant Adam Fitzner, the Team Two task unit's operations officer, said as he gave Chunk's hand a hearty squeeze.

Chunk felt a surge of adrenaline at being in Erbil, where only a day ago he might have actually run into his friend CJ. Now, he would be hunting down and killing those responsible for CJ's death. Bowman had had no hesitation about moving Chunk and a fire team to Erbil after hearing the intel on the social media post and Watts's and Yi's PsyOps theory. "Go get these fuckers before they hurt any more frogmen," he'd growled. "And let me know what else you need." Chunk imagined this was more to Watts's credit than his, and in no small part due to the way she'd single-handedly unraveled the al Qadar drone program. Bowman now gave heavy credence to her spooky working theories.

Chunk clapped his left hand on Fitzner's shoulder and met the other man's gaze. "I'm really sorry to hear about CJ. He was good people."

"Yeah," the SEAL said with a grimace. "Did y'all go back?"

"He was in my BUD/S class. I probably would have drowned during Hell Week if it wasn't for him," Chunk said with a chuckle.

"He was like that. The brother definitely hauled more than his fair share of frogmen out of the suck over the years, including my sorry green ass when I was new here. Gonna be rough around here for a while I reckon . . . but we'll sort it out."

Chunk gave his brother a tight smile and turned to Watts who was standing silently beside him. "LT, this is Whitney Watts. She pretty much runs our N2 shop and was the brains behind the operation that castrated al Qadar's combat drone operation a few months back. If you don't mind, I'd like her to join us for this conversation."

"Nice to meet you, Lieutenant," Watts said.

"Please, call me Fitz," the SEAL said, and they shook hands. "I know that shit's supposed to be compartmentalized, but I've heard good things about you, ma'am. Nice to meet you."

"Um . . . thanks," she said, and Chunk could tell she wasn't really sure how to respond to the surprising news that she had a growing reputation, however limited it might be, outside of the Tier One.

Chunk gestured to one of the vacant wooden picnic tables set up in the little dirt courtyard between two rectangular metal buildings. The trio walked over and took a seat, he and Watts on one side and Fitz on the other.

"Are you aware that there was a Facebook post about it?" Chunk asked.

Fitz nodded. "Just heard about it a few hours ago. That's fucked up, isn't it?"

"Yeah, but we don't think it originated from inside the NSW community like some folks are going on about."

"If not the community, then where?"

"Watts has a theory that the post was part of an emerging jihadi PsyOps program."

Fitz shifted his gaze to Watts. "If that was the case, why offer condolences? Why not brag about and publicize the victory over the Great White Satan?"

"I think the group we're dealing with here is operating with a different level of sophistication than those that came before them. I think the question we need to be asking ourselves is who was the target audience for this post? In my humble opinion, the answer is obvious. The target audience was the Naval Special Warfare community, and when I say *community*, I mean everyone—the command, the operators, and their families," she said.

"What's the endgame?" Fitz asked.

"To get inside our heads. Let us know that they've got our number. To reinforce the fact that counterterrorism is no longer business as usual." She turned to Chunk. "I gotta say, Chunk, this has a very Hamza al-Saud feel to it."

Chunk watched Watts's already pale complexion take on an even whiter shade as she spoke the words, which had an instantly chilling effect on him and lured his thoughts back to the conversation with the man he was convinced was *not* Hamza al-Saud.

I may have been pulled from the physical battlefield, but the spiritual war with the enemy of my God rages on. It does not matter where you keep this body. No matter the prison, I will witness your final destruction.

He turned back to Fitz. "Is there anything you can tell me about the op or the HVTs you've been hunting here that might shed a little light on what happened? Have you seen a change or elevation in tactics in the region before last night?"

The SEAL officer rubbed his bearded chin. "To be honest, I can't say that I have. That's something you really need to talk to the spooks about. No offense, Watts."

"None taken," she said.

"There's a pretty big OGA contingent at this compound and I'd say they definitely have their fingers on the pulse of what's going on in the region. I mean, from the operator perspective, up until last week it's been business as usual around here. You know what it's like—it's a frigging mess. We've got ISIL, the White Flags, PKK, the Peshmerga, GMCIR, PMF, a half dozen militias *claiming* to be PMF, and on and on. In Iraqi Kurdistan, everybody hates everybody, alliances change like the wind, and it's impossible to know who the hell is shooting at you on any given day."

Chunk glanced at Watts. "You familiar with PMF?"

"Popular Mobilization Forces—if I'm not mistaken it's an umbrella group composed primarily of Iranian-backed Iraqi Shiite militias," she said.

"That's right," the SEAL officer said. "And they're giving us fits. Pick a side assholes."

"Don't the different PMF factions take most of their direction from the Iranian Revolutionary Guard?" she asked.

"Yeah, which is pretty friggin' ironic considering they're on the payroll of the Iraqi Army, who we're supposed to be allied with."

"What else?" she asked. "Any other unusual activity or chatter we should know about?"

"Yeah, I got something that fits the bill," the SEAL said with a God-help-me look up at heaven.

"Go on," she coaxed.

"I know this is going to sound crazy, but one of my terps told me he was hearing rumors that the Lion of Ramadi was in Mosul."

"What!" Chunk said, reacting viscerally to a name he'd not heard in ages.

"My sentiment exactly," Fitz said.

"Impossible," Chunk said, pulling out a tin of Kodiak from his left chest pocket. "The Lion of Ramadi is dead. We took care of him fifteen years ago."

"I know," Fitz said. "But damn if there wasn't a sniper assassination in Mosul the next day."

"You talking about General Hassan?" Chunk asked.

"Yep, he flew up from Baghdad to meet with senior Pesh-merga officials. They were supposed to talk about coordinating regional security efforts against increasing pockets of Daesh activity cropping up all across the north, and he got capped walking to his car in the hotel parking lot before the meet-ing," Fitz said. "Single shot to the back of the head. They never found the bastard. Then a few days later, my unit is targeted by a sniper with legit skills . . . I'm just sayin'."

Chunk finished packing his lower lip with snuff and said, "No way in hell. He's not the only enemy sniper to emerge from this shithole battlefield."

"I don't know, dude. What if my terp is right? What if we really didn't get him, and he went into hiding only to resurface now, years later?"

Chunk looked from Fitzner to Watts. "What do you think?"

Watts inhaled deeply and then blew air through her teeth.

"My gut tells me the Facebook post and rumored return of the Lion of Ramadi are probably connected. Even if this sniper is not the actual Lion of Ramadi—which I agree seems unlikely—by using the legend, he instantly gains power and credibility. It's all part of the same endgame."

"Which is what?"

"To get inside our heads."

"Well, it's not going to work," Chunk said defiantly and spit a glob of brown tobacco juice into the dirt.

"Oh, really?" she said, cocking her head at him. "Because I think the fact that we're having this conversation is proof that it already has."

PART II

"People should be measured by the depth of their depravities. Virtue can be ignored, whereas our depravities leave an indelible mark upon everyone we touch."

—Whitney Watts

CHAPTER 12

With cold sweat trickling from his armpits, Qasim stepped out of the taxi onto Greenfield Road. A mere block from the East London Mosque—the first in London approved to broadcast the *adhan* on loudspeakers—the neighborhood was predominantly Muslim. In fact, the Tower Hamlets borough of London was 40 percent Muslim, and so his presence here was far from conspicuous. But that didn't matter. Hamza had put the fear of God in him during their last talk together, telling Qasim to assume he was being monitored by British Intelligence at all times and behave accordingly. Ever since, Qasim felt eyes on him wherever he went.

Paranoia is a terrible state of being.

This afternoon he was visiting al Qadar's secret cyber operations facility in London for the first time. His original inclination had been to make this visit at night, but he'd later decided that to do so only made his behavior appear more suspicious. A visit during daylight hours near the end of the workday gave the appearance of legitimacy. *I'm doing nothing improper . . . nothing to see here* was the message he wanted to project. Now, if only he could relax and look the part. The urge to look over his shoulder and scan the street for tails was overwhelming, but he resisted. It was imperative he looked confident.

They're watching you . . . surveilling you right now, the voice in his head warned.

Let them watch, he fired back, silently arguing with himself. *I'm just a Muslim man visiting an Afghan import shop to buy some spices.*

He exhaled, relaxed his jaw, and walked up to the entrance of the modest ground-level storefront. The trilingual sign above the door displayed Afghan Importers: Spices & Goods in English, Arabic, and Pashto. Bells jingled and rang as he pulled the shop door open. A fragrant aroma hit him a heartbeat later. Notes of cumin, coriander, turmeric, black pepper, cardamom, clove, and paprika—the principal spices of Afghan curry—flooded his nostrils. As he inhaled the savory mélange, a powerful wave of nostalgia washed over him and a once-forgotten childhood memory of his mother cooking and laughing with his sister, Saida, filled his mind.

"*As-salāmu alaykum,*" a middle-aged man of medium stature said, walking up to greet him, ruining the flashback. The man was dressed modestly in a gray sweater and blue jeans and kept a full but neat pepper-gray beard.

"*Wa-Alaikum As-salām,*" he replied.

"May I help you?" the shopkeeper asked in Pashto.

"Yes, I'm looking to buy some spices."

"You have certainly come to the right place, my friend,"

the man said, flashing him a mouthful of tea-stained teeth. "We sell bulk spices and blends. What are you looking for?"

"I'd like five hundred grams of the Anousheh blend," he said and saw a flicker of something chase across the man's face at the mention of the al Qadar code word.

"This is a very special blend that originated in the Pashto region, not known by many people. Very spicy and very delicious. Are you from the region?"

"Yes, my mother was from Mihtarlam and she was an excellent cook," he said, adhering to the challenge-response script he'd memorized to validate his identity and gain access to the secret operation in the basement.

"Ah, yes, I know this place," the shopkeeper said, nodding, and then asked Qasim a third and final challenge question. "In the town center, there is a sculpture if I'm not mistaken. Have you ever seen it?"

"Yes, it is twenty meters tall, so difficult to miss. At the pinnacle, there's a globe with an eagle perched on top," Qasim said and watched the shopkeeper's shoulders relax as they completed the protocol.

"Come," the man said and waved for Qasim to follow. "I wish to show you where the spices are blended."

Qasim strode after the man, careful not to bump into the merchandise displays crammed into the tightly packed store. In addition to spices, the little shop sold most everything one might find in a typical Afghan bazaar—handmade jewelry and trinkets, scarfs, pakol caps, Quran boxes, charms and keychains, and chai sets. The shopkeeper disappeared behind a maroon-colored curtain that hung in an opening at the rear of the shop beyond the cash register. Qasim had to duck his head under the curtain rod to pass through the low doorway. When he emerged on the other side, he locked eyes with a young

Muslim sitting in a chair in the corner holding a semiautomatic pistol in his lap. He did not recognize the young man
glowering at him, but why would he? The truth was, he knew
little about the breadth of the al Qadar network and how many
soldiers the terrorist prince had enlisted in his ranks. Admit-
ting to himself how little he really knew about Hamza's army
and all his master's plans made Qasim feel out of his league.

He nodded at the glowering man with the gun, who didn't
reciprocate any goodwill, and returned his attention to the
shopkeeper.

"This way," his host said and gestured to a dark cement
staircase leading down to a cellar.

Qasim had to hunch and duck his head all the way down
because of the low sloping ceiling. He took his time, not wanting to miss a step as his eyes were still trying to adjust to the
blackness. At the bottom, they stopped at a small landing
beside a metal door. The shopkeeper used his body to block
Qasim's view while he entered a six-digit code into a keypad.
An instant later, the keypad beeped, and he heard the lock
mechanism disengage. The shopkeeper pulled the door open
and stepped to the side to give Qasim room to pass.

"When you are ready to leave, ring the buzzer on the inside
of the door and I will escort you out," the shopkeeper said.

Qasim nodded but his attention had already moved on.
He counted a half dozen black hats working in a space lit
almost exclusively by the glow of the computer monitors they
were seated behind.

"Gazaaa!" a familiar voice exclaimed loudly as Qasim
stepped into the room, the shopkeeper shutting the door
behind him.

"Fun Time?" Qasim said, shocked to see the Chinese Uyghur
hacker he'd worked with during his first prolonged engagement

with al Qadar in Pakistan. Truth be told, Qasim was surprised to see the exuberant black hat alive. "I thought you . . ."

"You thought I dead?" Fun Time said in heavily accented English. Then, with a laugh, added, "I told you last time, I'm a badass Uyghur from Turkestan. No way no how no Navy SEALs ever catch me."

Qasim chuckled and walked up to shake the hacker's hand, but the stout Uyghur wanted a fist bump instead.

"Welcome to my operation," Fun Time said, his head bobbing to what Qasim could only imagine was some imaginary beat track playing in the kid's head. Qasim followed Fun Time's extended index finger as he introduced the other hackers in the room. "That's Tweem, Gru, Abdul, Kimchi Love, and The Prophet."

They were all men except for Kimchi Love, a young woman in a black hijab who looked to be of Malaysian descent. Only Abdul acknowledged Qasim's existence with a nod; the others ignored him completely as they typed away at their workstations, which were arranged in a horseshoe configuration. On the far wall at the bowl end of the horseshoe, three large flat-screen TVs mirrored select monitor feeds.

"Looks like you have quite the operation running here," Qasim said, following Fun Time into the middle of the horseshoe where he could see all their screens.

"I've been waiting for you for long time, Qasim," Fun Time said unwrapping a lollipop and popping it into his mouth. "Where you been?"

"Doing my job," Qasim said, not liking the insinuation implicit in the hacker's question.

"Hamza tell me your Facebook idea. It's good. We make it happen yesterday. We do like Russia, fuck the Americans on social media. Make them so crazy," he said with a grin that would have made the Cheshire cat proud.

"You're certain the Americans can't trace the Facebook account to us here?" Qasim asked.

"I never certain," Fun Time said, talking with the ball of his lollipop stretching out the side of his cheek "That's what make it fun time."

Ah, so that's where the nickname came from, Qasim thought, smiling and shaking his head.

"If you say so," he said and scanned the monitors of the other hackers to try to glean what they were doing. From a cursory sweep, every one of them was working on something different. "What are you guys working on?"

"Many things. Gru trying to hack USCENTCOM. Tweem building a database of all American Navy SEALs, where they live, who they marry, where they deployed, and hacking email and accounts. Abdul and The Prophet phishing at big defense contractors, and Kimchi Love running fake Twitter, Facebook, and Instagram operation. Multiprong attack, baby."

Qasim could not help but marvel at what he was seeing. Yes, he was a professional programmer. Yes, he was in charge of avionics software integration for the Valkyrie stealth UCAV program at British Aero. But he was no black hat. What these people did down here in the basement of "Afghan Importers" was as foreign to him as playing cricket would be to a basketball player.

"Hey, tall guy, you pay attention now," the hacker said, waving his lollipop at Qasim. "Hamza like your idea. He wants a big PsyOps job from us. But he also want more."

"Okay, what do you need from me?" he asked.

"Hamza wants to hack America drones. He wants to track them. He wants to hijack the data stream. Every op they use a drone we can influence."

Qasim shook his head. "We tried that before, remember? We couldn't crack the security on the satellite feed."

"You are programming drones for British Aero?" Fun Time asked.

"Yes, but I program the avionics software. I have nothing to do with uplink and downlink data transmission or ground unit command and control."

"Hey, buddy, you smart, you go figure out."

"I don't think you understand," Qasim said, his voice a tight chord. "If I start snooping around areas outside of my responsibility, it's going to raise red flags. The program is tightly compartmentalized. I don't have unfettered access to all information."

Fun Time bit the ball of his lollipop in half with a loud crack and growled, "Then get me access to British Aero servers and I do it myself."

Qasim had never seen the ebullient hacker angry before. "And how, exactly, am I supposed to do that?"

The hacker reached into his pocket and retrieved a USB thumb drive. "Insert in any computer behind firewall, open zip file, and install program. I do rest from here."

"What if they trace it back to me?" he said, accepting the hacker's cyber hand grenade.

Fun Time laughed and clapped Qasim on the shoulder. "Relax, okay. You can do it. This is *fun time*, remember?"

"Maybe for you," Qasim murmured as he grudgingly shoved the USB key in his pocket. Just the thought of trying to smuggle the hacker's Trojan horse into British Aero sent fresh, twin rivulets of cold sweat streaming down from his underarms as he turned to leave. When he reached the metal door, he pressed the buzzer just as he'd been instructed to do. A moment later the door opened and the shopkeeper greeted him with that toothy tea-stained smile of his.

"Time to go?" the man asked in Pashto.

Qasim nodded and followed him up the concrete stairwell, this time bumping his head on the low ceiling and then cursing himself for being distracted. When they reached the top, he didn't even bother glancing at the young sentry with the pistol. And why should he? This man was beneath him, nothing more than a guard dog. The shopkeeper pulled back the curtain leading to the store and a blaze of light made Qasim squint hard and reflexively raise a hand in front of his face.

"This is for you," the shopkeeper said and handed Qasim a plastic shopping bag.

"What is it?" he asked, accepting the sack.

"Spices, of course," the man said with a cautious smile. "You don't go shopping here and leave empty-handed. That would be suspicious."

Qasim thanked the man and let himself out.

I really need to get my head in the game, he thought, silently chastising himself for not thinking of that as he turned north on Greenfield Road. *Because things are about to get much, much more dangerous.*

CHAPTER 13

Chunk paced the tiny break room like a caged tiger at the zoo.

"Dude, what are you doing?" Riker said from the sofa where he was playing a game on a Nintendo Switch.

"Pacing," Chunk said.

"I can see that, but what's lighting this particular fire under your ass?"

"Just waiting on the spooks to get us a target, bro . . . I don't understand what's taking so long. I mean these assholes couldn't have gone far. Seriously, what's so difficult?"

"Damn it," Riker growled, and Chunk heard the sound effect for Riker's character dying in the game. "You killed me."

"What are you talking about?"

"You distracted me."

"I thought you were a steely-eyed frogman who was incapable of being distracted?"

"Let's go for a run," Riker said, tossing the Switch console onto the cushion next to him. "We could both use it."

"I don't wanna go on a run."

"Yes, you do. Hell, you've probably paced three miles already; what's another couple at speed?"

Chunk sighed. "You're probably right. A run would clear my head."

Riker popped to his feet. "I'm dressed and ready, how 'bout you?"

"Yeah, let me just grab a ball cap," Chunk said and followed Riker out of the break room toward their temporary berth at the end of the hall.

"Hey, Chunk," a voice called behind him, "you got a second?"

He turned to see Watts leaning halfway into the hallway from the office she was squatting in while they were here.

"Sure," he replied. "Whatcha got, Heels?"

She didn't answer just beckoned him with a come-hither curl of her fingers and disappeared back into her office. He followed her inside, leaving Riker leaning against the door frame looking in. On her desk, Chunk saw she had a hand-drawn pencil sketch of a man's face.

"This is the picture Edwards drew for me of the man with the ruined face," she said and handed him the drawing.

He'd heard plenty about the whole comic art fiasco, so when he saw this picture his first reaction was to chuckle. But on closer inspection, he changed his tune. The headshot sketch, while still graphic novelesque in its flair, was pretty damn good. "This ain't half bad," he said, holding it up to show Riker.

"Shit, that's good even for Edwards," his LCPO agreed.

Chunk handed the paper back to her. "Helluva lot better

than anything the rest of us could draw. Lucky he was the one to shoot this dude, I guess."

"Yeah, it's a huge improvement over what I had before. He really tried to give me what I asked for," she said, not taking the page from him and instead gesturing for him to hold on to it. "Please take a long, hard look at it, Chunk, and tell me if the face looks familiar. You too, Riker. You said before that you guys breached from the same side of the safe house as Edwards, right?"

"Yeah," he said looking at the sketch. "Truth is, I didn't really see this guy until after Edwards capped him," Riker said.

"How about you, Chunk? Do you recognize this face? Does it look like the man you saw?"

Chunk shook his head and set the paper down on the desk. "It was *pop, pop, pop* and over. Sorry, Watts, I wish I could be more helpful."

She nodded, propped her hands on her hips, and stared hard at it. "I took a digital photo of it and ran it through the database, but I think it's a little too generic. I'm getting too many returns," she said, deflating. "I just wish there was some way to take this and turn it into a photo-realistic CGI image."

Chunk scratched at his neck. "I might know a guy . . ."

She looked up to meet his gaze. "Really?"

"Yeah," he said, slow-nodding. "Did you happen to meet our new neighbors on the Tier One compound at MacDill before we deployed?"

"You mean the people working in that crappy trailer they brought in and set up on the other side of our little redneck barbecue courtyard?"

"Yep," he said.

"Can't say that I have. Who are they by the way?"

A conspiratorial smile curled his lips. "They don't exist . . ."

"Uh-huh," she said and folded her arms across her chest. "Sorta like this unit doesn't exist."

"Exactly . . . but way beyond JSOC-level secrecy. These dudes don't exist even at the highest levels of government. They are deep, deep dark."

"So, you're not going to tell me who they are? Is that what you're saying?"

He chuckled. "Shit, I'm not sure I'm fully read in on these guys. Me, Riker, Saw, and Trip have done a couple of righteous ops with them. I'm surprised we haven't augmented them on anything since you got here, to be honest."

"Probably because we've been a little busy, Chunk—or haven't you noticed?"

"Oh, they don't care about that," Chunk said, remembering how he and his guys had once been pulled out of high-tempo combat operations to augment a black op into Iran. It seemed like both forever ago and just last week.

"Is it some sort of blacker than black, off-the-books task force?"

"Yeah. They're called Task Force Ember. Super elite. Tiny footprint. You'll like them. Hell, I probably shouldn't introduce you or they'll try to poach you from us."

She smiled and shook her head. "I doubt it, but go on . . . you think they can help me with my facial rec problem?"

"If anybody can, they can," he said. "You got your secure sat phone on you?"

She didn't answer just squatted down behind the desk to root through her backpack and after a few seconds handed him the phone.

He dialed a number from memory. The call connected on the first ring and a serious male voice answered: "Ember Security Systems, Limited."

"Ian Baldwin, please," he said.

"Who's calling?"

"Lieutenant Commander Keith Redman."

"Just a moment," the voice said. He heard three clicks on the line and then the elevator music rendition of "Margaritaville" began to play.

"What's so funny?" she asked.

"It's the little things," he said, shaking his head and laughing. "You'll see when you meet them."

Several minutes passed, then three more clicks on the line.

"Commander Redman, to what do I owe the pleasure?" said the unmistakable voice of Task Force Ember's in-house technology maven and Signals Chief.

"Just calling because I missed you guys," Chunk said with a wide smile. "And I'm sure Lizzie Grimes has been dying to talk to me. Feel free to put her on the phone when you and I are done bullshitting."

"I see you haven't lost your sense of humor after your promotion and new tasking," Baldwin shot back. "Elizabeth is not here at the moment, so unfortunately you're stuck with me for the duration. How may I be of assistance today, Commander?"

Chunk walked Baldwin through some of the backstory and then explained what Watts was hoping to achieve. When he was finished, he said, "Is that something you might be able to help with?"

Baldwin's reply was exactly what he'd been hoping for.

"Child's play. Would you like us to send back the rendered image so that you can run the search yourselves, or would you prefer we take it from here and deliver the results?"

Chunk didn't even have to ask Watts to know her answer . . . so, he said the opposite. "Soup to nuts would be great, thank you. Do you want us to email you the sketch?"

Feeling Watts's angry laser beam eyes on him, he gave her his best dumb-guy shrug.

"We'd prefer you upload both the sketch and the photograph of the subject to a secure cloud server that we manage. Grab a pencil . . ." Baldwin said and rattled off the URL, a username, and a password.

"Got it. Thanks, Ian. I owe you one," Chunk said.

"Actually, I think it's the other way around—all the tally marks are on our side of the IOU status board. John will be happy to hear that you gave us an opportunity to erase one."

"How is JD, by the way?" Chunk asked, a smile curling his lips as he thought about his friend.

"John is as grumpy as ever, thank you very much."

"Good, then all is right in the world. We'll get the source material uploaded in short order," he said, but Watts cleared her throat. When he looked at her she mouthed, *How long will they take?* He nodded dutifully at her and added, "By the way, what sort of turn around are we looking at on this?"

"What sort of turn around do you need?" the Ember Signals guru asked.

"The sooner the better."

"I figured as much," Baldwin said. "Not to worry, I'll have Chip get to work straightaway. Give us eight hours and we should have something for you."

"Great," he said seeing Watts's grudging smile at the news.

"Commander, are you the point of contact on this, or is there someone else we should dialogue with in case we run into questions?"

Watts stuck out her hand and said, "Give me the phone, Chunk . . ."

Rolling his eyes, he handed her the phone.

"Hi, this is Whitney Watts," she said, pressing the sat

phone to her cheek. "I work with Commander Redman, and I'll be the point of contact going forward. I really appreciate your help with this, but there are other elements of the investigation that my colleague conveniently left out."

Chunk couldn't hear Baldwin's reply, but from the satisfied expression on Watts's face he imagined it was something to the effect of: *Yes, I, too, am saddled with the burden of trying to collect and analyze intelligence in the company of Neanderthals . . .*

After another back and forth and exchanging cordial goodbyes, Watts ended the call and glared at Chunk.

"What?" he said. "I just did you a solid."

"Yes, and thank you for that, but I would have preferred to run the image myself."

He smiled and said, "I know you would have, but this is an opportunity for professional growth. I think you'll be pleasantly surprised what happens if you just ease off the reins a bit and let these guys work their magic. I promise, you'll thank me later."

She narrowed her eyes at him, but he took it for the playacting that it was.

"Anything else?" he said, taking a step backward toward the door. "Cuz if not, I'm going for a run."

"No, that's it," she said. "I'll keep you posted as soon as I hear anything on this or about a mission package."

He nodded, then added, "While you wait on Ian you should also talk with the Team Two interpreter—the guy who heard the rumor about the Lion of Ramadi. Shake out where he heard it and what other gouge is floating around. These communities are tight-knit and you're never more than a degree of separation from the original source."

"Already on it," Watts said, her face saying, *Really? You don't think I thought of that?*

He nodded again, then chased away another image of CJ from his head. "Are you sure you don't want to come with us on this run? It's just me and Riker. I promise we'll keep it short and slow. I find it clears my head and helps me see things in a better light."

"And I find it helps me barf and clears my stomach," she fired back. "Apparently, you've already forgotten, I don't run."

"Fitness is a weapon," he said.

She pointed at the open door for him to leave.

"Just saying . . ."

"Go," she said and stomped her foot behind her desk.

"Someday, when you're doing a triathlon with me, I'm going to remind you of this moment," he said with a backward glance as he crossed the threshold.

"And the day after, we'll be ice fishing in hell, because it will have frozen over."

CHAPTER 14

JOINT SPECIAL OPERATIONS COMPOUND

NORTHEAST CORNER OF THE JOINT AIR BASE ERBIL

ERBIL, IRAQ

Chunk frowned as Riker stretched out his lead as they ran along the flight line, having completed their five-mile loop around the "white side" of the base. There was no way in hell Chunk was going to catch him, but he stretched his stride anyway and convinced himself he could close the gap on the final leg to the compound.

Images of CJ laughing at him over his shoulder throughout oceanside runs during the Chicks Beach town house days snuck into his head. A wave of grief tightened his chest, but the anger fueled his engine and he picked up his pace. Getting Bowman to authorize a hunting mission in Erbil had been easier than he'd anticipated, but it would be pointless unless they found a target. The idea that a new terrorist mastermind was at work in theater, someone who knew how to move all the chess pieces to lure a SEAL team into a kill zone, was terrifying . . .

perhaps even more terrifying than the al Qadar assholes with their drone. Being an operator was a dangerous business, but if they lost what made them so effective—anonymity and unpredictability—then his unit would not only lose their primary safety advantage but also their effectiveness.

He looked up and saw Riker had somehow stretched his lead again. The SEAL's long, powerful legs seemed almost to glide across the uneven surface, while Chunk simply beat the ground into submission with his tree stumps. But SEALs never quit, so he increased his speed to his personal redline and managed to close the gap a half dozen yards or so before Riker reached the fence and tagged it. Grinning in victory, the senior chief paced in a circle, hands on hips and catching his breath.

"Nice run, bro," Chunk panted, as he tagged the fence a moment later.

"Damn, you're fast for an old man—especially a short old man," Riker said and offered a fist bump.

Chunk laughed at the familiar joke, returned the bump, and forced himself *not* to bend at the waist and put his hands on his knees as he gasped for air. Motion caught his attention in his peripheral vision and he saw Watts jogging toward them inside the fence line.

"Damn, that girl is always on a mission," Riker said, already breathing normally.

"Yeah," Chunk said, still trying to recover his breath as he watched Watts punch in the access code from her side of the fence.

"I got something," she said, as the gate rattled and began rolling open on a series of wheels.

"That was quick," Chunk said as Riker followed him back into the compound.

"We talked to the terp," Watts said, punching the button to shut the gate and turning back toward the trailers. "The Team Two guys have an asset they've been working with. He's been helping coalition forces for as long as SOF and JSOC units have been in Erbil. Fitz said the guy is, and I quote, 'in the fight twenty-four seven, three sixty-five.' Supposedly, this guy has six kids and a wife and doesn't take Stateside rotation like our guys. He's really impressive."

"And?" Chunk pressed, needing almost desperately to hear what she'd learned. He well understood the passion many of the interpreters brought to the job and the incredible commitment they had to helping the community. Chunk had personally worked for two years to get a Group Two interpreter and his family asylum status after the Taliban had identified the man as a target. His efforts had been unsuccessful, however, and he often wondered what became of the man and his family.

"This rumor about the Lion of Ramadi comes into better focus when you dig a little deeper," she said. "Romeo—that's the terp—is reluctant to source details. He has concerns about naming people not wishing to be named because he doesn't want them to be targeted by any of the myriad, active terrorist cells in the area. But he did name one guy, a Kurd who's been working with some of the OGA guys . . ."

"Like a covered asset?" Chunk asked hopefully. "Someone inside the terror cells?"

"Not exactly," Watts said, stopping now beside the door to their long wooden building. "More like a well-connected midlevel observer. He has eyes and ears throughout the community and is considered a savant at sifting data, or so the CIA guys tell me. This Kurd hates ISIS as much as he hated al-Qaeda, which is no surprise since both groups have targeted the Kurds for genocide. He set up a spy network on his own when American forces arrived and now lives under the NOC Uthman Gamil, posing as an Iraqi, which allows him to snoop and gather intel under the radar."

"So, CIA is willing to help us dialogue with Gamil?"

"Yeah, in fact, they're doing us one better. Russ has set up a meeting for us with Gamil."

"This is great work, Heels. Really great," Chunk said, his breathing now normal after the run but his heart racing with excitement. "When?"

"We leave in thirty minutes. The OGA guy, Russ, is picking us up at the gate, so get cleaned up and put on civvies."

"Whoa, hold on, Heels," Chunk said, forcing himself to slow down and think this through. "I'm sure Gamil is well-vetted, but there's a terrorist hit squad actively hunting SEALs in this region. For all we know, this compound is under twenty-four-hour surveillance. The Lion of Ramadi could be lying in wait to take potshots at us the second we drive out the front gate. Serious thought needs to go into this meet. We're not meeting outside in a café or some shit like that."

"No," Watts said, nodding. "Gamil wants us to meet at his house. Or at least the house he uses in Erbil when he's working under his Iraqi businessman NOC. He won't meet us—or any Americans for that matter—at an outside location or even near a window. He says the Lion of Ramadi is real, is alive, and is on the hunt in Erbil."

Chunk pressed his lips together. "We need more time to prep. Call your OGA guy, Russ or whatever his name is, and tell him we need ninety minutes. Gamil clearly appreciates the threat level and so should we. I don't want us going from being the hunters to the hunted."

"Understood," she said.

He turned to Riker. "I want two vehicles that will blend

in, bro. And I want advanced security in place, including a countersniper contingency. We'll need to pull some Team Two guys to round out the force. Why don't we use Saw and their sniper on two points to cover us in and out and to run countersniper. Take Heels with you to get the geography figured out."

Watts shook her head. "Russ said he'd handle OPSEC and transportation."

"Yeah, well, I call bullshit," Chunk said. "Tier One is calling the shots today. Tell him what we need and why."

"Okay," she said, recognizing that he had no intention of backing down on this.

"On it, boss," Riker said and headed off toward the TOC at a jog, Watts trailing behind him.

"Jogging doesn't save us any time," she called after the SEAL. "You can't plan jack shit without me."

Chunk smiled, both at his teammates and at this new development. If this self-created Kurdish spy was as good as the CIA claimed, they might even have a target by tonight. And then it would begin—one hit after another until they'd tracked down whoever had killed CJ and meted vengeance . . .

Tier One style.

CHAPTER 15

The city of Erbil was laid out in a series of roughly concentric circles around the centralmost loop formed by Qatal Road and the Erbil Citadel. They were just inside the third major loop formed by Kurdistan Street and headed to the neighborhood that made up a good portion of the pie-shaped southwest district still inside the outermost loop formed by 120 M Road—or simply "the One-Twenty" to the operators who had spent time in Erbil. The SEAL compound was located just north of the airfield, in a spot where both CENTCOM and SOCOM could safely manage operations and have access to civilian flights several times a day. Though the distance from the base to the safe house was only a few miles, the trip had taken them over a half hour in the midday heavy traffic.

"Zeus One, Ares One—we are Scotch. Bourbon in two mikes," Chunk reported from the driver's seat of the F-250 pickup they were using for their infil to meet the Kurdish spy, Gamil.

Their legend for this evolution was posing as employees of an international construction company under contract for various infrastructure and public works projects in Erbil. Accordingly, Chunk was dressed in civilian clothes. He hated not having the familiar boom mike of his Peltor headset that was integrated into the helmet he wore when kitted up. But the low profile, in-ear transceiver he was using produced amazing sound quality, despite the irksome feeling he couldn't shake that his voice wasn't getting picked up by the device buried in his left ear.

"Ares One, Zeus—nothing to report. One vehicle at Bourbon. We see nothing suspicious. Ares Two confirm?" Saw said from his sniper roost, covering the west approach.

"All clear," came the follow-up call from the Team Two sniper whom Saw had positioned eight hundred yards east of the target house just south of Shanadar Park.

Riker, also hidden out of sight, was leading two ground teams set up in beat-up vans—one stationed north and the other south of the target. They were the QRF in case things went to shit.

"Check," Chunk said, while the thought occurred to him that a QRF was generally useless against a sniper. If they needed Riker, by the time he responded odds were they'd already be dead.

"Relax, man. It's all good," the CIA officer, Russ Profant, said from the back seat. "Gamil is a consultant and broker for the construction company NOC. We're here all the time. Trust me."

Chunk hated when spooks told him to "relax" and narrowed his eyes at Profant in the rearview mirror. He noted the man's tan face, well-groomed dark beard, and fit athlete's body, making him appear younger than what Chunk guessed was fifty. He had no doubt the dude had logged many years with Clandestine Services in the Middle East and knew a thing or two about meeting assets. But today's op required a whole different level of sophistication if they were to escape unnoticed and unscathed.

"Just ahead on the right," Profant said, pointing as Chunk piloted them onto Shanadar Street. "I know you're nervous but Gamil picked this house for some reason. No buildings with a higher elevation in a one-mile radius. We're through the gauntlet, so to speak."

Chunk nodded and pulled the gray Ford F-250 onto the paved driveway and inside the eight-foot cement-and-stucco wall and then up to the front of the sizable house with its large red front door. A thin young Iraqi gate attendant hustled past and pulled the gate closed behind them. Chunk parked, felt for the pistol on his hip, and then grabbed the short-barreled Sig MCX Rattler from the center console. Before stepping out, he scanned the small courtyard—complete with its little patch of grass that in Iraq said, "I am successful enough for a little patch of green grass"—and saw nothing alarming.

"Wait inside the truck a minute," he said to Watts and scanned the walls which completely blocked all lines of sight out of the compound. The high, solid walls, combined with the low-rise buildings in the neighborhood, had clearly factored into the selection criteria for the property, and together, provided a good measure of antisniper protection.

"You know sometimes you raise more flags trying to be careful," Profant said from his rear seat but smiled at him in the mirror.

"I don't disagree with that," Chunk conceded. "But personal protection is common in Iraq. I'm just a bodyguard doing my due diligence. Not like we have a whole fire team setting up."

"Oh, we're out here, boss," Riker said in his ear.

"All clear, Ares One," Saw added. The Ares call sign had been Saw's idea—the Greek god of bloodlust—and it felt right. But Riker had adamantly refused to use Greek cities as waypoints, so they'd fallen back on their old familiar list of favorite whiskeys.

Chunk exited the truck and swept his eyes across the yard and house, before striding to the passenger side door and opening it for Watts.

"Sure, I'll get my own door, thanks," Profant said with feigned injury, exiting the rear driver's side door. He walked past Chunk, posing as a successful businessman used to having bodyguards on his detail, and knocked on the red door. Watts stepped up to join Profant in front, but Chunk put hands on her shoulders and shifted her right and out of the "lane." Profant looked at him and cocked a knowing eyebrow. "So fuck me, I guess . . . Happy to be the two seconds for you guys," he said with a laugh, referring to the guys that died in the first two seconds it took to react if shooters were waiting on the other side of the door.

"Your asset," Chunk said with a shrug.

The door swung open from the inside.

Gripping his MCX, Chunk robotically scanned the foyer. The door had been opened by an attendant, who was armed but his weapon was holstered. The man they were here to see—Uthman Gamil, the Kurd asset posing as an Iraqi businessman—was standing twelve feet back from the door in the middle of the foyer. The way he'd positioned himself, well clear of any possible sniper angles through the open front door, was not lost on Chunk.

"*Marhaban*," Profant said and walked inside to embrace the man. "*Kayf haluk ya sadiqi? Min aljid ruyatuk, Uthman.*"

"It is good to see you too, my friend," the man replied in crisp, thickly accented English. "Business is good, I hope? You are spending my investment wisely?"

"Indeed," Profant replied with a big smile. "Booming in fact. That's why I've brought Ms. Fairchild to see you. She represents a large multicompany consortium wishing to bid on several projects in Erbil."

"I am honored to meet you, Ms. Fairchild," Gamil said, his right hand over his heart.

"The honor is mine, Mr. Gamil," she replied with a smile and a deferential nod.

The man laughed, a big and genuine laugh. "So formal, your friend," he said to Profant. "Please call me Uthman, Ms. Fairchild. And come in, and we will have tea and bread and get to know one another."

They followed the man through the well-appointed foyer, down a short hall, and into a great room that would be considered spacious in a US home but was palatial in Iraq. Two men, both in long gray shirts and trousers—but with clean and modern shoes, Chunk noted—stood beside a glass dining table where several laptops were set up.

"These are my associates, Ms. Fairchild—I should let you know they are associates from my *real* work here in Erbil, and I can personally vouch for them and their security."

"As can I," Profant added, shaking hands with both men. "Great to see you again, Masoud. You too, Hiram."

"We're secure," Hiram said, turning to Gamil. "No electronic incursions detected and our sentries report nothing out of the ordinary."

"Excellent," Gamil said, taking a seat and gesturing that

they should do the same on the sofas positioned around a modern, glass table. "Now, Ms. Fairchild, how can I be of additional assistance to the American CIA?"

"First, thank you for seeing us. I know taking this meeting is not without personal risk," Watts said. She waited until Gamil had nodded graciously before continuing. "We are interested in learning more about the rumors that the Lion of Ramadi is not only still alive, but that he is here, in Erbil, operating fifteen years after his supposed death."

Gamil sat back, fingers steepled, studying her.

"You refer to Juba—this is who you mean by the Lion of Ramadi?" he said.

She nodded.

"Many, myself included, believe that the Juba legend may have been a fiction—not one sniper but several, their kills aggregated and attributed to a single legendary sniper to instill fear and uncertainty into the Americans operating in Anbar at the time."

"Which worked, I can tell you," Chunk added. "Long after 2007 the white side troops spoke with fear of the Lion of Ramadi and had anxiety about whether he was really dead."

Gamil nodded at him, his eyes alive and intelligent. "Instilling fear is the *real* job of a sniper, is it not?"

"Yes," Chunk said. "So tell us, are the rumors true? Has Juba returned from the dead? Or was the sniper who targeted the Navy SEALs in Duhok merely resurrecting the name to capitalize on the legend?"

"Like you, I have heard these rumors. But as I said before, I believe Juba was a fiction and most of the snipers operating under this legend are dead. After 2007 the Juba legend seemed to fade away."

"Most?" Chunk said, not liking the nonchalance in Gamil's answer.

The man shrugged. "Who can know such things?"

"Well, what we do know is that a very talented sniper killed a Navy SEAL in Duhok and critically wounded another."

The Kurd held Chunk's hard gaze but his own eyes appeared full of compassion. "I understand this is a difficult thing for you. I am sorry."

"What can you tell us about that shooting?" Profant asked, perhaps trying to leverage the long relationship he had with the Kurd in an attempt to loosen his tongue.

It was only a gut feeling, but Chunk felt certain Gamil was being strategically evasive. There was more to the story, and he was happy to dance all day long with this guy if that's what it took to suss out the whole truth.

"I suspect that you are less concerned about the shooting and more concerned about the ambush itself," Gamil said.

"What do you mean by that?" Chunk asked.

"I mean that it would seem that this sniper *knew* your SEALs would be at this target that night. The shooting and the explosion that followed seem unlikely to have been an ambush of opportunity. A trap that was set. Of that I'm certain."

"And perhaps even baited," Watts added.

Gamil nodded. "Yes, I think so."

"Why do you know so much about it?" Chunk asked, feeling himself growing suspicious now.

"I know only what I hear, and much of that is the same as what you know. But I have been at this a long time, Ms. Fairchild," he said, turning away from Chunk to look at Watts. "And it is pretty obvious this is more than a simple attack."

"Russ tells us you are quite dialed in to the various groups here, so you must have heard something," she said, pressing him to get more specific.

"I am not some Iraqi—what do you call it in the States?"

Gamil said, pausing to try to remember the word, before looking up with a smile. "*Snitch*, this is the word. I am not some Iraqi snitch. I am not Iraqi at all. I live a life in a very dark world. And while I greatly appreciate all that America has done for me, and I hope you will continue to do, it is not for you or America that I risk my life and the lives of my wife and children. It is for my people, for Kurdistan. You see, long after you are gone, we will still be here."

Chunk sighed. He understood. America had not been a reliable partner the last decade, coming and going erratically and often leaving allies to fend for themselves after ISIS began to grow in the region. Few groups had paid for America's policy flip-flops as heavily as the Kurds. However, Gamil knew something and Chunk wasn't leaving here without answers.

"You know something you're not telling," Chunk said, steeling his gaze at the Kurd.

"I mourn with you for the loss of these men, these warriors," Gamil continued, "but I have to live with the consequence of every detail I share with you. Maybe I tell you a rumor about someone who could have provided support for the hit, what will you do? You will immediately conduct a capture/kill operation—probably tonight, knowing American Special Operations as I do. And what about tomorrow, when everyone here knows what you did, and what if the terrorists blame me? What becomes of the men in my employ?" He gestured to the two men by the sliding glass door behind him. "What happens to their families? What happens to the network I have developed over so many long and bloody years? What will the price be? What will Mr. Profant lose? You see . . . nothing is free of consequence."

Chunk ran his tongue between his teeth and lower lip. This guy knew something important concerning the attack in Duhok, and he wasn't sharing. Chunk turned to Profant, his patience all but burned up. "Look, no offense, but I say we take this guy back to the compound and continue our chat there. I have a feeling it will be more productive."

"Now wait a damn minute, Commander," Profant said, rising to his feet, his palms flat on the table. "While I'm happy to help you guys, 'cause we're all supposed to be on the same team, there is no way in hell I'm going to let you burn down everything this asset has built here. And for what it's worth, Gamil is right. When we rotate home, he'll still be here. I'm not going to sacrifice—"

"Wait a moment, Mr. Russ," Gamil said, his eyes sparkling with what appeared to be an epiphany. "Perhaps your Navy SEAL friend is right."

"Who the hell said I was a Navy SEAL?" Chunk said.

"Oh, please," Gamil said, rolling his eyes and laughing. "I know how to recognize Navy SEALs, Commander. But this is not the interesting point. I have an idea how to help you without jeopardizing my men or my legend. In fact, if executed properly, the outcome could make me even more valuable in my fight for Kurdistan, and also for the CIA in Erbil."

"What exactly did you have in mind?" Watts asked.

Gamil told them his plan, and Chunk smiled, feeling a new kinship and respect for this man.

"We can make that work," Chunk said with a grin. "We need a hood."

"Three hoods," Gamil corrected. "If you take only me, there will be suspicion that perhaps Masoud and Hiram gave me up to you." He tilted his head and Hiram hurried off, returning a few minutes later with three dirty cloth hoods. "Bind our arms as well, and I would ask you to please *not* be gentle. Perhaps even rougher than you might ordinarily be. We want the neighbors to hear."

Chunk smiled at the man. This guy was one cool cat.

"You catching all this, Zeus?" Chunk said.

"Gotcha, boss," Saw said.

"Ares Three, Zeus One—roll up with both vans right now. We're taking three crows off the X and we want to make a scene in the process."

"Ares Three, en route. Bourbon in two mikes," Riker came back.

"Breach the front gate," Chunk said and looked at Gamil. "Let's make it look like America's military is rolling us up."

"A nice, authentic detail," the Kurd said, nodding his approval.

"Be convincing," Chunk said to Profant. "I know you want to preserve your NOC."

"Don't worry," Profant said. "Not my first rodeo."

The three men allowed themselves to be flex-cuffed and have hoods pulled over their heads. A moment later, Chunk heard the sound of Riker and his two teams not so gently breaching the front gate for all the world to see.

"Ares is Bourbon," Riker called.

They exited the house and crossed the courtyard toward the gate leading to the street in front of the house. Chunk shoved Gamil ahead of him, his left hand tight on the back of the man's neck and his right gripping the Sig Rattler on his chest in a combat carry.

"Someone help me," Gamil screamed in Arabic, real terror in his voice. "The Americans are kidnapping me and I have done nothing wrong!"

"Shut up," Chunk shouted, then pressed his knee into the back of Gamil's left knee, driving him to the ground and holding his hooded face in the dirt by the back of his neck. "Cooperate, or we leave you behind with a bullet in your head."

Gamil began to sob, and for a moment Chunk worried he had hurt the man for real.

"I'm telling you, you're making a mistake," Profant hollered at him angrily from beside his TRW Construction truck. "This man is no terrorist. I can personally vouch for him."

The van doors slid open and six shooters, fully kitted up and ready to kick ass, streamed out. They took Gamil from Chunk and dragged him to the van. Two more SEALs came from the second van and grabbed Masoud and Hiram, dragging them into the other idling van.

"One more word from you, and I'll have your licenses pulled. We have zero tolerance for Americans who line their pockets by jumping in bed with terrorists," Chunk shouted, getting in Profant's face.

"He's not a terrorist, he's a businessman. I'm telling you," Profant fired back.

"We'll see about that," Chunk said, toe to toe now with Profant, his face red. "If you're lying, you're gonna end up with your sorry ass in jail."

Chunk spun on a heel and jogged to the nearest van and jumped in, the doors pulling closed behind. The van fishtailed with a squeal of tires, running over what was left of the damaged gate, then tore out onto the main road heading back toward Shandahar Road. He looked over his shoulder to see Profant flip him the middle finger, then pound theatrically on the hood of his pickup truck in frustration. Then, as if suddenly aware he was in real danger, Profant jumped into the truck and bugged out.

These CIA guys have got some serious chops over here. And that Profant dude is a shoo-in for the next Academy Awards.

He smiled and shook his head, and then leaned over to the hooded man beside him, resisting the urge to pull the hood off.

"You good, brother?" he asked, leaning in close to Gamil. "I didn't hurt you, did I?"

"I am okay," Gamil replied, all of the fear and desperation from before completely absent in his voice. "You were quite convincing back there. Good job."

Chunk caught Riker grinning from the rear bench seat. They locked eyes—reveling in the moment—and laughed at the theater of it all.

It's a crazy-ass world I work in . . . so thank God I've got crazy ass friends.

CHAPTER 16

Chunk watched Gamil as he meticulously prepared his tea with honey and lemon. Watts, resourceful as always, had somehow found a tea service on this base and brought everything on a tray for the interview. Chunk could see that her instincts were already paying dividends because Gamil seemed more relaxed and self-assured than before she presented it to him. The gesture was thoughtful but also an offering of respect—returning the humanity they'd stripped away from him during the fake abduction.

These things mattered, and Chunk wasn't sure if he would have thought of it on his own.

The parallels between this man and the married operators in Gold were not lost on Chunk. Just like Saw, Gamil had "deployed" away from his family—living a covert life in Erbil to help defeat ISIS and the other jihadi terrorists who would do his people harm. The man was a hero in the truest sense of the word, risking his life every day for his people.

Gamil has the heart of a warrior, Chunk thought as he took a seat across from the asset and next to Watts who was fixing herself tea now as well.

"Where are Masoud and Hiram?" Gamil asked, looking up from his cup.

"Don't worry," Watts said. "This is not some attempt to separate you and compare stories. Our team is getting them a nice lunch while we chat. I figured they probably weren't read into everything you might want to share—for their safety, or yours, maybe it's best if we dialogue this way."

"That is very . . . thoughtful," Gamil said, and Chunk wasn't sure whether the comment was meant to be genuine or wry. "So, let me tell you what I know, then. There is a group here in Erbil that fashion themselves true believers. Their operation is small and lacks funding, and so any opportunity to raise money, especially while supporting the global jihad, they pursue."

"Al-Qaeda affiliate?" Chunk asked.

"Dreamers," he said with a laugh. "Not posers, as you would call them. They represent an offshoot of Ansar al-Islam or AAI. When ISIL took control of the region, AAI was badly fractured with the more capable fighters joining the caliphate. In the void created by America's temporary absence, the ISIL caliphate seemed viable and quickly gained legitimacy. Ansar al-Islam collapsed, but this offshoot persisted and vied for power. They are small, but brutal, fanatical, and dangerous. These are the people who nail children to walls to impress the leaders of ISIL. They don't want to merge; they want to be recognized. This is the group that supported the sniper attack in Duhok."

Chunk felt his pulse quicken and his body involuntarily shift into what he thought of as his "predator" mode.

This is exactly what we need next. A target.

"Supported or orchestrated?" Watts asked. "Because the distinction is important."

"It is my understanding that they provided lodging for an outside team that carried out the attack."

"And you know this how?" Chunk asked, but already his mind raced forward to the capture/kill mission—emphasis on *capture*—that needed to take place next.

"This is my mission, Commander. I am the eyes and the ears of our resistance in this region. I live and work with my enemies so that I may be Kurdistan's CIA in Erbil. I assure you two things: one, my information is absolutely true, and two, I will not share with you the intelligence chain that allows me to say this with such certainty."

"And why is that?" Watts asked, looking fascinated with Gamil and the aura of self-confidence and power about him.

"Because one day—perhaps soon—you will have an interest that does *not* align with ours. I mean no offense when I say I have learned to never fully trust Americans. If you deemed it in your best interest, you would exploit my intelligence network and in the process, burn it to the ground. That day might not be today, it might not be tomorrow, but it is inevitable. American self-interest always trumps backroom promises made between friends over cups of tea."

Chunk nodded. The man's words were not without merit. "Fair enough. So, where can we find these people? And more importantly, are any members of this reincarnated Juba sniper team still with them, sheltering in place until things cool off?"

"Maybe . . . it is certainly a possibility. The location is thirty miles north of the town of Aqrah in the foothills of the mountains. Perhaps they are planning the next attack while they wait for the Americans to move on to other things."

"Do you know the layout of the compound?" Chunk asked, his mind a missile homing on the target, with no patience for *maybes* and *perhapses*.

"Yes. I have visited this place. It is a two-building compound—a primary building with a perimeter wall and a second structure outside the wall to the west."

"Would you be willing to sit with me and my planners so we can look at satellite imagery together?"

"Of course. But please understand I cannot accompany you on the operation."

"Nor would we expect you to," Chunk said and paused a moment, his mind returning to something Gamil had said earlier. "I know my government is not always a reliable partner to you and your people, but I want you to know I'm indebted to you personally for this information, and I take this debt seriously. I can't promise for the others, but my team will always have your back."

"I believe you, Commander," Gamil said, fire in his eyes. "Perhaps, when the time is right, I will feed you intelligence that will help save some of my people from enemies who would wipe us from the earth, and you will help stop them, eh?"

"I hope I get the opportunity to do just that," he said, rising now, the energy from getting a target too much for him to sit still any longer. Gamil rose as well and extended his hand. They shook firmly, sealing the deal warrior to warrior.

"Chunk, can I speak with you a moment please?" Watts interjected, ruining the moment.

Chunk nodded to Gamil and followed her out into the hallway.

"You sure about this, Keith?" she said, once they were alone and out of earshot.

"Uh-oh," he said with a smile. "I know there's a problem whenever you call me Keith."

"I'm serious, Chunk," she said, exasperated. "How well do we really know this guy? Are you sure you're ready to plan a hit off of a single data point?"

"Your own due diligence vouched that Gamil is thoroughly vetted. Profant has been working with him for years, and now that I've met him, my gut says he's the real deal. That's about twice as much confirmation as we usually get. We've hit people's homes with far less."

He watched her processing his words but realized he didn't really give a shit what she thought. She was an analyst—a brilliant analyst, but not an operator—and CJ was a brother. This was the only intel they had. If the masterminds behind the Duhok hit weren't there, at least they'd have crows to interrogate and the knowledge they'd shut down a compound full of terrorists.

Gamil's words echoed in his head: *These are the people who nail children to walls to impress the leaders of ISIL.*

The people Gold Squad was made to stop.

Oh yeah, they were going . . .

"Okay," Watts said, apparently sensing his mind was made up. "I'll get with Gamil and start pulling up satellite imagery of the area."

He gave her shoulder an *attagirl* squeeze. "And I'll go grab Riker, Saw, and Fitz so we can start planning the hit."

CHAPTER 17

Planning session complete, Whitney pulled her hair reflexively into a stubby ponytail as she walked to her temporary office. Her hair felt greasy. And her skin felt grimy. She glanced over her shoulder to make sure nobody was looking, then sniffed her left armpit.

I'm grimy, greasy, and stinky, she thought shaking her head. *Chunk is trying to turn me into one of his bros.*

When she got to her office, she dropped into the wobbly task chair, reached under the desk, and retrieved her backpack which she had stuffed inside the knee cubby. She unzipped the side pocket, pulled out a package of scented wet wipes, and drew two of the damp white sheets. Then, after folding them together into a compact little square, she reached under her shirt and commenced wiping herself down. As she did, a stout, burly shape in the hallway strolled past her open office door.

Please don't come back, please don't come back . . .

A split second later, like a movie being played in rewind, Chunk reappeared in the doorway, walking backward, and then stopped to look at her sideways with a wry grin plastered across his face.

"Taking a ranger bath I see," he said, eyeing her as she scrubbed away.

"Is that what you call it?"

"That's what *I* call it," he said with a chuckle.

"I'm sensing there's a story?" she said and tossed the wipes into the rubbish bin beside her desk.

"Oh yeah, there's always a story," he said with a nostalgic twinkle in his eye. "Ah, the good ole days of joint operations. If you ever meet a man claiming to be Jack Murphy, just ask him."

"I'll be sure to do that. Now can I please have five minutes without—you know—*you?*"

Chunk playacted pulling an imaginary dagger from his chest. "That stings, Watts. It really stings."

"Goodbye, Chunk," she said opening the screen of the notebook computer on her desk.

"I can take a hint," he said, disappearing out of view. "See ya later, Watts. I'm off to take a real shower . . . an *operator* shower."

"In other words, you're gonna roll around in some dirt?" she called after him, but he didn't take the bait.

As she leaned back in her chair, she thought about how he'd grabbed her by the shoulders and moved her aside at the front door when they'd gone to visit Gamil at his house. Like an idiot, she'd just walked up to take point, not even contemplating for a second that the bad guys could have arrived ahead of them and been lying in wait, assault rifles at the ready. But Chunk hadn't missed a beat. He was so good under pressure—fluid, calm, and methodical. He'd not even chastised her about it after.

That was one of the things she liked most about him.

He always had her back, no questions asked.

Or in this case, my front, she thought with a smile as she logged into the secure portal and checked her email.

A quick scan of her inbox showed a message waiting from Ian Baldwin, the Signals Director at Ember. She clicked on it. The message was short and to the point: *We've made outstanding progress on your unidentifiable man query. Contact me when you are ready to be briefed.*

"Yes," she said and pumped her fist in the air. Then she pinged Yi in the Tajikistan TOC on a secure video chat. Her partner in crime answered on the third chime.

"Hi," Yi said, greeting her from their shared bunk room back at the JSOC compound.

"Hi, how are you?"

"Good, you?"

"Pretty good. We just got done interviewing a Kurd informant who seems like he might be able to help us out with some intel on what went down here," Whitney said and filled Yi in on everything they'd learned.

"That's good you're making some headway."

"Yeah, but that's not why I called. I got a message from that Signals guru, Ian Baldwin, at that spooky task force back home. Looks like they have something for us on our faceless man. Are you free to jump on a video conference with them?"

"Hell yeah, let's do it," Yi said.

"Cool," Whitney said and clicked on the teleconference link Baldwin had provided. A few minutes later, they were all looped together.

"Greetings," Baldwin said, sipping from a mug with a

white string dangling a square paper tab that read, Darjeeling. "I've asked Chip to join us if you don't mind, as he deserves the lion's share of the credit for the identity reconstruction work."

"Hi, Chip," Whitney said, smiling as a twentysomething man-boy with shaggy hair slid into frame. He was holding a can of Olipop Vintage Cola and wearing a T-shirt that read, Keep Calm and Call Dempsey beneath a graphic of St. Edward's Crown.

"Hi," Chip said and scratched at the side of his nose. "So, I used our own in-house CGI neural rendering engine—which is very similar to the PaGAN II platform—to work on your John Doe, or in this case, your Fulan al Fulani." When nobody got the joke, he blushed and continued, "Our Generative Adversarial Network works similarly to Pinscreen's, but it is a little more flexible when the input parameters are degraded. In this case, I had to tweak the ML algorithm to be generative rather than iterative because of how badly—"

"Thank you, Chip," Baldwin said, cutting him off. "But I'm not sure they're interested in the nitty-gritty. Perhaps we move straight to the results."

"Sure, yes," Chip said, "but all I was going to say is that—"

"That it was very complicated and very hard—yes, Chip, I think we can all appreciate that," Baldwin said, with an empathetically paternal look that Whitney took to mean, *The children don't care* how *Elsa was made, they just want to see her use her ice powers and sing "Let It Go."*

"Sure, okay," Chip said, deflating just a bit, and then he put up a photo-realistic image of a handsome man with Middle Eastern features and skin tone. "Here are where things settled out."

Whitney gawked at the picture on the screen, which looked so realistic she could not believe it was a computer-generated image. "That's incredible," she said, studying the man's eyes. "Is that the same technology people are using to create deep fakes?"

Chip glanced at Baldwin and then looked back at her and simply said, "Yes."

"So that's what he looks like," she murmured, noticing elements of Edwards's comic sketch come to life in the face staring at her on the screen.

"No," Chip said, taking her by surprise. "That's what the neural engine predicts he looks like given the data you provided. It's purely speculative. This is what he really looks like . . ."

A new picture popped up on the screen beside the CGI character. The new image lacked the clarity, perfect lighting, and refinement of the rendered image because it was a scan of a real passport photo. The similarity of the faces, however, was unmistakable.

"Say hello to Eshan Dawar, born in Nangarhar Province, Afghanistan in 1990," Chip said and after a pause added, "and also to Mani Sadot who travels with a Maltese passport, and Javad Ahmad who travels under a UAE passport. These last two were the most recent aliases we found that Dawar used, but I would not be surprised if he has more."

"Interesting," Whitney said as three passport photos of the same man popped up on the screen. "How long has he been traveling with aliases?"

"Three years," Chip said. "Give or take."

"How do you know this guy is our guy?" Yi asked. "Was the CGI reconstruct so accurate that Eshan Dawar was the only hit you got?"

"Certainly not," Baldwin said, fielding this question with a chuckle. "We got dozens of possible matches, but we took the liberty of narrowing the field before we called you. At Ember, we never do anything half-asked."

Whitney crinkled her brow. *Is it really "half-asked?" I always thought the expression was "half-assed." Maybe it was supposed to be "half-asked" and people bastardized it to "half-assed," which actually is pretty stupid because half an ass is arguably—*

"Did I say something wrong, Ms. Watts?" Baldwin asked, snapping her out of her pointless rumination.

"No, no, sorry," she said. "Is there anything else you want to discuss before we sign off and dig in?"

Chip shrugged and glanced at Baldwin who said, "I think it's all fairly self-evident, but I might draw your attention to Dawar's international travel the month before the attack on Kandahar Air Base. He was quite active with trips to London, Dubai, and Kabul. If this were my tasking, I would start there."

"We'll take a look," Whitney said and then flashed Baldwin and Chip her best gratitude smile. "Thank you, guys. Amazing work. Serious respect."

"Anytime," Chip said with a low-key smile that she took to mean, *Coffee sometime when you're back in Tampa?*

She mirrored back his grin. *Maybe . . . could be a nice change of pace from my redneck rodeo existence.*

She ended the video conference with Ember but kept her connection with Yi intact. "Looks like we've got work to do."

"I'm literally dying here in the Batcave by myself. How long are you going to be in Erbil?" Yi said.

"Don't know—as long as it takes, I guess."

"You sound like Chunk," Yi said with a feisty grin.

"And I smell like him too," she said with an eye roll. "I just took a bath with a wet wipe, Michelle. Seriously, I can't even . . ."

"Been there, done that," Yi said with a knowing chuckle. "How do you want to split the work?"

Whitney paused a moment. They were working two problems, both of critical importance. In her mind, the al Qadar network clearly had more global implications. But if there was another sophisticated terror group targeting Americans in Iraq, that certainly rose to nearly the same level—and with the potential for a much shorter threat timeline. What struck her as most chilling were the similarities she saw in the two different taskings—that both seemed to involve terrorist organizations who had risen to new, and unprecedented, levels of technological and operational sophistication. The jihadi terrorist threat was evolving, and they'd damn well better evolve with it or more American lives would be lost.

"Whitney?" Yi prompted.

She smiled sheepishly at Yi on her screen. "Sorry. Tell me something, Michelle . . . Is there anything about these two threats that strike you as similar?"

"It's funny you ask that," Yi said, "because I was just thinking about that very thing. Both of these threats are more sophisticated than what we've seen before. It's a little unnerving."

"And what does it suggest to you?" she asked.

"A new paradigm," Yi answered without hesitation. "A fresh perspective, born from youth, technological savvy, and perhaps education. I think we're dealing with the next generation of Islamic terrorism."

"Not your daddy's al-Qaeda . . ." Whitney said absently, but the joke fell short. There was something else, just out of reach . . .

"Makes you wonder if there's a connection."

"What?" she said, returning from another rumination. "What did you say?"

"A connection," Yi repeated. "I mean, we could simply be seeing an evolution of the way the bad guys engage in general as a younger generation rises in the ranks, but . . . it also feels a little too coincidental."

Whitney nodded. It was a common analyst mistake to force connections where it was convenient to do so, but if there was a link between the two groups . . .

"I'm going to be tied up on this op with Chunk for a while," she said, "but why don't you start digging deeper into Eshan Dawar and his connections."

"And circle back when I have something?"

"Perfect," Whitney said and severed the connection.

Despite the plan she'd just made with Yi, she downloaded the zip file Chip had forwarded to her and opened the files on Eshan Dawar.

"Just a quick look," she murmured, unable to resist.

She clicked on a folder labeled Torkham with a data stamp three weeks before Dawar's death at the safe house in Mingora. Inside she found two subfolders. The first appeared to contain a digital copy of Dawar's border crossing from Afghanistan to Pakistan processed by Pakistani border control—no pictures, just a digital log of the clearance. The other folder, labeled Coalition Checkpoint Screening, was much more interesting. Torkham was one of the busiest, if not *the* busiest, crossing between Pakistan and Afghanistan and it happened to be located in the heart of terrorist country. Not surprisingly, Torkham crossing was one that the US Intelligence Community kept a close eye on and maintained a near-permanent OGA presence on the Afghan side.

She found three JPEG images and a PDF document. The first JPEG was an image of a vehicle license plate, which she assumed was the car Dawar was occupying at the crossing.

The second image was of the passport he used at the crossing, which was his UAE passport and alias. The third image was a photograph of Dawar seated inside a vehicle in what she deduced was the driver's seat. She couldn't help but be taken by the man's smile—relaxed, confident, genuine.

"How can a terrorist be this happy?" she said to herself.

Whitney glanced back and forth between Dawar's photograph, the passport headshot, and Ember's CGI rendering of the man. She took a second to marvel at what advances in technology allowed her to accomplish in her profession that would have been impossible to do just ten years ago. Feeling pretty good about this unexpected turn of events, she was just about to close the JPEGs and move on to the next folder when something caught her eye. She squinted at the picture of Dawar in the vehicle, but before she could enlarge it, her computer chimed with a video chat request from Yi. She accepted the call and a video window opened on her screen.

"Sorry, I know we said we'd talk later, but I think I got something," Yi began, her face lit with excitement. "Open the file labeled Torkham—"

"Are you talking about the photo with the legs visible in the passenger seat?" Whitney said, grinning. "I couldn't help myself. I was just looking at that same picture."

"There's someone else in the car," Yi said, practically bubbling with excitement.

"I know, I was just about to call you."

"This is getting weird, Whit. It's like we're sharing a brain or something."

"Well, Chunk's always going on and on about the Tier One family and all that. Maybe there's something to it," she said. "So, you wanna figure out who the passenger is or should I?"

"I don't think it will take long," Yi said. "There's a date and time stamp on the photo. I'm sure whoever took this picture photographed the passenger as well. We just need to query the same database for a photo logged at the same time."

"Sounds like you got this. Wanna call me back?"

"Just hang on a second, I'm logging in now. It won't take long since we know what we're looking for."

While Yi ran the search, Whitney opened and read the PDF document in the folder, which turned out to be the filing report from the stop:

Occupants in vehicle: two males. Driver: UAE citizen . . . Passenger: British national . . . no hits on GTD, TSDB, TIPOFF, or Interpol FTF databases . . . stated reason for travel is to attend a wedding . . . no suspicious behavior or visible items in the vehicle . . . photographed and cleared for travel.

"Got something . . . Looks like there was only one other passenger in the vehicle—a Mr. Qasim Nadar who was traveling under a British passport," Yi said. "Sending you his picture and passport image now . . ."

Whitney's computer chimed, and she opened the two images—one of Qasim Nadar's passport and the other of a man sitting in the passenger seat. Unlike Dawar, Nadar was not smiling. In fact, he looked quite put out in the photo—his expression equal parts dismay and irritation.

"I wanna build a file on this guy," she said. "Who do we know at MI6?"

"Actually, I think it would be MI5 who would keep records on this guy since he's a British national. MI5 handles domestic counterterror," Yi said.

"Yeah, yeah, you're right," Whitney said. "I don't know anyone there. How about you?"

Yi shook her head. "Nope."

"All right, well, you dig up whatever else you can on Nadar

and Dawar, and I'm going to make a few calls. Let's circle back in an hour or so."

"Roger that," Yi said and signed off.

Whitney slumped back in her chair, the adrenaline rush she'd been feeling just moments ago suddenly tempered by the realities of her pathetically tiny network of IC contacts. And therein lay the irony of her job—for a modern intelligence analyst, technology could replace a thousand or ten thousand or even a million human memories and eyeballs, and yet for all its value-added benefits, technology was still nothing more than a tool. The Intelligence Community was a labyrinth of walled gardens, each carefully tended by its own gardener and protected by a gatekeeper. When she was at NCTC, the only relationship she'd cared about was the one she had with her boss. As long as he was happy with her reports and assessments, then she was golden. Besides, who had time for relationships when your caseload was stacked up to the virtual ceiling? Now at the Tier One, she realized how wrong she'd been. In the *real world* of intelligence, relationships were king. The meeting she'd just stepped out of with their Kurdish source was proof of that—all the intelligence he'd harvested had been from relationships, not some CT database.

With a sigh, she picked up her secure mobile phone and dialed one of only a handful of relationships she'd managed to cultivate over the past few months.

The phone rang twice and a baritone male voice answered, "Theobald."

"Hey, Bobby, it's Whitney Watts," she said and when he didn't say anything for a second, her heart dropped, suddenly worried that he'd forgotten who she was. "Bob, can you hear me?"

"Oh, I can hear you all right," he said, and she thought she heard a smile in his voice. "But after what you put me and my team through the last time I took your call, I was seriously contemplating hanging up on you."

"I deserve that," she said, trying some Tier One operator humility on for size. "And if I were in your shoes, I'd probably do the same."

"Ah, Watts, I'm just screwing with you—how the hell are you?"

"Well, I just took a bath with a wet wipe behind my desk in Erbil," she said with a smile. "That pretty much sums it up."

"Ranger bath," he said with a laugh. "Been there, done that. Well, with you hanging out with a bunch of frogmen for a living, I suppose it was only a matter of time. Welcome to the club."

"Thanks, *I guess* . . . So, hey, do you remember the night we hit the al Qadar safe house and hangar in Mingora? That was a stupid question, of course you remember."

"Yeah, that's one night that's pretty much burned into my memory forever. You still hunting those assholes down?"

"Yeah, and we've got a lead on a British national I'd like to follow up on. Do you have any contacts at MI5 you could put me in touch with?"

"MI5, huh? British domestic is not exactly my wheelhouse but give me a couple of hours and I'll see what I can do."

"Thanks, Bobby. I appreciate it," she said.

"Well, what can I say . . . when Navy falls down, Army is always waiting with a helping hand."

CHAPTER 18

Pounding on the front door woke him.

Qasim sat up in bed, listening for a moment to see if the noise was real or something he'd dreamed. He looked over at Diba in the dim light of their bedroom, but her closed eyes and rhythmic breathing confirmed she was asleep. Three more sharp raps on the door gave him a start and panic welled in his chest.

What if it's the police? What if they are coming for me?

He debated staying in bed, hoping and pretending the midnight caller was not a SWAT team from MI5 but rather a local drunk who'd stumbled home to the wrong flat after a night at the pub. But he knew in his heart he was not so lucky. The British had finally reconciled his involvement with al Qadar, and tonight they'd come for him.

Do I dare risk Diba's life because I'm too craven to face my enemy?

No. It would be better to answer the door indignant and with the presumption of ignorance than force them to breach his flat with guns blazing. He steeled himself with a deep breath and swung his legs off the bed. Resigned to his fate, Qasim went to the front door.

Three more knocks reverberated, hard and angry.

"I'm coming, I'm coming," he called, fetching his jacket from a coat hook in the hall.

He looked through the security peephole expecting to see a gaggle of black-clad operators huddled just outside and armed to the teeth with assault rifles. Instead, a lone figure stood on his stoop, back to the door. The man appeared to be of medium build and wore slacks and a dress shirt. Something about his shape looked familiar. Qasim reached for the dead bolt latch, but his fingers stopped short.

Something felt wrong . . .

Better to err on the side of caution.

"May I help you?" Qasim called through the door.

"It's me, Qasim," the man said with his best friend's voice, not turning around. "Open the door."

Eshan!

Suddenly light-headed, Qasim fumbled with the lock before managing to disengage the bolt and throw the door open.

"Praise Allah, how is this possible?" he said, his heart practically taking flight with joy.

The figure turned.

Qasim gasped with equal parts terror and disgust as he back-pedaled into his foyer. The visage that met him was not a face, but rather a bloody, mutilated horror—cratered in the middle by a high-velocity round that had torn away his best friend's nose and upper jaw and punched a hole out the back of the skull. The bottom of the left eye socket was missing, and the eyeball dangled from a sinewy, bloody stalk to stare at the floor.

"No, no, no . . ." he stammered.

The thing at the door took a step toward him. "Is this how you greet a brother?"

"Eshan, what is happening?"

The monster smiled at him with its savaged half-face—if one could call it a smile—and said, "I have returned to you, Qasim, in your time of greatest need."

Qasim's right heel hit the baseboard behind him and then his back found the wall. "No, please . . ."

"They did this to me," the Eshan zombie said, stepping up to him. "And yet you have done nothing?"

"That's not true," Qasim said, voice trembling and hands going up to stop the thing from getting any closer. "We used the drone. We hit their base of operations."

"You have not avenged my death," it screamed, spraying Qasim's face with cold, wet blood from its ragged, gaping maw. "Find the men who did this to me—make them pay!"

Qasim sat bolt upright in bed—heart pounding, T-shirt drenched in sweat.

Diba was awake beside him, her soft hands tenderly rubbing his back. "You had a nightmare, Qasim. But it's over. You're awake now."

"It's not over," he said, his voice little more than a dry, hoarse croak. "I failed him . . ."

"What are you talking about, husband? Who did you fail?"

"Eshan . . . I failed Eshan," he said and this time swung his legs off the bed for real.

"No, Qasim. What happened to Eshan was not your—"

"Silence," he snapped, whirling. "You know nothing."

He watched her wilt under his glare and her outstretched

hand recoil to her lap. When she cast her gaze downward and did not challenge him, he turned and walked to his closet. With great haste, he went to the toilet, got dressed, and shoved his mobile phone into his pocket. Then he walked to the foyer where he laced on a pair of shoes. Diba joined him a moment later, still barefoot but having shrugged on the cozy shawl she preferred on cool evenings. He felt her expectant eyes on him, but he ignored her and collected his wallet and keys from the drawer of the console table beside the front door.

"Where are you going?" she finally asked, waiting until he reached for the door handle.

"That does not concern you. Go back to bed, Diba," he said and stepped out into the night.

As he walked along Cambridge Road toward town, he used an app on his phone to hire an Uber Exec. The black Jaguar sedan picked him up at the corner fifteen minutes later.

"Are you Qasim?" the Pakistani driver greeted him.

"Yes," he said, sliding into the leather rear seat.

"Seventy-nine Greenfield Road in East London?" the driver said, confirming the address.

"Correct."

"It's a long way," the driver said as if double-checking that Qasim was in his right mind. "It could take nearly an hour, even at this time of night."

"Just drive."

"You want to listen to some music or do you prefer silence?" the man said as he looped the Jag through the roundabout and onto Burlington Street. In moments, they'd be on the A3 which would take them north and all the way into central London.

"Silence," Qasim said, shooting the man a leave-me-the-fuck-alone look in the rearview mirror before shifting his gaze out the window.

The driver kept his pledge and drove in silence. Forty-two minutes later he dropped Qasim off in front of Afghan Importers on Greenfield Road in the heart of East London. Qasim tipped the driver 10 percent and waited for the sedan to drive around the corner before he walked up to the darkened spice-and-sundry-goods shop. He entered a six-digit code into the keypad next to the door and an LED light flashed green. The lock clicked.

Inside, the miasma of fragrant spices hit him immediately. He inhaled deeply and—just like every time he came here—felt an instant nostalgia for his childhood home. But he had no time for such things, and he pushed the distracting and pointless emotions from his mind. Using his mobile phone as a flashlight, he navigated the shop's narrow, tightly packed aisles until he reached the back of the store. He stepped through a pair of drawn curtains and into the shopkeeper's office, which was empty but dimly lit by a night-light plugged into the opposite wall.

He turned right and used his flashlight to illuminate the pitch-black concrete stairwell leading down to Fun Time's underground cyber lair. At the bottom of the steps, he entered a different six-digit code into another keypad, earning him another green LED blink and another lock click. A flashbulb memory of Eshan's grotesque and mutilated face appeared before his mind's eye. He shivered as the specter's parting instruction echoed in his head.

Find the men who did this to me—make them pay.

"I'm sorry I failed you, my brother," he whispered. "I promise to avenge you this time."

He pulled the door handle a split second before the timer on the lock reset, then stepped into al Qadar's hacker central. All the black hats in the room looked up when he entered but then, instantly indifferent, turned back to their keyboards and monitors. Qasim made a quick head count and noted that Abdul and Fun Time were both missing. He walked over to see Tweem, the hacker with whom he'd logged the most time. Despite making a genuine effort the last few times he'd come, he'd failed miserably to develop a rapport with the man.

"Hey, Tweem," Qasim said, walking up beside the man's terminal.

The hacker didn't respond, just kept typing.

"Is Fun Time here tonight?" he asked.

"He's in the loo," Tweem said with profound indifference, not even taking his eyes off his screen.

A sudden and unexpected flash of anger blossomed in Qasim's chest.

Who the hell do these assholes think I am? Hamza al-Saud put me in command of this operation. How dare they treat me with such disrespect?

With a fury that took even himself by surprise, Qasim flipped Tweem's chair over backward with the hacker still in it. The chair hit the concrete floor with a resounding crash, hard enough to knock the breath out of the hacker's lungs.

"What the fuck did you do that for?" the hacker called Gru said, popping to his feet, while Qasim was staring down at the pathetic gasping fish at his feet.

Qasim was not a powerfully built man, but at six foot four, his stature was imposing. He didn't work out, but he did have a naturally wiry, muscular frame. In two strides, he closed the gap to Gru. He grabbed the Arab programmer by the throat right under the chin and pressed up. And while he wasn't strong enough to pick the kid up off the ground, the aggressive move had the desired effect. Gru's eyes popped wide with fear and his cheeks flashed crimson.

"Hey man, what the fuck you doing?" Fun Time called from somewhere behind him.

Qasim shoved Gru backward by the throat, causing the hacker to stumble over his chair and fall. He whirled on Fun Time. Qasim had a full foot of height advantage on the stalky Chinese Uyghur, but the little man did not back down.

"You need to teach your people the meaning of the word *respect*," he said. "They would be best to remember their place in this organization."

Fun Time laughed in Qasim's face. "What up your ass today, tall guy?"

Qasim struck Fun Time with an open hand across the left cheek so hard the slap echoed in the room. "I'm tired of your insolence. You disrespect Allah and you disrespect me every time I visit this place. I am Qasim Nadar, second in command of al Qadar. It's time for *you*," he said, spittle flying from his lips as he dragged his gaze like a laser beam over all of them, "for *all of you* to remember that."

Silence hung in the air like a suffocating fog, no one speaking or challenging him, and Qasim realized he liked it. He'd never behaved this assertively in his entire life, having always been afraid to offend, always afraid to make waves . . . But to what end? So that he could be pushed around by lesser men—men with half his intellect and half his talent? Well, no more. The terrorist prince had chosen Qasim as his right-hand man. It was time to stop letting Hamza down. Qasim returned his gaze to Fun Time and saw murder in the normally gregarious hacker's eyes, but this time the stocky Uyghur held his tongue.

"What was that?" Qasim said, boring a hole in the other man's forehead with his gaze. "I couldn't hear you."

"Please accept my humble apologies," Fun Time said through gritted teeth, switching to Arabic. "How can we serve you?"

"That's better," Qasim said, standing to his full height. "I have additional tasking for you."

"Tell me," Fun Time said. "What is it?"

"I want you to shift your focus to discovering the identities of the team of American operators who attacked our safe house and hangar in Mingora three months ago. I want to know where they live. I want to know the names of their family members. These men killed my best friend, and now it is time for them to know the same pain and loss that I have suffered."

"Should we no longer be working on the hack using information from British Aero?"

"Work on both problems, but this is time sensitive. I trust you to divide the labor as needed to work both problems."

I might never be able to know the drone pilot who killed my sister and my father, but the Navy SEALs who murdered my best friend . . . these men I can find.

These men I can punish.

CHAPTER 19

160TH SOAR MH-60M

CALL SIGN: STALKER ONE

EIGHT MILES NORTHWEST OF THE TARGET COMPOUND

JUST NORTH OF AQRAH, IRAQ

THIRTY MILES EAST OF DUHOK

0025 LOCAL TIME

The list of things Chunk loved about being in the Tier One was practically endless, but as he watched the ground scream past below his dangling feet—so close he could practically drag his heels through the dirt—he decided that working with the Army's elite 160th Special Operations Air Regiment "Night Stalkers" ranked near the top. The pilots and crews of the most daring and respected aviation unit in the world were among the best of the best. And they'd saved his bacon when Gold had been ambushed in the Hindu Kush during his first Tier One op a few months earlier.

"Five minutes," the crew chief called in his headset, marking the time left before the hover at the infil point—code-named 11th Street after the surfboard company favored by Fitz. Chunk's hands flew over his gear with a mind of their own while the other SEALs performed their own prefast-rope rituals and gear checks. Chunk was struck by the differences between his guys and the Team Two guys with whom they were sharing the helicopter. Perhaps only a half dozen or so years separated the operators, but those were years spent in continuous combat operations, making even Georgie and Trip look aged by comparison. Most of Fitz's guys looked no more than twenty-two or twenty-three years old. But the fire in their eyes came from the loss of their teammates, and for them, this operation would be deeply personal, he had no doubt.

"Two minutes," the pilot reported, and everyone shuffled into position.

All told, they had a total of ten operators, a pretty good-sized force for this kind of op, but Chunk wanted plenty of manpower to pull live crows from this terrorist nest. This op was, more than anything, an intelligence-gathering operation—the desperately needed information to find who controlled the operation targeting American SEALs, before more Team guys were targeted. But given that their enemy was highly attuned to their tactics and methods, Chunk wasn't taking any chances. He'd prepositioned Saw and Georgie several hours earlier as a sniper/spotter team northeast of the compound along with a Team Two sniper and spotter northwest for overwatch and covering fire.

The helicopter slowed, nose rising, and then settled into a static hover. The rope master kicked both bags out the side openings, and seconds later Fitz and Riker started their slide. A heartbeat later, Chunk was on the rope, and two seconds after that his booted feet hit the hard, rocky ground. He moved clear of the drop zone, took a knee, and scanned for threats as the Night Stalker bugged out. As the quiet returned, Chunk counted off a full two minutes in his head.

"Mother, Ghost is Farina," he whispered softly into the boom mike of his Peltors.

"Show you Farina. Eagle shows nothing between you and Walden," came a cool but unfamiliar voice from the Team Two coordinator in the Erbil TOC, reporting on the imagery from the MQ-9 Predator drone overhead. Chunk grinned at the sudden mental picture of Watts pacing back and forth behind the dude, ready to snatch his headset at a moment's notice.

"Apollo One, Ghost—sitrep," Chunk said, querying Saw while mentally picturing his brother sighting on the compound, Georgie on the spotter scope beside him.

"Doesn't look like you raised any alarms on infil, Ghost One," Saw called back a moment later. "Apollo Two, you see anything?"

"All quiet as far as I can see," the SEAL Team Two sniper they called Spicolli confirmed.

Chunk exhaled. The helo portion of infil had been his biggest worry. The terrorist compound sat on top of a hundred-and-fifty-foot plateau, making an approach from the east untenable. The walled compound was flanked to the north by mountains and to the south by a large cluster of homes and buildings stretching like a long tongue from the city of Aqrah. That left a single infil path to the west, up the narrow valley, and then down a moderate grade of hills before the land flattened out for the last kilometer of the approach. This was the route he'd chosen. But the bad guys also knew the topography and had set up two sentry teams of three men each in the hills of the western approach, a development the SEALs had discovered using the Predator drone's thermal imaging.

Chunk turned in the direction of the compound and signaled his five fellow SEALs to move out. "Ghost en route to Walden."

Walden, the next checkpoint, was located a half kilometer from the target. The plan was for Apollo One and Two to take out the enemy sentries just before Ghost made the checkpoint, then Ghost would split into two three-man teams and haul ass to the X before the sentries were missed. It was a gamble, but with the added firepower from Predator drone and the two MH-6 Little Birds orbiting nearby, Chunk felt confident they could handle whatever the bad guys threw at them.

The time slipped by as they made their approach along the creek flowing through the valley. As they closed on Walden, they diverted from the creek bed to covered positions along the slope side, north of the valley. Moving among the boulders and scattered trees, Chunk evaluated each footfall with increasing care so as not to slip or send rocks tumbling down the hill, thereby alerting the enemy sentries to their presence.

"Closest tango is on top of the ridge on your left, out of line of sight from you still," came the cool voice from the TOC, as if reading his mind and reassuring him they were still safe from detection.

He double-clicked his mike and quietly led his team into position behind a pair of boulders kissing each other halfway up the northern slope. Sighting around the upper, he called in. "Mother, Ghost One—Ghost is Walden."

"Roger, show you Walden. Stand by," the coordinator said.

Chunk and his teammates scanned their sectors, waiting for the updated imagery from overhead.

"Ghost One, still no indication you have been detected. Six sentries on the north ridge in two groups of three. Compound head count is unchanged, with four thermals in Building Two—all appear to be sleeping. Seven thermals in Building One—three bodies in the south corner, all upright and moving, four appear horizontal and sleeping. Only one tango outside, walking back and forth between the buildings about every half hour. We've seen him make two trips to the roof of the north building during his rounds to scan with binos."

"Copy all," Chunk said, then to Saw: "Apollo, do you have lines on all six sentries on the ridge?"

"Roger that, Ghost," came Saw's quiet reply. "We're dialed in. Just make the call when you're ready."

"Roger. What about the rover that goes up on the roof? Can you get him?"

"Apollo Two, you probably have a better line. I'm obstructed," Saw said, referring to the twenty-foot-tall tower with a TV dish that Chunk remembered on satellite imagery during the brief.

"Yeah, I got an easy shot," Apollo Two confirmed.

Chunk turned to Fitz. "You ready?"

"Hooyah," Fitz replied and fist-bumped Chunk's left hand with his gloved fist.

"Apollo, go to work and call us clear."

"Apollo," Saw said, acknowledging the order for both himself and his fellow sniper.

Chunk rolled his head, getting a satisfying crack from the bones in his neck, and pictured Saw and the Team Two sniper lining up their shots. They would have already worked out the geometry and order of shots between them on their private channel.

Saw's voice came back over his headset, but he was counting down for Apollo Two. "Three . . . two . . . one . . ."

Chunk didn't hear the suppressed shots, but he imagined the enemy sentries falling to a cadence in his mind.

Matching his mental rhythm, Saw checked in a moment later. "Ghost, Apollo—you're clear."

Chunk double-clicked and the six SEALs were up and moving fast, splitting into two three-man teams north and south, covering the ground as quickly as stealth would permit. They crossed the half kilometer in under five minutes, the sound of their boots and Chunk's breathing loud in his enhanced ears. As the low perimeter wall of the compound came into view, the two elements split farther apart, with Fitz taking his Team Two SEALs along the south wall and Chunk leading Riker and Trip toward the northwest corner of Building Two. Once in position, Chunk's element spread out, pressed against the wall, and waited for Fitz to position at Building One.

"Ghost Two in position," the Team Two officer reported a moment later.

"Roger, Two," Chunk said. "Mother, Ghost is Kechelle."

"Show you Kechelle, Ghost. Be advised your roving sentry is moving to the roof of Building Two."

"Apollo?" Chunk said softly, prompting his snipers.

"Apollo Two has him," came the Team Two sniper's reply. "On your mark."

"Ghost Two, breach when the roof tango is down."

A double click told him Fitz had heard the order.

"Apollo Two—take him," Chunk said.

This time he did hear the shot, followed by the high-pitched whistle of the inbound bullet and the soft thud of the 6.5 mm Creedmoor round striking its target.

"Tango down," the Team Two sniper said in his ear.

"Ghost Two—go," he called while spinning around and scanning over the low wall. Seeing no close threats, he signaled Riker and Trip to advance. He covered them as they vaulted over the wall, quickly scanned the rooftop of Building Two and the courtyard with his surreal X27s, then rolled over the wall himself. Once on the other side, he led Riker and Trip noiselessly to the door of the target building and knelt. Feeling completely vulnerable and exposed, he waited for Fitz to call in position to breach Building One. The several seconds it took felt like an eternity, but finally, the call came.

"Ghost Two—set," Fitz said in his Peltors.

Chunk rose and covered the left side of the door, Trip the right, as Riker backed up two paces.

"Three . . . two . . . one . . ."

On zero, Riker took a big step forward and planted his left boot into the door. The door fractured at the handle and swung in, while Riker tossed a flash-bang into the gap. At the sound of the dull *whump*, Chunk opened his eyes and sprinted low and fast through the door, moving left, as Trip mirrored him to the right. His corner was clear and he vectored forward, the left side of the arrowhead formation as Riker surged up the middle. Movement left drew his scan to a bearded man—still blinded by the flash-bang—pointing a rifle roughly toward the door they had just entered. Chunk dropped the terrorist with a quick double tap to the head and then continued forward. Riker fired from ahead of him and another man fell to the ground.

"We need crows," Chunk reminded his teammates. Overflight had held four thermals in this building and half of them were now dead.

Two other men sat up in their cots, stunned but searching the blackness for their attackers.

"*La totliqu alnār!*" the man in the center bunk hollered, begging not to be shot while his neighbor threw his hands up in surrender.

Chunk sighted on the door while Riker and Trip wrestled the two remaining terrorists to the floor and had them flex-cuffed in seconds.

"Ghost One is clear," he called, while gunfire echoed from Building One where Fitz and his element were engaged.

From the sounds of it, Fitz was being forced to put down more tangos than Chunk hoped. He looked at the two dudes they'd just cuffed—trembling and blubbering on the floor—and grimaced. With 100 percent certainty, he knew that neither of *these guys* was the Lion of Ramadi.

CHAPTER 20

Ducking low inside the cramped attic loft, Ahmed Nazari met his young spotter's terrified gaze and lifted his index finger to his lips—*shhhhh*. Putting on a brave face, he mouthed the words, "It's going to be okay."

But it was not going to be okay.

There was no conceivable outcome in which *this* was going to be okay.

The SEALs had come like Ahmed had feared they might, and escape was not only improbable—it was impossible. And yet, his decision to shelter in the hidden loft had already proven prescient and would hopefully buy him the precious time he needed. Juba and the woman sniper, Nurbika Abdulayeva, had already departed the safe house separately to travel to their next assignments, and as far as Ahmed knew, they'd both slipped through the American's web undetected. As for himself, he was still waiting on tasking, and unfortunately, his time had run out.

Inshallah.

With controlled, smooth movements, he stretched out on the floor and pressed his cheek into the buttstock riser of his Dragunov SVDN2 sniper rifle. He let out a long slow breath and sighted through the PSO-1M2 scope. His normally slow, rock-steady pulse pounded in his temples as he scanned through the slats of the front gable window. He positioned his reticle at chest height in the open doorway of the building housing the AAI fighters who owned this compound. To call this raggedy group Ansar al-Islam did a disservice to the twenty-year history of AAI in Ahmed's mind. This newer, self-proclaimed "Pro-AQ faction of AAI" was little more than a loose collection of radical malcontents with rifles. The men in this compound would give up easily and would not hold up to interrogation by the Americans, and that was a problem.

Juba and his chain of command had to be protected at all costs.

It would be an honor to martyr himself for the cause.

"We'll escape out the back window and down the cliffs to the east," he whispered, playing to hope so his spotter could find the courage to be still and quiet.

"Inshallah," the young man whispered back.

The sound of gunfire directly below sent Ahmed's pulse soaring. They had only minutes before the Americans discovered the little loft. It was well-concealed, the only access via a hidden ceiling panel and a ladder he pulled up at night, but the Americans were no fools. They had drones and satellites peering down from above and would be able to see his thermal outline. The trick was to capitalize on the period of uncertainty while the operators tried to reconcile the body count of the dead and captured on the ground with the imagery from above. They would depart while they tried to rectify the two unaccounted-for heat signatures.

He pushed the thought from his mind and returned his attention to his scope.

Someone passed in front of the door to the other building, and Ahmed slipped his finger inside the trigger guard of the Dragunov. He adjusted his cheek on the riser, and let out a long, slow breath, feeling his pulse slow. He had been trained well. For fifteen years, he'd embraced his mentor's tutelage. For eight of those, he had racked up his own impressive list of kills, a résumé second only to Juba himself. Tonight he would repay Zain for all the years the man had invested in him.

A kitted-up American operator stepped out of the doorway, clearing left and right before entering the courtyard. Ahmed let his targeting reticle hover briefly over the man's chest. To send a 7.62 mm round through the Navy SEAL's heart would give him great pleasure, but his mission wasn't about pleasure. The lead SEAL moved off to Ahmed's left and then two more operators emerged, both escorting shuffling AAI fighters whose wrists were flex-cuffed behind their backs. He could take all three SEALs in mere seconds. But first, he had to take care of the liabilities . . . No matter what, the Americans could not know that this compound had housed Juba and Nurbika Abdulayeva. If they thought that Juba and his accomplice had slipped through their fingers, they would intensify their search, and whatever the mission Juba and the Chechen woman embarked on would be at risk. His job now was to give them cover and protect their next operation.

Ahmed shifted the reticle onto the bowed head of the first captive, who was being shoved forward by an American operator. He exhaled, feeling a paradoxical peace flood over him, before he squeezed the trigger. The man's head snapped back, and he collapsed, pulling the SEAL off balance as Ahmed sighted in on the second captive and squeezed again . . .

CHAPTER 21

BUILDING TWO

ANSAR AL-ISLAM TERRORIST COMPOUND

NORTH OF AQRAH, IRAQ

At first, Chunk thought Trip had stumbled, but when the terrorist he was escorting collapsed to the ground, Chunk knew they were in trouble. Riker's captive took a round to the throat next. Blood spraying in an arc, the jihadi screamed while he tried desperately to free his hands from behind his back. The screaming stopped a heartbeat later when the top of the terrorist's head disintegrated in a puff of red.

"Sniper!" Trip hollered as both he and Riker got low and sprinted for cover.

Another suppressed *whump* followed, and a third hand-cuffed captive—this one being marched out of Building One by a Team Two SEAL everyone called Slappy—hit the dirt.

Chunk spun around the corner and pressed into the wall. He exhaled, took a knee, then quickly popped out to scan Building One for the shooter they'd somehow missed.

"He's got to be on the roof," he called, his voice calm but tight.

"Negative, Ghost One," said Saw's voice in his ear. "The roof is clear."

Chunk pulled back as a high-velocity round slammed into the corner inches from where his head had just been.

"Got him," Riker called. "Ghost, sniper is inside Building One, shooting through a louvered window in a gable."

"Apollo, Ghost Two—did you say *inside* Building One?" Fitz said. "We're secure inside."

"No, you're not, there's a shooter on the upper level," Riker said.

"There is no upper level . . ." Fitz said, confused.

"Can you take him or not, Apollo?" Chunk said, worried less about why they were in this mess and focusing instead on how to get out of it.

"Negative, One. All I can see is the suppressor peeking out from the wooden slats."

"Shit, there must be an attic hide or something above us, Apollo. Give me a sec," came Fitz's frustrated reply.

Chunk heard multiple bursts of gunfire kick off inside Building One and knew it was Fitz going to work, probably shooting into the ceiling.

"Squirters out the back of Building One," Apollo Two called with urgency. "Two tangos—just saw them drop out of an upper window on a sweep but now my line is obstructed."

"Which way are they going?" Chunk asked.

"They're running east," the Team Two sniper said.

"Ghost One, Apollo One—I got 'em," Saw called. "Want me to take them?"

"Negative," Chunk said moving quickly around the corner in a combat crouch, sighting over his rifle. "We need them alive." He sprinted toward the northeast corner of the other building, scanning rapidly back and forth as he did. "But don't let them fucking shoot me either," he added.

He sprinted, full tilt, toward the wall at the east end of the compound. The smaller jihadi was carrying an AK-47 slung over his shoulder as he fled. The other squirter, who was taller, was holding a long gun with a suppressor out in front as he ran.

A sniper and his spotter?

Chunk grinned as he ran. This had to be him—the Lion of Ramadi, or more likely that asshole now living in the legend of the infamous sniper.

"*Qiff!*" he shouted, ordering the terrorists to stop as he took a knee and sighted in.

Instead of stopping, the smaller fighter spun on a heel and brought his weapon up. Chunk fired three times, the first grazing the fighter's neck and the next two hitting center mass, knocking him onto his back.

"I said stop!" Chunk yelled at the still-fleeing sniper, who was pumping his arms and legs with everything he had and making for the wall.

"Son of a bitch," Chunk mumbled, robotically putting his sight on the back of the man's head . . . but instead of squeezing the trigger, providence stayed his finger.

This dude was the last living soul on the X.

They had to take him alive, or it was all for nothing.

He toggled his rifle to three-round burst, lowered his aim to the man's legs, and fired a volley. The fleeing shooter dropped instantly, spinning as he fell. Chunk popped up into a combat crouch and advanced, sighting over his rifle in case the wounded terrorist had his heart set on paradise and virgins today. But the man did not appear to be wearing a suicide vest, and instead of going for his weapon, both of his hands clutched his left leg just above the knee as he howled in pain.

Chunk kicked the black Dragunov sniper rifle away from the man's reach with a booted foot while keeping his muzzle trained on the jihadi's forehead. "*'arini yadaik!*" he barked in Arabic, ordering the man to show him his hands.

"I cannot," the man said replied in English. "If I let go, I bleed to death."

"If you don't show me your hands, you'll bleed to death from the next five bullets I'm about to put in you," Chunk said. "Now show me your hands."

The man flashed his bloody palms, up and empty toward Chunk, but then quickly grabbed his leg again when blood sprayed from the wounds.

Chunk moved in, still aiming at the center of the man's head, and placed a boot on his chest as he called on his radio. "Stalker, Ghost One—ready for immediate exfil."

"Ghost, Stalker, roger. Five mikes," the helo pilot said.

Riker was coming up beside him now with Trip in tow.

"Get a tourniquet on this guy's leg," Chunk said.

Trip dropped to a knee beside the wounded sniper and pulled a blowout kit from his right cargo pocket as he did.

Riker picked up the wounded man's sniper rifle. "Look at this, boss."

Chunk pulled the wounded man's blood-soaked hands from his leg and secured them with a zip tie, while Trip fastened the tourniquet. Next, he patted the man down, double-checking for hidden explosives. Satisfied they were safe, he glanced over at where Riker held up the Dragunov, hoisting it like it was the Stanley Cup. Then his SEAL brother slung it over his shoulder and moved in on the badly bleeding jihadi at his feet.

"Is this what you used, motherfucker?" Riker snarled,

holding the rifle over the man. "Is this what you used to murder my brothers?"

For a moment, Chunk was afraid that Riker was about to connect the heel of his boot with the wounded sniper's temple, perhaps hard enough to kill the man, but then his brother regained control. The senior chief let out a rattling breath and turned away. Just beyond, Chunk saw Fitz and Slappy jogging over.

"You got him?" Fitz asked, his eyes ticking over to the sniper rifle in Riker's hands, and no doubt struggling with his own bloodlust at the sight of the sniper who had likely killed CJ.

"Yeah," Chunk said. "Whaddya got in Building One?"

"Five KIA, unfortunately," Fitz replied, unable to tear his eyes away from the Dragunov. Slappy, despite the goofy nickname, took a knee and scanned in an arc for any incoming threats like the professional SEAL he was.

"Stalker One, this is Ghost One. We have one crow who is an urgent surgical, all others are KIA," Chunk said. "Keep Stalker Three in orbit for air support. Stalker Four exfil Apollo. LZ is secure."

"Ghost, Stalker, roger. Three mikes," the lead pilot said.

"Stalker Four, roger," said the little bird pilot in charge of picking up their sniper duos from the ridgeline.

"Fitz, grab whatever you found in Building One for the N2 guys and let's haul ass," Chunk said turning to the Team Two officer.

"Check," Fitz said and then he and Slappy jogged back to Building One to button things up.

Chunk looked down at the sniper at his feet, the man's eyes now glazed with early stages of shock. "Get this piece of shit to the LZ," he said, turning to Trip and Riker. "And whatever you do, don't let him die on us. The Lion of Ramadi's got a lot of talking to do."

CHAPTER 22

The long gray building, once home to the Army Airborne's 28th Combat Support Hospital, stood nearly empty. Chunk paced the cavernous space, sized for thirty-two hospital beds, while Riker watched. Now, it was used for storage, with crates and boxes stacked along the north wall, dust covering most of the surfaces. A makeshift lounge had been set up in the middle of the room—with three well-worn sofas arranged in a U, one wooden crate doing double duty as a coffee table, and another serving as a stand for a seventy-two-inch television. Behind the TV spanned a row of industrial shelving containing food, video games, and DVDs, flanked by two full-size refrigerators, one with a large red label reading, Hazardous Waste—a joke Chunk decided. At the far end of the space, a section had been partitioned off with gray, industrial-style curtains which hung floor to ceiling, bright-white light streaming through the breaks in the five different panels.

His gaze went to Watts who was sitting on the center sofa, a notebook computer open on her lap, chatting in low tones with the CIA man, Russ Profant. She, at least, was trying to use her time productively, which made this the perfect opportunity to pester her.

"Hey, Heels," Chunk called.

She turned and looked at him, her eyes shooting daggers that he dare use her unofficial nickname in front of someone outside the unit—especially a fellow spook from her world.

"Yes, Commander Redman?" she replied, emphasizing the honorific in case the ire in her gaze was somehow lost on him.

"I thought you said our boy was waking up," he said, referencing the last update she'd given him what felt like eons ago but was probably fifteen minutes. "I've been pacing for hours over here and nobody's called us yet."

"Last time I checked, I wasn't the attending," she said, parrying his passive-aggressive good ol' boy comment with one of her own. "I imagine the docs will get us when he's conscious and able to form complete sentences."

As if waiting for just that cue, a tall, solidly built fellow emerged from between the curtains, his broad chest stretching his OR scrub-style shirt, which had been cut from Army camo cloth. The doc strode toward them, and Chunk intercepted him at the far end of the lounge.

"Hey, Doc," he said and stuck out a hand. "Appreciate you taking care of this guy for us."

"Yeah, no problem," the man answered in a Texas drawl. "I'm Ray. Which one of y'all shot that dude?"

"That'd be me," Chunk said, grinning over the wad of snuff packed in his lower lip. "He was running away, so I had to stop him, but I really needed to talk to him too . . . if you catch my drift?"

"I hear ya," the surgeon said with a knowing grin that suggested this wasn't his first rodeo with Special Operators. This top secret medical unit from Fort Bragg only supported Special Operations task forces and mostly the JSOC elements. Chunk figured this guy had seen it all by now. "Well, you walked that line pretty tight, bro," he continued. "Nice work to whoever placed the tourniquet, 'cause otherwise he'd a died turning transport. One of the bullets shattered the femur, shredded the femoral artery, and transected the nerve. Not fixable, so he wound up with an AKA."

"AKA?" Watts asked, stepping up beside Chunk along with Profant.

"Above-knee amputation," the doc said, hands on hips.

"You cut his leg off?" she asked, her eyes open wide.

"Yep," the surgeon said. "Too much tissue loss to repair. Most of the muscles around the knee and lower thigh were toast. The nerve was gone. The artery was shit. He ain't gonna be running away from you again, I can guarantee that . . . Anyway, he's up now. Sorry to keep you waiting but he emerged from sedation pretty combative, so I was trying to find a nice balance where you could talk to him, but he wouldn't be overly combative. He's pretty toasty now, so he should be chatty for you."

"Thanks, brother," Chunk said shaking the man's hand. "Where you hail from, Doc?"

"Grew up in Lubbock," the surgeon said. "College at UT and then med school at Baylor. I really hate leaving Texas, but hell, even Erbil is better than Fort fuckin' Bragg."

Chunk laughed. "I hear that. We owe you guys a case of something, so we'll see what we can do."

"Ah, that's not necessary," the surgeon said, "*but* if you insist, I happen to be partial to Redneck Riviera."

"You and me both, Doc," Riker chimed in. "Might just be 'cause I love John Rich, but man, that's my whiskey for sure."

The surgeon drew open a space between two panels of gray curtain for them. On the other side there were four ICU-style beds, each with an impressive array of monitors and rolling equipment carts, including ventilators. Bright light filled the space from OR grade light fixtures atop aluminum poles, one in each corner.

"Pretty impressive," Profant said. "I had no idea you guys were even here."

"We're not," the surgeon said with a wink. "We got tasked to set up here when Team Two came to town. We were in Baghdad before that." He waved his arm indicating the setup. "Got everything we need and nothing we don't. Pirated the ICU gear from stuff left behind by the 28th CaSH. We don't usually travel with big base hospital equipment, but this stuff is packable, so we kept it. The OR is on the other side of the curtain—we set up two tables when you launched your op— just in case you needed us."

Chunk nodded, suddenly overwhelmed with gratitude knowing these guys were within arm's reach for no reason other than to keep his team alive if something terrible happened. It was a comfort during every pre-op brief to know they had medical on standby, but being here, meeting the docs in person, drove the point home.

"Your dude is over here," the surgeon said, ending the awkward silence. He walked Chunk and the others to the far corner where the sniper with the well-trimmed beard lay motionless with his eyes closed. Another doc, who was dressed in BDU pants and a brown T-shirt, was slowly pushing a syringe full of medicine into the IV bag hanging from a pole at the head of the bed.

"Hi, Ray," said the man with the syringe, greeting the surgeon. Then, turning to Chunk and the others added, "I'm Tank, the unit PA and sometimes anesthesia guy. You here to meet my new friend?"

"Yup," Chunk said with fresh malice brewing as he looked down at the man who was, in all probability, the sniper that had shot CJ in the head.

The Iraqi, who Chunk guessed was midthirties at the most, presented nothing like a typical jihadist. While his age did not preclude him from being the original Lion of Ramadi, Chunk still believed Watts's theory that this was a new fighter, living in the legend for obvious PsyOps reasons. With his clean young face and slight build, this guy looked like a barista in an upscale coffee bar, not someone executing SEALs with a Dragunov rifle in a war zone, but perhaps this was the evolution of the new generation of jihadi. Chunk's gaze drifted from the sniper's face to the bandaged bulge where the man's left leg now ended abruptly at midthigh.

"Wake up, sunshine," Tank said, patting hard on the right side of the man's face. Chunk saw now that the terrorist's wrists were secured to the sides of the bed with soft restraints.

The man's eyes flickered and then opened. He looked at the party of Americans around him, confused at first, and then, as if remembering where he was, settled his gaze on Chunk. A hint of a smile formed in the corners of the enemy sniper's mouth, and it took all of Chunk's discipline not to cave in the man's face with his fist.

"I got this," Profant offered, perhaps sensing Chunk's simmering rage.

The CIA man stepped between Chunk and the prisoner

while Watts circled the bed to stand on the other side. Chunk, for his part, folded his arms on his chest and glared at the man from the foot of the bed.

"*Marhaban,*" Profant said in greeting. "*Ismee Russ. Inta a-seer.*"

"Oh, I think he knows he's a prisoner," Riker said from beside Chunk, his voice thick with the same vitriol Chunk was feeling.

"*Shis-mek?*" Profant asked.

"This dude speaks English," Chunk said, irritated. "What's your name, asshole?"

"He spoke English pretty good for us . . . Just so you know," Tank said, confirming Chunk's deduction.

The terrorist looked at Chunk for a long time, the smile no longer in the corner of his lips, and then replied, "*Ismee Juba.*"

"You say you are named Juba?" Profant said, making no effort to hide his surprise at the claim.

The Iraqi nodded.

"Well, Juba, that would have made you something like fifteen years old back in 2005 when Juba was operating. You were pretty badass for a kid, huh? Where are you from?"

"I am from Iraq," the sniper said, his eyes still locked on Chunk. "I am a son of Iraq and have spent my life protecting my country from invaders like you."

"Where in Iraq?" Profant pressed.

"I am from everywhere, since I was young."

"Where is your family?"

"I have no family except all of the people of Iraq."

"Oh, I see," Profant said with a chuckle.

"They say Juba was Syrian. You don't look Syrian to me," Chunk said from where he stood, eyes locked with the unlikely-looking killer.

The sniper responded with a wry smile, then abruptly looked over at Watts. With a disgusted look on his face, he said, "You let your woman dress like this in my presence? I will not talk while your whore is here."

There was a blur of motion and, before Chunk knew it, Riker had pushed past him. The senior chief grabbed the sniper's stump with both hands and squeezed.

"Don't you ever disrespect my teammate, you piece of garbage," Riker growled as the Iraqi howled in pain.

"Soooo, I'm gonna grab some coffee," Tank said and disappeared through the gray curtains.

"Say you're sorry," Riker said, his gaze locked on the sniper's face.

The terrorist gritted his teeth, his eyes squeezed shut in pain, but said nothing.

"I said apologize," Riker demanded.

Chunk approached Riker and gave his shoulder a gentle squeeze—*enough*.

"I . . . am . . . sorry . . ." the terrorist breathed, and only then did Riker release his grip on the stump.

The man looked down at his leg and his eyes widened, tears filling them and spilling onto his cheeks. Chunk thought the tears were less from pain and more from the epiphany that his left leg was gone. Chunk motioned with his head for Riker to return to the foot of the bed. Then he looked at Watts, whose pursed lips conveyed her apparent displeasure at what Riker had done.

"My leg . . . *Shi' rijli* . . ." the sniper said, his tone equal parts whimper and dismay.

"Yeah, it's gone," Chunk said. "Shoulda thought about that before you started shooting at us."

"So," Profant said, "you want us to believe you're Juba,

the Lion of Ramadi—a sniper who was operating in his prime when you were only a kid?"

"I *am* Juba," the man seethed through a grimace.

"Uh-huh," Profant said, his tone suggesting he wasn't buying it. "Here's what I think . . . I think Juba was your sniper daddy and we killed him dead, and now you're here trying to resurrect the legend. The problem is, nobody believes it."

"The Navy SEALs think they are superman, but I showed the world they are nothing but men." The sniper shifted his gaze to Chunk. "I made you and your friends bleed and suffer, just like my people have."

Chunk felt a swell of anger at the taunt but swallowed it down.

"Who do you work for?" Watts asked, her question slicing through the testosterone-fueled red tape of posturing and threat-making they were engaged in.

The man glared at her, but then his eyes ticked back to Riker and he chose his words carefully. "I work for the people of Iraq."

"Mm-hmm," she said. "Who is funding your operation and setting up your logistics? Who connected you with the AAI here in Erbil?"

"I make the connections myself over many years. I am funded by many groups who need my talents. I kill traitors. I kill infidels. I am Allah's instrument of justice. I have killed hundreds in his name."

"Then why did you shoot the Ansar al-Islam fighters who gave you shelter?" she pressed.

The sniper looked at the ceiling.

Her question was the same one that had been burning in Chunk's mind since the firefight at the AAI compound. He followed the thread. "Answer her. Why did you snipe your brother fighters? They were not Kafir. This is not permitted by the Quran."

"I was trying to kill you," the terrorist snapped, but then something else flashed in his eyes. "I regret my aim was not true, but it is an honor for any fighter to be martyred for Allah."

"Hold on," Chunk said, clawing out the spent tobacco from his lip and tossing the wad in a trash can on the floor. "First, you claim to be the Lion of Ramadi, the most revered sniper in the history of jihad. Then you claim you're a sniper for hire who's killed hundreds of infidels and Kafir as Allah's instrument of justice. But if you're such a badass sniper, then how come last night you missed all the SEALs and shot your own jihadi brothers in the head? Were those all *accidental* kills?"

The man looked away, his gaze returning to the ceiling.

"I didn't think so," Chunk said with victory in his voice, then turned to Watts and gestured for her to follow him out of the curtain partitions.

"Let's talk about where you were born," Profant was saying as they walked across the open space out of earshot. Riker followed them and stood beside Chunk for this three-person huddle.

"What do you think?" Chunk asked her.

"He prepared a narrative and he's sticking to it. Which, given his circumstances, is pretty impressive," she said with sympathy in her eyes that Chunk suddenly found annoying.

"Well, he's not the Lion of Ramadi," Chunk said. "That's for damn sure. Too young."

"I agree."

"But you think he was part of the operation that ambushed SEAL Team Two?"

She nodded. "Too many coincidences not to be, but there's still a piece we're missing. He claims to be a hired gun working for the jihadist movement du jour, but I think that's also part of his script. The lone-wolf narrative doesn't work. To pull this attack off he would have had to have logistical support."

"And intelligence support," Riker said. "Somebody had to provide the intelligence on where Team Two would be and then bait the trap. This guy is an instrument, but not for Allah. He's working for somebody . . . somebody a helluva lot smarter than your average tribal warlord."

"And we know *that* guy had to be the brainchild behind the weird PsyOps Facebook post," Chunk added. "Because the two operations are linked."

"I agree," she said, then bit her lip.

"What?" Chunk said, seeing something fresh was on her mind.

"What do you think about me showing him pictures of Eshan Dawar and Qasim Nadar? It might be interesting to see what his response is."

"No offense, Heels, but talk about confirmation bias. I mean, there are dozens of splinter cells out there," he said, playing devil's advocate. "Al Qadar is operating in Pakistan and eastern Afghanistan. We don't have a single thing to make us think they have any presence here."

She nodded and sighed. "Yeah, I know, it's just this operation has a similar vibe . . . if there is such a thing in counterterror."

"You mean a similar evolution in tactics and sophistication like we witnessed with al Qadar's combat drone program?" Chunk said.

"Exactly," she said.

"I think the priority is to press this guy hard and figure out if there's still an active operation underway," Chunk said, wondering if the sniper attack on Team Two was only *phase one* of some broader plan. "Bowman won't let us stay here in Erbil indefinitely, especially now that we got this guy and wiped out the compound. We need to figure out who else is in play before we get pulled back to Taj, okay?"

"Of course," she said, nodding. "I'm on it." She started walking back toward where Profant was interrogating the self-proclaimed Juba.

"Hey, Watts," he called after her and she turned, eyebrows up. "Maybe show him those pics anyway . . . Why the hell not?"

"Sure," she said with an inscrutable smile.

Why do I have a feeling she was going to do it anyway? he thought with a smile of his own. *Best to let her tug at her knots.*

"I want to stay," Riker said.

Chunk looked at his LCPO with surprise. "Really?"

"Yeah, I wanna make sure the guy talks. He's hiding something."

Chunk imagined Riker giving Juba's stump another squeeze. With a sigh, he clapped his hand on Riker's shoulder. "I feel ya, bro, but let's let the pros do their thing, okay? Heels is all over this."

"Yeah, okay," Riker said after a grudgingly long pause. "Wanna go for a run? Happy to kick your ass again."

"How about we hit the weights first? Maybe you can dead-lift half what I can today."

"You're such a dick," Riker said with a chuckle. "I'll take that bet."

As they walked out of the hidden hospital, Chunk had to acknowledge that something was still missing. This was just too simple to be the end of it—a new generation Juba, hired by low-level shitheads like AAI to kill SEALs . . . nobody in that equation had the sophistication to have pulled the hit off. But if anyone could put the pieces all together, it was Watts. And the CIA guy, Profant, seemed to have his act together too. It was just going to take time, discipline, and patience.

And therein lay the rub.

That's the thing about hunting, he thought, rolling his shoulders in anticipation of hitting the gym. *Shooting a buck is easy. Properly positioning your blind and lying in wait until you lure him out into the open . . . well, that's the hard part.*

CHAPTER 23

Whitney stared at the black screen of her laptop, which had timed out and gone dark while her mind wandered. "Juba" had stuck doggedly to his script, and despite her and Russ Profant's best efforts, they'd not managed to shake actionable intelligence loose. She'd showed him the photos of Eshan Dawar and Qasim Nadar and neither picture had elicited recognition. And the sniper *had* looked at the images, if for no other reason than to satisfy his own curiosity. His nonreaction shouldn't have surprised her, but it did. She'd been sure her hunch that al Qadar was tied to the Erbil sniper attack had been right.

Her secure mobile phone rang, vibrating on her desk next to her computer. She glanced at the caller ID and grinned. It was like the universe anticipated where she needed to go next.

"Hey, Bobby," she said, pressing her phone to her ear and leaning back in the wobbly task chair.

"I got some good news and some bad news," said the former Delta operator turned spook. "Which one do you want first?"

"Ooo, I love conversations that start off this way," she said and meant it. "I'm a good-news-first kinda girl. Hit me."

"I reached out to a fella I know at MI5 and after a good bit of begging—and the promise of a very expensive bottle of scotch, which you're paying for incidentally—I got him to agree to connect you with a British joint counterterror task force that has Qasim Nadar on its watch list."

"That's great news," she said, pushing off with her right foot and spinning a full circle in the squeaky chair. "What's the bad news?"

"The bad news is the team ain't happy about it. In fact, don't be surprised if the response you get is downright hostile."

"I'm not worried. Collaboration is the name of the game in today's counterterrorism world. I'm sure I can sweet-talk my way into their good graces."

He chuckled. "Good luck with that. I'm sending you the contact information for the officer in charge on your high side. His name is Holden McLean. He's with MI5, and he's the task force lead."

"Thanks, Bobby. I really appreciate this," she said. "And do send me the bill for that scotch."

"Anytime, Heels," he said, using her insider nickname. "Oh, and one more thing, don't make the rookie mistake and call them *agents*. What we call *informants*, the Brits call *agents*; what we call *agents*, they call *officers*."

"Roger that, thanks for the tip."

"Don't be a stranger, Watts."

"Back at you," she said and ended the call.

She refreshed her confidential inbox over and over again

until Theobald's email showed up. She clicked on it, noted the name and phone number, then glanced at the clock icon in the upper right corner of her screen.

No time like the present to get shit done, she reminded herself and dialed the number.

"McLean," a male voice said after the third ring.

She'd only made it halfway through her introductory spiel before he interrupted her.

"Let me stop you right there," he said. "Watts, you said your name is, eh?"

"That's right."

"How do I put this delicately, Ms. Watts?" he said with uniquely annoying British indifference. "I don't think this is going to work."

"I don't understand," she said. "I haven't even told you what I need yet."

"Right, I know, but see there's the kicker, because it doesn't really matter what it is. Whatever it is, it's of enormous importance to you, but not to us. When I connect you to Lucy Kim, our agent runner on the task force from MI6, she's going to tell you to piss off straightaway. No feigning interest or nothing—just a *piss off, mate* and then a hang up. She's like that and who can blame her? A third of East London are potential Islamic jihadists on paper. But you'll be miffed, and rightfully so—us being close allies in the war on terror and all—so you'll call me back and complain. Make no mistake, I'll take the call and listen sympathetically, probably all the while checking my exploding high side inbox and maybe wondering what, if anything, my knackered wife will warm up for my dinner when I get home late tonight for the hundredth day in a row. Then I'm going to apologize and sound like I care, but let's be honest here—I really don't. And why would I? I don't know you. Everybody here is very busy. We all have our own jobs to do, don't we? We certainly don't have time to do other people's jobs, especially for the Americans who seem to have their own resources and budgets. And so, I think what would be best is if you submit your request in writing, and then I'll have one of my junior targeters put together a nice, tidy package of everything we've got on Qasim Nadar and transmit it to you. All right? How's that sound?"

Whitney pursed her lips, considered her reply, and decided to go with brutal honesty.

"That was quite a long-winded monologue, Officer McLean, and in the time that took, you probably could have had me on and off a conference call with your colleague. I know how hard you work, but it was still a shit response and not the level of professionalism or courtesy that I expected. So, let's try this again. Hello, my name is Whitney Watts, and I believe that one of *your* countrymen might be a high-ranking member of a terrorist organization that launched two drone strikes that killed a dozen of *my* countrymen. I personally happened to be on the receiving end of one of those attacks. And while I narrowly avoided being dismembered myself, I was lucky enough to help identify the charred remains of a CIA colleague I'd been standing next to only moments before."

"I'm sorry to hear that," he said, his voice taking on a more serious timbre now.

"Have you had the privilege of smelling barbequed human flesh, Mr. McLean?"

"I can't say that I have."

"That's good, because every night before I go to sleep, I wish to God I could extract the memory of that smell from my brain." An uncomfortable silence hung on the line, but she let it linger until he broke.

"I'll talk to Officer Kim and have her contact you at her earliest convenience," he said.

"I'd prefer to video conference with her. Let's schedule it now," she said, knowing it was harder to be a passive-aggressive asshole when you had to do it to someone's face.

In the background, she could hear him talking to someone and she pictured him cupping his hand over the phone while he whispered to his MI6 colleague.

"All right," he said through a defeated sigh. "Give us thirty minutes. You have my email address?"

"Yes, I'll set it up and send you a secure link. Talk to you both then," she said and ended the call.

Thirty minutes gave her just enough time to use the facilities, grab a snack, and make herself a cup of coffee before logging into the call a few minutes early as the host. Chunk had turned her onto Bonefrog Coffee—a veteran-owned coffee company started by a retired SEAL—and damn if she wasn't drinking two cups a day because it was so damn good.

Mug in hand, she returned to her desk and was relieved that her British counterparts did not ghost her. When the video conference went live, she was greeted by a window featuring a middle-aged, pale-skinned man with a receding hairline of curly dark hair sitting beside a woman of Asian descent who looked to be in her late twenties or early thirties.

"I'm Lucy Kim, the agent runner on this task force. McLean tells me you want to get into my knickers?" the woman said with an angry estuary English accent that would make Ricky Gervais proud. "Why are you looking at me that way? Yeah, this is how I talk. I'm second-generation British-born Korean, grew up in New Malden."

Whitney felt her cheeks get hot, taken aback by Lucy Kim's onslaught.

"Nice to meet you, Lucy, I'm Whitney Watts. I work in the N2 shop for the Naval Special Warfare JSOC element presently prosecuting the al Qadar terrorist network in Pakistan, Afghanistan, and abroad. We've flagged one of your naturalized citizens, an Afghan-born immigrant who goes by the name Qasim Nadar, as a person of interest. We have limited information on him, but we believe he has ties to Hamza al-Saud and is connected to a series of drone strikes conducted by al Qadar three months ago in eastern Afghanistan against American and coalition forces."

"The Kandahar attack?" Kim said.

"That's correct."

The MI6 officer nodded, clearly aware of the incident.

"You said you're the agent runner for your task force?" Whitney said, assuming that *agent runner* was MI6 vernacular for what the US Intelligence Community called *asset handlers.*

"Yeah, that's right," Kim came back.

"You wouldn't happen to be running Nadar by any chance, would you?"

Kim cocked a questioning eyebrow at McLean.

"I vetted her credentials," he said. "She's cleared at the highest level."

The MI6 woman nodded and turned back to the camera. "The answer to your question is no. But Nadar is on our Level One watch list and a person of interest given his immigration status and occupation."

"What is his occupation?" Whitney asked, pen at the ready.

"He works at British Aerospace as the engineering lead for avionics software integration on the Valkyrie stealth UCAV program."

A lump instantly materialized in Whitney's throat as this new and confirming puzzle piece clicked into place. *Chunk's going to flip when I tell him that Nadar is a drone avionics engineer.*

"You look like you've just seen a ghost," Kim said.

"That's highly pertinent information that we were not aware of," Whitney said, her mind racing a thousand miles an hour. "Nadar traveled to Pakistan fifteen weeks ago. We believe he was in the city of Mingora when the al Qadar drone strikes were conducted. Now that I know he is an avionics engineer with expert drone knowledge . . . it changes everything."

"It could be coincidence," McLean said.

"I don't think so," she said. "Does the name Eshan Dawar mean anything to you?"

"That name sounds very familiar," McLean said, turning to Kim.

"Yeah, Dawar is on our watch list. He also uses the alias Javad Ahmad, but he disappeared from our radar several months ago."

"That's because Eshan Dawar was killed during a hit we conducted on a safe house in Mingora before the drone attack."

"That answers that question," Kim said with a look at McLean. "The Yanks blew his brains out."

Whitney grimaced. "Yeah, it's unfortunate. Sometimes the boys get a little trigger-happy."

"But how does Dawar relate to Nadar?" McLean asked.

"They traveled together from Afghanistan into Pakistan. We photographed them in a hired vehicle at Torkham crossing fifteen weeks ago . . ." She stopped as an absurdly ridiculous, but possibly brilliant, epiphany occurred to her.

What if Chunk's "fake Hamza" theory is right? Is it possible that Qasim Nadar and Hamza al-Saud are the same person?

"You looked like you were about to say something important," Kim said. "Go on, spit it out."

Did she dare read them in on Hamza? Could she trust them with the crown jewel of her investigation? Whitney refocused on the computer screen and met Lucy Kim's eyes—guarded eyes that had greeted her with suspicion and mistrust from the get-go. But in those guarded eyes Whitney thought she saw her own reflection—a kindred spirit, a young CIA analyst who was trying to do the same impossible job in a "guard my rice bowl at all costs" environment. She remembered the MI6 officer's opening salvo:

I'm Lucy Kim, the agent runner on this task force. McLean tells me you want to get into my knickers . . .

Who talks like that to a fellow professional they've never met? Someone who's been burned but is still playing with fire. An agent runner whose carefully cultivated sources had been exploited and compromised by "colleagues" and "partners" she thought she could trust. A cynic who expects the worst but hopes for the best . . . *Someone like me.*

Yes, I think I can trust Lucy Kim.

Whitney took a deep breath and said, "We have Hamza al-Saud checked into one of our luxurious five-star detention facilities."

Kim and McLean traded looks once again.

"You better not be taking the piss out of us, Miss Watts," McLean said, turning back to fix her with a hazel-eyed stare.

"I don't know what that means," she said.

"It means you better not be fucking with us," Kim said, her interest suddenly piqued for the first time in this conversation.

"I'm not fucking with you," she said, but not quite ready to float Chunk's body-double theory.

"Then why haven't we heard anything about this?" Kim asked, turning to McLean. "If al-Saud was off the board, why didn't anyone tell us?"

"A good question," McLean said and looked at Whitney. "It would have been nice if you blokes had let us know you had Hamza al-Saud. Would have saved us a lot of work hunting for him."

Screw it, she thought and blew air through pursed lips. *I'm going all in.*

"Look, here's the deal. We snatched al-Saud out of Pakistan on an unsanctioned operation while trying to stop that drone strike on Kandahar. In the three months that we've had him in custody, we've failed to extract a single piece of actionable intelligence from the man. At first, we thought it was because he was just that good. But the longer it has dragged on, the more we're beginning to have doubts. There are some people, and I include myself on the list, who believe the man in that detention cell claiming to be Hamza al-Saud is a body double—one of al-Saud's lieutenants who gave himself up as a living martyr to throw us off the real al-Saud's trail. Our failure to harvest intelligence from the man we have in custody prompted us to revisit assumptions we'd made about the al Qadar chain of command . . . You wanted to know what I was thinking earlier, well, here it is: Do you think it's possible that Qasim Nadar and Hamza al-Saud are the same person?"

"Unlikely," McLean said, the speed and certainty of his dismissal taking Whitney by surprise.

Kim, however, was not so quick to dismiss the idea. "I don't know, boss, it's an interesting theory."

"I say bollocks. GCHQ has been all over Nadar since he made that trip to Afghanistan and came home with his new wife. They've harvested no viable SIGINT at all. Nothing. How does a man running an international terror organization like al Qadar do it without communicating up and down the chain of command?"

"This new generation of terrorists are smart," Whitney came back. "For God's sake, you just told me that Nadar works at British Aero on your country's next-generation stealth combat drone. Any terrorist capable of circumventing your background checks—"

"Now wait just a bloody second," McLean said, cutting her off. "We have not confirmed that Nadar is a terrorist. Yes, we are watching him, out of an abundance of caution. But Nadar is a British citizen, and to date, we have no evidence tying him to al Qadar."

"I just told you he was photographed in a vehicle with Eshan Dawar at Torkham entering the Khyber Pakhtunkhwa province three weeks before the drone strikes which we know originated in Mingora," Whitney said, but she could already see the gears of damage control spinning in McLean's head at the prospect of having failed to thwart a major intelligence breach on his watch.

"Yes, but you just shared that information with us five seconds ago," McLean said.

"But if what she says is true, then we have a major fucking problem," Kim said, vocalizing Whitney's private thoughts quite eloquently. "I want to step things up with Diba. I think I can land her."

McLean scrubbed his face with his hands and murmured a string of curses Whitney couldn't quite make out before looking back at Kim. "Fine, do it."

"Who's Diba?" Whitney asked.

"Nadar's wife," Kim said. "I've been . . . cultivating a relationship with her. Just in case."

Ahhh . . . so they're more worried about Nadar than they let on.

She looked back and forth between her two new friends on the screen. "I think this was a very productive exchange."

"So do I," Kim said, smiling at Whitney for the first time.

"So . . . does this mean we're officially cooperating now?"

"It would appear so," McLean said and seemed to deflate on screen. "I'll make the necessary calls."

"We should probably step up surveillance on Qasim," Kim said. "Put twenty-four-hour eyes on him. Maybe bug his flat while he's at work. I can invite Diba for a lunch."

"Agreed," McLean said and then turned his attention back to Whitney. "Are you planning to come to London?"

"I hadn't thought that far ahead," she confessed. "Just taking it one step at a time, to be honest."

"Understood. If you do decide to join our little party, I would appreciate some advanced notice. You Americans have a rotten tendency to show up uninvited and immediately start making lots of demands. Rubs people the wrong way, and by people, I mean me," McLean said.

Whitney smiled. "That's not how I roll. Let me talk to my Head Shed and get back with you. We've got some other pots on the stove at the moment, so as much as a trip to London sounds interesting, I don't see that happening anytime soon. But I'll never say never."

"Let's stay in touch, Watts," Kim said, her demeanor softening to something resembling cordial. "I'm going to put the squeeze on Diba and see what happens. If she talks, I suspect we'll learn new information. If she panics and runs to Qasim, that will be informative too."

"Thank you," Whitney said, and then taking a page from Chunk's interpersonal management playbook, added, "I know it's a pain having someone show up asking to play in your sandbox. I appreciate you guys being so accommodating."

McLean and Kim nodded, said their goodbyes, and logged off.

Whitney got to her feet, pocketed her mobile phone, and—feeling quite proud of herself—set off to find Chunk to fill him in on the news that was going to rock his world.

CHAPTER 24

Qasim rode the elevator down to the lobby from his office feeling completely consumed but unable to put his finger on what was consuming him. It wasn't a thirst for vengeance, or at least for vengeance alone. It felt more like a calling—a duty to fulfill some supernatural purpose that Allah had set aside for him. His burst of anger at the hacker safe house the other night had been more than just his frustration boiling over. It had been him finding his inner strength.

Violence is a necessary part of my evolution—my rebirth into the man I need to be.

To fulfill his true calling, he had to be more than just an engineer, more than just a victim of Western aggression, and more than just one of Hamza al-Saud's loyal followers. He had to grow into the al Qadar leader that Hamza had encouraged him to be. He could no longer afford to allow anyone to regard him as less. He could no longer allow people to disrespect him. Even the armed, rough fighters he'd feared when he'd first met Hamza in Pakistan must come to fear and respect *him.*

He crossed the lobby and gave a cursory nod to the friendly night security guard behind the reception desk.

"Burning the midnight oil again I see," the guard said.

"For God and country," Qasim said with a chuckle, his Received Pronunciation getting better by the day.

He'd been working diligently at stripping the Afghan undertones from his speech to sound more like a native-born speaker. He'd become quite the chameleon of late, and he was getting better at managing the two identities always warring for his attention. At times, it seemed almost inconceivable that his career at British Aero had once been his real passion and joy, and not just a cover for his secret life. At other times, when sussing out a thorny aeronautical engineering challenge, it felt like his other life as an al Qadar warrior was a hangover memory from a terrible nightmare. But this was his life.

He was Janus—the two-faced god of beginnings and endings, duality, and change.

Qasim left the building, exiting onto the B283 just south of Dukes Avenue. Tonight he was meeting Hamza, but he needed to perform a series of countersurveillance activities before he did. London was the CCTV epicenter of the universe, so he had to be methodical and careful.

Assume people are watching you and behave in a way that makes them feel foolish for bothering to do so, Hamza had told him.

So Qasim walked to the corner and then feigned a sudden realization he had forgotten something. He turned back and entered the Tesco convenience store at the corner of Apex Tower. Once inside, he forced himself *not* to scan the store for anyone who might be watching him. Instead, he wandered to the aisle where the over-the-counter medicines were located and selected two different brands of painkillers, flipping them over as if to compare the ingredients. In his peripheral vision, he watched as a heavily disguised Hamza al-Saud entered the store. Hamza browsed for a while before making his way to the aisle where Qasim pretended to shop.

"Excuse me," Hamza said in an altered accent as he reached for a bottle of Calpol.

"Certainly," Qasim said, stepping aside for Hamza to reach the shelf. "By the way, do you think Calpol works better, or Nurofen? I can't decide."

Hamza shrugged and smiled. "My wife swears by Calpol, so that's what we take."

This preplanned exchange told Qasim that it was safe to meet. Had Hamza answered Nurofen, he would have aborted and walked straight home.

"Cheers, mate," Qasim said, placing the Nurofen back on the shelf and walking to the register.

Outside again, Qasim crossed over the B283 at the circle and then headed east on Dukes Avenue as was the plan. He forced himself to walk slowly, a man alone with his thoughts, the bottle of painkiller swinging from his right wrist in the little white plastic bag the clerk had given him. It took great effort not to scan the streets for would-be British agents who might be following him. That was Hamza's job now—to clear his tail and make sure he was not being followed.

At Malden Hills Gardens he turned right and slowed his pace. Inside, his pulse was pounding as he worried if he was under surveillance by MI5 or some other British agency. A block farther, that worry morphed into fear as he approached the corner of Kings Avenue and still Hamza had not texted him with the all clear. Without the message, he would abort and walk home, but just as he reached the corner, his phone chirped. He fished the burner mobile he was carrying tonight from his pocket. In keeping with standard computer programming protocol, a one meant the meet was on and a zero meant it was off.

He checked the screen and saw the number one.

His heart a bass drum in his chest, he turned right and headed west, counting off residences as he did. For some reason, he had a very bad feeling that tonight was the night he was going to be arrested. He'd been far too lucky for too long . . . Why did Hamza have to come in person? On reaching the eighth home, he turned and walked to the front door. The flat was dark inside and no exterior lights had been left on. He squatted, retrieved a key from beneath the doormat, and let himself inside. Movement in the dark room to the rear caught his attention and fresh panic washed over him. He balled his fists, peering into the dark, ready to defend himself . . .

"It's only me, Qasim," the familiar voice said as a table lamp clicked on, illuminating Hamza who was standing beside a leather chair. "I entered through the back door. Please, come and sit. There is nothing to worry about, this house is perfectly safe. There are no listening devices here, no CCTV cameras, no one across the street listening with laser microphones. I have spent a small fortune to have this face-to-face meeting with you tonight because I do not know when the opportunity will present itself again."

Qasim nodded and let out a shaky exhale as he slipped into one of two high-backed chairs, his body still burning off the adrenaline dump. On the wall behind Hamza hung an oil painting of a naval battle between two tall-masted ships from a lost era—maneuvering in gray, rolling seas set against storm clouds and lightning in the background.

"How are you, Qasim?" Hamza said with unnerving casualness, taking a seat opposite him.

"I'm well," he said, setting his briefcase and plastic bag on the floor beside his chair.

"I understand from Fun Time you paid a recent visit to the cyber team," the terrorist prince said with an inscrutable smile.

Qasim nodded nervously.

But instead of reprimanding him, Hamza said, "I was pleased to learn you asserted your rightful dominance. Never let lesser men disrespect you."

A chilling memory of Hamza ordering the murder of a subordinate in Mingora flashed in Qasim's mind. Hamza's bodyguard had practically cut the man's head off as Qasim had looked on. Qasim had nearly pissed himself with fear in that moment, but now he understood why Hamza had been forced to give that order. To be respected in this world, you had to be feared. To be feared, you had to demonstrate strength and the willingness to punish. Fun Time and the other hackers had disrespected him because they hadn't feared him. They'd seen him as weak, and it had been necessary to change their perception.

"They needed a reminder of who was in charge," Qasim said at last, wondering if he could give an order to kill like Hamza, should the situation demand. "However, despite their insolence, Fun Time and his hackers are very talented."

"Bring me up to date with their progress," Hamza said, his voice ripe with conspiratorial interest rather than accusation or concern.

A very good sign . . .

"As discussed, we're mining social media to build a database of American operators. We've made good progress unmasking the identities of SEALs and Green Berets, connecting them with specific commands, identifying their home addresses, spouses, and what schools their children attend and so on . . . This database creates many new opportunities for us."

"What are you suggesting, Qasim?" Hamza asked, leaning in, forearms resting on his thighs. "That we attack schools in America? That we kill women and children? Then we would be no better than the animals who attack us in *our* own country—the animals who killed your sister at her own wedding."

"That's not what I'm suggesting," Qasim said, but felt unsure if that was true. Did not the American animals, as Hamza called them, deserve to suffer the same pain and anguish he suffered? To feel the same loss? But then, what would that make him? "What I suggest is that it might be possible to target the operators on American soil when their guard is down. We could hit them on the way home from the grocery store, or the base, or while out on a run in the neighborhood. What impact would *that* have on the Special Operations community? What psychological impact might that have on the families? Can you imagine the outrage? The Special Operations commands would become paralyzed. Many active duty personnel would resign for fear of their families being targeted. Would that not take our PsyOps program to the next level?"

Hamza stroked his well-trimmed beard. "Interesting that you propose this, Qasim. I would not have expected it from you."

"Can we operate inside the United States? Do we have that capability?"

Hamza stared at him for a long moment, and Qasim wondered suddenly if Hamza fully trusted him.

"Yes," the al Qadar leader said finally. "It could be done but operating on American soil is the ultimate challenge. There is a high likelihood of losing all members of the team, but what you suggest could be worth the cost. It also might help solve the ultimate objective that all my operations attempt to influence."

"Which is what?" Qasim asked, feeling himself relax with Hamza seeming to confide in him, to even brainstorm with him like a colleague—perhaps one day as an equal.

"The Americans have been in the Middle East a long time. Their network of intelligence assets has been developed for decades. They are so firmly entrenched it is nearly impossible for us to be effective—even with them officially out of Afghanistan, they are always just over the horizon. Just like they rooted out our operation in Mingora, they found our safe house outside Erbil—thankfully only one of our snipers was in residence at the time of the hit, but it was a big loss." Hamza let out a heavy sigh. "We need the Americans to lose their stomach for war. They are not like us, Qasim. Tribal peoples have known war for generations, but this is the longest the Americans have ever been at war and their people grow weary. It is why your suggestion carries such promise. This would send a message that their lawless presence in the Middle East is driving terrorism back to their own country. Your strategy might create a sea change in US foreign policy and accelerate a full-scale withdrawal from the region, not just from Afghanistan. I will consider it carefully. Thank you for having the courage to share it with me."

"When Eshan introduced us . . . when my journey began, I was filled with so much fear and uncertainty," Qasim said, overcome by a strange and overwhelming compulsion to unburden himself to this man. "I find myself flip-flopping back and forth about whether violence against our fellow man is Allah's true will."

Hamza laughed and patted him on the leg. "I have always known that about you, brother. To be called to Allah's purpose is terrifying and at times uncertain. We all struggle with such feelings."

Qasim raised his eyebrows and stared at his mentor. "Even you?"

"Most especially me," Hamza said, his face soft and his tone patient. "Men who do not contemplate such things are not warriors, but sociopaths. Extreme violence is unnatural for introspective men like us. You and I are, at our core, men of peace. Our faith teaches us to be so. But only a few are called—and Allah knows only a few are able—to be a sword for peace in a world governed by warmongers. I struggle with this seeming contradiction constantly, brother. If you did not share the same struggle, I could not trust you as I do."

Qasim nodded and considered the sage words from this complicated man he both respected and feared.

"Your words are a comfort to me, Hamza. Especially as I ask what I am about to ask." Qasim took a long cleansing breath. "I wish to know more . . . What other operations do you have planned? I desire a greater role. I'm ready to do more for the cause. Will you read me into the full breadth of al Qadar operations?"

Hamza smiled broadly and his already infectious charisma seemed to glow even brighter. "I have been waiting for this day."

Qasim felt his cheeks flush with pride, and he wondered why pleasing this man mattered so much to him. Over the next hour, the terrorist prince read him into the details of multiple concurrent operations, their Juba sniper program, his efforts to acquire another Chinese UCAV, and future operations he was planning on British soil. But the terrorist prince did not stop there; he also patiently fielded Qasim's questions about al Qadar recruitment pipelines, the organization's financing channels, and cell locations. As Hamza talked, Qasim was floored by the amount of information Hamza had committed to memory.

"How is it that you can remember all of this detail without a computer?" Qasim said, truly flabbergasted.

"I would like to say it is by choice, but by necessity is closer to the truth," Hamza said with a tight grin. "When the day comes that you succeed me, you will have to do it too."

Qasim nodded, not sure how to respond to that comment. Most men in positions of power would do anything and everything to protect their power, and here was Hamza practically gifting Qasim with the keys to the kingdom. This was the difference between enlightenment and greed. Hamza considered his al Qadar leadership position as a tour of service, and he had chosen Qasim as his successor.

"There is something else we must talk about," Hamza said before Qasim had a chance to respond. "I am planning an operation in Dubai, at the Middle East Defense Expo."

Qasim's heart skipped a beat. "An attack? At the Middle East Defense Expo? But, I'm . . . I'm scheduled to attend that conference. I thought we talked about a meeting there, but you are planning an operation there?"

"I know," Hamza said with a vulpine smile. "You said you wanted to do more . . . well, this is your opportunity."

Qasim listened as Hamza laid out his plan for Dubai—infiltrating the conference with snipers and multiple attackers to target key executives from the world's largest and most powerful defense contractors. The mission was audacious, but if anyone could make it succeed it was Hamza. And yet, instead of feeling excited by being read into the operation, Qasim felt confused and unsure.

"You do not approve?" Hamza replied with a curious narrowing of his eyes.

"The plan is brilliant, but it seems out of step with our guiding principles. We just agreed that we would not target innocent civilians."

"And I am adhering to that vow. These men are not innocent women and children. They are part of the defense industrial complex who arm the American and British military to kill our people, Qasim," Hamza said, folding his hands in his lap as if they were debating a work of literature rather than a plot to kill hundreds of people. "To separate the West's military apparatus from the actions and policy of their military leaders is naive. Not only do companies like Raytheon, Lockheed Martin, Textron, and your own British Aero provide the very arms that murder our countrymen, but they also, by their very nature, drive defense policy. It would be like saying that the man who buys a gun and then gives it to another man whom he pays to murder someone is innocent of that murder. This is more than legal reasoning, Qasim—it is common sense. With this attack and our propaganda campaign to follow, we will make it clear that we hold accountable all who are involved in the murder of our people. I believe that this is entirely in keeping with the philosophy of al Qadar. Remember we are trying to change policy. These companies are like drug dealers. They want every country in the Middle East to be addicted to war. While we kill each other and turn our cities into piles of rubble, they take our money and call us terrorists. We cannot let this continue. The men responsible cannot go unpunished."

Qasim thought of that night when an invisible drone fired a missile, vaporizing his sister and his father in the blink of an eye. He remembered how he'd felt when piloting such a drone himself, as he'd delivered some modicum of revenge just a few months ago on the air base at Kandahar. And then, for a moment, he thought of his colleagues at British Aero. They never talked about the profound violence and murder their handiwork inflicted on their fellow men. They spoke only of the mathematical solutions to the engineering problems before them. But did that make them innocent? Of course not. Willful ignorance is not the same as innocence. They knew what they created, what it was used for, where it was used, and who was targeted. But then how did he resolve his own, willfully ignorant decision to join a defense contractor in the first place? He longed for the engineering challenges, but he knew the purpose as well as any. He had rationalized his hatred for terrorism and had perhaps bought into the Western dogma that it was the Islamic extremists like the Taliban who perpetuated the violence and terror inside his country.

"You're right," he said at last. "The defense contractors who manufacture the drones are just as culpable as the generals who order the strikes and the pilots who pull the trigger."

Hamza nodded, seemingly pleased. "It is important to consider all avenues and perspectives when planning strategy. To achieve what Allah envisions for us requires us to be pensive, calculating men. Men of faith, but men who understand the complexities of our enemy."

A sudden, unexpected thought occurred to Qasim, his mind going back to the upcoming operation in Dubai. "Who have you targeted at British Aero?"

He felt no guilt in the asking, only perhaps a morbid curiosity. There was no one at the company he wished targeted for elimination and, conversely, no one he would lobby to save.

"It was a difficult decision," Hamza said, "but in the end, I decided that we would not target any executives at British Aero. Your position there is far too valuable to our operations. I don't want to do anything that would bring unwanted suspicion or attention to you personally or professionally, especially now."

Qasim stood abruptly—nervous energy from his sudden epiphany making it impossible to sit. He began to pace and talk at the same time. "That is a mistake, brother. It may have the opposite effect and bring more scrutiny on me, especially if British Aero is the one major player spared. In fact . . ." He spun around, raising one raised finger above his head, excited by where his brainstorm took him. "We could use this as an opportunity to solidify my position in the company and in the British media."

"What exactly did you have in mind?" Hamza asked, his expression pensive.

Qasim smiled. "What if we make me, if not a hero, at least a sympathetic victim in this attack?"

Hamza smiled. "I'm listening . . ."

Buoyed with nervous energy and pride at being able to plan an operation one-on-one with Hamza, Qasim shared his idea for what would be the most dangerous role-playing gambit of his double life.

CHAPTER 25

Diba watched her husband finish getting dressed for work. He'd worked so late last night that she'd been asleep when he got home. She remembered giving him a groggy kiss when he'd climbed into bed, but they'd not talked. This morning, he looked particularly handsome. And tall. Qasim had always been tall—it was one of the things that even as a girl of fifteen she had found attractive about him—but lately, he looked a giant.

Imposing, confident, and—

"I'm going on a business trip," he announced, interrupting her rumination. "I'm leaving the day after tomorrow. I'll be gone for the better part of a week."

"To the conference in Dubai?" she asked.

He turned to look at her. "How do you know about that?"

"You told me about it two months ago," she said, meeting

his gaze, confused now. "That you were hoping your boss would ask you to come and how excited you were that he had."

"Oh, that's right . . . I'd forgotten," he said, nodding.

"It is wonderful news, Qasim. Congratulations, you deserve this."

He returned her smile with a frown. "I have brown skin and speak Arabic, so it is not surprising. I'm certain it is only because of my heritage and the fact the conference is in Dubai, that they want me to come. They did not have me attend the European Expo last month."

"Why must you always look for the negative?" she's said, her tone jocular and gentle rather than critical, as her husband did not respond well to criticism.

He made a little grunt but did not engage.

"I've always wanted to go to Dubai," she said, imagining herself shopping and dining with him in the Middle East's most iconic and prosperous city. "Traveling with wives is a very Western thing to do. Maybe I could come with you?"

The question seemed to take him by surprise and his expression morphed like she'd just thrown a glass of water in his face.

"Of course not," he snapped. "This is an important business trip. The last thing I need is you tagging along and distracting me."

The rapid vehemence of his answer stung, and she looked away from him. Instead of anger, she felt diminished.

Don't cry, she silently chastised herself. *Don't let him see . . .*

"I'm sorry, Diba," he said after a moment, his voice losing its edge. She felt a hand on her shoulder and looked up, and when she did she saw the *old* Qasim gazing down at her with the empathetic, tender eyes she'd fallen in love with. "I'll tell you what," he said, taking her hand and sitting beside her on the edge of their bed, "why don't you get on the internet and look for a place you want to visit in France or Ireland? We can take a long weekend holiday. Sometime soon after I get back. Just you and me . . . spending a nice time together. Okay?"

She nodded, and despite her conciliatory smile, a single tear ran down her right cheek.

He wiped it away with his thumb and kissed her on the forehead. "I love you, Diba. I'm sorry I was short. I'm under a lot of pressure. That is all it is."

"I love you too," she said.

He left after that, kissing her deeply and tenderly at the door, a kiss that took her breath away. Alone, she busied herself until lunchtime—cleaning the kitchen, which was already clean, and folding laundry. She listened to her English language audio program, talking aloud as she did her chores, all the while trying not to revisit her conversation with Qasim. She was disappointed that she could not travel to Dubai—it would have been very exciting—but she soothed her bruised ego with thoughts of a trip to France. She had always wanted to visit France, and she wondered if his offer for a long week-end holiday applied to *anywhere* in France. Her preference would be to see Paris, but she knew it was very expensive and predicted he would try to talk her out of visiting the capital and into a holiday in some smaller lesser city.

No matter, she thought, smiling. *I'll wear him down with affection and persistence.*

By eleven thirty her stomach was growling and she decided to go to Nando's for lunch. If memory served, Soo Jin should be working today. Maybe she could ask her friend for advice on where to go and what to see in France. Feeling buoyed by the thought of chatting about Paris, Diba changed into Western attire, donned her headscarf, and set out on the short walk.

She smiled at everyone she passed on High Street. The weather was sunny but brisk, and she felt light on her feet. When she arrived, a middle-aged British man on his way out held the door for her. The courtesy took her by surprise, as it was something that had *never* happened to her, not in Afghanistan nor in England.

"Thank you," she said in her best English, and he responded with a polite smile and perfunctory nod.

As soon as she stepped inside, she scanned the restaurant for her friend who she spied delivering beverages to a table of seated patrons. Soo Jin's face lit up on seeing Diba and she held up her index finger asking for a minute. Diba nodded and waited just inside the door instead of stepping into the queue of would-be diners. Soo Jin walked over to her a minute later and greeted her face-to-face with a beaming smile.

"Guess what?" Soo Jin said.

"What?"

"I got my manager to agree to let me take my lunch break now, so I can eat with you."

"Really?"

"Yes," her friend said, nodding. "I put in an order for us, so we can take a seat and wait."

"That is wonderful, but you don't need to pay for me," Diba said.

"Don't worry, I wasn't planning to," Soo Jin said through a laugh. "I'm going to run separate checks after we eat. I'm not *that* rich."

"Good," Diba said, relieved to not have to carry the guilt of her working-class friend paying for her lunch.

Soo Jin selected a table in the corner and they both sat.

"How are you?" Soo Jin asked, leaning in to put her elbows on the table and plopping her chin into her upturned palms.

"I'm well," Diba replied, a little taken back by the attention. She considered Soo Jin a friend—or as close to a friend as she had in the UK—but this was all a little unexpected. Delightful, but unexpected. "I am studying English all the time; it is nice to have time to practice with you."

"Then we should do this more often," Soo Jin said. "I don't have a lot of friends here, but I always enjoy your company. I just never have time at work to hang out with you, until today at least." The pretty Asian woman smiled and patted the back of Diba's hand. "If you want, I can tutor you in English. Not for money, but as a friend."

"Yes, but not to miss your lunch every time," Diba said with a chuckle.

"Right, and I don't want to get sacked from my job, but we could always go for a coffee either before or after my shift."

Diba nodded, excited by the thought. "I would like very much."

"Good, it's settled then. How about we try for twice a week?"

"Yes, I can do this . . . thank you," Diba said and looked out the window, trying to think of what to talk about next, surprised at what came out of her mouth when she turned back to look at her friend. "A man hold the door for me today," she said.

"Oh . . . how proper of him," Soo Jin said with a wry grin.

"No one has done this for me since I came to England. It made me feel . . . I don't know the word?"

"Respected?" Soo Jin offered.

"Yes, respected is it."

"Well, we need a lot more of that. Gentlemen behaving like gentlemen . . ."

"Have you travel to Paris?" Diba asked, unable to resist jumping to the topic she really wanted to discuss.

"No, I'm afraid not. But that would be lovely," Soo Jin said. "Why do you ask? Are you going there on holiday?"

Diba flashed her a dreamy smile. "Qasim told me to pick place for holiday and I thought to go to Paris."

"Do you travel together a lot?"

"No," Diba said, shaking her head. "We take no trips recent, but he is going to Dubai for—how do you say—a business holiday?"

"A business trip . . . most people would say."

"Yes, a business trip. Thank you."

"So, Dubai, eh?" Soo Jin said. "I've heard it is a remarkable city. Very clean and modern."

"Yes, this is what I know too. I asked Qasim for me to come, but he said no." Diba immediately wondered why she'd just confessed so much.

"Does he travel to Dubai a lot for work?"

"No, this is first time to Dubai."

"Oh," Soo Jin said, nodding. "What does your husband do . . . if you don't mind me asking?"

"He is engineer for British Aerospace. I do not know his exact job, but he is working very hard all the time."

"I'm sure. I could never be an engineer. I don't have the mind for that kind of work. Formulas and maths were never my thing."

Diba nodded, but her schooling had ended at age twelve, so she could not even speak intelligently on the topic. Their food arrived and gratefully the conversation shifted from school to food. Since coming to England, she'd grown very self-conscious of her lack of education. It was probably the reason why she'd thrown herself into learning English. Gaining knowledge was empowering. Being able to speak English in England was doubly so. Maybe someday, if

Qasim permitted her, she could go to school and try to earn a degree.

Their lunch entrées were delivered by one of the other servers. Soo Jin ate quickly, more quickly than Diba would have liked, but her friend was supposed to be working after all.

"When did you say your husband is leaving for Dubai?" Soo Jin asked, after finishing off her last bite of chicken and rice.

"He is leaving not tomorrow but next day," she said.

Soo Jin nodded. "Well, maybe while he is away, I could come to your flat and practice English with you . . . That is, only if you want to?"

Diba looked down. Qasim did not approve of her sharing information about their personal lives. She'd told her friend far too much already, and the idea of Soo Jin visiting her at home made her terribly nervous. If Qasim learned she'd invited a stranger into their home—

"Great, it's settled then," Soo Jin said, despite Diba having not agreed to the arrangement. "It must be quite lonely for you when he travels. Does he at least spend evenings with you when he's in town, or is he always off to the pub with his mates like most men?"

"Qasim is working long hours, but like me has no friends here. He spends his time after work with me." Her mind went to Asadi Bijan, the man she had grown to loathe, showing up unexpectedly and skirting her husband away. She was grateful for Bijan's generosity in paying for her travel and wedding in London, but at what cost had that generosity come? She felt Soo Jin's eyes on her. "It is sometimes lonely while Qasim is gone, but this is okay."

Soo Jin smiled and took Diba's hand in her own, "Well, we'll have some girl time while he's off having fun in Dubai. How's that sound?"

Diba wiped a tear from her cheek, feeling unexpectedly emotional—angry that she'd shared too much while feeling touched by Soo Jin's friendship and thoughtfulness.

"Ah, love, it's nothing to get weepy about. He'll be back before you know it." Soo Jin gave her hand a pat and let go. "I have to get back to work, okay?"

Diba nodded and then, reluctantly, exchanged mobile phone numbers at Soo Jin's suggestion. She'd not given anyone her mobile phone number since Qasim had bought her the phone. She liked the idea of having a friend in her otherwise empty contacts list. Hopefully, Qasim would not be angered by it. The question of his reaction tumbled around in her head during her walk home. Eventually, a lump began to form in her throat as she thought about everything she'd shared in her lunch conversation with Soo Jin.

I should not have told her about Qasim and his business, she thought. *He would be very angry . . . but then again, maybe not. This is his real job. The trip to Dubai is for legitimate purposes.*

She shook her head, realizing that his paranoia was beginning to rub off on her.

Living in fear is no way to live. I need to try harder to get him to say goodbye to his double life as a . . .

I'm not going to say it.

I need to be patient, and encouraging, and persistent . . .

I need to give him something—something more.

Maybe if I can give him a son, she thought, her right hand going to her belly. *Maybe then he would choose us over jihad.*

CHAPTER 26

SHOWER TRAILER

TOP SECRET JOINT SPECIAL OPERATIONS

    TASK FORCE COMPOUND

THIRTY-FIVE MILES NORTH OF THE AFGHANISTAN BORDER

QURGHONTEPPA, TAJIKISTAN

Whitney lingered in the shower longer than she knew she was supposed to. Hot water was a luxury, and she was probably using all of it . . .

But damn it, I deserve it, she thought as she removed five days' worth of stubble from her right calf with a fresh razor in long, gliding swipes. When she finally turned off the water and towel-dabbed herself dry, she felt like a new woman. She'd even used conditioner on her hair, for the first time in weeks, and damn that felt good too. She stepped out of the shower stall wearing her lime-green shower shoes and a towel wrapped around her torso and walked over to one of the sinks where she looked at herself in the mirror. Her complexion looked better than usual—a hint more golden. She was one of those people who basically didn't tan. As a teenager, she'd figured out early that her skin had only two states of being: pale or burned.

She and her melanin had a very binary relationship.

But after having been in the Middle East for seven weeks, and despite all the hours she logged in her Batcave, she'd actually managed to pick up a little color on her cheeks and neck. Nobody else in the world would have noticed, but she did and it made her smile—a smile that lingered until her gaze continued south and saw the faint blue veins snaking this way and that across her chest. It was always something she'd been self-conscious about. Her first boyfriend had made a joking comment about it once in bed, tracing one of the "tributaries" snaking over her left breast, but she'd never forgotten it.

There are just some things you don't say to a woman . . .

Her smile returned as she silently cursed Brayden Holly-field and decided wherever he was these days, it certainly wasn't at the tip of the spear stopping the world's most dangerous terrorists like she was. She thought about how different her Tier One door-kicking bros were than her ex, about how Chunk could probably break Brayden in half over his knee.

Literally, in half, she thought, her mind flashing to a memory of the stout SEAL deadlifting some ungodly tonnage the last time she went to find him in the gym. She shook off the thought, towel-dried and brushed her hair, and got dressed. On the way out of the trailer, she stopped to look in the mirror one more time, this time wearing a pair of coyote-gray cargo pants and the ridiculous T-shirt that Chunk and the guys had bought her as a predeployment gift. On the front it read, Guys Dig Chicks with Guns and on the back, Chicks Dig Guys in Body Armor.

I'm not the same person I was before. I don't know who the hell I am now, but I'm definitely not the girl who showed up to MacDill in heels and a pantsuit.

Toiletry kit in hand, she walked out of the shower trailer and headed back to the bunk room she shared with Yi. She was glad to be back in Tajikistan. Not that the accommodations were better than Erbil, but she'd made herself at home here, and just being immersed back in the familiar lowered her anxiety level.

"Guess what?" Yi said when she walked into the room.

"What," she said stepping up to her locker.

"That agent runner from MI6, Officer Kim, sent us her field notes on a lunch she had with Diba Nadar."

"Seriously?" she said, turning to look at Yi with surprise.

"Seriously."

"Did you read it?"

"Yeah. It appears Qasim Nadar is traveling to Dubai for a conference."

"When?" Whitney asked, closing her locker and dropping into the vacant task chair behind her desk.

"Tomorrow."

"Do we know why?"

"The first annual Middle East Defense Expo is being held at the Dubai International Conference Centre. British Aero is an exhibitor," Yi said.

Whitney combed her fingers through her damp hair. "Is that all Kim reported?"

"Pretty much," Yi said. "The report is in your high side inbox."

"Did she recruit the wife?"

"The notes didn't specify, but I don't think so."

"Are they bringing Nadar in?" she asked.

"Again, the report didn't specify, but it sounds to me like they're going to leave him in play," Yi said. "The report does make mention that they've bugged his flat and are going to step up surveillance on him."

"Does Chunk know about this yet?"

"Not yet. I figured you'd want to tell him yourself after you read the report."

Whitney nodded and opened the attachment from Officer Kim. After skimming it, she popped to her feet and walked over to her al Qadar case wall. As soon as she'd arrived from Iraq, she'd added Qasim Nadar's picture next to Eshan Dawar, who now had a face. She pulled the thumbtack and moved Nadar's headshot next to the headshot of Fake Hamza at the top of the hierarchal pyramid of terrorists. She stood there for a long moment, staring at it and rubbing the trefoil knot tattoo on the inside of her left wrist.

"Is that supposed to mean what I think it's supposed to mean?" Yi said behind her.

"Just trying it on for size," she said without turning.

"How's the fit?" Yi asked, and Whitney could hear the smile in the other woman's voice.

"A little baggy, but I kinda like it," she said wondering if there was any possibility this crazy brainstorm could be true.

"Wanna go read in Chunk?"

"Yeah, let's go," she said and led Yi out of the bunk room.

They found Chunk in the gym, and this time instead of deadlifting he was bench-pressing with Riker spotting. He had so much weight on the bar it actually bowed in the middle. She watched him finish his last rep before greeting him.

"Hey, Chunk," she said.

"Hey, Heels," he said, sitting up on the bench red-faced, sweaty, and grinning. "You wanna pop in here for a set?"

"Sure, and after, maybe we go for a six-mile run," she said.

"Hooyah!" he said and got to his feet and turned to Riker. "What do you think? Start her with a twenty-five on each side?"

"Dude, that's called sarcasm," Riker said, folding his tattooed forearms across his chest. "Heels doesn't lift."

"No way, man. She's got her Chicks with Guns T-shirt on, and she brought Yi and everything. She's here to work out, for real this time. Ain't that right, Michelle?"

Whitney shot Yi a don't-you-friggin'-dare look.

Yi shook her head. "Un-uh, I'm not letting you rope me into this rodeo."

"I'm just havin' fun with y'all," Chunk said. "Whatcha got? Something new from Juba, I hope."

"No, I'm afraid not," she said. "I checked in with Russ a few hours ago, and Juba is still insisting he was working for Ansar al-Islam and has been for months. Russ is gonna source it, but we know it's a lie. OGA will take a harder crack at him in a while and wants to know if they can take him to a black site?"

"Hmm," Chunk said, wiping his face with a camo-green towel. "What do you think about relocating him to the same site where Fake Hamza is? We'd have way better access if our new amputee friend was here . . ."

She nodded and understood his need for control over this one, especially with so many unanswered questions. "I think the odds are pretty unlikely given his medical condition, but I can float the idea."

"Please do and let me know what they say."

"Sounds good, but Chunk, the sniper isn't the reason we're here . . . there's been an interesting development we need to read you in on."

Chunk raised his eyebrows. She did a quick glance around the little gym just to make sure she recognized all the faces before reading Chunk in on Qasim Nadar's travel plans obtained by their British besties.

When she was done, Chunk scratched at the scruff on his neck and said, "All right, I guess we wait and see what happens?"

"Or . . . we could go to Dubai," Whitney said slyly. "Tail Nadar, see who he meets, maybe even pop a bag over his head and find a nice quiet room to ask him about his recent trip to Pakistan and his association with Eshan Dawar."

"Whoa there, cowgirl," Chunk said holding up his hands. "For a second there, it kinda sounded like you want us to travel under NOCs to a strategic partner nation we have no permission to operate inside, grab a foreign national we have no authority to grab, and interrogate him *without* telling the Brits . . . but I'm sure I misunderstood you."

"No, that's exactly what I'm proposing," she said, her expression deadly serious.

Chunk turned to Riker and they both started laughing.

"What's so funny?" she said.

"You are," he said, in between chuckles. "Where's the girl who always says, 'I don't know if that's a good idea, Chunk,' or 'we don't have permission to do that, Chunk,' or 'no way, we can't operate there . . .' What happened to that girl?"

She shrugged. "That girl took a shower and now she wants to go to Dubai."

This response just garnered more laughter before Chunk finally settled down and got serious. "You think this guy Nadar has legit ties to the real Hamza al-Saud?"

"Yeah, in fact, I'm starting to wonder if Qasim Nadar *is* the real Hamza al-Saud," she said, floating her wild theory for the first time.

"Hold on, Heels," he said, glancing at Yi and then back at her, his expression incredulous. "Are you having another one of those clairvoyant, spooky nerd attacks like you did when you figured out al Qadar was flying a Chinese combat drone out of Mingora using line-of-sight transmitters? Because if you are, I need to know."

"Maybe," she said. "I don't know . . ."

"Dude, when the girl's on fire, she's on fire," Riker said. "We don't have shit going on unless OGA shakes something more from that Juba dude. I bet Bowman would authorize a quick trip, just in case something pops."

Chunk nodded slowly, and Whitney knew he was playing out the hypothetical conversation with Bowman in his head. Then he blew air through his teeth. "Do we have anything else? Comms or a SIGINT intercept, or anything more concrete than just your intuition on this one?"

She shrugged. "Just the confirmation that Qasim Nadar— who is a friggin' combat drone engineer at British Aero—was photographed in a vehicle with Eshan Dawar entering western Pakistan a few weeks before the drone attack on the convoy and Kandahar. Other than that, I'm sure he's harmless."

Chunk glanced at Riker.

"The force is strong with this one," Riker said and gave her a fist-to-palm kung fu salute with a head bow.

"All right, all right—I'll call Bowman and see if I can make it happen," Chunk said through a sigh. "But put any thoughts about staying at the Burj Al Arab out of your head right now, cuz I can tell you *that* ain't gonna happen."

PART III

"Many a man has failed because he had his wishbone where his backbone should have been."

–Ronald Reagan

CHAPTER 27

MERCEDES-BENZ S550 LIMOUSINE

E11 HIGHWAY, SHEIKH ZAYED ROAD

SOUTHWESTBOUND FROM DUBAI INTERNATIONAL AIRPORT

DUBAI, UNITED ARAB EMIRATES

0035 LOCAL TIME

For many months, one of Qasim's coworkers at British Aero had gotten in the habit of telling people they looked like "a young wanker on their first visit to Disney World" whenever they were excited or amazed by something. Qasim got the meaning, but he didn't fully appreciate the sentiment until now. Staring out at the Dubai cityscape, he decided that this was one of those moments. Each high-rise they passed seemed to have been built to outdo the grandeur of the one before.

London is a remarkable city, but Dubai is unlike anything I've ever seen, he thought staring at the towering Burj Khalifa in the distance.

His companion in the back seat of the luxury limo, Merrell Thompson, made a snorting sound so loud he woke himself from dozing. As he came to, Thompson seemed uncertain where he was for an instant, before looking out the window.

"You must be chuffed to be back to your old stomping grounds, eh, mate?" the Brit said with a smile. "Good to be home, right?"

Qasim smiled to conceal his irritation at the man's ignorance.

"Yes," he said, instead of pointing out that Dubai was not only more than a thousand miles from his childhood home but also a thousand *years* more evolved as well. Until he'd traveled to Kabul with his father at age eleven, Qasim had never seen a building more than two stories tall, much less skyscrapers of sloping metal and colored glass, stretching toward heaven like sculptures made by Allah himself.

"Look at the size of that tower. Tallest building in the world, the Burj," Thompson said, following Qasim's gaze. "Amazing what your people were able to do with all that oil money."

The comment might have made him angry were he in the right frame of mind, but instead it simply made him sad— for both of them. Then contemplative, nostalgic Qasim was replaced in a flash by new Qasim who reminded himself that very soon boorish Merrell Thompson would not have occasion to denigrate him ever again.

Because Merrell Thompson would be dead.

He smiled warmly at his colleague.

Yours is one of the names at the top of the list I shared with Hamza, my asinine friend. Enjoy this moment of superiority while you can.

Since his last covert meeting with Hamza at the safe house in New Malden, Qasim had neither seen nor heard from the terrorist prince. He assumed there would be communication between them soon—some way to let him know the plan— but he'd heard nothing. When would the attack come? Where did he need to be positioned at that time, and how would they keep him safe while also making him look like the sympathetic victim? To pull this off—to play the part he had written for himself in Hamza's plot—he needed to know the details of the attack.

Then, a new fear overtook him—what if Hamza had not contacted him because he'd been pinched by MI5 or perhaps even killed? What if everything had disintegrated and all that remained was for the British or, worse, the Americans, to piece it all together and arrest him?

What would become of Diba?

A slap on his right knee made him startle.

"You hear me, mate?"

Qasim blinked twice and Merrell Thompson's screwed-up face came into focus in the rear of the dimly lit limousine.

"I'm sorry, what did you say?"

The Brit laughed. "I said, you're going out with us while we're here, right?"

"I don't know, we shall see," Qasim said with a placating smile.

"It's okay to let loose and lighten up from time to time, Qasim. Yes, we're British Aerospace engineers with a reputation to uphold, but that doesn't mean you have to be so bloody serious all the time. Now that we're in Dubai, maybe we can see the fun side of you, eh? I've never once seen you on a bender. This is your chance. Plenty of alcohol, plenty of beautiful women—even Muslims are allowed to drink and party in Dubai. Did you know that?"

"I am married," Qasim said, and his mind went to Diba. She had so wanted to come with him, and a part of him had wanted to bring her, but this was no vacation. With great effort, he swallowed his distaste for Thompson's impertinent comments and forced the smile back onto his face. "But this might be an opportunity to get to know the team better, I agree. I have a hard time unwinding back home in London."

The Brit gave him another laugh and patted his knee; Qasim barely resisted the urge to recoil.

"That's all I'm saying, Qasim. Being part of the team is about more than just the work. These conferences don't come along every day, so let's have some fun, shall we! It'd be great to have you with us, especially since you can help us navigate the language barrier and cultural bits. You'll keep us out of trouble, right? Especially those of us who don't take our marriage vows so seriously as you, eh?"

So there it was—the harsh truth. No one really wanted him to go out with the team, or at least this fat piece of rubbish didn't. They needed him to be their interpreter and help them stay out of trouble.

Looking at Thompson, he thought about what Juba's sniper round would do to the man's head . . . imagined it splitting open like a sledgehammer taken to a pumpkin.

"Okay then, I'll go out with you," Qasim said, savoring the gruesome mental imagery as he said it. "Let's make this a trip to remember for everyone."

"Brilliant," Thompson said, slapping Qasim's knee again. "I knew we could count on you."

Moments later the limo pulled into a circular drive that looped around a fountain constructed of concentric bowls lined with gold tiles. Qasim wondered if the tiles were plated in real gold and decided that they might well be as his gaze was drawn to the sprawling building complex with its modern architecture and stunning two-tone blue glass. Such decadence and yet such beauty—he couldn't even imagine how many starving children in neighboring Oman could be fed with the money wasted on just the cosmetic aspects of this building.

"Have you stayed here before, mate?" Thompson asked as he hauled his fat ass out of the seat and exited the limo. Qasim followed him, amazed at the ignorance of westerners when it came to the Middle East.

"No," he said simply.

"Did you know you can't stay at the disgusting Safestay Hotel at home for what British Aero booked us into these luxury apartments for? Hell of a thing, the exchange rate here. It just goes to show you, the British pound still carries weight everywhere you go."

Qasim nodded but didn't comment, lest he encourage the man to keep talking.

"God, I'm knackered. I'm going to check in and go straight to bed. Good night, Qasim," Thompson told him as he headed for the entrance, leaving his bags for the driver who was already at the trunk.

"Good night," Qasim called after him. Thompson waved over his shoulder as a smartly dressed bellman opened the door to the hotel for him.

Qasim accepted his roller bag from the driver at the trunk, as well as his computer bag and satchel, both of which he slung over his left shoulder.

"*Marhaban*," he said with a slight nod at the driver and handed him a crisp twenty-pound note.

"My pleasure, sir," the driver said in English with a smile. He handed Qasim a business card. "Let me know if I can serve you again during your stay, sir."

Qasim nodded, pocketed the card, and headed for the entrance set in between two twenty-foot-tall brushed-metal columns embedded with soft light panels. He crossed the clean, contemporary lobby to the wooden desk and moments later was checked into his prepaid room, which he was told was a one-bedroom duplex residence on the fifteenth floor.

"Your conference materials and your package have been placed in your room, sir, along with some essentials we have stocked in your kitchen to make your stay more pleasant," the woman behind the desk said. Despite her Middle Eastern appearance, she wore makeup and her dark hair down and uncovered by a hijab. He smiled, uncertain about this supposedly Muslim city, and thanked her.

He rode the gleaming modern elevator alone to the fifteenth floor and followed the signage to his room. Upon arriving at the door, he swiped his key card and his mouth dropped open as he entered the palatial hotel room. He passed first through a sleek, modern kitchen with a stainless steel refrigerator, microwave, and full-size oven set into dark wood cabinets. On the counter sat two bottles of wine—one red and one white—with a basket of fruit and a note saying, "Welcome British Aero to Dubai," signed Oliver Payne, VP Unmanned Aviation Systems. Payne, who was Qasim's former boss and had been promoted up the chain at the same time Qasim had gotten his own promotion, was the high-value target for the upcoming attack. Payne's death would pave the way to Qasim's opportunistic ascension in the ranks.

He passed through the kitchen and walked to the six-person glass-and-metal dining table, above which hung a chandelier that reminded Qasim of a jeweled necklace. On the table, two envelopes sat waiting. The first—a large white envelope with 1st Annual Middle East International Defence Expo DWTC written across the front—was addressed to him. The second envelope, of the brown paper variety, simply had his room number written on the front.

As expected, the first envelope contained all his conference materials—a program booklet, his name badge and lanyard, a map of the Dubai World Trade Centre, a booklet listing all the breakout sessions, scores of loose advertising flyers from area restaurants and clubs, and a complimentary ink pen. Bored, he shifted his attention to the second envelope, looking for anything else that might suggest who it was from. His heart rate picking up, he tore open the flap. Inside he found a simple, older generation mobile phone with a yellow Post-it stuck to the packaging. The handwritten note simply read, *The beginning*. He pulled the phone from the box and powered it on. The screen immediately prompted him for a seven-digit password.

This can only be from Hamza, he thought, pursing his lips. *The beginning . . . what does he mean the beginning?*

Seven digits was unusual. Generally, mobile phone passwords were four digits, sometimes six, but seven? He was not familiar with a common seven-digit code format, other than dates.

Could it be a date? The date we met in Mingora . . . the beginning of my journey? Is that the beginning he's referring to?

It didn't feel right, but he couldn't put a finger on why as he paced back and forth in front of the glass windows overlooking the well-lit luxury of Dubai. He would likely get only three attempts before the phone would lock and purge whatever data it held for him.

He thought back to all the conversations he'd had with Hamza. Not the tactical and strategic discussions, but the philosophical ones. Hamza was a deeply spiritual and contemplative man, and his knowledge of the Quran rivaled that of any imam . . .

A smile curled his lips.

Could it be that simple?

For Hamza, the beginning would mean one thing.

December 22, 609 CE—the date the Quran was verbally revealed to the Prophet from God, relayed to him by the angel Gabriel. The first revelation of the Quran began when Muhammad was forty years old on December 22, 609 CE. The revelation ended twenty-three years later at the moment of the Prophet's death.

He tapped in the numbers 1-2-2-2-6-0-9 and the lock screen disappeared.

"Yes," he said and pumped his fist in the air.

Feeling triumphant, he looked at the tiny color LCD screen. The burner phone had no apps, not even a notepad function where a message might have been left. The only thing he saw was a red circle with the number one next to the envelope icon indicating that a single message waited for him.

He selected it and played the message:

"Greetings, my brother. I am excited and proud that we are on this journey together," Hamza's voice said. "I know you must be anxious for instructions and were hoping I would leave them for you in this message, but as you know, I refuse to entrust our fate to the security of electronic devices. Sometimes, the old ways are the best ways, which is why despite the risks, I want to meet in person. I will be watching you. Go out with your British Aero colleagues tomorrow night. It doesn't matter where, just go where they tell you. I will make contact with you there. Until then, brother, may Allah's strength and peace go before you."

The message ended and Qasim deleted it immediately. Setting the phone on the table at first, but then thinking better of it, he tucked it into his badge holder instead so as not to absentmindedly forget to dispose of it tomorrow. He renewed his pacing, eyes on the Dubai skyline, mind running over with nervous anxiety.

I can do this, he reassured himself. *I will do this . . .*

He was on a mission.

Thompson, Payne, and two other British Aero executives had been targeted for elimination, along with senior players at a half dozen other defense companies who profited from the murder of Muslims. That Allah would want him to hold them accountable made more sense than anything at all in his entire life.

Except maybe for his love for Diba.

A second wave of exhaustion hit him. He checked his watch to see it was well after one in the morning local time. As much as he wanted to climb directly into bed, he had one more obligation to fulfill. He put an AirPod in his left ear and dutifully dialed Diba at home. He spent the next twenty minutes talking to his wife, making every effort to comfort her fears and make her feel happy, safe, secure, and loved while he unpacked his suitcase.

Undoubtedly, she would hear the news of the attack at the conference before he next called her. She would worry and wonder if her husband was dead, and he felt a modicum of guilt knowing he would have to put her through that. But it could not be helped.

It was for her salvation, as much as his own, that he answered Allah's call.

CHAPTER 28

Chunk helped Riker load the last of their luggage into the cargo hold of a brand-spanking-new, blacked-out Chevy Suburban Z71 idling on the tarmac. At nearly nineteen feet long and 7,700 pounds, this ute was a brute and the automotive personification of their Tier One unit: American-made, intended for off-road operations, fully kitted up with all the bells and whistles, and most importantly, badass looking from every angle.

"Anything else I can do for you fellas?" the ground crewman said as he climbed back into the TUG he'd driven over from the C-17 they'd hitched a ride on from Bagram.

"We're all good, Sergeant," Chunk said with a nod. "Thanks for the helping hand."

"Easy day," the sergeant said with a knowing look in his eyes. "Y'all be safe out there."

"Will do."

Riker closed the tailgate. "I'm driving."

"Like hell you are," Chunk said, holding his hand out for the keys. "Saw's driving."

"Dude, you put Gramps behind the wheel, and it'll take us four hours to get to Dubai. I'm driving, Saw can take a nap in the back." The tattooed SEAL headed for the driver's seat.

Chunk sighed, flipped on a pair of Skeleton Optics Scout sunglasses, and made his way to the front passenger seat. The rest of the team—Trip, Saw, Watts, and Yi—were already waiting in their seats.

"Why is it that the two most senior members of this element were the ones who loaded the luggage?" Chunk said, turning and looking at his crew with theatrical condemnation.

"Oh, I thought it was obvious," Trip said from the middle row. "Because just like on family vacation, it's Mom and Dad's job to pack the car."

The comment garnered a snort from Watts in the back row, a chuckle from Yi, and a fist bump from Saw. With a shit-eating grin on his face, Chunk turned around in his seat and chopped a sarcastic hand toward the windshield. On this cue, Riker slammed his foot down on the accelerator, the engine roared, and the big SUV laid a strip of rubber on the tarmac.

"Dude, slow down," Saw barked from the captain's chair behind Chunk. "You're gonna kill somebody."

"Told ya," Riker said, flashing Chunk a sideways grin. "Gramps don't like to go fast."

The drive from the air base to Dubai did not take four hours, it took less than ninety minutes with the bulk of it spent cruising on the impeccably maintained, eight-lane E11 highway connecting Abu Dhabi to Dubai. With the exception of the occasional scrub tree or palm, khaki-colored sand stretched off in both directions as far as the eye could see. The afternoon sun shone bright and hot in a cloudless blue sky, cooking the desert sands and the pavement and causing heat mirages to hang over the road ahead. Thankfully, the Z71, with its super-sized air conditioner and dark-tinted windows, kept the inside of their ride a frosty sixty-nine degrees . . . much to the displeasure and incessant protest of Watts and Yi.

They arrived at the gleaming Conrad hotel, which was located across the street from the Dubai World Trade Center, and checked in. All of the logistics and planning for the op had been taken care of in-house. Moreover, they hadn't informed the US Embassy, the OGA folks in country, or the British Joint CT task force of their presence in UAE or the nature of their mission. This trip to shadow Qasim Nadar was übercompartmentalized and a little outside the unit's typical wheelhouse. Truth be told, it was an operation tailor-made for the blacker than black Task Force Ember team who was sharing space with them on the Tier One compound at MacDill. But the short fuse nature of the op and the fact that nothing precluded Chunk's team from conducting ISR under NOCs had tipped the scales in favor of doing it themselves. Yes, they were a direct-action unit, but they were also the Tier One.

They weren't white side SEALs anymore.

Getting spooky from time to time was now part of their MO.

"Duuuude," Riker said, flinging open the door to the fifteen hundred square foot, two-bedroom family suite. "I think this hotel room is bigger than my apartment back home."

"And a helluva lot nicer," Trip said, nudging Riker as he walked by, carrying his duffel on his left shoulder.

"Saw, you're with me," Chunk said, veering toward the bedroom on the left side. "I need a break from Riker's farts."

"That hurts, bro," Riker said, pounding a fist to his heart. "Hurts me right here."

"Dude, I need a break from that shit too," Trip said, vectoring to follow Chunk. "Why don't you and I take the room and put Saw with Riker?"

"Because you fucking snore, Trip," Chunk said, waving off the SEAL. "And I really need to get some sleep on this boondoggle."

Saw, grinning triumphantly, pushed past Trip and into the bedroom with Chunk. "Which bed do you want, boss?"

"I don't give a shit," Chunk said. "Do you?"

"Nope," Saw said and tossed his bag onto the double bed closer to the door.

Chunk nodded and dropped his own duffel onto the foot of the other double bed. He then walked over to the floor-to-ceiling plate glass window and looked at the waters of the Persian Gulf in the distance. "Hell of a view . . . Too bad you're here sharing a room with me instead of Ellie."

"Man, she would love it. A Dubai getaway without the kids. She could hit the spa, I could eat like a king," he said with a wistful smile, "and we'd probably end up with another kid nine months later."

Chunk laughed.

"Speaking of kids, mine love you, bro," Saw said. "You're really good with them . . . Is having kids in the cards for you someday?"

Chunk ran his tongue between his lower lip and his gums and then swallowed. "Honestly, I doubt it. I'd have to find the right girl and . . . I just don't see that happening. Besides, this unit is my family. And I certainly don't have time to manage anybody else's bullshit beyond this crew." He clapped Saw on the back and walked into the shared common room.

"Where are the girls sleeping?" Trip asked, clearly still trying to angle for an alternate arrangement. "Do they each have their own room or are they sharing too?"

"They're sharing a deluxe suite," Chunk said. "And even if they weren't, nobody's gonna swap places with you."

Grumbling, Trip carried his bag into Riker's room and got last pick of the beds.

An hour later Watts and Yi showed up to brief the Nadar op for the evening. The palatial common room with its expensive carpets, designer sofas, and dining table would serve as their TOC for the duration of the operation—a five-star upgrade from their typical digs. As Chunk settled into one of the unoccupied upholstered chairs, he felt a strange, almost dystopian disconnect from reality wash over him.

Something about hunting terrorists from the forty-ninth floor of a luxury hotel just feels wrong.

He listened as Watts walked them through all the SIGINT and other intelligence that had been collected on Nadar since they'd left Bagram. Using the published British Aero conference schedule and mobile phone intercepts, she and Yi had pieced together Nadar's rough itinerary for the next seventy-two hours.

" . . . so our first viable opportunity to surveil Nadar is tonight," Watts was saying. "The British Aero contingent reserved a VIP table at the Cavalli Club for the last dinner sitting, and we expect Nadar will be in attendance. Consequently, Yi booked a table for two at the same time so we can have eyes on. The objective is to observe Nadar, document everyone he interacts with, and see if he makes contact with any third parties."

"Hold on, Heels," Chunk said, leaning forward in his chair. "The Cavalli Club? Isn't that one of those fancy-schmancy joints where supermodels, actors, and gangsters hang out?"

"Winner, winner, chicken dinner," Riker said and put his right index finger to the tip of his nose. "Not it."

Around the room fingers flew to noses and Chunk and Whitney were left staring at everyone in disbelief.

"Looks like it's settled," Riker said, doing a little overbite dance in his seat. "Chunk and Heels will be the ones getting their groove on tonight."

"Un-uh," Chunk said, shaking his head. "We are the world's most elite direct-action covert element. We do not make critical tactical decisions using elementary-school playground methodology."

"For once," Watts chimed in, "I have to agree with him."

Nobody lowered their fingers from their noses.

"C'mon, guys," Chunk said. "Don't make me pull rank."

This earned him a round of pitying smiles but the mutiny held.

"Ah, man . . . you guys know I'm terrible at this sorta shit. Trip, dude, why don't you go?"

"Oh, I see how it is," the SEAL said with a smirk. "*Now* you want me to have your back? Well, you should have thought about that when you decided to rebuff my generous offer to bunk together. But noooo, you picked Grandpa and stuck me with Senior Chief Stink-Ass. Consider this your penance."

Chunk turned to Saw, looking for help.

"Look, boss, as much as I hate to say it, out of this lot the two of you are the prettiest. To blend in at this place, we need to send eye candy. Put some lipstick on Heels, get you a little haircut, and the two of you are gonna make one hot couple."

Chunk let out a groan that sounded very much like an angry bear. He looked at Watts and raised his eyebrows: *So, are you in?*

"I'm sorry, but I have nothing to wear," she said, her cheeks going rosy.

Trip theatrically checked his watch. "Plenty of time to go shopping. I'll even go with you and pick out something for our intrepid leader to wear, otherwise he'll go out in an NSW ball cap, Forged T-shirt, and 5.11 jeans."

"All right, fine," she said, acquiescing. "But you guys owe me big-time for this . . . big-time."

CHAPTER 29

His heart rate elevated, Chunk completed a round of four-count tactical breathing to center himself. Then he opened his eyes and looked at his teammate.

"Dude, are you sure about this?" Trip asked, meeting Chunk's gaze. "Cuz there's no going back once I start."

"I know," Chunk said, with a fatalistic exhale. "Just do it."

Trip clicked the power button on the Wahl hair clipper and it buzzed to life. In the mirror Chunk watched his SEAL barber go to work grinning like the Cheshire cat.

Oh man, what have I done? he thought as his hair began to fall in tufts to the marble tile floor.

He watched as his brother frogman transformed him from shaggy roughneck into a redneck hipster—if there was such a thing—over the course of the next fifteen minutes. Trip barbered an expert fade from Chunk's ears up to the crown but left the hair long on top which he slicked up and over from the side part in a James Deanesque gelled sweep. After finishing with his hair, the SEAL went to work on Chunk's beard— creating a perfectly groomed lumberjack chic look one might find featured on the cover of *Cigar Aficionado*.

"All right, bro," Trip said, stepping back to admire his handiwork. "Check you out."

"Dude . . . what in God's name have you done to me?" Chunk said, getting his first completely unobstructed view of himself in the mirror.

"I took you out of the honky-tonk in Carthage and put you into the Roosevelt Room in Austin," Trip said with a proud nod.

Chunk shook his head and chuckled despite himself. "If you say so . . . What am I supposed to wear? I didn't bring anything but jeans and a polo shirt."

"I got your back there too. After the intel brief, I did a little shopping." Trip ushered him out of the bathroom to his hotel room suite where a tailored dress shirt and a five-button tweed waistcoat were laid out on a chair.

"You want me to wear that?" Chunk asked, confused.

Trip nodded.

"With my jeans?"

Trip nodded again.

"Shouldn't there be a suit coat or jacket or something to wear over it?"

"Nope, just the shirt and the vest. That's the look, bro."

With a resigned sigh, Chunk reached to put the dress shirt on over his T-shirt.

"Whoa, whoa, whoa, dude, you gotta ditch the T-shirt first," Trip said. "Bare chest underneath, man."

"Really?"

"Yeah," Trip said and then screwed up his face at Chunk. "Seriously, boss, have you never been to a club before?"

"Lots of times," he said as he pulled off his gray Don't Tread on Me tee and shrugged on Trip's dress shirt. "Just . . . the kind with country music, boots, and beer."

"Well, where you're going tonight ain't that kinda place," the younger SEAL said with a laugh.

"I don't think this shirt is big enough," Chunk said as he fastened the buttons up the chest.

"It's supposed to be tailored. Just don't Hulk out and you'll be fine."

Chunk arced his arms in a bear hug move, and the fabric got instantly taut across his back and shoulders.

"I said *don't* Hulk out," Trip said. "Or you're gonna rip it."

"It's too tight," Chunk complained.

"Dude, nobody moves their arms like that in real life. You're not in some bodybuilding competition. The shirt's perfect. Now stop being a baby and put on the vest."

Grumbling, Chunk put on the gray tweed vest and fastened the buttons. Then, feeling very constrained, he undid the shirt cuffs and rolled up his sleeves. Feeling Trip's eyes on him, he said, "Sorry, forgot to ask, am I allowed to roll up my sleeves?"

"I'll permit it," Trip said with a laugh.

Chunk walked over to the full-length mirror on the bathroom door and surveyed himself from head to toe. "I look like a bartender at a speakeasy."

"That's the point. You're gonna make all the girls thirsty, bro. All right, final touch."

Trip pulled a watch, an elegant blue-faced watch with a black leather strap from his pocket. Instead of handing it to Chunk, he took the bulky Suunto from his boss's wrist and put the watch on for him.

"I know how to put on a watch," Chunk grumbled. He took a closer look. He liked the look, just couldn't imagine where in the hell he would ever wear such a luxury timepiece. "Dude, you bought a damn watch for me to wear?"

Trip laughed.

"That's mine, bro," he said. "Be careful with it, it's a Declan James. Believe it or not, the company is owned by a former frogman. His stuff is drip."

"Whatever that is," Chunk said, his hands into his pockets and rolling his eyes.

I look ridiculous, he thought, and suddenly, the urge to pack a dip was overpowering. "I suppose dipping is out of the question at this club?"

"Yeah, better get your fix now," the SEAL said and tossed him a tin of wintergreen Copenhagen.

Chunk packed the snuff with a snap of his wrist and his index finger hitting the side of the can. After three slaps, he twisted off the lid, grabbed a heaping pinch, and stuffed it in his lower lip.

"Have you been to trendy, rich clubs like this before?" he asked as he tossed the tin back to Trip.

"Of course," Trip said and looked like the question had offended him.

"Please tell me I'm not going to have to be out there on the dance floor with Heels all night."

"Would Watts grinding on you for a couple songs really be so bad?"

"Not gonna happen. Gotta keep things professional," Chunk said, looking around Trip's hotel room for something he could use as a spitter.

"Dude, seriously, sometimes you're like a thirty-five-year-old dad. How can you be so chill as a SEAL and so lame as a man?"

"What the fuck is that supposed to mean? I'm twice the man you'll ever be."

"Yeah, dude, in Alabama in 1955—you do know it's 2022."

Chunk flipped Trip the bird and then used the water glass on the bedside table to deposit his dribble of brown tobacco juice.

"I was drinking out of that, dick," Trip said.

"I know," Chunk said with a wry grin. "Where the hell is Heels, anyway? Shouldn't she be ready by now?"

"She's a chick, dude. They take longer."

"Yeah, but you gave me a haircut and a beard trim. All she had to do is put on a dress," Chunk said, pacing and spitting. "I just wanna get this over with."

"Seriously, Chunk. You need to chill and just go with it. This is probably the only time in your operational career you're gonna get to NOC out at Club Cavalli in Dubai on the government's dime. Would you rather be in some shithole in the Hindu Kush right now?"

Chunk shrugged. "Hell yes, wouldn't you?"

Trip shook his head. "You're a lost cause."

A knock came at the hotel room door, and Trip popped to his feet and trotted excitedly to answer it. "Oh man, I can't wait to see what Heels looks like."

Chunk turned and watched as Trip opened the door to reveal a lithe beauty standing in the doorway dressed in a shimmering, barely there silver cocktail dress.

"Holy shit, Heels!" Trip said, theatrically stumbling backward with his hand over his heart. "You look like friggin' Kendall Jenner."

"This is Yi's fault," she said and stomped into the room. "I'm literally naked and it's horrible. All I want to do is— Oh my God, Chunk is that really you?"

Chunk, for his part, couldn't believe his eyes either. This was the first time he'd seen Watts with makeup, and he'd never seen her wear anything remotely resembling the sexy slip dress she wore now.

Blink, dude, you've got to blink or she's gonna think you're a perv . . .

"May I get you a martini, ma'am?" he said, his Texas twang coming on a little thicker than normal.

This made her laugh so hard she actually let out a little snort in between breaths.

"See, Trip, you made me look ridiculous," Chunk said turning to his brother SEAL. "She's laughing at me."

"No, I'm really not," she said, her hand over her mouth. "I just . . . I just wasn't prepared for you to look so . . ."

"So metrosexual?" Chunk said, cocking an eyebrow at her.

"I was going to say *hip*."

"Uh-huh," he said and used his index finger to claw out the wad of tobacco from his lip and then plop it in the spitter. He then handed the sullied glass to Trip, wiped his finger off on his jeans, and extended his hand to her. "C'mon, let's get this over with."

"You got your earbuds in?" Trip asked, backing them up.

Chunk tapped the microtransmitter where it sat deep and virtually invisible in his ear canal. "Yep, thanks for the backup."

Watts nodded. "Me too."

By the time they got to the hall, the rest of their teammates were waiting outside to catcall as they walked by. Chunk chuckled and shook his head while Watts gave them a beauty pageant wave as they strutted to the elevator. The jeers and whistles continued until they'd stepped inside and the doors closed behind them.

"Well, that was fun," she said, breaking the super awkward silence as the elevator began to descend.

"Yep . . ."

She let go of his hand and, seemingly unsure what to do with her arms, she crossed, then uncrossed, then crossed them again over her deeply exposed cleavage. "I hate not wearing a bra," she said, almost talking to herself.

"Thanks for sharing."

"I'm serious. It's why I never wear these kinds of dresses. It shouldn't even be called a dress. At least with a bikini, it's on tight. Look how loose this is. I'm a wardrobe malfunction just waiting to happen. With my luck, it will probably happen while we're walking into the club in front of everyone."

"You're going to be fine." After an uncomfortable pause, he added, "You look really good, by the way. Seriously, Heels, smokin' hot."

"Really?" She turned to him with a tentative smile. When he nodded, she said, "Thanks, so do you . . ."

"As for me, I feel naked in a different way . . . not carrying," he said, hating the fact he was not carrying a concealed weapon tonight. The decision to go to the club unarmed had been his, but it didn't mean he had to like it.

"Do you always carry? I mean, wherever you go when you're off base?"

"Certainly on mission. Back in CONUS when I'm bumming around town, I usually don't." Suddenly feeling the tug of duty, he asked, "Enough of that, you ready to go to work?"

She exhaled through pursed lips. "Yeah."

"It's gonna be loud and crowded, so we're going to have to work as a team," he said. "We need to photograph everyone Nadar interacts with."

"Then we're going to have to pretend to take lots of selfies with Nadar in the background," she added. "Otherwise, we risk him noticing."

"Yeah."

"We didn't talk about this, but um, do you want me to hit on him?" she asked. "Try to get him drunk and chat him up."

Chunk considered for a second, thinking about the pros and cons. "I don't know. The risk/reward seems pretty skewed to risk. He doesn't seem like the type that's going to spill his guts in a club to some random girl. I assume you're not thinking about trying to coax him back to your hotel room."

"No way in hell," she said. "I'm not *that* kind of spook."

"I know," he said, his cheeks getting red this time. "I didn't mean to imply . . ."

"No worries. Just making sure we're both on the same page."

The elevator slowed to a stop at the lobby floor and a chime sounded. She uncrossed her arms and once again gave him her hand, which he took. They stepped into the hotel lobby, and Chunk felt more self-conscious than he could ever remember. He felt dozens of pairs of eyes on him. *Hold on, they're not looking at me . . . they're looking at Watts,* he realized. He glanced at her, wondering if she felt it too, but she was strutting like a supermodel who gobbled up gazes for a living. He cued off her, imagining himself as someone who was better than all these people.

The walk to the Cavalli Club didn't take long as it was located on the ground level of the Fairmont hotel next door. Yi had booked them a VIP table for two, and Chunk couldn't help but wonder how much coin they were going to be dropping on this little surveillance operation. *Certainly less than the cost of a Blackhawk ride to and from the X on a typical op.* The thought made him realize how biased his thinking was toward the strategic and human cost of Special Operations without ever worrying about the financial cost. *If I had to run my unit like a business, how many ops would I forgo because of the price tag?*

Thankfully, that wasn't his job.

That's what the bean counters in the Pentagon were for.

In the circle drive in front of the club entrance, exotic sports cars, luxury sedans, and Range Rovers were dropping off VIPs dressed to the nines for a night of clubbing and partying. When a candy-apple-red Lamborghini pulled up, Watts squeezed his hand and he watched the scissor-style doors swing open like a gull's wings. Out of the cramped front passenger seat, not one, but two supermodel-caliber women emerged in dresses so short they barely covered the curves of their respective asses. The driver, a middle-aged Middle Eastern man in a dark-purple suit, tossed the keys to the valet and trotted around to catch up to his two dates who were posing for pictures being taken—not by paparazzi—but instead by a small gaggle of tourists standing off to the side, watching the spectacle that was the Cavalli Club.

Massive vertical flat panel displays outside the entrance showed curated video footage of what lay in wait for them inside the hottest club in the Middle East. Chunk didn't care about the Hollywood crowd or read the tabloids, but even he recognized a face or two in the Cavalli Club's highlight roll of the global movers and shakers who'd dined and drank inside. Chunk felt Watts slip her hand out of his and reposition her grip to the inside of his elbow, which he bent and extended to her on cue.

He glanced at her, and in a quiet voice with a French accent, she said, "I'll do the talking, *ça va?*"

He didn't know what *ça va* meant, but her accent sounded convincing enough so he nodded and went with it. Strides in sync, they stepped onto the red-carpeted approach and walked up to the trio of suits at the entrance, who Chunk decided did double duty as hosts and bouncers. Despite still being outside the club, it was already hard to hear thanks to the speakers broadcasting what he presumed had to be the music playing inside. Watts rattled off something to one of the bouncer-hosts who looked them both up and down before gesturing to the club entrance. Chunk gave the dude a bro nod and led Watts toward the double doors, which were held open for them by two other less intimidating dudes in suits.

"Welcome to the Cavalli Club," the one on the right said.

"Have a nice time," the other man said with practiced disinterest, his gaze locked on Watts's assets.

Neither of them replied—they were too important to interact with the help—as they stepped into the parallel universe that was the Cavalli Club. The first thing that caught Chunk's attention were the chandeliers. Massive and draped with thousands of crystals, they looked like enormous shimmering jellyfish floating in midair. Although they weren't moving, the light show inside the club reflecting and refracting off of them created the illusion of movement, like the phosphorescing creatures that inhabited the ocean deep. The second thing that grabbed his attention was a woman—barely clothed in a nude-colored bodysuit—dangling upside down from a pair of silk ribbons while performing an inverted split. Defying gravity, she performed feats of aerial acrobatics that the SEAL in him recognized as requiring a core strength to body weight ratio that he was certain eclipsed his own.

"You've got a little drool running down the side of your beard," Watts said in his ear. "You might want to close your mouth."

"Ha ha, very funny," he said, shifting his gaze from the acrobat to her. "Do you know how much friggin' core strength that requires?"

"Her core strength, really, that's what you're thinking about?" she said with a mischievous grin.

"Your table is this way," a hostess said, stepping in front of them. "Follow me."

The young woman led them to a small round table with two club chairs upholstered in faux leopard-pelt fabric. The hostess pulled out Watts's chair for her before Chunk had a chance to do it himself, then gestured to his vacant chair.

"Thank you," he said as he dropped into his seat, which was more comfortable than he predicted it would be.

"A server will be with you momentarily," the woman said, smiled at Chunk with want-you eyes, and then strode away.

For all the eye candy inside of the club, the air reeked of cigar and shisha tobacco smoke, and he saw Watts crinkle her nose as her gaze settled on three Arab men smoking, laughing, and drinking at a nearby table. The United Arab Emirates was subject to Sharia law, but that strict code of conduct did not apply inside the Cavalli Club or others like it. Dubai was an oasis of Western debauchery where alcohol consumption, cohabitation of unmarried couples, and immodest female attire were permitted. As so often was the case with the world, when dogma and capitalism collided, an uncomfortable and unspoken agreement of cooperation and tolerance was forged . . . an "I'll scratch your back while you pretend you're not itchy" arrangement.

Without trying to look like he was surveilling the joint, Chunk methodically scanned the cavernous club for Qasim Nadar. In the middle of his sweep, his gaze crossed Watts's own scan, two lighthouse searchlights in the night.

"Do you see him?" he asked.

"No," she replied.

A waiter appeared tableside, interrupting their effort.

"Good evening, can I interest you in a cocktail and our Midnight Brunch?"

"What is the Midnight Brunch?" Watts asked, still using her authentic but strangely comical French-accented English.

"It is a three-course meal with drinks included for two hundred and fifty Dirham per person. We start you with an antipasto *sulla piramide* with thirteen tastes. After that, you choose a main—tonight's entrées include *petto di pollo* with olive reduction, salmon over risotto, or beef medallion served with truffle gnocchi. After this, you have a choice of desserts."

"We will have the Midnight Brunch, and I will have a prosecco," she said.

"Beer for me," Chunk said, shifting his weight in the chair.

"Excellent, someone will have your drinks right out to you while I put in your order. Incidentally, is this your first time dining with us?"

Chunk nodded.

"Just so you know how it works, this is the last dinner sitting. At midnight all the tables are cleared away to make room for the dancing. For now, enjoy the show," the man said, and as if on cue, a trio of scantily clad women stepped out onto a little stage and began performing "All That Jazz" from *Chicago*.

Chunk watched the lead vocalist sing for a few measures and then looked at Watts, whose attention was fixed on the performance. His gaze swept from her face to the tattoo behind her left ear—a small α symbol inked in black in the tiny patch of skin between the back of her ear and hairline. From there, his gaze drifted to her back where he noticed another tattoo, one he'd not seen before and only visible because of the plunging back of her cocktail dress. The

Hebrew characters הלבק were inked in a vertical line along her spine, positioned high on her back between the shoulder blades. He leaned forward and squinted to see if he could make them out.

Just then she turned to catch him looking at her. "Checking out my ink?"

"Yeah."

"You haven't seen that one before, have you?" she said.

"Nope, can't say I have. At work you usually have more clothes on."

"I know! Stop reminding me."

"Are those Hebrew characters?" he asked.

"Yeah," she said. "It spells the word *Kabbalah*."

"What is Kabbalah?"

"In early Jewish esotericism, Kabbalah described parallel loops representing the physical and spiritual realms. When the loops are clasped together a nexus is created—a place where knowledge of the metaphysical universe can be received," she said. "But it also has a gematria, so with this tattoo, I'm celebrating both the mystical and numerical significance of the word."

"I have absolutely no idea what the hell you're talking about, Heels. What is a gematria?"

She laughed. "Gematria is the ancient practice of assigning a numerical value to a name, word, or phrase. It's all about the power of numbers—gematriot are prevalent in mysticism but were also used to create ciphers in the era before digital encryption."

"Okay, so what's your Kabba-whatever tattoo's gematria?"

"One hundred and thirty-seven," she said, not missing a beat.

"One hundred and thirty-seven," he echoed, thinking

about the seemingly unremarkable number. "Is that a special number or something?"

"Oh yeah," she said with a laugh as if he'd just asked the dumbest question in the world.

"Fine, I'll bite. What's special about it?"

"First of all, it's a prime number, but not just any old prime. It's a strong prime, a twin prime, an Einstein prime, a Stern prime, a Pythagorean prime, and a primeval number. In geometry, one hundred and thirty-seven degrees is the golden angle, and the multiplicative inverse of one hundred and thirty-seven is the fine structure constant of the universe."

Chunk laughed and shook his head. "I have no idea what any of that means. You might as well be speaking Greek."

"No, this is Greek," she said with a chuckle and pointed to the α tattoo behind her left ear. "Alpha is the symbol for the fine structure constant. I also have one hundred and thirty-seven tattooed inside a triangle *somewhere* else. There's power in threes."

"*Somewhere* else, huh?"

"Yeah, somewhere not visible, even with this skimpy dress," she said, blushing.

"Sounds like you *really* like that number. Okay, I'll bite . . . what's so important about it?"

"Many theoretical physicists and mathematicians believe the fine structure constant is the key to quantum mechanics, string theory, and unraveling the mysteries of the universe itself . . . but other than that, not much."

"Oh my God, Heels, you're such a nerd. I thought your fascination with knots was weird but this—" He stopped midsentence as he saw her attention shift. "You see something?"

She laughed theatrically, as if he'd just made a legit joke, and reached out to touch the back of his hand. "Oh stop," she said, her gaze ticking back to meet his. "Quebec is charming this time of year."

She'd spoken the assigned code word, Quebec, for their target.

It appeared that Qasim Nadar was officially in the house.

CHAPTER 30

"Damn, dude, what does it take to get a beer in this place?" Chunk said loudly. He sat up in his chair and pretended to look around for their server. He swept his gaze across where Watts had been looking and confirmed that, yes, Qasim Nadar had just arrived along with three other men, all white with Anglo-Saxon features. He watched them get seated at a four-top table twenty-five feet away. He scooted his chair back from the table and retrieved his mobile phone from his pocket. "Hey, darling, why don't you come over here, sit on my lap, and we can take a selfie?"

"Any excuse to get me on your lap, eh cowboy?" she said with a little laugh, playacting perfectly and getting up from her chair.

As she settled onto his lap, he realized just how slender and diminutive she was. His last girlfriend had been super into fitness and had a real density to her, but Watts was like a bird—hollow-boned and featherweight. He raised his phone and lined up the front-facing camera to take a picture of Qasim Nadar's table with him and Watts squeezed to the very edge of the frame. He pressed and held the shutter button down, forcing the camera into burst mode, and took two dozen pics in rapid-fire succession.

"Would you like me to take your picture?" a voice said in accented English beside them.

Chunk released the shutter button and glanced with annoyance at the server who had just shown up with their drinks. "No, thank you," he said, with no intention of handing his mobile phone off to anyone regardless of the situation. "We like the selfie look."

"As you wish," the waiter said with a nod, placed their drinks on the table, and departed.

"Check the pics before I get up," Watts said.

He nodded and went to the photo library to review the images. "Not bad," he said, seeing that he'd caught Nadar in profile, a second dude head-on, and a third in profile. The last guy, with his back to them, was not visible in the picture. Only problem was, they were too far away and the low-level light made it worse.

"Let me take one," she said and took the phone from him.

She scooted her ass farther up his lap and reclined, draping herself against his chest so that their heads were cheek to cheek. He resisted the urge to look down the front of her dress—which from this angle undoubtedly left zero to the imagination—and kept his eyes on the phone screen. He watched her use her thumb and index finger to zoom to maximum magnification and then snap another burst of pics of the British Aero table.

"That should do it," she said, lowering the camera for them to look at the new crop of pictures.

"Much better," he said, as she swiped through the deck of photos.

"I'll try to get a pic of the guy with his back to us later." She gave the side of his thigh a friendly pat and returned to her chair.

"Roger that," he said, keeping his voice below the din as he texted the best photo of the lot to Yi. "Just messaged the pic to your partner in crime."

She nodded and, without discussing it, they both subtly adjusted their chair positions so neither of them had their back to Nadar's table. Their first course of appetizers arrived a few minutes later—thirteen distinct small bites served on a metal wire pyramid. Chunk gave Watts first pick which she argued about, only to acquiesce when he refused to move a muscle.

"Oh my God, this is amazing," she said, forgetting her accent as she took a bite of a tiny pastry shell filled with something. She offered what remained of the morsel to him. "You have to try this."

"Uh, okay." He leaned forward and let her pop the other half of whatever it was in his mouth. It tasted salty and rich and had a slight tomato flavor. "What was that by the way?"

"I have absolutely no idea," she said.

He rolled his eyes and picked a little gem off the stand for himself and popped the whole thing into his mouth. As he chewed, he saw her glaring at him. "What?" he said, still chewing.

"What the hell?" she said. "I don't get to taste that one?"

"I didn't realize we were sharing every single one."

"I don't see two antipasto pyramids on this table, do you?"

"My bad," he said with a chuckle, selected another

appetizer, extended it to her to take a bite, and then ate the remainder, grinning. And so it went until they'd tried everything and the pyramid was empty.

"Which one was your favorite?" she asked.

"That cracker with the Wagyu beef," he said. "What about you?"

"I think that was my favorite too. Kinda wish I would have taken a little bigger bite first," she said which made them both laugh, and for the briefest of respites Chunk lost himself in the moment. Despite his ridiculous outfit and this ridiculous glam club with its jellyfish chandeliers, leopard-print chairs, and food with names he couldn't pronounce, he was having a great time. And probably it was because of Watts. He'd never seen her so relaxed and funny before. Most of the time she had her guard up around him, even the times when they were alone. Probably because he kidded her incessantly, all the while making sure to reinforce that he was her boss and she his subordinate. In their NOCs tonight, however, she'd somehow managed to turn the tables. For this operation, they were equals . . . partners even . . . and that felt okay. Maybe even better than okay.

"I'm going to make a trip to the ladies' room," she said, slipping her tiny handbag over her shoulder. "See if I can get a good look at Nadar and snap a selfie with the guy we can't see in the background."

"Be careful," he said and she disappeared into the crowd.

While she was gone, the waiter delivered Chunk a fresh beer along with their dinner entrées. Assuming she'd want to split these too, he pulled her plate over to his side and divided both meals. While he waited for her to return, he checked his phone for any text messages from Yi.

There were three.

Confirmed identities of three
persons in pic. Nadar and two
British nationals.

What's going on?

Sitrep?

He snapped a picture of one of the female aerial acrobats and texted it to Yi. Then he typed an accompanying message.

Watts is a little drunk and
showing off. Did you know she
could do this shit?

Chuckling at his cleverness, he waited for Yi's reply. A laughing emoji with tears came back seconds later. He typed another string, this one serious.

Nothing new to report.
Position watchdogs per plan.

A thumbs-up emoji came back.

Watts returned a few minutes later wearing a look of accomplishment.

"Did you get him?" Chunk asked.

"*Oui*," she said with a little grin, her French accent returning. "I took a panorama of the club, pretending I was trying to document the whole spectacle."

"Nice."

"Hey, look, they split our entrées for us," she said, smiling and pleased. "Unless . . . Did you do that?"

He shrugged. "I figured it was the only way to make sure the portions were fair. I couldn't let you do it after the Wagyu beef incident and all."

This earned him a flirty slap on the arm and a smile. While they ate and talked, they worked in tandem to continuously scan the club and kept a close eye on the British Aero table. No surprise, Nadar and his colleagues were doing pretty much the same thing everyone else in the club was doing—eating, drinking, and gawking at the spectacle of it all. Ever since Watts's bathroom trip, however, Chunk noticed periodic glances at their table from Nadar's table. Not so much from Nadar, but from the dude sitting on the left. All his looks were at Watts, and Chunk recognized this as *carnal* as opposed to *tactical* surveillance. Half the club had undoubtedly noticed her during her last flyby, putting her on plenty of single guys' radars now.

Probably not a bad thing, Chunk thought. *If they're looking at her, then they won't be looking at me.*

They finished their entrées—the salmon and beef selections—and moved on to desserts, which they also split. Chunk didn't catch the Italian names, but one was chocolate cake and the other was some kind of mousse with hard biscuit-like cookies. A few minutes to midnight, their server asked them to clear their table in preparation for clubbing time. A small army of staff quickly transformed the Cavalli Club from a dining room into a dance floor, removing the tables and pushing the chairs to the perimeter.

"Time to up our game," Chunk said, putting his arm around Watts's waist and pulling her close to him. "It's about to get loud and crowded."

"Should we move closer to Nadar?" she asked.

"Not yet," he said, keeping their target in his peripheral vision.

Five minutes later the bouncers opened the main doors and a crowd of people flooded in, quadrupling the number of patrons and filling the club close to capacity.

"Let's reposition," he said and, like a blocking fullback moving in slow motion, methodically cleared a path toward the lounge area where the British Aero guys were hanging out and sipping cocktails.

He found a patch of unoccupied standing room only fifteen feet from Nadar. He brought his half-drank, gone-warm beer, and she her prosecco, so they'd have something to sip on. They pretended to have an engaging conversation while they surveilled Nadar. To Chunk's bewilderment, multiple dudes came up to hit on Watts while they were together. What's more, they were utterly shameless, persistent, and unintimidated by both his presence and his bulk. He could have dropped every one of them with a single punch, but Watts dismissed them like spam callers, callously and bluntly, and he never once had to intervene.

Some "big deal" DJ and entourage entered the club to a raucous cheer and took the stage. The crowd swooned for the guy, but Chunk couldn't give a shit. He understood why actors and singers garnered fame and followers, but why the hell anybody gave a damn about a DJ was beyond him. The music changed, became instantly ten decibels louder, and a light show commenced. The dance floor transformed into a living, undulating organism of gyrating bodies. Sexy female dancers climbed into gilded cages that seemed to appear from nowhere, and the acrobat from earlier in the night now glided overhead, sitting on a trapeze swing. Despite the noise, the eye candy, and aerial distractions, Chunk stayed on mission and kept his attention focused on Nadar. He was just about to suggest to Watts that they relocate closer when Nadar walked away from his three colleagues.

"The package is on the move," he whispered in Watts's ear. "Looks like he might be headed to the bar."

"Check," she said and then loudly announced, "I'm going to the bar to get another drink."

Chunk grabbed her arm, stopping her. "Hold up . . ."

Something interesting was going on—an Arab dressed in a trendy suit had just bumped into Nadar and the two men were having words. They were too far away for Chunk to make out any of what was being said and he had no training in reading lips, so he focused on facial expressions and body language. The encounter didn't seem particularly friendly, but not heated either. They'd not greeted the other with a hug or handshake and they parted company the same way after the exchange.

"What do you think that was all about?" he said to Watts.

"Don't know. Could have just been they ran into each other, apologized, and parted company," she said. "Or it could have been something more."

"We need to get a picture of that guy, send it to Yi, and see if it gets a hit."

"Agreed."

"I'm gonna shadow this guy, see if I can get the pic," Chunk said. As he spoke the words, in his peripheral vision he saw the handsome Arab turn and look in their direction.

Chunk kept his gaze where it was, ten degrees behind the man, careful not to make eye contact. After a reasonable pause, he turned to Watts and whispered in her ear. "I just saw him scout us. Laugh and pretend I made a joke."

She did as told and looked convincing. "Looks like he's heading to the restrooms," she said with a demure grin while rubbing his upper arm affectionately.

"I'm going to make a pit stop in the men's room," he announced. "Back in a minute."

"I'm going to the bar," she said, after downing the last sip of her drink. "*À tout de suite.*"

He leaned in to give her a peck on the cheek, but she turned and took it on the lips.

"We're together, not siblings," she said with a coy grin, their lips mere centimeters apart.

He inhaled her breath, hot and sweet in his nose. "Unmute your earbud."

She nodded and he stepped away.

As he fell in behind he pulled his mobile phone from his pocket, unmuted his earbud in the surveillance app, and trailed the new target to the men's bathroom. When he entered the crowded restroom, he didn't see the Arab anywhere. Concluding the man had gone into a toilet stall, Chunk capitalized on the opportunity to empty his own pressing bladder into the first available urinal. After finishing, he washed his hands slowly and fastidiously, buying time for the target to emerge. He played that game as long as he could, then pretended to adjust his waistcoat and fix his hair. Finally, the Arab came out of a stall, and Chunk couldn't help but wonder if the man had truly been defecating or if he'd chosen the stall to use his mobile phone in privacy. The handsome, thirtysomething Middle Easterner stepped up to the sink beside Chunk and began washing his hands.

"Quite the spectacle, this place," the Arab said in British-accented English while glancing at Chunk in the mirror.

"I've partied at better places," Chunk said, dropping his native Texan tongue for a flat American accent.

"In that case, you must be quite the globe-trotter," the man said as he turned off the water and took a paper towel to dry his hands.

"You could say that," Chunk said with a wry smile.

Just not the kind of globe-trotter you're thinking of, bro. My everyday vest isn't tweed. It's made of Kevlar and stuffed with magazines and grenades.

"The woman you're with—the one in the silver dress—is she your wife?"

The question caught Chunk off guard, and he hesitated a microsecond before responding. "If I say no, are you going to start hitting on her like every other dude in the club?"

"Certainly not, I'm married," the Arab said with a chuckle. "But like every other man, I can't help but notice beautiful things, and your woman is very beautiful."

Watts is not my *woman . . . even if we were a couple*, Chunk thought and was surprised that the comment kinda pissed him off. *Dude, that's just how these guys think. What do you care?*

Chunk gave the standard bro nod, acknowledging the sexist compliment, and met the man's gaze in the mirror.

"*Ilal liqaa*," the man said with a nod, turned, and walked out of the bathroom.

Chunk's Arabic was rudimentary, but he understood the difference between this particular farewell and other common Arabic goodbyes.

Until we meet again . . .

Irritated and feeling that this guy had somehow just gotten the better of him, he counted to five and exited the men's room. Scanning the crowd, he spied his new friend a few seconds later heading for the bar and walking straight toward a lithe figure with her back turned wearing a silver cocktail dress . . .

CHAPTER 31

"Whiskey, you've got Tango Two incoming," Chunk said, using Watts's call sign for the first time and praying she could hear him over the din of the club.

The Arab was closing in on her position and walking with purpose. Chunk's heart rate picked up and that old familiar precombat tension crept into his muscles.

What the hell is this guy doing? Are we blown? Is he making a move on Watts? No way he's targeting her in a crowded club, he thought, his mind a whirlwind of paranoia. *Terrorists kill people in public all the time. That's what they do. Maybe this guy is with al Qadar . . .*

He tried to scan the man's hands for a weapon, but the club was too crowded and there were too many people blocking his line of sight. The only thing he could see clearly was the man's head moving through the crowd.

"Watch your back, Whiskey," he said with urgency in his voice. "I can't see his hands."

"*Merde!*" he heard Watts exclaim on the comms circuit a heartbeat later, followed by, "*Je suis désolée*— Look what I did. I'm so sorry."

Even with his view blocked by the crowd, Chunk knew what had happened. Watts had whirled at the last second and collided with the man, spilling her drink on him. It was a heads-up maneuver, taking control of the situation and putting her in a face-to-face position to survey the threat and react accordingly.

"No apology necessary," he heard the smooth-talking Arab say. "It's my fault. You were turning and I surprised you."

"At least it wasn't red wine," she said with an apologetic laugh. "You're going to smell like prosecco, but no stains, thankfully."

"Indeed. A small price to pay for an opportunity to meet a woman as beautiful as you. I am Asadi Bijan . . ."

"Adrienne," she said.

"Nice to make your acquaintance, Adrienne," he said. "Please allow me to buy you a replacement drink? It's the least I can do."

"That won't be necessary," Chunk said, shoving past the last dude in his way and taking his place at Watts's side.

"I said we'd meet again, and look . . . here we are," Bijan said, a superior smile stretching across his face.

"And you also said you weren't going to hit on my girl, and look . . . here we are," Chunk fired back.

"Mere coincidence, I assure you. I was walking to the bar to get a drink and Adrienne here was just leaving. Our paths crossed . . ." Making a show of wiping his wet shirt and suit coat, he added, "And I seemed to have paid the price for it.

Now if you'll excuse me, I'd like to get what I came for—a Vesper."

"Why don't we have a drink together?" Watts said, smiling while her eyes sent Chunk an altogether different message. "No reason to part company on bad terms."

What the hell is she doing? This was not part of the plan . . .

Bijan looked at Chunk. "I would say yes, but I wouldn't want to upset your friend."

The operator in Chunk hated the idea of drinking with this guy, but the Tier One officer recognized this sudden twist of events for what it was—an opportunity to interact and photograph someone who was feeling suspiciously and increasingly relevant with each passing minute.

"Sure, why not," Chunk said and grudgingly stuck out his bear paw. "I'm Charles."

The Arab clasped his hand and shook it. "Asadi."

They ordered a fresh round of drinks—which Bijan insisted on buying—and then wandered as a trio to the lounge area along the perimeter. Chunk maneuvered himself to take a chair with his back to the wall, while Watts took the seat that gave her line of sight on Nadar. Bijan seemed none the wiser, taking a seat opposite them while chatting happily about the not-to-miss attractions of Dubai. They talked for an hour, Watts questioning the stranger about his business, which he happily elaborated on. Bijan pitched himself as a financier for urban development projects throughout the Middle East. He went on to speak quite passionately about entrepreneurship, education, and empowering the next generation of Muslim youth with the technology and opportunities necessary to change the Arab world. Bijan said his dream was to create start-up incubators throughout the region modeled after successful incubators in the US, thereby transforming the Middle East into a beacon of hope and prosperity.

". . . not unlike the city of Dubai itself. But first, I must raise the capital," the polished conversationalist said. "As they say, my new friends, cash is king."

Chunk had to hand it to the guy, he had charisma. The longer he listened, the less convinced Chunk became that Asadi Bijan was a terrorist. Terrorists didn't talk like this. Villains dreamed of vengeance, not entrepreneurship and education. Truth be told, he was beginning to get bored. And annoyed. He wasn't sure how much longer he could endure watching Watts flirt so shamelessly with the guy.

He ran his tongue between his lower lip and his gums, his nicotine craving presently a throbbing eleven on a ten-point scale.

Beer was a crappy substitute for dip . . . a very, very crappy substitute.

"I've been blathering on for a fortnight," Bijan said with a chuckle. "Tell me about you. Are you vacationing in Dubai together, or are you here on business?"

"To be honest with you, we are simply here for the party," Watts said, her French accent seeming more and more authentic as the night wore on. "We met in New York City, became lovers, and now we travel. Not as exciting or important as your big dreams, but *maintenant* we are young, so why not have fun."

Better hope this dude doesn't know French, Chunk suddenly thought. *Or she's gonna look like an idiot.*

As if reading his mind, the Arab rattled off something in French to Watts.

Chunk's stomach lurched and he looked at her, but to his surprise and relief, she laughed and answered Bijan in French. They conversed for several minutes, but the only word he was able to extract from the soup was *Brittany*.

"As you can see, I'm not fluent," Bijan said, finally switching back to English, "but I travel to Paris from time to time and I've picked up a little French along the way. I like to learn languages. It makes me feel . . . connected."

"*Non*, I think you did quite well. In Paris, sometimes the people are not patient with beginners, that's why you should visit Brittany. The people there are very nice. Plus, it's not so expensive, and you can practice your French with everyone," she said.

"I'll keep that in mind, Adrienne." He checked his watch and blew air through his teeth. "It's late and I have a busy day tomorrow, so I'd best call it a night. It was very nice to meet both of you."

Bijan stood and they followed suit.

"Before you go, we must get a picture," she said.

"Maybe next time. I really should be going," Bijan said, stepping away.

But Watts was on her game and having none of it. "I insist," she said and hooked her arm around the man's waist.

Chunk was quick to act, his mobile phone out and snapping pictures before the Arab could protest.

"Perfect," she said and then exchanged kisses on the cheek with the now frowning Bijan.

When it was Chunk's turn to say goodbye, he shook the man's hand. Unable to resist, he put a Texas-sized squeeze on just to let the dude know who the *real* man was at the table. To his credit, Bijan did not wince, but Chunk thought he saw a flash of malice in the man's eyes as he released his grip.

"You need to follow him," she said once Bijan had stepped out of earshot.

"What?"

"Something's definitely up with that guy. Nadar was eyeing us while we were talking to him the entire time. You need to follow him, Charles," she said, her gaze insistent. "I'll stay here and shadow Nadar."

"I'm not leaving you here alone."

"I won't be alone. Riker and Trip are outside. Trust me," she said, her eyes on fire. "Go, before you lose him."

"Copy all," Riker's voice said in Chunk's earbud, making his presence known for the first time all evening. "I'm with Whiskey. Bravo Two is bringing our vehicle around front to pick you up."

The prompt from his senior chief tipped the scales in Watts's favor.

"Check," Chunk said, and with a grudging backward glance at his spooky girl in the svelte silver dress, he set off after Asadi Bijan.

CHAPTER 32

Chunk tailed the man calling himself Asadi Bijan toward the Cavalli Club exit while doing his best to maintain a reasonable standoff. The Arab seemed to navigate the crowd with an almost unnatural fluidity, like sand slipping through spread open fingers. Whereas Chunk felt like the steel ball in a pinball machine, colliding with seemingly every patron in his path.

"Just finished running Whiskey's pic of Tango Two through the facial rec database," Yi reported in his ear. "I got a hit under the provided name, Asadi Bijan, a financier operating under an Emirates passport. He travels frequently between Dubai and London and shows trips to Cyprus, Riyadh, Paris, Tel Aviv, and Lahore. He's not on any watch lists and appears to have a clean but truncated history."

"What do you mean, truncated history?" Chunk asked.

"Well, there's not much on this guy before eighteen months ago, and he really stepped up his travel recently."

"How recently?"

"Over the past three months," Yi said.

Chunk nodded to himself. "All right, sounds like a secondary NOC he might have slipped into full time. Keep digging."

"Roger that."

"Bravo Two, sitrep?" Chunk said, checking in with Trip.

"I'm third in the pickup queue out front. Describe your boy," Trip came back.

"Arab in a black tailored suit, light-purple shirt, no tie. Medium height, lean build, handsome features, short beard."

"Check, I've got eyes on your boy. Just exited the club . . . Now he's climbing into a black Range Rover."

"Copy," Chunk said, picking up his pace and pushing out of the exit instead of waiting for the attendant to open the door for him.

"Hurry," Trip said. "They're getting away."

Chunk jogged to the Suburban and climbed into the front passenger seat. The vehicle in the queue in front of them, a Mercedes G-Wagon SUV, was still loading passengers. "Go around them," Chunk said.

Trip did as instructed, and as he did, the driver of the Benz tried to pull out only to slam on his brakes and honk as the big American SUV zipped in front and cut him off.

"Yankee, do we have eyes in the sky?" Chunk queried.

"Negative," Yi came back.

"Damn it," Chunk murmured, scanning the road ahead as Trip whipped around the side of the Fairmont hotel via an access road and onto the one-way two-lane frontage road that ran parallel to the E11, which bisected the heart of Dubai.

"I don't see him," Trip said. "Do you think he already turned?"

"There he is! Three cars ahead, in front of that Maserati," Chunk said, spying the Rover.

Trip pressed the accelerator and the Z71's V8 roared under the hood, propelling the four-ton behemoth down the road. When they'd closed to within two vehicles, Trip eased off the gas and fell into a standard trail.

"Dude, tell me you brought weapons," Chunk said, feeling suddenly quite naked. He'd managed to effectively suppress his angst at being unarmed while immersed in his NOC at the Cavalli Club, but now that he'd put both physical and mental distance between then and now, that vulnerability felt tangible.

"Puh-lease," Trip said in mock offense. "There's a vest behind your seat on the floor and a Sig underneath it."

Chunk nodded and grabbed the oh-shit handle on the A pillar, fighting the urge to pull the Sig right now. Technically, Asadi Bijan had done nothing wrong, and getting pulled over in Dubai packing heat would land them in jail and trash their NOCs.

"Chunk, dude, relax. Why are you so jumpy?" Trip said.

Chunk ignored the comment. "They're turning west at that KFC a block ahead."

"Yeah, I see it . . ."

Chunk ran his tongue back and forth between his lower lip and gums. "I need a dip."

"There's a tin in the cup holder," Trip said, turning right without signaling at the intersection where the Range Rover had gone. He accelerated to close the distance to the taillights ahead.

"Yankee, this is Charlie," Chunk said. "You tracking us?"

"Roger, Charlie," Yi said. "I hold you heading northwest on Fifty-Seventh Street."

"What are we heading into?" Chunk asked as he packed his lower lip with snuff. "We appear to be leaving the fancy part of town."

"Looks like mixed-use zoning on the satellite imagery—residential and light commercial," Yi said.

"Check," Chunk said, scanning out the windshield and side windows. The towering hotels and office buildings were now in the rearview mirror and they were entering a section of Dubai dominated by townhomes and duplexes, intermixed with one- and two-story storefronts along the road. In keeping with the rest of Dubai, everything was clean and well-kept. The neighborhood seemed far from a slum—solidly middle-class by UAE standards, Chunk imagined—but possessed none of the opulence or self-importance on display in the business and shopping districts.

The Range Rover continued straight for two more blocks then turned north. Three blocks later it turned left, off the four-lane Al Wasl Road, and onto a two-lane spur leading into a neighborhood of single-family homes, each surrounded by a stucco wall or an iron fence.

"If I turn here, he's going to notice," Trip said.

"And if you don't, we'll probably lose him. We don't have eyes, remember. Yi's on a GPS app, that's all."

Trip slowed, giving a little distance, and then made the turn just in time to see the Range Rover turning into the neighborhood.

"Perfect," Chunk said. "Before you make the next turn, kill the headlights."

Trip nodded and did as instructed. They turned north, following the path the Rover had taken. A block later, Bijan's luxury ute turned right and disappeared behind a wall. Just beyond stood a white stucco four-story tower with arched windows, a domed roof, and a balcony. It was taller than the surrounding buildings. Chunk recognized the structure instantly as a minaret.

"Yankee, confirm a mosque near our pos?" he asked Yi.

"Confirmed. Al Wasl Hassan Masjid Mosque," she came back. "Sixty meters northwest."

"Copy," he said and turned to Trip. "A twelve-pack says he's in the mosque parking lot."

"I ain't taking that bet," Trip said and turned left. As Chunk predicted, Bijan's Range Rover had pulled into the mosque parking lot and was sitting at idle, the brake lights on. Trip cruised past the parking lot entrance. "What me to loop around?"

"No—turn right at the next intersection and park along the curb. Make sure our ass end is blocked by that stucco wall," Chunk said, stripping off the tweed vest and unbuttoning his dress shirt as he talked. Once he had his shirt off, he reached behind his seat and grabbed the black Kevlar vest off the floor. He quickly slipped it over his torso, fastened the Velcro tabs, and put his already slim-fitting dress shirt back on. Thanks to the extra girth from the vest, he could barely get the buttons fastened.

Trip laughed.

"What?"

"You move your arms at all and you're gonna rip that shirt."

"I know," Chunk said and reached for the Sig under his seat. As he did, he heard a stitch pop behind his right shoulder. "Shit . . ."

"Hulk smash," Trip said, dropping his voice an octave.

"Yeah, well, you wish you had this body."

"No . . . I really don't," the SEAL said with a snigger. Then, getting serious, he asked, "You gonna surveil on foot?"

Chunk nodded. "Yankee, what are my options?"

"Looks like there's an empty lot on the northeast side. It abuts the north side of the mosque and the parking lot," Yi came back.

"Copy." Chunk stuffed the Sig in his waistband and pulled the handle to open the passenger side door. "Stay frosty," he said, glancing at Trip.

"Here, take this," Trip said and handed Chunk a SiOnyx Aurora Pro monocular scope.

"Thanks," he said and stuffed it in his pocket.

"Charlie, this is Whiskey," Watts said in his ear. "Tango November is leaving the club along with his British Aero colleagues. I'm going to tail him with Bravo One as my escort."

"Roger that, Whiskey," Chunk said, relieved that Riker had hung back to be Watts's plus-one. "Happy hunting."

He stepped out of the Suburban onto the sidewalk and shut the door behind him. He walked with purpose northeast, passing three connected duplex homes that backed up to the mosque on the west side. After clearing the last one, he saw the vacant lot Yi had mentioned, but her imagery was outdated. A building of some sort was going up and a construction fence encircled the perimeter.

Chunk scanned a one-hundred-and-eighty-degree arc for eyes on him. As expected at this late hour, the street and sidewalks were empty except for him. He spit a glob of tobacco juice on the sidewalk, then did a pull-up using the top crossbar and slipped over the fence, popping a few more threads in his shirt in the process. He landed with a muffled thud on the hard-packed sandy earth and quickstepped into cover inside the building under construction.

Keeping to the shadows, he dropped into a tactical crouch and shuffled to the fence running along the north property line. Through the chain-link mesh, he could see the Range Rover in the parking lot—lights completely off. He couldn't tell if the driver's seat was occupied or not because of his angle and the Rover's tinted windows. He identified three other vehicles in the parking lot—two commercial vans and a midnight-blue four-door sedan. He shifted his gaze to the mosque itself, scanning each of the six windows on the north facade.

"I can't see shit," he grumbled, looking through the monocular scope.

"Say again, Charlie," Trip said. "I didn't copy."

"This sucks, I can't see anything. I'm going in for a closer look."

"Unadvisable, boss. You've got no backup."

"Oh c'mon, he bought me a drink at the Cavalli Club. We're best buds now. What's he going to do, shoot me?" Chunk said, pocketing the scope and pulling his Sig.

"Yes, he will definitely shoot your redneck ass."

"Just be ready to pick me up if this thing goes south," he said and moved to the chain-link fence on the back side of the lot.

"Roger that."

He was just about to jump for the top crossbar when an east-facing door leading to the mosque parking lot opened. A triangle of light appeared on the pavement and male voices cut the silence. Chunk immediately got small, dropping to the ground in the prone position. He couldn't make out what was being said, but two men emerged pushing a tall rectangular aluminum cabinet on wheels.

What the hell is that thing? he thought as he pulled the scope from his pocket for a closer look.

The thing made a terrible metallic racket as the two men

rolled it across the parking lot toward one of the vans, rattling and shaking on its hard caster wheels. The man guiding it in front yelled at his colleague in the back about the noise, and the guy in the back rattled off something derogatory at his accuser. A few feet later, one of the casters hit a divot in the pavement and the cabinet tipped violently to the side. Everything inside shifted, causing even more metallic ruckus. The guy pushing from the back moved quickly and caught the cabinet before it fell.

What a couple of dumbasses, Chunk thought as he watched the two guys argue and struggle to load the entire thing into one of the vans while keeping it upright.

"Hassan's Delight Catering," he murmured, reading the appliqué graphic on the side of the van.

"Charlie, this is Whiskey," Watts said in his ear.

"Go," he whispered back.

"Tango November is back in his room at the Fairmont. Bravo One tailed him and the other British Aero persons of interest." Then, as if reading his mind, she added, "And I'm back in the TOC with Yankee, safe and sound and no longer half naked . . . just in case you were wondering."

This last comment made him smile and he clicked twice with his tongue in acknowledgment.

As the first two catering dudes headed back inside, a second pair came out, this time carrying a massive Igloo cooler. Even in the dim light, he could see the strain on their faces as they struggled with the weight. The first pair of men returned pushing another aluminum box on wheels, this one fatter and shorter than the last one. Just like before they were bickering like two little old ladies, until Asadi Bijan stepped out to reprimand them. The loading operation went on for another twenty minutes, and during that time Chunk snapped pictures with the scope which was equipped with a thirty-two gig micro SD card for image and video capture. In all, he photographed seven persons—Asadi Bijan and six adult males, not one of whom Chunk would have pegged as a *catering professional.* After they'd finished loading the vans, he waited and watched.

When twenty minutes had passed, he checked in with Trip. "Two, One—something doesn't feel right about this. I'm going in for a closer look. I need to see what's in those vans."

"Then let me loop around. I want to be ready to intervene and provide cover if they make you," Trip came back. "I'll reposition east just before the turn into the parking lot."

"Check," he said, liking the idea because that would make emergency exfil possible.

Chunk held until Trip called in position a few minutes later. Before making his move, he scanned the north-facing windows of the mosque one more time with his scope. Satisfied he wasn't being watched, he shifted into a crouch, jumped, and grabbed the top crossbar of the chain-link fence. In one fluid sequence, he pulled up and rolled over the top, landing with a soft thud on the other side in a deep squat.

He sprinted low and fast across the parking lot to the far side of the row of parked vehicles and slid behind the first of two cargo vans, his back pressed up against the front bumper. Pulse pounding in his ears, he held . . . listening for any sounds indicating he'd been spotted. The compulsion to pull his Sig was overpowering, but he resisted. Shooting a visually unarmed civilian in the public parking lot of a mosque, even a civilian snooping around in the middle of the night, was probably something these guys would not risk. Of course, if these dudes were terrorists working for Qasim Nadar, then all bets were off.

Getting into the vans was going to be a bitch, no question about it. They were pulled into their parking spots nose first with the rear doors facing the mosque to facilitate loading, so going in the back was a nonstarter. Each van had a driver's side slider door, which was his best option for access. Picking the lock or breaking a window was out of the question. If he didn't get lucky with an unlocked door, he'd have to abort. He performed a round of four-count breathing to clear his head, pivoted one hundred and eighty degrees, and crept low and slow around the front driver's side wheel well. Crouching, he reached up and pulled on the slider door handle. It wouldn't engage. He tried the driver's door and, not surprisingly, found it locked also.

Staying low, he reversed course and crept back around the front of the first van and then over to the second. He sighted the gap between the vehicles, looking at the east-facing mosque doors. The lights were on in the foyer beyond, but he didn't see any figures or movement. With a determined exhale, he crabbed between the vans. For the sake of thoroughness, he tried the front passenger door of the second van, but it was locked as expected.

To his great satisfaction, the driver's side door of the van engaged with a click and he opened it a crack. But at the same time, the cabin lights inside the van turned on.

Shit . . .

He pivoted around the door, opened it partway, and methodically scanned the driver's console for the lighting control switches. He found the rocker switch for the interior lights and flipped it from Auto to Off and then glanced over his shoulder at the mosque. Through the entry doors, the foyer was lit inside but he saw no threats. He exhaled with relief, eased the door shut, and then slowly and quietly pushed the slider door open. When the gap was big enough, he slipped inside the cargo compartment.

Inside the van it was too dark to see, so he pulled the Aurora Pro scope out of his pocket and night became day thanks to the scope's magic tech. Chunk scanned the inside of the van, which was packed with insulated coolers, crates, and catering supplies. Taking care not to knock anything over, he opened the lid of the biggest cooler and found it packed with bottled water and soft drinks. He closed the lid and scooted to the middle of the van, his eyes going to the tall rolling cabinet. Something about that thing bugged him, but he couldn't open the door because of all the other crap packed in around it. Grumbling, he started moving boxes, making mental notes so he could put everything back the way he'd found it. Once he'd created clearance, he opened the aluminum cabinet door. The cavity resembled the inside of a large vertical oven, with over a dozen sliding food trays on racks. Each rack was wrapped in aluminum foil.

"Sitrep?" Trip's voice said in his ear.

"In the van, looking."

"Hurry up, you're coming up on four minutes."

"Check."

He pulled the top rack one-quarter of the way out, peeled back the foil six inches, and peeked underneath to find pastries. Methodically, he put the foil back, slid the tray back onto the rack, and checked another. This tray had more pastries. The next tray felt heavier and required more of a tug to get it to move. But, again, he found more pastries. Shaking his head, he set down his scope and slid the tray fully out of the rack. He peeled back the foil all the way to find four black plastic bags taped to the tray behind the first five rows of pastries. He felt one of the bags, pressing with his fingers, and traced the outline of a pistol.

Tricky, tricky bastards, he thought.

He returned the tray and pulled out the tray above it and found the same trick—pastries in the front and weapons in the back, except this time, instead of pistols, he found grenades and long knives. With a low growl, he replaced the foil and slid the tray back into the cabinet.

"Two, One," he whispered. "We've got a problem. I just found weapons in the catering van. Looks like these guys are planning on delivering more than just pastries."

"Copy. What do you want to do?"

"Not sure. Gonna exfil to you and we'll decide."

He methodically put everything back in the van the way he'd found it and crabbed backward to the slider door.

This is the part of the movie when they come out to check on the vans, he thought.

Blowing air through his teeth, he pulled his Sig and readied himself. If they caught him, he'd have to end things here and now. He had the grenades to do it. Teeth clenched, he quietly and slowly opened the van's slider door. Once the gap was two feet wide, he held and listened. Hearing nothing, he slipped out into a low crouch between the two vans. He shut the slider door and then ducked around to the front and out of view. At this point he had two options, jump the stucco wall of the duplex residence straight ahead, or try to sneak out the mosque parking lot to the street without being noticed. Both had counterdetection risks, but he decided to hop the wall and travel through the backyards to the street where Trip was idling.

He sprinted the twelve feet to the shoulder-height stucco perimeter wall and vaulted over it with ease. After landing with a thud, he scanned for threats but the little courtyard he found himself in was deserted—save for a tricycle and a kid's soccer ball. He moved like a shadow to the east, hopping another wall

and crossing a second backyard to get to the street where the
Z71 Suburban sat idling, lights off, along the curb. He slipped
his weapon into his waistband and then walked casually to the
SUV and climbed in the front passenger seat.

"Sometimes, I hate being right," Chunk said, turning to
Trip.

"What do you want to do?" Trip said.

"Head back to the hotel, grab Riker and Saw, kit up, and
hit these guys here before sunrise—I think that's our only play.
Otherwise it's gonna be pastries and bullets for somebody
somewhere."

CHAPTER 33

Something bothered him about how things unfolded and he put a hand on Trip's forearm as the SEAL pulled the gear lever to Drive.

"Hold up," Chunk said, stopping Trip before he pressed the accelerator.

"See something?" the SEAL asked, scanning out the windshield.

"No," Chunk said, rubbing his temples. "We don't have eyes in the sky, so we need to stay put. If these guys leave before we get back, we'll have no friggin' idea where they went. Let's just brief it now on the party line. Whiskey, are you back with Yankee?"

"Roger," Watts came back.

"What about Romeo and Sierra?" he asked, referring to Riker and Saw since they'd never bothered to assign proper call signs for the op when it was just going to be ISR.

"They're here," she came back.

"Everybody up to speed on the situation?"

"Yes, and no one likes it," she said. "We can't hit a mosque in Dubai, even with justification. First of all, we're not authorized for that. We haven't read the Head Shed in on any of these developments. Second, it would be a political disaster. Nobody in the local government knows we're here. And third, we have a vehicle problem—you guys are in the only one we have."

"All true," he said and clawed out the spent tobacco from his lower lip. "So, let's fix each of those action items."

"We're already working on it. Yankee put in an urgent request for another vehicle with the air base when it looked like there was a chance that things could get complicated. It should be here inside an hour."

"Bravo Zulu, Yankee," Chunk said liking Yi's foresight. "All right, here's what I'm thinking—Romeo and Sierra you guys kit up. When the new wheels arrive, load our kits and the long guns and reposition north of the mosque. We have no idea when these a-holes are leaving or what their target is, but if I was a betting man, I'd put money on the Defense Conference. In the meantime, we need eyes in the sky and everything you can find out about Asadi Bijan, who is obviously not a financier interested in promoting entrepreneurship across the Middle East like he claimed to be. I'll call Charlie Oscar and read him in on what's going on and see if we can't make this operation official, or at least get some local support."

"I've already put in the priority request for satellite coverage—did it at the same time as the vehicle ask," Yi said. "We'll have eyes at 0400."

Chunk checked his watch: 0149.

It was gonna be a long night. He grabbed the tin of snuff

from the cup holder, packed a fresh lipper, and said, "We'll maintain a close-in position here until we get eyes in the sky, then we can establish an offset just in case they've made this vehicle. Whiskey and Yankee you are now Mother, we're Alpha One and Two, and Romeo and Sierra are now Three and Four."

"Check," Watts said. "Does this operation have a name?"

Chunk pursed his lips, thought for a second, then grinned. "Why yes it does, Operation Nutcracker."

This earned a chuckle from Trip and although he couldn't see it, most certainly a collective eye roll back in the hotel room TOC.

The next four hours went faster than Chunk thought they would. The call with Bowman was interesting, but the salty CSO took the news like a frogman who'd wrestled with Mr. Murphy enough times to expect nothing less. The second vehicle showed up at the hotel, and the driver, a Marine gunnery sergeant who'd clearly read the tea leaves when Yi's request came in, enthusiastically agreed to stay on as "tactical chauffeur" for the op with no questions asked. The Bravo element—Riker and Saw—arrived on station about the same time the satellite fell under their operational control. Chunk and Trip repositioned a block south, and Bravo element took station a block north of the mosque, but not before dropping off two coffees and a box of TORQ energy bars, compliments of Saw—whose wife insisted he eat *clean* and packed his luggage full of them. Chunk would have preferred a bagel or a banana, but he ate four of the things and they weren't half bad.

At 0449, Chunk drank his last sip of coffee.

At 0518, he pissed in an empty water bottle, filling it to the very top while narrowly avoiding spillage.

At 0549, Trip ripped a fart that required emergency ventilation.

And at 0632, the terrorist caterers got underway.

"One, the train has left the station," Watts reported. "Three-vehicle convoy, two vans and the Range Rover. We have eight warm bodies—four in the Rover and two in each van. They are turning west out of the mosque parking lot . . . and now they're turning north at the corner."

"Copy all," Chunk said and nodded to Trip, who put the transmission in Drive and pulled away from the curb. "They're heading your way. Take lead and we'll follow."

"Check," Riker acknowledged.

They trailed the catering convoy north and east across the E11 and into the Dubai World Trade Center complex.

"What did I tell you?" Chunk said as the full complexity of what they were facing hit home. "Mother, you need to get on the horn with DWTC security and inform them we have a terrorist threat from Hassan's Delight Catering—"

"They're splitting," Riker interrupted. "Catering vans just turned west, off Al Mustaqbal just ahead of the complex, but the Range Rover is continuing straight."

"Two, follow the catering vans; we'll follow the Rover. We can't let them unload and disappear. Take them in the parking lot if you have to," Chunk said.

"Rules of engagement?" Riker said, uncertainty ripe in his voice.

"Just hold them at gunpoint until security shows up. We know those vans have weapons inside. All we need to do is prove it."

"Understood."

"Mother, sitrep on the Rover?" Chunk said as Trip made the turn onto Al Mustaqbal Road. They were a quarter mile from the lead vehicle and did not have a visual on Bijan's SUV.

"The Rover just turned west on the road immediately

south of the Novotel World Trade Dubai. That's the second tower you'll pass at the front of the complex. The road doesn't seem to have a name . . . Seventh Street maybe. He's turning into a multistory paid parking tower," Yi came back.

"One, we've got a fucking problem," Riker cut in. "A truck pulled out in front of us and is blocking the access road the catering vans turned down. We're dead in the water and we've lost visual."

"On it," Yi said. "Looking . . . Shit, I don't see them."

"What do you mean, you don't see them!"

"It's like a big loading area between all the complex buildings," Yi explained. "I think this area is for all the vendors and contractors to load and unload. On top of that, the area appears to be under construction. There's a big tent, probably for shade, and what looks like metal awning carport structures. Maybe they pulled under one of those. I don't know."

Riker's mike was on vox because Chunk heard him blast his car horn and then yell, presumably out the window, "Move that fucking truck right now!"

"Damn it," Chunk cursed, his guts going to knots as the situation continued deteriorating in real time. "Are you having any luck contacting DWTC security?"

"Whiskey is on the phone with them right now," Yi said.

Trip steered their Z71 Suburban past the Novotel hotel tower and onto the road leading to the parking garage. "Pursue inside?"

"Check," Chunk said. "Two, sitrep?"

"We're around the interference, but our tangos are nowhere in sight. It's like a loading dock back here. There are roller doors everywhere. They could have pulled the vans into any of a dozen places. What do you want us to do?" Riker said.

"We need options, Mother," Chunk growled, anger seeping in to spoil his normally clearheaded optimism.

"You're going to have to look for them on foot. The N2 shop worked with the DNI to get you priority clearance and conference access yesterday because we assumed you'd be surveilling Nadar over the next two days. DWTC issued security badges for the four of you," Yi said. "They're at the security personnel entrance which is located on the south side of the convention center main gate."

"That's slick, but we can't go wandering around the expo in full battle rattle," Riker said.

"No, you can't, but these badges permit you to conceal carry in civilian clothes. No rifles, no kits, but at least you're not going to have to worry about being stopped by security personnel everywhere you go," Yi said.

In the background, over Yi's open mike, Chunk heard Watts unleash a string of curses that would make Davy Jones proud. "Is there a problem, Mother?"

"Yes, there's a friggin' problem," Watts said, now on the line. "DWTC security has no record of Hassan's Delight Catering. They're not a registered vendor at the conference, which tells me these guys have people on the inside working for them. I bet the truck that cut off Bravo team was no accident. The catering vans disappearing from sight was also no accident. And worst of all, the security manager I was talking to was an arrogant dick who patronized me the entire conversation and said before they panic over a potential false alarm, he needs proof that the threat is real. I asked him if it would be fucking real enough for him when there were a hundred dead bodies in the exhibit hall, and he hung up on me. Can you believe that? He hung up on me!"

"Okay, everybody take a deep breath," Chunk said,

including himself in the *everybody* category as he swept his gaze across the parking stalls for Bijan's black Range Rover. "We need to work this problem methodically. Two, go to the south security entrance, get our badges, and let them know what's going on. Maybe you'll have better luck in person. If we can get the conference evacuated or at least suspend letting people in, that's a start. Mother, see if you can get access to DWTC's security camera feed. And I also want you to generate a list of probable targets. There have to be some serious defense industry VIPs in attendance today. Is there a keynote address they might be targeting? Or are they going for mass carnage? We need to prioritize our search."

"Check," Riker said.

"Copy all," Watts said.

Trip braked and pointed. Chunk's gaze went to the spot and he spied the Range Rover parked nose out, the front two seats vacant.

"We just found Bijan's Range Rover parked in the garage," Chunk said while gesturing for Trip to loop around behind it. "It appears to be empty, but we're going to confirm."

"Be careful, Alpha One," Watts said. "It could be rigged with explosives."

"Copy," Chunk said and knew she was right. He guessed the odds of being blown up in the next few seconds at a stomach-churning 50/50.

If Riker were here, I wouldn't be worried, he thought with a pitying sideways glance at Trip, *but there's only one lucky SOB on every SEAL team.*

Reaching the back side of the garage, Chunk slipped out of the Z71 with his Sig P365 SAS clutched in his right hand. Crouching low, he advanced on the Range Rover from the back. Its interior cabin was impossible to see into thanks to the dark tint on three sides. As he scanned through the Sig's FT bullseye sight, he swallowed down the distracting and dreadful feeling that this op might finally be the one he didn't get to walk away from. He reached out a hand for the handle . . .

CHAPTER 34

NOVOTEL WORLD TRADE CENTRE HOTEL PARKING GARAGE
AL MUSTAQBAL STREET 9622
DUBAI, UNITED ARAB EMIRATES

The Range Rover did not explode and rifle fire did not blow out the SUV's windows and cut him down, but he still felt the tension of the unknown, that feeling that his head might yet be in the crosshairs of some fighter's scope. He preferred a straight-up fight, guns on guns, to this sneaking around.

Chunk completed his sweep around the Range Rover and confirmed it to be unoccupied.

"Clear," he said and slipped his Sig into his waistband. "It's still possible they rigged this thing to blow, but I don't see any visible payload."

"Check," Trip said.

Chunk pointed to the set of double doors leading from the garage into the hotel. "Park our ride over there along the wall."

"Roger that."

As Trip drove the SUV around, Chunk pulled a three-inch

Kershaw folder from his pocket. He flicked the blade open with his thumb and then methodically slashed all four of the Rover's tires, relieving Asadi Bijan and his crew of one of their getaway vehicles.

Assuming, that is, they're not planning on martyring themselves . . .

"Alpha One, this is Two . . ." Riker's voice said in Chunk's ear. "We're at the security entrance at the convention center's main gate. I have our badges."

"Did you brief them on the threat?" he said, jogging to meet up with Trip at the doors.

"We did."

"And?"

"They assured us that they have everything under control," Riker came back.

"Are they going to evacuate the expo?"

"Doesn't look that way, boss."

"Shit. All right, we're en route to you," he said, striding shoulder to shoulder with Trip as they made their way through the hotel that abutted the DWTC complex.

Minutes later he and Trip were badged and through security and standing with Riker and Saw. His objective now was narrowing the search and to do that effectively, he needed the on-site security personnel's help. The dude he was talking to now, must have been the same one who'd hung up on Watts because even Chunk—who prided himself on having a ridiculously long fuse—was on the verge of losing his cool.

" . . . you must put yourself in my shoes," the security chief whose name tag read Saleh was saying. "Your credentials were approved yesterday, but I don't know you. And since you won't tell me which American counterterrorism department you work for, it makes it difficult for me to put trust in your words.

I understand that you believe there is an imminent threat, and I am not actively impeding your investigation, which I could easily do. I have let you into the DWTC with weapons and the freedom to patrol the entire complex. But you must understand, your report is the only source of information on this threat. I have no confirming evidence from my organization, from Interpol, or the Dubai Police Force. Imagine if I showed up at your place of work claiming a terrorism threat but not sharing my true identity or all the details I know. You would be skeptical, would you not?"

"I ran a search on this guy, Saleh," Watts said in Chunk's ear. "He's Jordanian, former General Intelligence Directorate. Undoubtedly, he left for a bigger paycheck than he could make there. Jordanians are actively recruited throughout the Middle East in the private sector."

"Saleh is a Jordanian surname, is it not?" Chunk said, using Watts's timely data dump to try a different approach with this guy.

A look of surprise momentarily washed over the man's face. "It is."

"And from the way you talk and carry yourself, I wouldn't be surprised if you're former GID?"

"And what if I was?"

Chunk met Saleh's frown with an easy smile. Lowering his voice, he said, "I know what you're thinking, Saleh. You're just trying to do your job when a group of American assholes shows up out of nowhere, squawking about a terrorist threat without giving you the bare minimum intelligence you need to neutralize that threat. Believe me, I get it—this conference is huge. It's the first time all the Western defense contractors have attended and presented at a single event in the Middle East. If you shut it down on the opening day over a false alarm, you'll be fired and word will spread and your reputation in this business will be ruined."

Saleh nodded.

"But you also know how this game is played," Chunk continued. "Me and my guys, we're not actually here. There's no paper trail. If we stop this attack, you're the guy who's going to get the credit. If we fail, you're the guy who's going to take the blame. Six hours from now, no matter the outcome, we'll be gone. But you . . . you'll still be here. So, what I'm asking you to do is to take off your DWTC security chief hat and pull out your old dusty GID hat and put that on. I have a feeling you've worked with American covert operators before. You know how the game is played. I promise, we're not here to fuck you. Let's work together, save a bunch of lives, and you can go home to your family tonight a hero."

Saleh held Chunk's gaze for what felt like an eternity, but Chunk didn't break eye contact. Finally, the Jordanian spoke. "Okay, what do you want?"

"First and foremost, we need eyes. Can you share access to your CCTV security feeds with my team?"

"I am willing to do this," Saleh said.

"We need remote access," Watts said in Chunk's ear.

"Great, my IT folks will need remote access to your system. Let me put them in touch with—" But Saleh cut him off.

"No remote access. I cannot risk potentially compromising our network. I will permit one person in our control room. I'm sorry, but this is your only option." His voice was a hard line.

"I'll take the sky bridge over from the Fairmont," Yi said on comms. "If I run, I can be there in ten minutes or less. My NOC name is Suzy Bae."

Chunk nodded at Saleh. "Okay, my colleague Ms. Bae will be that person. She's en route as we speak. In the meantime, we're going to start our sweep. We need a map and a schedule of events."

Saleh snapped his fingers at one of his men and rattled off an order in Arabic. The man bolted to an information kiosk and returned with four Expo program guides.

"Here," Saleh said, pointing to a page in the guide Chunk held. "This is opening day. The conference kicks off with a coffee-and-pastries meet and greet event. The twelve anchor exhibitors are hosting a continental breakfast service in Concourse Two. That runs from 0730 to 0900. At 0900, the keynote address is being given by the CEO of Lockheed Martin in Sheikh Rashid Hall."

Chunk glanced at the color-coded map in his hand and then looked left down the massive, three-story atrium in front of him. "We're looking at Concourse Two, aren't we?"

"Yes," Saleh replied.

"And that's Sheikh Rashid Hall?" Chunk said, pointing to the imposing, curved structure that stuck out into the middle of the atrium.

"Correct. It is the main auditorium."

"What a friggin' nightmare," Chunk murmured to himself as he scanned the heart of the convention center, with the dozen exhibitor breakfast booths and a second-story balcony opposite the entrance to the auditorium. As he surveyed the layout, the tactician in him put on his bad-guy hat. He'd faced off against so many clever, ruthless terrorists over the years that he well understood how they thought. He had no trouble contemplating the machinations of murder and mayhem . . . hell, it was what the US government paid him to do. He looked back down at the map and then scanned the right-hand side of the concourse, opposite the hall. He pointed at a row of open doors under the cantilevered second-story balcony. "Exhibit Halls Six, Seven, and Eight are through those doors?"

"Yes, these exhibit halls are the premium booth floor space due to their proximity to the convention center entrance and the main auditorium," Saleh said.

"And what about these booths out here in the atrium? I see signs for British Aero, Boeing, Lockheed Martin, General Dynamic . . . They're not the exhibit booths for the twelve anchor vendors?"

"No," Saleh said. "These are like pop-up cafés. Very informal, a place to relax and make connections. All of these vendors have their main booths inside Halls Six, Seven, and Eight. Most are very big, with two stories and lounge areas and office rooms."

"Are the three halls connected or separate spaces?"

"They can be partitioned or open to create one large exhibition hall. It depends on the size of the conference and the nature of the event. Sometimes we have multiple conferences at the same time."

"And for this conference?"

"The partitions are removed. This conference is very large—all of DWTC has been reserved."

Chunk looked at Saw, who was studying the second-story balcony, undoubtedly looking for possible sniper hides. "What do you think?" he said.

Saw frowned. "It's a kill box. Sorta like shooting fish in a barrel. If I was them, I'd wait until fifteen minutes before the keynote. Everybody will be out here, getting their last-minute coffee and donut before heading into the conference hall."

Chunk slow-nodded, imagining the scenario Saw had just painted in his mind. "Yeah . . . it would be a bloodbath. Or maybe they intend to target the keynote, once everyone is seated inside and the doors are closed. How many people does the auditorium hold?"

"We have it configured with four thousand seats. Twenty-five hundred tiered and fifteen hundred on the flat," Saleh said, his complexion starting to ashen as Chunk and Saw's war-gaming began to sink in.

Chunk checked his watch and then swiped his tongue back and forth between his lower lip and gum and said, "It's 0723. The doors open in seven minutes and it's going to start to get crowded. We know these guys are dressed as caterers and waitstaff and that the breakfast event somehow factors in. We need to find them and take them out of play before they get into position. Four, I want you guys to sweep the kitchen and catering spaces with Saleh's guys. We'll sweep Concourse Two and the auditorium. Depending on what we find, we'll regroup and sweep Halls Six, Seven, Eight."

"Do you need radios?" Saleh asked.

Chunk tapped his right ear. "No. We have microearbuds on a secure, cellular channel."

"You have me concerned now. I want to augment your search team. I'm going to put six of my people on a sweep," the Jordanian said and then stuck out his hand to Chunk. "Also, I will notify the Dubai Police Force, just in case. Let's work together, okay?"

Chunk clasped the former GID man's hand. "Now we're talking, brother. Let's find these assholes before they can get a single shot off."

CHAPTER 35

SECOND-FLOOR ATRIUM

DUBAI WORLD TRADE CENTRE INTERNATIONAL CONVENTION

    & EXHIBITION CENTRE

TRADE CENTRE 2

DUBAI, UNITED ARAB EMIRATES

0802 LOCAL TIME

It's times like this I wish I had X-ray vision, Chunk thought as he weaved his way through the atrium, looking for terrorists in disguise.

And was bulletproof . . .

And could fly . . .

Unfortunately, I'm not Superman . . . just a SEAL.

He blew air through his teeth as he performed a threat assessment the old-fashioned, non-superhero way—scanning the crowd with unaugmented eyes for people who looked nervous, shady, or suspicious.

"Alpha One, this is Yankee," Yi said in his ear, resurrecting her letter call sign from earlier, now that Watts alone was Mother. "I'm with Officer Saleh in the control room, which they call *Central*. They've got good eyes."

"Copy, Yankee," he said. "We need to go back into the

recorded surveillance and look for the two catering vans that we lost in the loading area. If you can see where they pulled in, then we can try to better ID the shooters on film when they climbed out of the vans."

"Roger, One," Yi came back. "Saleh says they do have limited surveillance of that area. It's called the Marshalling Yard. We're on it."

"Ask him if they have surveillance of the Novotel hotel parking garage. That's where Bijan's Range Rover parked. There were four warm bodies in that vehicle we need to track."

He heard Yi relay his question and Saleh answer her in the background: "Unfortunately, the answer is no. The hotel has its own security."

"Did you catch that?" Yi said.

"Roger. Then we need to get somebody over to the hotel security center and try to pull their footage. Because maybe the three shooters with Bijan are not dressed as catering staff. If that's the case, they're going to be even harder to find. You need to move on that ASAFP," he said.

"Copy all," Yi came back.

Chunk checked his watch: 0805. The conference had been open for over thirty minutes and they'd not ID'd a single terrorist. His heart rate ticked up a notch as he felt their time cushion slipping away while the atrium filled with civilians. "Four, sitrep?"

"We're walking the service areas behind the exhibit halls and asking everyone about Hassan's Delight Catering," Saw came back. "Getting a bunch of funny looks, but no hits yet. No joy on finding the two catering vans either."

"Check," he growled, his irritation rising.

"One, Mother," Watts said in his ear. "This isn't working. I think you need to get more invasive."

"You just read my mind, Mother," he came back. Then, to Yi in DWTC Central, he said, "Yankee, One—tell Saleh we're running out of time. We need to step things up. Ask him to set up a security frisk station inside Sheikh Maktoum Hall. It's the smaller auditorium next to the main one. Nothing is going on inside there that I can see."

"Copy," Yi came back. "What's the purpose?"

"I want to start marching anybody in a waiter or catering uniform in there for a full-body pat down. If they pass, they get a colored sticker on their name tag. It's the only way we're going to find them," Chunk said.

"Roger that," Yi said. "Standby."

"Good call, One," Watts said. "Mother concurs."

"One, Yankee—you've got the green light," Yi said. "Saleh is going to make it happen personally. Start bringing folks over now and he'll meet you there with three staff."

"Hooyah, Yankee," he said. "Three, Four, did you catch all that?"

"Copied all," Riker came back. "You want us to do the same?"

"The loading docks and service areas are too far away. You'll waste too much time escorting people there and back. Execute locally."

"Stop and frisk?"

"Exactly."

"Roger that," Riker said, his voice brimming with renewed enthusiasm. "This is going to be fun."

It's the little things, Chunk thought as he fixed his gaze on a twentysomething Arab in a catering uniform pushing a cart with pastries from station to station. "Two, One—have you got visual on me?"

"Check," Trip came back from his position in the atrium.

"Watch all the servers closely in the area around me when I execute this first inspection grab. If any of them react nervously or try to exit, intercept and detain."

"Copy that, One."

Chunk approached the server with the pastry cart and loudly said, "Excuse me, sir, I'm with conference security. I need you to come with me for a brief safety inspection."

"But I am not understanding. I need to deliver this pastries," the man protested.

"Bring your cart. It will only take a minute." Chunk grabbed the caterer by the upper arm and gave it a hard, flesh-compressing squeeze. "This way."

As he led the caterer toward Maktoum Hall, he scanned the faces of the other servers who'd been within earshot of the encounter. Several of them were eyeing him warily now, but none were—

"We got a runner," Trip said, interrupting his scan.

Chunk stopped midstride and looked over his shoulder. He spied Trip first, then followed the SEAL's gaze to a man in a server's uniform exiting the atrium at a brisk pace for the double doors leading to Hall Seven. A second before the man disappeared from view, Chunk saw him raising a mobile phone to his ear. "He's got a phone," Chunk said.

"Check," Trip said, running in pursuit.

"We just lost power in Security Central," Yi said in Chunk's ear. "All the camera feeds went dark."

"Shit, it's happening," Chunk said and whirled toward the sound of footsteps pounding toward him.

"Mr. Black!" Saleh called the impromptu NOC Chunk had given as he ran toward him with three uniformed DWTC guards.

"Security Central just lost power," Chunk said.

"I know," the security chief said and, then in Arabic, ordered his two subordinates to take the caterer in Chunk's custody to be frisked. "Mr. Black, follow me."

Chunk handed over the caterer to the two DWTC guards and jogged after Saleh who was moving quickly through the crowd. "Where are we going?"

"To the circuit breaker room," Saleh said.

"I need to be here, in the atrium. We're about to be outgunned."

"I got a radio report of a man matching the photograph your Ms. Bae provided of Asadi Bijan," Saleh explained, glancing with knowing eyes as they ran, stride for stride, beside each other. "He was seen entering the circuit breaker room and my man pursued, but now my man is not answering his radio."

"Check," Chunk said, but his mind was torn between the opportunity to nab Bijan and being on the scene where he sensed an attack was imminent.

I should have heard from Trip by now.

"Two, Mother—sitrep?" Watts queried, dialed in like nobody's business.

Trip didn't answer.

Instead, a single gunshot echoed behind Chunk, followed by screams, then by controlled, repeated rifle fire.

CHAPTER 36

Saw was patting down a man dressed in a server's uniform when he heard suppressed gunfire in the exhibition hall behind him. He turned his head and listened. The cadence, the shot interval, the distinctive muted crack of a suppressed supersonic round . . .

There's a sniper in the building.

"One, we have a sniper in the exhibition hall," Saw said, reporting the bad news to Chunk. "Four will pursue and neutralize."

It was a bold claim—considering he didn't have a rifle—but he was the team sniper which made this both his specialty and his responsibility.

"Sniper targeting the British Aero booth in Hall Seven," Trip reported. "I see three bodies down, covering."

Saw sprinted out of the vendor prep area at the back of

the exhibition hall and into the chaos—people were screaming and running mindlessly in every direction, knocking into each other, and toppling booth signage and furniture.

"Yankee, I need a long gun," Saw shouted over the pandemonium. "Can you get me one?"

"Saleh left Central Command," Yi came back, "but I can try . . ."

"Check," he said but knew by the time she came through it would be too late.

Three more sniper rounds echoed. The short but precise firing interval told him two things: one, the shooter was using a semiautomatic rifle, and two, he had an excellent level of proficiency. Saw scanned in the direction he perceived gunfire originating, looking for the sniper's hide. Most of the booths didn't offer any height advantage and only a handful had two levels, which still didn't make them effective hides. This realization drew his eyes overhead where exposed ventilation ducts, trusses, cable trays, and an electrical conduit—all painted matching white—zigzagged this way and that. His gaze swept across the ceiling looking for something, when he spied a catwalk which he traced to a six-sided hanging structure with large flat-screen displays playing a flashy promotional video, ironically featuring British Aero products. While not as massive as the Jumbotrons at indoor sports arenas, the design principle was the same, and this hexagonal display was definitely large enough for a person to hide inside.

That has to be it.

"Four, Mother—I have another long gun option for you," Watts said in his ear. "What is your current position?"

"Back end of Exhibition Hall Seven, looking in the direction of Concourse Two," he said.

"Sig Sauer has a booth in Hall Six, just like every major defense company. One of our Sig reps, Jason Wright, is on the attendee list. I just called his mobile and he's sheltering in place and said he will pull an unsterilized Cross 6.5 Creedmoor from the lock case for you," she came back. "But you've gotta go to him."

"Smart thinking, Mother," he said and turned right. "Guide me."

"Booth 1024 in the middle front third of Hall Six," she said.

"Check," he said and set off in a sprint through the mayhem, like a running back bumping and weaving his way out of a crowded backfield.

Normally, given his size and bulk, he took great care navigating crowds but not now. Every second that sniper was allowed to work meant another dead body on the floor, so he plowed through the sea of people like a battering ram, knocking them out of his way and bowling some over. In his ear, Watts guided him to the Sig booth almost as if she had a visual on his position, calling out booth numbers and names like signposts for him to navigate from. When he reached the Sig booth, he scanned for the rep he'd met several times back in Tampa.

"Saw! Over here," Jason called from where he was crouching beside a large metal display cabinet.

Saw quickstepped to the Sig rep's side in a low combat crouch.

"What the fuck is happening?" Jason said.

"Multiple active shooters. They're dressed as catering—"

An explosion cut him off, followed by a wave of screams.

"Was that a grenade?" the rep asked, fresh worry in his eyes.

"Yes, whatcha got for me?"

Jason flipped open the rifle case resting on the floor

between them, revealing a Cross, bolt-action, 6.5 Creedmoor variety fitted with a Tango6 optics package and a Sig suppressor. The weapon appeared immaculate and already had a magazine installed.

Saw grimaced.

"What?" Jason asked.

"Has this weapon been fired and sighted, or is it fresh out of the box?"

The Sig man clasped a hand on Saw's shoulder. "You know I wouldn't do that to you, bro. It's new but I had one of our Sig ambassadors, Eli Crane, spend the day with it on the range. It's doped up and dialed in to a gnat's ass."

Saw nodded and picked up the rifle. In another circumstance, he'd have made a joke about the SEAL-turned-entrepreneur's skills with a long gun, but Eli Crane was a badass frogman and if he'd doped this gun up, it was good to go. Facing off against an enemy sniper was already a harrowing proposition but doing it with a virgin weapon was damn near suicide. His was a profession where precision ruled the day, and he did not have time to make dozens of calibrations in the fight.

Gunfire echoed in the hall to Saw's left—pistol rounds, not sniper rifle fire this time.

"Multiple tangos engaging civilians in Hall Seven," said Trip's voice on the comms circuit. "Alpha Two just dropped the shithead who threw the grenade."

"Watch yourself," came Riker's reply. "We've got a sniper in the room . . ."

"Shooter is in the Jumbotron," Saw said, providing tactical guidance to the team. "Cover accordingly."

"Check," came the replies from Riker and Trip on top of each other.

Jason handed Saw a polymer AICS magazine. "There's a

round in the chamber and five in the mag and here's a spare. Wish I could give you more, but that's all I've got."

"Thanks, Jason, you're a lifesaver."

"Actually, the hero stuff's your job . . . I'm just the *backpack* guy," Wright said.

Saw smiled, catching the *Jumanji* reference but his brain had already moved on to work the problem. His gaze swept across the exhibition hall in the direction of the suspended digital hexagon-shaped display. If he'd been holding an M4 with a thirty-round magazine, he'd probably just unload everything into it right now and hope for several blind hits. But to try that with the bolt-action rifle was a death wish. The sniper would triangulate on Saw's position on the floor and drop him before he had time to change mags, maybe sooner. No, his best chance was to get on elevation and sight through the gaps.

He looked back to Jason and then up at the catwalk running transverse across the exhibition hall. "You wouldn't know how to get up there by any chance?"

"No, but he might." Jason pointed to an Arab dude dressed in black coveralls cowering under a table at the back of the Sig booth. "He's a DWTC facilities guy. Was working on fixing our lighting when the shooting started."

"Thanks, bro," Saw said and gave him a nod of gratitude. "Now you should probably get your ass out of here."

"Godspeed, frogman."

Saw sprinted over to the facilities technician under the table. "Do you speak English?"

"Yes," the man said, his terror-stricken gaze fixated on Saw's weapon.

"Listen to me," Saw said, grabbing the man by the upper arm and squeezing to get his full attention. "How do I get up to that catwalk?"

"You want to go up there?" the man said, confusion plain on his face.

"Yes, there is a sniper hiding inside that thing." He pointed to the mini Jumbotron. "I need to take him out."

"Not a good idea. The catwalk will shake. The person shooting will feel you coming," the man said, seeming to find some courage now that Saw had given him a task. "I have a better idea. Follow me."

Saw nodded and followed the maintenance technician as he jumped to his feet and ran toward the front of the exhibition hall in the direction of Concourse Two. Saw fell in behind the tech, in a combat crouch sighting over his rifle, scanning for threats as he moved. As they passed the second to last row of booths, commotion on Saw's left drew his attention. He swiveled ninety degrees and saw an Arab man wielding two large knives slashing and stabbing at fleeing conference-goers. Saw paused and sighted. Placing the reticle on the terrorist's forehead, he squeezed the trigger. The bullet found its target a couple of centimeters left of the mark. He made a mental note of this as the jihadi fell. Reflexively, he cycled the bolt handle to eject the spent cartridge case and chamber a new round as he scanned for a second target. At the same time, his SEAL mental stopwatch was counting down. The sniper would have heard his round, so he had three seconds to shoot and move. Finding no new targets, he swiveled and chased after the maintenance tech who was just disappearing out of the exhibition hall into the Concourse Two atrium.

Saw dropped into a combat crouch and hustled after the smaller man.

Seconds later he exited the hall and spun left, looking for his guide.

"This way, this way," the man shouted and waved for Saw to follow.

A second grenade explosion rocked the facility, this time inside the Concourse Two atrium. Saw reflexively hit the deck as shrapnel flew in all directions—cutting down a dozen innocents and breaking glass in multiple places. Saw looked up, relieved to see his guide was still alive.

"Hurry, hurry, we need to go," the man said, sprinting up a flight of stairs.

Saw popped to his feet and took the stairs two at a time.

"There is a control room for the screens," the man said in breathless pants as they ran along the balcony overlooking the atrium. "It looks into the exhibit halls."

Unable to help himself, Saw scanned the expansive atrium lobby below as they ran, looking for threats. His mind was in full targeting-computer mode, and his vision locked on one body in the crowd not moving like the others. "Hang on a second," he said and abruptly stopped to swing his muzzle over the railing.

Sight . . .

Exhale . . .

Trigger squeeze.

The round exploded the terrorist's head just as he was pulling a second grenade from a pocket. Saw clicked in a quick correction on the scope, as this bullet had also skewed a hair left, then he backpedaled, moving position to be harder to kill. The maintenance technician muttered something in Arabic and then attempted to unlock a security door with shaking fingers. Seeing the man was trembling so badly he couldn't get the key into the lock, Saw stepped up, took the keys, and unlocked the door for him.

"Thank you," the man said and ushered Saw into the room then locked the door behind them. "This is it, the control room."

Saw scanned the space, which reminded him of a sound

booth at a recording studio. His gaze quickly went to the plate glass window that looked out over the giant exhibit hall below. Fifty feet away, at eye level, hung the mini Jumbotron.

Instinctively, he took a knee and got low.

"Is this two-way glass?" he asked.

"Two-way glass . . . I don't understand," the man said, mimicking Saw and dropping into a crouch.

"Can the people see into this room from outside?"

"No, no, it is a mirror on the outside," the tech said, shaking his head.

"Can you open the window or is it a fixed pane?"

"It does not open."

"Okay," Saw said, popping back to his feet and quickly setting up his nest.

His rifle didn't have a tripod, so he flipped a computer monitor onto its face on the control desk so that the support bracket faced up. With methodical efficiency, he ejected the spent case, chambered a fresh round, and pulled the spare magazine from his pocket, setting it on the desk. Next, he took a knee, rested the rifle's polymer handguard on the monitor bracket, and sighted out the window at the mini Jumbotron. Because of its hexagonal design, the shooter had six vertical firing slots—one at each of the junctions between the six giant flat-screens. He estimated the gap between the screens at six inches, which meant that the sniper would have at least a twenty-to-thirty-degree field of fire from each corner. Limiting, yes, but still plenty of coverage to wreak havoc. He scanned the first vertical gap, which was oriented to face directly at the control room window.

"Four is God," he reported on the comms channel.

"Copy, God," Riker's voice came back. "The sniper is still working the room. He's suppressed and using good muzzle discipline. I don't know which of those slots he's shooting from."

"Check," Saw said, scanning for the shooter and not seeing anything. After several seconds, he cursed under his breath.

"What is wrong?" the tech asked.

"There's no lighting inside the structure. It's completely dark behind those TV panels and I can't see shit. Have you been inside that thing by chance?"

"Yes, one time."

"Describe it to me," he said, sweeping his targeting reticle vertically along the gap, looking for anything resembling a human form in the shadow.

"There is a platform for standing near the bottom, to give access to all the cables on the back of the displays."

"Is it big enough to lay down on your stomach?"

"Not really, and there is a metal ladder in the middle."

"I'm trying to imagine the body position of the sniper. Is he prone, sitting, kneeling, or standing to take his shots? Do you understand?"

"Yes, I understand . . . but I have never shot a gun. I don't know."

"What's your name?" Saw said, his eye still on the scope.

"Kaaf," the tech said.

"Listen to me, Kaaf. The first round I fire is going to break this window. That's going to alert the sniper to my presence. My second shot has to hit because it's probably the only one I'm going to get. What is the elevation of the maintenance platform inside that structure?"

"Probably one-half meter above the bottom," Kaaf said.

Saw imagined himself inside the mini Jumbotron—standing on a platform with an interfering ladder in the middle, trying to manipulate a long gun and find a firing stance that allowed him to achieve the necessary down angles to hit targets below. As he did, his own words came back to him from earlier: *Like shooting fish in a barrel . . .*

"He's standing," he murmured, then turned to Kaaf. "Can we control the lights in the exhibition hall from in here?"

"Yes," Kaaf said.

"Do you know how to do that?"

Kaaf shook his head. "I'm only a maintenance technician."

"We need to figure this out, Kaaf, together and quickly," he said and started scanning the control room panels.

"Okay," Kaaf said and then, just as Saw suspected, knew a little more than he let on. "I think this is the main lighting panel."

Saw stepped to Kaaf's side and scanned the myriad buttons which were engraved with English labels and had Arabic printed stickers next to most placards. A joystick labeled *Spotlight* caught his eye.

"Where is this spotlight physically located?" he asked.

"It is in the front of Hall Seven. Outside this window in the ceiling about ten meters back. Sometimes they set up a stage at the front of the hall for music or awards. They use the spotlight for this."

"God, if you're going to do something about that sniper, do it quick," Riker said in his ear. "It's a bloodbath down there."

"On it," Saw said, then looked at Kaaf. "Can we turn the spotlight the other way? Aim it at the Jumbotron display where the sniper is?"

Kaaf nodded, his expression flickering with hope. "Yes, yes, I think so."

"Okay, listen to me very carefully," Saw said as a plan took shape in his mind. "Here's what we're going to do . . ."

CHAPTER 37

Chunk ran stride for stride with Security Chief Saleh toward the electrical room while chaos erupted behind him. Guilt wracked his brain with each footfall as the voice inside his head chastised him for running "away from the fight," but if he caught Bijan it would be worth it.

Or would it?

How many lives lost today could be justified by stopping future attacks planned by Bijan? Were ten lives lost today worth it if his choice potentially saved twenty tomorrow? *Probably*. What about a hundred? *Certainly*. But this fuzzy logic assumed that Asadi Bijan, not Qasim Nadar, was the mastermind behind today's attack. Maybe Asadi Bijan was the real Hamza al-Saud, not Qasim Nadar.

What if they'd been wrong about Nadar?

"Does anyone have eyes on Nadar?" Chunk queried the team.

"Negative," Riker came back.

"One, Yankee—I had Nadar at the British Aero booth in Hall Seven before we lost power," Yi reported.

"Copy, Yankee. We can't let him leave the complex."

"Understood," Riker came back, answering for all.

Saleh halted beside the body of a security guard—throat slit and lying in a puddle of blood—on the tile floor beside a door marked Electrical Service.

An Arab man dressed in a white thobe and wearing a red-and-white-checkered kaffiyeh with a black iqal shouted at them in Arabic.

"He says he saw two men run that way," Saleh said and pointed toward several pairs of revolving doors twenty feet away.

"Where does that exit lead?"

"To a courtyard with cafés and a drop-off roundabout for the Trade Center Apartments," Saleh said.

Pistol in hand, Chunk took off toward the exit in a full sprint. "Mother I need eyes."

"On it," Watts said. "Got them—two men fleeing down a long alley between two massive rectangular buildings. When you exit the exhibition gate, bear right and follow the curved facade of the building on your right. Then take the first right."

"Check," he said, arms pumping and legs churning ferociously.

He was through the revolving door and into the courtyard seconds later, sprinting along the curved glass facade of a building matching Watts's description. He heard footsteps and panting behind him as Saleh tried to keep pace.

"Target just slowed to a walk," Watts said. "Probably trying not to draw attention, but I have good eyes. The alley is a thousand feet long. They're two hundred feet in. You can still catch them, One."

Chunk didn't reply, his mind slipping into a state of hyperfocus. He dug deep and found an extra gear, sprinting like an Olympian toward the finish. No way in hell was he going to let that bastard get away. He rounded the corner into the alley and scanned for his target. The alley wasn't really an *alley*, more like a narrow promenade between exhibition halls. Decorative planters lined both sides of the walkway and a series of metal awnings—shade relief from the desert sun—created a checkered pattern of light and dark down the corridor. He spied Bijan and a male accomplice walking north, two hundred feet ahead just like Watts had said.

Gaze fixed on his targets, Chunk closed the gap rapidly, ready to shoot at a second's notice. When he was thirty yards away, Bijan turned and they made eye contact.

Everything happened in a blur . . .

Bijan took cover behind a ceramic planter while his companion whirled and pulled a machine pistol from inside his suit coat. Chunk squeezed off three rounds from his compact Sig as he dove behind a planter on his right. His rounds skewed wide, while the enemy shooter sprayed bullets in his direction, shattering the plate glass window beside Chunk. A heartbeat later, the urn-shaped planter in front of him exploded. The ornamental shrub it contained toppled onto his back as the planter collapsed under its own weight, spilling sandy soil out in all directions. His cover gone, Chunk crabbed forward in a low crouch squeezing off three more rounds at the shooter who was dodging and shooting with surprising skill.

"I'm hit!" Saleh cried somewhere behind him, but Chunk knew better than to take his eyes off his target.

Four rounds left, the voice in his head reminded him, as

the little Sig held ten rounds—one in the pipe and nine in the magazine.

Trigger squeeze, trigger squeeze . . .

At least one of the bullets found its mark because the shooter's torso spasmed and he stopped firing. Chunk shifted his green FT bullseye sight to the shooter's forehead as the man brought his weapon back up.

Trigger squeeze, trigger squeeze.

The jihadist's head snapped back and he dropped like felled timber. In Chunk's peripheral vision, he saw a blurry shadow careening toward his right ear. He ducked and dodged left simultaneously. When he turned to face his opponent, he saw that he'd narrowly avoided being stabbed in the side of the neck by the polished blade in the terrorist's left hand. They locked eyes and recognition flashed in Bijan's eyes.

"I knew last night that you and Adrienne were agents," the terrorist said with a confident, superior tone. "You took my picture, but I took your pictures too . . . We know who you are. We know who all of you are, and your blood will run in the streets."

Chunk didn't reply to the terrorist's bravado, but his mind went to CJ and the internet post about his death. These assholes were targeting the Teams directly now, somehow. But that was for later. That was for Watts. This chapter was over, and perhaps that would close the entire book. He didn't bother turning his gun on the terrorist—his magazine was empty and they both knew it. Instead, he did something unexpected— threw the compact pistol at his assailant's face. His aim was true, and the Sig bounced off Bijan's forehead, stunning him for an instant.

Chunk capitalized on the moment. He catapulted himself forward, like a defensive lineman off the snap, and drove his right shoulder into Bijan's chest, tackling the man. Most of Chunk's two hundred and ten pounds of bulk slammed down on top of the terrorist, driving the air from the terrorist's lungs. The knife popped out of Bijan's grip and clattered on the pavement beside them. Chunk pressed up to his knees and looked down at the gasping terrorist.

"You're coming with me," Chunk said and then punched Bijan in the nose. He felt and heard the man's nose flatten and break under his knuckles. Blood exploded from both nostrils and poured over the jihadist's upper lip and into his mouth, instantly turning Bijan's gleaming white teeth a greasy red.

Chunk wanted to punch him again, to smash that stupid smile off the terrorist's face, but the sound of gunfire in his earbud stayed his fist. "Is there a bomb inside the exhibition hall?" he growled, his eyes burning into the other man like lasers.

Finally catching his breath, Bijan spat blood onto Chunk's shirt and said, "Your days are numbered. We know where you live."

"What did you say?"

With the speed of a serpent strike, the terrorist snatched the knife and drove it home. Chunk moved to block, but he missed . . . He missed because *his* jugular was not the target.

Instead, Bijan slit his own throat.

"No!" he shouted, wresting the blade from the terrorist's hand and chucking it thirty feet down the promenade.

"*Ilal liqaa*,*" Bijan said, his Arabic words little more than a gurgle.

Until we meet again . . .

Chunk looked down at the self-inflicted wound and knew there was nothing he could do to save the man. Cursing, he pressed to his feet and scanned the ground for his Sig. He found it five feet away, picked it up, and then trotted over to where Security Chief Saleh was lying unmoving and sprawled on the concrete.

"God, if you're going to do something about that sniper, do it quick," he heard Riker say in his ear on the open comms channel. "It's a bloodbath down here."

I gotta get back in there, Chunk told himself as he knelt beside the Jordanian whose eyes were unmoving and glassy. "Saleh? Can you hear me?" he said, checking for a pulse on the man's neck.

"Damn," he murmured, finding none.

With renewed fire in his belly, he got to his feet, radioed in the body count in the alley, and took off in a sprint toward the exhibition gate to rejoin the fight.

CHAPTER 38

Saw looked at Kaaf, searching for any signs of confusion or doubt on the man's face. He could not pull this off alone and if the maintenance technician lost his nerve, froze, or chickened out then they were screwed.

"You understand the plan?"

"Yes, yes," Kaaf said, crouching behind the lighting control panel. "I turn off the lights, you shoot out the window, then I turn on the spotlight."

"Promise you're not going to freeze or panic on me, Kaaf."

"Do not worry. I can do this," the Arab said and his voice did not waver.

Saw nodded and took his place behind the Cross 6.5. He settled in against the adjustable cheek weld on top of the buttstock and slipped his right index finger onto the two-stage match trigger. Next, he positioned his targeting reticle four feet above the base of the mini Jumbotron and dead center in the vertical slot between the right and left angled TV panels. With his left hand, he smoothly raised his Sig P365 pistol until the muzzle was parallel to the rifle barrel and pointing at the control room plate glass window which he would blow out before firing his rifle.

"Nutcracker, God—stand by to go dark," he said, prepping his teammates below for lights out. At the same time, he squeezed his eyelids shut to give his eyes a head start.

"Copy," Riker came back.

"In three . . . two . . . one . . . Kill the lights."

Kaaf rapidly flipped nine toggle switches, turning off all the overhead lights in Halls Six, Seven, and Eight. The cavernous exhibition space went dark, and Saw unloaded with his pistol on the window. It took five 9 mm rounds for the stout glass to lose enough structural integrity to shatter and collapse under its own weight.

He set the pistol down, opened his eyes, and placed his left elbow into a stabilizing position on the desktop.

"Spotlight," he ordered as he brought his left hand into that old familiar tuck against his chest and readied himself for the duel to come.

Kaaf illuminated the spotlight. The alignment was off, the yellow beam cutting a swath through the darkness below and to the right of target. Saw had expected this, however. Kaaf had tried to position the head in advance as best he could, but they were not so lucky as to nail it out of the gate.

"I fix it," Kaaf said and started working the joystick.

Saw decided not to wait. The light scatter from the beam provided enough illumination that he could see the dark vertical gap between the screens. His aim had drifted while firing the pistol and he brought the crosshairs back to center . . .

Exhale.

Trigger squeeze.

With lightning speed, he released the rifle grip, grabbed the bolt handle, and indexed a fresh cartridge. A heartbeat later, he put a second round through the gap at a lower elevation than the first. A blinding light settled into his scope's field of view as Kaaf dialed in the spotlight and focused it on the mini Jumbotron. Saw squinted as his pupils contracted to shift from processing super dim to super bright light and chambered the last cartridge from his magazine.

Critical details came into focus as his vision adapted.

A cylindrical shape moving in the shadowy gap between the TV panels.

The enemy sniper's suppressor coming up . . .

A glint of light from inside the slot: the spotlight reflecting off the front lens off his opponent's optical scope.

In a sniper dual, any number of variables in any number of combinations could tip the scales to determine the winner. Experience, distance, position, covering geometry, lighting, weapon characteristics, optics, spotting skills, the element of surprise . . . these things all mattered. But if there was one commodity Saw would trade for all others, it was time.

Time was the advantage he would never cede.

And right now, he had a one-second lead.

He squeezed the trigger and the Cross kicked into his shoulder. The 6.5 Creedmoor round sailed across the convention hall at nearly three thousand feet per second. He'd assumed the sniper was a right-handed shooter and placed the round just to the right of the glint off his opponent's scope which would send the bullet through the shooter's left eye.

"Lights on," he ordered and dropped low behind the desk, taking his rifle down with him. He'd fired his last round and needed to swap magazines.

Kaaf flipped the same nine switches to turn the lights back on in the exhibition halls.

"Get down," Saw barked, looking over at the maintenance technician who was standing behind his panel.

Kaaf dropped to hands and knees on the floor behind the light control console. "Did you get him?" Kaaf called.

"I think so," Saw said. "But I need visual confirmation."

"God, Three," Riker chimed in. "Enemy sniper appears to be down but stay frosty. By my count, we still have one possible tango in play."

"Check."

Saw swapped magazines and cycled the bolt handle to eject the spent cartridge and chamber a new round. Then he brought the Cross back up and scanned the mini Jumbotron to validate Riker's report. The primary indicator of victory was seeing the terrorist's sniper rifle muzzle sticking out and unmoving at the bottom of the vertical slot between the display panels. His secondary confirmation was blood dripping from the near corner of the standing platform.

"Kaaf, I need you," Saw said as he lowered his scan to sweep the crowd below for targets.

"I'm ready."

"Keep an eye on the muzzle of that sniper rifle sticking out of the Jumbotron. Do you see it?"

"Yes, I see it."

"Watch that muzzle like a hawk. If the weapon moves, you tell me."

"Okay, I understand. I got your back," Kaaf said with commitment.

A smile curled the corners of Saw's lips as he scanned left. The maintenance tech had turned out to be one hell of a wingman. It had been years since Saw had had a dedicated spotter, and truth be told, it was kind of nice.

A blood-chilling scream reverberated in the exhibition hall below. He pulled his eye off the scope and scanned in the sector where his ears had triangulated the cry. There he saw a man dressed in a catering uniform walking down the aisle in front of the anchor exhibitors—a pistol in each hand—shooting at a handful of fleeing civilians.

Saw leaned into the buttstock, placed his crosshairs on the murdering jihadi's forehead, and squeezed the trigger.

"Tango number eight is down," he reported with calm detachment.

By the numbers, it was over, but he would remain overwatch until Chunk secured him. Until that happened, he continued his scan. Just in case they were wrong . . .

CHAPTER 39

Qasim leaned his head against the giant British Aero logo that spanned the back wall of the booth, feeling dazed and sick to his stomach. Convincing security personnel that he was in shock would prove easy, as he realized he actually *was* in shock. The feel of the sticky, drying blood on the side of his face, along with other substances too horrifying to think about, brought on a wave of nausea and he vomited.

His stomach now empty, he stole a glance at the corpse on the floor beside him.

Merrell Thompson stared up at the ceiling with his one remaining eye. The entire right side of his head was missing from just above the brow. A cavernous hole gaped open to reveal the parts of his brain not spattered on the wall and Qasim's face and inside his left ear. The smell of excrement hit him an instant later, undoubtedly from Thompson relieving himself of the previous night's debauchery at the moment of death.

Qasim heaved again, but little came up except bile.

"Over here," someone shouted in Arabic, and moments later uniformed men surrounded him, one carrying a large orange box that he set on the floor between Qasim and Thompson. The man stole a glance at Thompson and let out a raspy sigh. "This one is gone," he reported.

"We have two dead back here," one of the man's colleagues shouted. "Both shot through the head."

"Can you talk?" the man asked, turning his attention to Qasim.

"What?" Qasim said in English, magnifying the level of shock he felt. "What did you say?"

"I am a medic," the man said in English. "Are you hurt?"

"I . . . I don't know," Qasim said, looking down at his gore-stained clothes. He wiped his forearm across his face and looked at his shirtsleeve. "Is this my blood?" he asked, his voice quivering as tears spilled onto his cheeks. "Am I shot?"

He felt gloved hands running over his body, then pulling his shirt up to inspect his torso. The medic shined a light into his eyes and asked him to open his mouth, which he did. The man looked inside, though for what reason Qasim could scarcely imagine.

"You are not shot, sir. This is not your blood," the medic said and pinned a green square of paper to Qasim's shirt. "What is your name?"

"Qasim Nadar," he said through a sob. "I need to call my wife."

"Stay here. Security personnel will come to help you," the medic said and rose.

He reached out and grabbed the medic's arm. "You're leaving me?" he said, with as much fear as he could muster.

"There are many wounded. I have to help others, sir. Someone will come and take you to a staging area. I'm sorry, just hang in there a few more minutes."

And he was gone.

Qasim put his face into his hands and sobbed, for anyone else who might be watching or for the security cameras which were always recording.

Had the female sniper managed to escape after the carnage she wrought? How many of the high-value targets had been executed? He knew the knife-wielding killers who had been slashing their way through the crowds had been dispatched, and it suddenly occurred to him he could have been killed by one of those men. How could they possibly have known who he was? Hamza had not mentioned the indiscriminate killing. Every victim was supposed to be targeted, but it had not gone down like that. Had some of the martyrs gone rogue in the heat of the moment? Perhaps it was all by design. Or maybe after the shooting started it was impossible to control the chaos . . . yes, that was more likely the case.

"Qasim Nadar?" a male voice said above him.

Qasim looked up to see a stoutly built, bearded American, left hand on his hip and right hand behind his back, staring down at him. Beside him stood a second man, dressed in khaki cargo pants and an open-collar shirt, with his tattooed arms folded over his chest. He looked at the badge hanging from a lanyard around the shorter, well-dressed man's neck, identifying him as Keith Black. Beneath, in smaller letters, the badge said, US Military—Central Command.

"Yes, I am Qasim Nadar. Are you here to help me? I need to call my wife in London. When she hears about this, she'll be frantic." He sobbed again and wiped an arm across his face, conscious of the importance of making his British accent as apparent as possible and minimizing any residual underlying accent from home. "Can someone get me a towel and some water please?"

He let the sob grow into genuine weeping.

"Are you injured?" the man ID'd as Mr. Black said, squatting beside him. His right hand came around and slipped a pistol into a holster inside the waistband under his shirt.

"No, I don't think so. The medics put a green square on me. Does that mean I'm okay?"

"Yes, Mr. Nadar. You'll be fine, I promise. We're Americans working with a joint US-British counterterrorism task force here in Dubai. We're going to take you to a secure location. Sometimes there's a second wave in these types of attacks. Come with us, Mr. Nadar, and we'll get you somewhere safe and then you can call your wife."

"Okay," Qasim said, struggling to his feet.

What the American said seemed reasonable. Surely the US and British governments had security personnel on-site to augment the British Aero security team and local police. It made sense. But there was something naggingly familiar about this man. Or perhaps Qasim was just being paranoid.

"Homeplate, we've found another on the list—a Mister Qasim Nadar. No other British Aero members at the booth to evacuate. Three KIA. Send Charlie team to identify the bodies. We're headed to the secure location," Black said. Qasim saw no radio on his belt or earpiece; the American must be using a microtransmitter of some sort.

Feeling Qasim's eyes on him, Black turned and added, "I know this has been terrifying, but I promise you're safe now."

Qasim nodded and managed to choke out a thank-you.

But where were they taking him? He knew that British Intelligence was probably looking for him in the aftermath. As a native Afghan working at a key British defense contractor, he would be a person of interest for the Home Office . . . so why were the Americans running point? Maybe they would hand him over to the British at the secure location.

It's all part of the plan, he reminded himself. *Surviving the attack and getting rescued from the evil terrorists as a victim.*

He suppressed a grin as they led him out of the exhibition hall and into a back hallway. A sterile silence replaced the chaotic din of the convention center. An unsettled feeling washed over him as they marched down the corridor with its bare cement floor and painted cinderblock walls. Stacked chairs and folding tables lined the wall on the right-hand side, but the hallway was otherwise completely vacant.

"Clear ahead," Mr. Black—clearly in charge—ordered. The tattooed man hustled down the hall in front of them. "Two, fall in on us. We're exiting the rear and will cross south of the Ibis hotel. We have Mr. Nadar. He's uninjured and we're escorting him to the secure location for evaluation and debrief."

"Thank you so much," Qasim said, regaining both his real and fictitious composure. "I know that Merrell Thompson . . ." He made a show of closing his eyes tightly. "That he didn't make it. Is anyone else from British Aero . . . you know . . . dead?"

"We're still sorting everything out, Mr. Nadar," Black said as they pushed out the back doors. "We're just glad you're okay."

Once outside the expo, the Americans picked up the pace. A third American agent joined them, dressed similarly.

"Hey, boss," the new man said, falling in on the other side of where the "boss" gripped Qasim's arm.

"This is Mr. Nadar," the boss said. "We think he's okay, but we're gonna get him to the secure location and check him out."

"Cool," the younger man said. "You're in good hands, Mr. Nadar."

"Thank you," Qasim said, but felt a growing dread in his chest. Why would they commit three men to securing just him? There were hundreds of American and British citizens back at the convention center who needed attending to.

Something was wrong.

If this was the beginning of an inquiry into his possible involvement in the attack, then all he could do was play dumb and stick to the script, so showing apprehension at being whisked away by Americans would make no sense at all and would only increase their suspicion. If they knew nothing, then he would give them nothing. If they already knew he was working with al Qadar, then the game was up.

Inshallah . . .

"So much blood . . ." he said, tossing a choked sob in for good measure. "Thank you for getting me out of there. If I had to stay in there another minute—beside Merrell's body . . ."

"We're almost there, Mr. Nadar," the boss said as they made to cross the normally busy Sheikh Zayed Road. A carnival of flashing lights at either end of the enormous roadblock surrounding the World Trade Centre complex announced that the local police and military response to the attack had finally arrived. After crossing, they turned north toward the opulent Conrad hotel.

"Copy that," the boss said to someone Qasim couldn't hear and then turned to him.

"We're going to use the rear entrance where my team has a service elevator standing by to take you up to the secure suite. We'll check you out and get you connected to your wife."

"Okay," he said, but his voice must have betrayed his doubts because the American made another thinly veiled attempt to reassure him.

"Don't worry, Mr. Nadar. We're just trying to avoid the media and any photographs before we get you cleaned up, okay? With the way you look right now, the rear entrance is the only way to make that happen. We're almost there."

Qasim nodded, recognizing the merits of that argument, but he was now certain these heavily muscled men with side-arms were not mere Good Samaritans doing their best to help him phone home. He tried to swallow the growing lump in his throat, but it persisted as he came to realize that how he performed over the next few minutes would likely determine whether he ever saw Diba again.

CHAPTER 40

TWO-BEDROOM SUITE
TWENTY-FOURTH FLOOR, CONRAD HOTEL
DUBAI, UNITED ARAB EMIRATES
0934 LOCAL TIME

When Chunk was at SEAL Team Four, the command master chief once told him that a good SEAL, especially an officer or NCO, was "sometimes mistaken but never in doubt." Over the years, Chunk had tried to lead by that motto, and it had served him well. Making no decision was almost always worse than making a poor decision when operating in a highly kinetic environment. But leading Gold Squadron was already teaching him myriad exceptions to the rules that had served him well before. The Tier One world, with its darkly covert nature and need to remain covered at all times, brought a new level of complexity to operations that didn't fit nice and neat into a black-and-white world.

Qasim Nadar, who was sitting in a chair while Trip cleaned blood and spatter off him with a hand towel, was the source of Chunk's burgeoning doubt. With trembling hands and tear-laden cheeks, Nadar was not behaving like any terrorist Chunk had grabbed off the X before. Not that all terrorists followed a uniform script—some were aggressive and belligerent, while others begged for their lives. Some glared at him with murder in their eyes, while others were unable to make eye contact. But this man was behaving very much like every civilian hostage Chunk had ever rescued. His post-traumatic response looked and felt genuine, and so far, there'd been no red flags.

"Are you bringing other people here as well? What about the other British Aero survivors?" Qasim asked. "I . . . I need to know if everyone else is okay."

Chunk looked at Watts, who was standing beside him, and saw her purse her lips.

She's having doubts too.

She'd altered her appearance—donning eyeglasses, baggy clothes, and a ball cap—as well as hardened her demeanor before entering the room for the interview. Chunk knew she'd done it to reduce the chance of Nadar recognizing her from last night. The irony of the situation, however, was that her normal endearing and spooky nerd self was just as far removed from the sexy, French model she'd portrayed last night as this character. Also, he wasn't sure if Nadar recognizing them was necessarily problematic. In Chunk's mind there would be a logic behind being recognized. Bad guys and professionals watched their six and worried about being surveilled. Innocent everyday civilians did not. If Nadar recognized them it might be a tell.

A phone chirped.

Watts pulled out her encrypted sat phone and looked at the number. "It's the Head Shed," she said and handed it to Chunk.

"One," he said and excused himself from the bedroom they were using as an interrogation suite, leaving the door cracked so he could still hear what was going on.

"Sitrep," Bowman demanded, his voice all business. "Clearly, we didn't stop the attack."

"No, sir," he said. "But our presence saved hundreds of lives, sir. Saw took out their sniper, but not before the sniper capped three executives in the British Aero booth. I'm glad we were able to contain it to just that booth before he could target others, but still. We were able to neutralize all the attackers in the crowd. They used grenades, but there were no suicide bombers or IEDs found on the premises. Watts and I think it was a targeted attack rather than something designed for mass casualties. It could have been much, much worse."

"Check," Bowman said simply. "Do you have the target?"

Chunk exhaled.

By *target*, Bowman meant Asadi Bijan, whose dead body he'd left lying in the promenade behind the DWTC exhibition hall. Was Asadi Bijan the real Hamza al-Saud? *Maybe*. Bijan's involvement in the attack today was indisputable, but whether that proved he was the terrorist mastermind behind al Qadar was something Watts and the rest of the spooks would have to figure out. How Nadar factored into the equation was still a big fat question mark in Chunk's mind.

"Bijan is dead—martyred himself when capture was imminent. Whether he's the real al-Saud or not, we don't know. We did bring in Qasim Nadar, however. He's secure here and we're just beginning to talk to him, but my gut tells me he's no jihadist."

"You don't think he's involved then?" Bowman asked.

"Not sure, sir. I need to hear what he has to say and gauge his reactions. But sir, he was nearly killed in the attack himself. When we found him, he was sitting with a colleague's blood and brains all over him—couldn't have been but a foot away when the sniper fired."

"Nearly killed, huh?" Bowman said, and his voice suggested he was mulling that over. "If he's al-Saud, a near miss would be a pretty convenient alibi, wouldn't it?"

"Yes, sir," Chunk agreed, but still had trouble thinking of the guy in the other room as anything but a traumatized engineer. "We'll know more soon."

"Keep me looped in," Bowman said, "and either hand Nadar over to the Brits or get him out with you if you believe he's connected. Either way, you need to exfil in the coming hour or two, Commander. This joint American-British security team NOC we created won't hold up much longer."

The line went dead before Chunk could comment.

He returned to the living room of the luxurious suite where Nadar was now sipping from a water bottle, his hands still trembling to the point where water sloshed into his lap.

"I know this has been a traumatic event for you, Mr. Nadar, but we need to ask you a few questions," Watts said, glancing at Chunk who nodded.

"Of course," Nadar said and let out a long, shaky sigh. "I'm afraid I don't know very much. I had just arrived at the booth when it happened. Well, it's more than a booth. We had reserved nearly fifteen hundred square feet for our displays and even had a lounge with sofas and a coffee table. Anyway . . ." He looked up at Watts, and she smiled and took a seat—softening her demeanor to good cop rather than standing accusingly over him.

"Go on," she said.

"Anyway, the breakfast reception was the opening event for the conference. British Aero was one of the cosponsors—it was mandatory we all attend. Merrell Thompson, my colleague, had returned from getting drinks—mimosas I believe. I don't drink because I was raised Muslim, and just, I don't, I just never did."

"What happened when you got there, Qasim? May I call you Qasim?" she said.

"Yes, of course," Nadar said with none of the misogynistic aggression toward Watts that both Fake Hamza and Fake Juba had exhibited during their interrogations. "So, I got there and just as I said hello to Merrell, he just . . . he just . . ." Qasim took a swig, water dribbling onto his chin, but he seemed not to notice. "I didn't, like, hear a gunshot or anything. Just one minute he was laughing about something with two drinks in his hand, and then it was like his head just exploded. And I felt stuff, wet and warm stuff, on my face. I think I screamed. And then I did hear sort of a *poof* sound, and then people on the other side of the partition screamed. Right after that there was an explosion—not near us, but like from the other side of the room. I think I dropped down to hide, but I don't remember doing it. I just remember that I was on the floor and then there were more screams. And then some gunfire. I just lay there on the floor and did nothing."

He looked up, tears streaming down his face which he didn't wipe away.

"It's okay, go on," Watts said.

"I don't know how long that was. It seemed like minutes or, I don't know, longer. I was in shock. I could see inside of Merrell's head . . ."

Nadar put his face in his hands.

Chunk leaned down and whispered in her ear, "Picture from the border crossing."

Watts nodded and went to the dining table where Yi sat, watching from a distance and recording everything quietly on her computer. She whispered to Yi who handed her a large photograph which she in turn handed to Chunk.

He pulled a chair over, spun it around to sit backward in it, and leaned in. "Do you know this man, Qasim?" he asked, holding up the photograph.

Nadar looked up and glanced between his interrogators for a moment, then looked at the photo. His eyes widened with what, to Chunk, seemed like genuine shock.

And then fear.

"Oh my God," he said, taking the picture in his shaking hands. "Please tell me he is not the one who did all this. Please, tell me Eshan is not involved."

"So that's a yes?" Chunk said. "You know this man?"

Qasim nodded.

"How long have you known him?" Watts asked, and Qasim turned to her.

"My entire life," he said, and Chunk noted what seemed to be genuine pain in the man's eyes. "Eshan was my best friend since childhood. He married my sister, before she died." He turned to Chunk. "So, this is why I am here? Because you wish to know about Eshan?" He suddenly thrust the picture back at Chunk and, with angry fervor in his voice, said, "Ask me anything. I will tell you everything I know. This man betrayed my family and all the values I hold dear."

Chunk hid his surprise at the comment and set the picture in his lap. "When did you last see him?" he asked, watching the man's eyes very carefully now.

"A few months ago," Nadar said. "He came to London to tell me he'd met someone and that he'd fallen in love. After my sister died, Eshan went to a very dark place—we all did—but he took it especially hard. But when he came to my flat, quite out of the blue I might add, he seemed happy—like the Eshan

I remembered from the old days. He told me he'd proposed to the woman and wished for me to be at his wedding, and I gladly agreed. I took a holiday and met him in Kabul. He picked me up at the airport and drove me to my childhood home in the Kameh Valley outside of Jalalabad. That was my first time home in many years and it was . . . both a joyous and painful experience." Nadar sighed, his eyes dark now at the memory. "I fled Afghanistan for a reason, after all," he added, looking up again. "After we visited with my relatives, Eshan told me his wedding was actually in Pakistan and that we would need to travel across the border. That's when I realized I had made a mistake."

"What mistake was that?" Watts asked.

"Trusting him."

"I don't understand," Watts said, playing dumb.

"I told you . . . after my sister's death, Eshan went to a very dark place. As it turns out, during that time he abandoned everything we believed in."

"What did you believe in?"

"Good," Qasim said simply, looking at his hands. "We believed—my sister perhaps most of all—in the goodness of man, despite all that has happened in my country. My whole life, I have been grateful for the British and Americans who have fought and died trying to liberate Afghanistan from the Taliban and other forces wishing to keep us in the past—in the Stone Age, to put it bluntly—and in oppression. Like all people, Afghans mostly just want to be free. But at the wedding, I learned that Eshan had been seduced by the tenets of radical Islam. To put it simply, he had become a terrorist, embracing the very path I have dedicated my life to fighting against."

An uncomfortable pause hung on the air as they contemplated Nadar's words. Finally, Watts broke the silence. "How did your sister die, Mr. Nadar? I'm sorry to ask, as I'm sure it's painful to talk about."

"I have moved beyond the pain. It is what drives me to this day. My sister died during an attack targeting terrorists in our town. Unfortunately, Saida was in the wrong place at the wrong time. Eshan blamed America for her death and fixated on retribution."

"But you didn't?" Chunk challenged, watching the man carefully. "You didn't blame the Americans for your sister's death?"

"Why would I?" Qasim said, and for the first time Chunk heard fire and confidence in the man's voice. "Did the Americans invent the Taliban and their reign of terror over my people? Do the Americans come to our villages and execute teachers who teach girls to read? Do the Americans burn down homes with people inside because a twelve-year-old living there took candy from soldiers? It is not the Americans or the British who have destroyed my country. Men like Eshan came to view them as invaders because they believed the lies of those who would control them. I saw—and still see—the American soldiers for what they are."

"And what is that?" Watts asked, her voice now suggesting fascination with the engineer's story.

"Liberators," Qasim said and took a sip of the water again. "My sister died that night because of the Taliban. The Americans were targeting a terrorist that night, not my sister. The missile fired from that drone did not target the wedding hall. It targeted a car with a Taliban member driving away. My sister should never have run to that car."

A second hard silence lingered. Nadar took a drink of water, collected himself, and then continued.

"When I was at Eshan's wedding, I saw men I was certain

were Taliban loitering in the crowd, watching everyone . . . keeping an eye on things like they love to do. They were the same type of men who used to harass my father and sister. When I confronted Eshan about them, he told me that they were not Taliban. He said they were trusted *friends*. I didn't believe him. I wouldn't let it go, and when I pressed him hard enough, he confided that he was working with a new type of terrorist group—his word was *new*; to me they are all the same and nothing ever changes with such zealots—but was adamant that this organization was different. We fought about it. I'm a British citizen. I work for British Aero Defense Systems for God's sake. The position he put me in—jeopardizing my citizenship and my career—it was unacceptable. After we argued, I left." He looked up at Chunk. "I never saw him again."

"I'm sorry," Watts said, with what sounded like real empathy in her voice.

"There is always good from life's trials," Qasim said with a sad smile on his face. "On that visit I reconnected with Diba, the love of my life. We had been in the early stages of romance before the death of my sister. When I left for the UK for university, I knew I would never return to Afghanistan and the romance ended. But finding her again was worth the pain of my encounter with Eshan. Diba is now my wife," he added, beaming with pride.

"The story has a silver lining, at least," Watts said.

Nadar nodded then, looking suddenly pensive, said, "Do you know what I do at British Aero?"

"No," Chunk lied. "What do you do?"

"I help develop the next generation of combat drones. Yes . . . I know, it is ironic, isn't it, since my sister died during a drone attack. But do you know why I do this?"

"Why?" Chunk asked, mesmerized.

"For my country," Qasim said. "And when I say this, I do not only mean the UK; I'm talking about Afghanistan as well. By helping perfect drone technology, I give British and American forces tools to protect my people from the terrorists who would murder my brothers and enslave my sisters. The Taliban regime is a regime of oppression. They must be stopped. I am proud of the work I do at British Aero. Through better engineering and technology, I will make sure that drone pilots have more tools and more precision to target the enemy, while lessening the risk of collateral damage. In that way, Saida's death will not be in vain. It is more than a job for me—it is a calling. I will never forgive Eshan for selfishly putting that calling at risk. Now tell me . . ." Qasim leaned in with fire in his eyes. "Was my childhood friend Eshan responsible for the attack today? Is he responsible for the murder of my friends and colleagues? And if so, how can I help you to hunt him down?"

Chunk stared at the man a long moment, and then looked over at Watts who took the cue and threw Nadar a ninety-mile-per-hour fastball straight down the middle.

"Mr. Nadar, did you assist the al Qadar terrorist organization with operating a Chinese combat drone in Pakistani and Afghan air space to launch an attack on Kandahar Air Base?"

Nadar hesitated a second before answering. "Okay, now I understand," he said, his shoulders relaxing. "It didn't make sense to me why the American CIA was questioning me instead of British Intelligence, but of course you would be interested in this connection. The answer to your question is no, I had nothing to do with that. But I have thought about this incident so many times, and I am convinced that Eshan tried to recruit me because of my technical expertise and knowledge of drone technology."

"Did Mr. Dawar discuss al Qadar's drone program with you the night of the wedding?" she asked.

"No."

"Did he hint at it or give you any reason to believe that al Qadar *had* a drone program?" she pressed.

"No," he said. "But I know the details of the incident you're talking about. I have security clearance at British Aero. After the attack, management tasked my group with stress testing the firewalls and safeguards in all of our models to make sure that foreign actors cannot hack into and take control of our UCAVs. This is a very serious threat."

She watched him for a long moment before looking at Chunk and smiling. "That's all I've got. I think we're done here," she said.

He nodded and turned back to Nadar. "Thank you, Mr. Nadar, for your candor and openness in answering our questions. I'm sorry for the ordeal that you have been through—both today and in your past. My colleague and I need a moment to talk in private. We'll be right back."

They walked out of the bedroom, closing the door behind them, and stepped into the common area where Saw was waiting.

"Hey, boss," said Saw, who held a black gun case in his right hand and a backpack slung over his shoulder.

"Hey, bro," Chunk said and gestured toward the bedroom. "We're just finishing up the debrief with Mr. Nadar from British Aero. I think the plan now is to escort him back to his hotel and turn him over to the Brits."

"Okay," Saw said, his neutral voice conveying he understood he had a lot he needed to get caught up on. "FYI, I recovered Bijan's mobile phone before the Dubai Police Force got to the body. Took pictures and got a DNA sample while I was at it."

Chunk gave his sniper a fist bump, loving the fact his brother SEAL was in full Tier One mode on his own. Movement in his peripheral vision got his eye, and Chunk turned to see Nadar standing in the bedroom doorway—the door he'd closed now hanging wide open. The engineer was staring, eyes wide, directly at Saw.

"Are you okay, Mr. Nadar?" Chunk said. "We told you we'd be back with you in a second."

Nadar shook his head, as if shaking off a bad dream. "Yes . . . I'm sorry, I just . . ." He pulled at his face with both hands. "Is that a rifle in that case? I'm sorry, I just have never been close to such weapons and to real soldiers since leaving Afghanistan. I know it seems crazy, considering what I do and the systems I design, but being so close to guns after what just happened . . . I apologize, I mean no offense. I admire the work you do, it's just . . ." He wiped a fresh tear from his cheek. "It's been such a horrible day."

"I understand," Chunk said and nodded with what he hoped to be a sympathetic smile. "We forget sometimes that not everyone is part of this mad world we work in. If you could please go back in the bedroom. It will just be a moment."

Nadar nodded and did as instructed, closing the door behind him.

"Well?" Chunk said, turning to Watts. "What do you think?"

"The jury is still out in my mind," she said, with that look she got when her words didn't scratch the surface of the complex thoughts churning through her head.

"Come on . . . this guy's clearly not the mastermind of al Qadar. And he ain't Hamza al-Saud either—that's for damn sure," Chunk said in a low voice, folding his arms.

"I don't know," she said, pulling at the stub of her ponytail which was sticking out the back of her black, unmarked ball cap. "So many threads pull through him," she added, and her knot metaphor was not lost on Chunk, "but everything he said makes sense and is consistent with what we know. And he was insanely forthcoming. He sounded like . . ."

"Like someone telling the truth?"

She nodded. "Or at least, like someone with nothing to hide."

"Look, our decision point here is simple. Either we black bag this guy and take him with us, or we let him go. We left a footprint today and the Head Shed wants us wheels up as soon as possible. From my perspective, I think we got all we're going to get from him. Like you said he was an open book. Zero hostility. Zero evasiveness. He answered every question we asked and volunteered details for questions we didn't."

"Agreed," she said.

"So, what do you want to do?"

"We should let him go," she said, but he didn't like the lack of conviction in her voice. "I'll debrief the British task force on everything and turn the Nadar piece of the puzzle over to them. If our investigation into Bijan yields anything suspicious, we can always ask the Brits to question him again."

"Okay. Sounds like we're on the same page. I'll have Trip take the guy back to his hotel." He nodded to Trip.

"Sure, boss," the SEAL replied and went to fetch their guest.

Before his departure, they gave Nadar a fresh shirt to wear, relieving the man of his blood-soaked Oxford. The engineer thanked them and made a point to shake both Chunk's and Watts's hands before departing with Trip.

Once they were gone, Chunk turned to Watts.

"I noticed you didn't ask him about his run-in with Bijan in the Cavalli Club."

"Neither did you," she pointed out with a defensive laugh.

"That's because I was letting you take the lead. I didn't know if you wanted him to know we'd been surveilling him— that he had been a target for us."

She nodded. "I thought about it, but when I gamed it out in my head there seemed like nothing to be gained. If Nadar is a terrorist working with Bijan, then he's the best liar I've ever met, and he's going to pretend the interaction was accidental. If Nadar is innocent, then the interaction was accidental. Either way, we learn nothing and tip our hand in the process."

"Sounds about right," Chunk said, agreeing with her logic. Turning to Saw and Riker, he added, "Let's pack it up and get ready to roll. It's time to put Dubai in our rearview mirror."

CHAPTER 41

A new rage simmered in Qasim as he closed his hotel door.

He stood in the foyer of the enormous suite, arms by his side staring at the immaculate tile. Then, in a fit of unbridled ire, he ripped the shirt the Americans had given him off and hurled it—only to watch, unsatisfied, as it fluttered gently to the floor. Fuming, he stomped into the suite and began to pace back and forth behind the sofa in the living room, his mind filtering through a million thoughts. His balled fists were so tight that his fingernails were digging into his palms, and he forced himself to open and close his hands.

What he did next might truly be a matter of life and death, and not just for him.

I am sorry, Diba, he thought, knowing that her fate would likely mirror his own. He pushed the guilt away. Diba wasn't the priority right now. The *cause* was all the mattered.

Hamza was dead.

His instincts to open the bedroom door and eavesdrop had been on the mark, allowing him to overhear an essential snippet of conversation. The face of the bearded man with the rifle—the man bragging about taking Hamza's mobile phone and DNA samples—had been the final blow. The universe, it seemed, was not without a sense of irony. This man, the man who undoubtedly had killed Hamza, was one of the men he'd seen in the portfolio of operators Fun Time assembled from his social media interrogation efforts. That man had been flagged because of a recent move from Virginia Beach to Tampa, where his wife had posted pictures of their new house before she had abruptly disappeared from social media after the sniper attack in Erbil. At the sight of him, Qasim had nearly passed out, though he believed he concealed the reason for his shock well and to the apparent satisfaction of the American the others called "Boss."

He also felt he'd concealed his shock at seeing the picture of Eshan quite well. He'd not expected that. The Americans had been better prepared than he'd imagined and it had taken all of his inner strength to stay in character. Hamza had taught him to use real emotions to fuel his fictitious reactions, and he had done just that—turning his rage at the Americans at seeing his childhood friend killed in Mingora and transferring it to fictitious rage at Eshan. As guilty as it made him feel, Qasim had harbored real anger toward Eshan. Anger for how he'd duped him into becoming involved with al Qadar in the first place, anger that Eshan had not trusted him with the truth or to make his own choices, and finally, anger that Eshan had died on him and left him alone, as crazy as that seemed.

Above the anger hovered guilt—like a dark halo he could never seem to rid himself of, radiating blackness and toxicity down on him at all times. Had Qasim been stronger, Eshan might not have felt the need to trade places with him that night—in which case Eshan would not have been in the safe house at all when the Americans had attacked. Had Qasim not been so damn weak, perhaps Eshan would be alive today, and they would be working together for al Qadar. Instead, Qasim was here, alone, now more alone than ever.

If Hamza is dead, then that means . . . I'm in charge now.

The realization hit him like a punch to the stomach.

As of this moment, he was now the leader of al Qadar. The crown of the terrorist prince had passed to him, and all of Hamza al-Saud's followers were now his army.

But do I want that?

He suddenly felt light-headed and lowered himself to sit cross-legged in the middle of the floor.

Head swirling, he realized he was at a crossroads.

If the Americans didn't know he was with al Qadar—and their conversation in the hotel room most certainly suggested they did not—then he could simply walk away from it all. Right now, forever . . . All he had to do was one more round of Q&A with British Intelligence, and he could go back to work at British Aero where he would, most certainly, be promoted. He could put this all behind him and walk away from jihad, vengeance, and killing forever. He and Diba could start a family. Their life would be good and safe and happy.

Or . . . he could rise.

Qasim closed his eyes and, for the first time in a long time, said a silent prayer—asking God for direction and guidance.

Instead of an answer, he felt only a burning rage grow even larger inside him as memories of his sister's body blown to pieces filled his mind, followed by a parade of other horrible images—the burning car with his father inside, the security

camera footage Hamza had shown him of Eshan being shot in
the face by the American SEALs, and now Hamza . . . lying
murdered and lifeless in an alley somewhere in Dubai.

A new image entered his mind—the confident, smiling
face of the bearded American with the gun case that he carried
as if he'd just returned from playing a round of golf. Besides
Hamza, who else had this man killed with his precision instrument of war? Almost certainly he'd killed Nurbika. He had
likely killed many other believers during the attack as well.
And yet, he seemed so calm. So at peace.

*Might he be the man who shot Eshan in the face? Is that
possible? There are hundreds of Special Operators, thousands even,
and yet . . .*

The rage grew inside him to levels he had never experi-
enced, and his rib cage felt like it was being ripped open from
the inside.

He opened his eyes.

Was this feeling Allah's reply? Was his rage Allah's call? He
knew what Hamza would have him do. He'd made his expec-
tations about the transition of power abundantly clear during
their hours-long one-on-one talk in New Malden. Al Qadar
was his responsibility now.

Decision made, Qasim stood, and he realized he could feel
Hamza's ghost standing beside him. His mentor would always
be with him—whispering, counseling, and guiding. He felt
it now, as he scanned the hotel suite for places where cameras
might have been placed. The Americans, and no doubt the
British, clearly had some doubts about him. They'd built a case
file on him; they had questions prepared. Certainly, there were
cameras in the suite, or at least listening devices?

*No problem. My performance in front of the Americans was
far beyond what I knew I was capable of. I know now what is*

inside me—what gifts Allah has bestowed in me to fulfill his purpose.

He walked to the bedroom, intent on continuing the charade for whoever might be listening. He walked to the dresser into which he had unpacked his clothing and opened the top drawer. As he made a show of shuffling through the clothes, he palmed the ZTE Axon smartphone Hamza had passed him in the Cavalli Club. The phone had contained all the information the al Qadar luminary had committed to memory, as well as communication protocols and instructions enabling Qasim to access financial accounts. Now, it was his turn to do as his mentor had done. But that would take time.

First, he needed to make certain Hamza's murder did not go unpunished.

He grabbed a shirt to cover the phone then, feigning a sudden wave of nausea, sprinted to the bathroom where he dropped to his knees in front of the toilet. The shirt and hidden phone now on the floor between the toilet and the vanity, he retched, surprising himself by actually producing a considerable amount of vomit, the strain of the moment and toll of the last hours more than he had imagined. When he'd finished, he draped one arm over the porcelain bowl and hung his head in exhaustion, while using his free hand to pull the phone from beneath the shirt.

As he panted, he connected the phone to the internet using a VPN and sent an encrypted message to the contact labeled simply "4."

2 is now 1

Execute Tampa Operation.

Authentication Dagger.

2 sends.

After that, he pretended to dry heave a few times for effect, wrapped the phone in the shirt, and placed it on the bathroom vanity beside the sink. He flushed the toilet and proceeded to clean himself up—brushing his teeth and then showering. After, he changed into clean clothes, collapsed on his bed, and used his mobile to call Diba.

She answered on the first ring and he slipped back into character for the next act of the play he was performing. They talked for forty-five minutes, him recounting the horrors of the morning and her sobbing and trying to be supportive. But all the while, his mind was on the phone wrapped inside the shirt in the bathroom. He would need to download the data from the phone, encrypt it on his laptop computer, and dispose of it before traveling, in case British Intelligence brought him in.

Maybe Hamza had a photographic memory, but I most certainly do not. Without that data, there is no al Qadar.

As he listened to Diba drone on in her soft, empathetic voice, he felt calm envelop him. He would manage as best he could, do the things he needed to do, and the rest he would accept as out of his control.

Inshallah . . .

CHAPTER 42

UNITED STATES AIR FORCE C-17
CLIMBING TWELVE THOUSAND FEET OVER THE PERSIAN GULF
NORTHWESTBOUND
1418 LOCAL TIME

Whitney was exhausted, and yet she paced, her finger absently tracing the trefoil knot tattoo on her wrist, as she had a half dozen times in the last days and weeks. She wanted to let it go, pat herself on the back for having predicted and foiled yet another al Qadar attack, and yet she couldn't. She'd been a half step behind Hamza al-Saud once again, and once again innocent people had died. Yes, their intervention had saved hundreds of lives. And yes, Chunk had defeated Asadi Bijan—the man that all evidence seemed to indicate was the real Hamza al-Saud—but was it really a win?

Was it really over?

Behind her, Michelle Yi let out a long and distinctively unladylike snore from the hammock she slept in, cocooned deep inside a sleeping bag. The SEALs, spread out campground-fashion on the floor of the cargo jet near the aft ramp, had also drifted to sleep after burning off their operational adrenaline.

Why am I the only one who seems to have this problem? she thought.

Footsteps behind her made her turn and she saw Chunk walking up to greet her.

Okay, maybe I'm not the only one . . .

"Dude, Watts, what are you doing?" he said with a Texas-sized grin. "Take a load off and get some sleep. It's over, we're done; you can chill out now."

She heard his message, but for some reason all she could think about was the fact that he'd called her *dude*. Was it weird that she kinda loved that?

"I can't," she said, wanting to unload all her misgivings but managing to restrain herself.

"Seriously, how many cups of coffee have you had?"

"Zero."

"Then we have a problem." He blew air through pursed lips. "All right, let me hear it. What's got you all spun up?"

"It doesn't make sense. We came to Dubai because of Qasim Nadar. We thought Nadar might be the real Hamza al-Saud, and that's why we conducted ISR. In the process, we run into Asadi Bijan and he orchestrates an al Qadar signature attack, giving very strong credence to the conclusion that Bijan, not Nadar, is the real Hamza al-Saud." The words came out in a torrent.

"Yeah, that's right," he said, seemingly unperturbed.

"But we didn't know about Bijan before," she said.

"So? We know about him now."

"But we came here because of Nadar. We didn't know anything about Bijan. If it hadn't been for us thinking Nadar was Hamza al-Saud we wouldn't have come. Don't you see the problem?"

He chuckled. "No, I don't see the problem."

"Seriously, you don't see the problem?"

"I just said I don't see the problem," he repeated, this time with a dash of frustration.

She let out an aggravated sigh. "There has to be a connection between Nadar and Bijan because we didn't know about Bijan before."

"Because otherwise the coincidence of them being in the club at the same time is too much for you to stomach?"

"That and the Dawar connection, and the fact that Nadar was in Pakistan in temporal proximity to the Bagram drone attacks, and he is a combat drone engineer . . . Ahhhh, it's driving me crazy," she said, running her fingers through her hair.

He put his bear paw of a hand on her shoulder. "Look, Whitney, I'm not telling you to walk away from this, but I am telling you to take a break, decompress, get some sleep. Not only do you deserve it but you need it. Okay?"

She gave him her pout face but nodded.

A soft ding from behind her—barely audible, but her ear was tuned and waiting for it—caught her attention.

"Your computer just chimed," Chunk said looking over her shoulder at it.

"I'm going to take this," she said.

"Of course you are."

She literally sprinted back to the shipping crate she was using as a desk and took a seat on the bulkhead bench seat. The square in the upper corner had become a video chat box, and the passive face of a smiling Ian Baldwin waited patiently, cleaning his glasses with a microfiber cloth. She put on her headset and connected to the chat.

"Ah, Ms. Watts, such a delight to see you again. Are you well?"

"Quite well, thank you, Dr. Baldwin." Her last encounter with the man suggested that attempting to dispense with the formal pleasantries would be pointless, frustrating, and likely delay her receipt of information even more. "How are things for you and your team?"

"Quite well, which is to say we are taxed beyond our limit with the never-ending string of emergency requests from our organic team here, but that is the life I've chosen."

Her chatting had woken Yi, who climbed out of her sleeping bag and hammock to join her. Whitney switched from her headphones to the laptop speakers.

"We greatly appreciate your finding time and resources for us," she said as Yi dropped onto the bench beside her.

"Please, call me Ian."

"Thank you, Ian," she said, nearly bursting with the need to know what he had found from Bijan's mobile phone, which she'd connected to her computer and given the Ember team remote access to. "Any luck mining the phone?"

"Not directly, no," he said, smiling, and she felt herself deflate with disappointment. "But we will, I assure you. There is a tricky bit of code we need to sneak around and any misstep will result in the wiping of all data from the device with no hope of recovery. We've written a rather interesting algorithm to attack such problems. I won't bore you with the details, but, in essence, it's a passcode cracker that deletes the memory of each attempt so that we don't trigger the wipe—which generally is set for X number of failed attempts. Picture yourself walking backward, sweeping with a broom to remove your footprints as you go. That's a rather crude analogy, but not far from what we are doing . . ."

"But you said you did find something?" she prompted.

"Ah, yes. Something rather important, I think. While

we're not into the phone yet, we have the number and have traced the last forty-eight hours of cellular network transmissions. This device communicated with a device in Tampa, Florida."

There was a ding on her computer and an email appeared. She clicked it open.

"There's reason to be concerned. I wish we could offer you tactical support, but I'm afraid all of our Special Activities Division personnel are otherwise engaged overseas. That said, Signals Division remains available and at your disposal should you need us again."

"Thank you," she said, nodding.

He smiled and was gone.

She read the message:

Tampa operation authorized.

Commence on schedule.

Authentication Dagger.

1 sends.

Whitney turned to Yi, who looked up from the computer screen wide-eyed.

"Asadi Bijan sent that coded instruction?" Yi said.

She nodded.

"Does that mean . . ." Yi let the unspeakable go unsaid.

"I'm afraid so, Michelle," Whitney said, her own mind spinning.

It was natural, she supposed, to immediately think they were the target, and yet there was no way she could imagine an attack on the Tier One compound on MacDill Air Force Base. Access to the base itself would be difficult—if not impossible—and unauthorized access to the Tier One compound was inconceivable. And anyway, only a handful of people read into NSW activities at the highest level even knew that the Tier One SEAL Team existed.

She shook her head.

No way they were targeting the Tier One specifically . . . But then, what?

"Michelle, I gotta let Chunk know about this transmission. Get to work and find the target. It could be MacDill, perhaps, but that seems like a low probability of success for these guys. So where? What else is in Tampa or what's going on there in the coming days? I'll be right back."

She took off at a near sprint toward the rear of the plane.

Chunk saw her before she got halfway back and must have recognized the look on her face for what it was, because he slipped out of his own improvised hammock, said something to the team that got a laugh, and headed her way.

They met before she was two-thirds of the way back.

"I thought I said you need to chill," he said, his voice the frat-boy prankster. But seeing the look on her face, his own expression turned deadly serious. "You found something . . ."

"Come with me," she said.

As they headed forward again, she summarized the call with Baldwin, finishing as they arrived beside Yi who hunched over the makeshift desk.

"So it's not over," he said and ran his tongue between his teeth and his lower lip. "Well, they can't possibly be targeting the Tier One. Only a fraction of the US Intelligence Community even knows we're up and running. And even if they knew we existed, the security on the compound is impenetrable.

From a probability standpoint, they're gonna pick a softer but high-value target like they just did in Dubai."

"My thoughts exactly," she said. "Michelle is working on it."

"And I may have it," Yi said looking up at them and pointing to the laptop screen. "The SOCTIC starts at the Tampa Convention Center tomorrow."

"SOCTIC?" Whitney asked. The name sounded like about a hundred other acronyms she had learned so far.

"It's the Special Operations and Counterterrorism Industry Conference," Chunk said. "A very military-centric conference held once a year. I've attended a few times myself. It partners industry leaders with DoD decision-makers in the realm of counterterror operations."

"Same playbook as Dubai," she said, her concern deepening but her instincts telling her this had to be it. "That's just the kind of thing they would do—hit similar targets in multiple geographic locations. Amplify the impact."

Chunk nodded. "All right, listen. Get me a list of any other defense-related conferences starting in the next ten days. There could still be other targets."

"We need to notify FBI," she said.

"Give me a minute first," Chunk said and headed aft.

"Where are you going?" she called after him, confused. "We need to get operators in motion immediately."

"I know," he called over his shoulder, "which is why I want to get Bowman's permission to divert to Tampa. If al Qadar is coming for us at home, I want this team there to stop them."

CHAPTER 43

SPECIAL OPERATIONS AND COUNTERTERRORISM INDUSTRY

CONFERENCE MAIN EXHIBIT HALL

TAMPA CONVENTION CENTER

333 SOUTH FRANKLIN STREET

TAMPA, FLORIDA

THE NEXT DAY

1015 LOCAL TIME

Chunk walked down the aisle between the exhibitor booths in the main convention hall. On his left, a rescue litter dangled from a cable in the overhead—the exact same litter that Black-hawk helos used during MEDEVACs. On his right, the 5.11 Tactical booth had tactical clothing on display in a setup rivaling one of their brick-and-mortar stores. He scanned the handful of people standing inside the booth area, sipping coffee or restocking racks of backpacks and holsters. Unlike the rest of the Tier One SEALs who were fully kitted up and maneuvering through the back hallways, ready to engage, he and Riker were incognito—dressed in khakis, sports shirts, and jackets, armed only with Sig Sauer pistols. Still, with Saw in place on his sniper rifle and a full contingent of kitted-up Tier One operators from their sister squadron—along with a legion of FBI HRT operators outside the exhibit hall and, more importantly, electronic and airborne ISR supporting them today—they were infinitely more prepared and capable than they had been in Dubai.

The only problem was they'd found nothing at all to support the theory of an impending attack.

Over the last twelve hours, the FBI had worked with another joint interagency counterterror task force to review the vetting of every damn vendor, waiter, maintenance worker, and custodian, as well as the third-party providers on-site. All of the support staff for the attendees and vendors sponsoring the conference had been similarly vetted, a much easier task since these folks had been vetted for security at least once already. That exhaustive search had uncovered nothing except a handful of outstanding warrants for mundane crimes, none of which were even remotely terror-related.

"God—sitrep?" he said softly, knowing his invisible earbud would pick it up, but longing for the familiarity of the flexible boom mike of his Peltors.

"God is clear. Nothing to report," Saw said.

"Mother?" he pressed.

"Nothing new, One," came Yi's reply. "We have thermal imagery from multiple angles and show nothing suspicious in likely sniper hides. Nothing new on intel from any source. No relevant chatter."

"Gray One?"

"Zip," came the reply from SBCS Brad Tenet, the Senior NCO running the SWCC team positioned in the waterways on both sides of the convention center. The Special Boat operators from the Tier One Special Boat Squadron assigned to them were in civilian boats to blend with the water traffic including recreational boaters and the police. The three Sea Ray Sundancer 320s looked like luxury cabin cruisers but were up-armored and used ballistic glass. Inside the boat cabins, instead of kids or bikini-clad women, four fully kitted-up SWCC Operators waited with fifty-caliber machine guns, ready to drop into deck mounts should they be called into action.

Yeah, we're way more prepared than for Dubai. So, where's the action?

He caught Riker's eye as the SEAL passed in front of the display for some new tactical backpacks—which looked to Chunk like all the other tactical backpacks. Riker shrugged and gave him a look that said, *I ain't no crystal ball.*

"What key events are on tap for the conference today?" he asked softly.

The last of the breakfast stragglers had all but left, with most attendees now gone from the vendor room and off to attend a huge variety of talks and breakout sessions. His new working theory shifted to having the right target, just the wrong time and venue.

"There's snacks and drinks during the lunch break," Yi reported. "We're scouring the presenters and attendees for the key breakouts and talks to see if we can discover a likely potential target in lieu of the conference itself."

"Check," he said.

They were missing something, but what?

"There's an exhibitor cocktail party at 1700 hours," Yi continued. "That one is invitation only, so probably some heavy hitters in attendance on both the government and civilian side of the coin."

"That sounds promising," Riker's voice said in his earbud.

He agreed, but they couldn't just keep guessing. They needed more.

"Any progress on the device decryption? Do we have a timeline on cracking Bijan's phone, Mother?"

"Negative and negative," Whitney answered this time. "Ember Signals is still working it, and we also have other agencies working simultaneously."

Chunk sighed.

"Get you a coffee, sir?" a voice asked.

He turned to the attractive blond, decked out in tactical pants and boots and a 5.11 shirt.

"No thanks," he said, smiling back, tempted like hell to take her up on the offer. But things could change any second.

"Stay sharp, fellas," Chunk said. The guys were getting restless. "We keep doing what we're doing until Mother sends us in a new direction. Two, let's you and me make a pass of the breakout rooms on Level One. Meet me at the front. Blue One, take a pass here in the exhibit hall."

"Gold Two," Riker said, acknowledging the order.

"Blue One," responded Lieutenant Commander Derek Malkin, Chunk's counterpart for Blue Squadron.

Chunk headed toward the escalators, gritting his teeth.

This was not what the Tier One was created for—scouring faces in a crowd and stalking conference halls. They were a direct-action unit, not a security force or crime scene investigators. But until Watts and Yi found them an objective for that direct action, there was little to do but bide their time and hope they had not gravely misjudged al Qadar's target.

CHAPTER 44

Zain al-Masri stood naked on the cool white tile in the bathroom. With the water already running in the shower behind him, he raised his hands, bowed his head, and closed his eyes.

"*Bismillah*," he whispered, his voice tight with urgency, eager that his prayer of intention be heard.

Although performing the *wudu*—the basic ritual cleaning before prayer—would satisfy the Prophet, he felt compelled to perform the more complete *ghusl* cleansing. In all likelihood, this would be his final cleansing and opportunity to pray. If he died today, there would be no imam to perform the *ghusl* on his corpse. Allah would be understanding, but he would also appreciate the commitment and effort of performing the *ghusl* now, before the midday prayer.

With the *niyyah* complete, he stepped into the shower.

Peace descended on him as he washed—first his right hand

and fingers to the wrist and then his left, then his private area with his left hand, then rinsing his mouth and nostrils . . .

He wished it were possible to perform the ritual with rainwater, but again, he knew that Allah would understand and approve of his effort. He bowed his head beneath the shower three times, then, cupping the water in his hands, he washed his shoulders and back. Finally, his feet.

Purified, he stepped from the shower, said a prayer of thanks, and then whispered the *Shahada.*

"Ash-hadu-Alla-ilaha-illallah   wa-ash-hadu   anna-mu-hamaddan ab-duhu wa rasuluhu."

When he opened his eyes, he saw himself in the mirror, stoic and proud, water dripping from the beard on his chin. He hoped Allah found him worthy, should he die today. He prayed that all he had done for jihad had been recorded and that he may enter paradise. The operations today, both of them, carried intimate personal connections that would slake his thirst for vengeance. Hamza al-Saud's death had upset him more than he'd imagined. He did not know the details—and given the tight operational security, he could not expect to—but a transition of power had definitely occurred. Hamza had approved the operation, but the second message with the instruction to execute had been given by the acolyte. The phrase "2 is now 1" signaled that Qasim Nadar—a man al-Masri had never met—was now in charge. Maybe that was a sign. That his own personal jihad would end here, completing al-Saud's final mission felt like Providence.

After nearly eighteen years of constant war . . . Paradise will be a welcome relief.

Al-Masri padded on wet feet back into his suite, glancing at the clock beside the bed. He had a few minutes before the call to Dhuhr Salat—the midday prayer—enough time to call his young accomplice.

"Greetings, brother," the young warrior said, answering the phone.

"Is the equipment ready?" he asked, his gaze going to the impressive weapon mounted on the robotically controlled stand by the hotel window.

"It is," the other man said and in confirmation, the barrel of the fifty-caliber machine gun indexed down a few degrees.

Al-Masri would have preferred to have had Ahmed by his side today, but the man on the phone had other talents that both he and Ahmed did not. Just as there was no need for pilots in a future where drones ruled the skies, so would there be no need for snipers in a world where guns could shoot by themselves.

"And are *you* ready?" he said, asking a very different kind of question. "Do not neglect the *Dhuhr Salat*, my brother. It may be our last."

"Inshallah," the young man replied. "I am devout, my brother."

"One hour, then," al-Masri said and ended the call.

From his eleventh-floor hotel room, the remote-controlled machine gun positioned at the window would be able to rain down death and destruction on the convention center across the street. And when it happened, nobody would be in this hotel room. He looked at the gun case holding his antiquated Russian sniper rifle and then back to the internet-controlled war machine with its laser targeting system and high-definition cameras.

"Lion of Ramadi," he murmured with a smile. "A name that used to strike fear now sounds like a joke."

Nurbika was dead.

Ahmed was either captured or killed . . .

"Either way, I'm the last of my breed."

Resigned to his fate, he pulled his prayer rug from the side panel of the suitcase and unrolled it on the floor. Using the compass app on his phone, he found 234.8 degrees and positioned himself to face the Kaaba in the city of Mecca, 11,736.5 kilometers away.

Then, flush with anticipation for the events to come, he placed his hands on either side and pressed his forehead to the rug and prayed.

CHAPTER 45

Chunk wandered past half of an actual UH-60 Black Hawk helicopter, divided lengthwise and part of a massive integrated display perched atop a twenty-five-foot-tall wall with four orange ropes where sales reps demonstrated vertical ascenders to a crowd of uniformed military members crowded below. His eyes caught Riker moving across the T-intersection of booths he approached, and his fellow SEAL raised his eyebrows and shook his head at the circus they were presiding over.

Nearly seven hours now they had combed the conference, vetted attendees and staff, inspected carts, and searched every nook and cranny for possible threats. Outside, their SWCC brothers were watching the waterways while the FBI HRT team secured the perimeter on land. Local police were controlling traffic and checking vehicles seeking access to the drop-off/pickup lanes and the parking lot.

"Maybe they saw the increased security and aborted," came the soft voice of his Blue Squadron counterpart, Derek Malkin, in his ear. "We got a lot of operators moving in the access spaces, FBI overtly present outside, increased cops, boats, helicopters—I don't know, maybe we spooked them."

"Maybe," Chunk said, but his gut told him they were missing something. This attack was likely Hamza al-Saud's final order, likely issued moments before Chunk had chased him down outside the Dubai World Trade Center. There was no turning it off from the grave.

"There have been at least two highly evolved al-Qaeda affiliated terror cells taken down in the Tampa Bay area the last several years," Yi reminded them. "One of them was just blocks away from USF and included professors and students."

"And al Qadar has shown they are far more sophisticated. If this was set up in advance and the cells are all completely autonomous, there may be no chatter to detect, Blue One," Watts said.

She was right, but where did that leave them? At least they had plenty of detection equipment in place, as well as dogs. No one was bringing explosives into the hall undetected, so the bombings like they'd seen in Dubai seemed unlikely, and the same went for handguns.

"Gold and Blue, stand by," came an urgent call from Yi in his headset. "Gold One, we have two Mercedes Sprinter vans headed at high speed south on Franklin Street toward the Tampa Police checkpoint at the corner of Platt."

Chunk resisted the urge to reach for the subcompact pistol under his jacket on his right hip. "And?" he said, not sure what this report meant. These could be delivery vans headed to any of the hotels or to the residential communities on Harbour Island.

"I can't explain," Yi said, her voice frustrated. "It's the way they're driving—reminds me of Iraq and Afghanistan."

With that, Chunk understood instantly. He'd seen lines of cars or trucks downrange, and they did move in an acutely recognizable way . . . with haste and intent.

"Keep an eye and let us know what Tampa PD decides to do," he said, tension creeping into his muscles.

"Oh, shit," Yi exclaimed in his ear, and then immediately regained her cool, controlled tone. "Gold One, the TPD checkpoint is under fire. Make that heavy fire!"

"Coming from where?" Chunk said.

"Unclear," Yi said.

"Gold One, Blue team is moving now to assist," Malkin called in his ear.

"The lead van just slammed through the checkpoint," Yi said. "Van two is following at high speed. TPD is pinned down by heavy fire and can't engage."

It's by design—clear a path for vans loaded with explosives.

Chunk pulled his pistol and as he scanned the crowd for sleeper agents about to activate, said, "Mother, have HRT snipers stop the vans in place. Stop them now!"

CHAPTER 46

TACTICAL OPERATIONS CENTER
TIER ONE SEAL TEAM COMPOUND
MACDILL AIR FORCE BASE
TAMPA, FLORIDA
1458 LOCAL TIME

Whitney watched helplessly as mayhem unfolded at the convention center, her gaze transfixed on the wall of monitors livestreaming video from multiple sources. Her high side phone rang in her pocket, but she ignored it, unable to tear her eyes from the action. The terrorist's heavy machine gun had just shifted from the TPD vehicle checkpoint to the front of the convention center where security personnel were scrambling for cover.

"Is that a fifty-cal unloading on them?" she asked Yi.

"I think so," Yi said.

"Where the hell is it coming from?" she murmured, glancing from one screen to the next trying to triangulate the source of fire using the various angles she had.

"Gold One, Mother—HRT snipers are engaging the vans but they're still incoming," Yi reported, informing Chunk and the rest of the team that this new threat was far from neutralized.

A helicopter zoomed past on one of the monitors, flying at low altitude. On another monitor, SWCC Operators poured out of the boats, setting a perimeter on the back side of the convention center while crewmen dropped heavy machine guns into deck mounts.

By the fifth persistent ring, she angrily pulled her phone and looked at the caller ID.

Ian Baldwin.

She pressed the green icon to connect the call. "We're in the middle of a—"

"Yes, I'm aware, but this is equally important," Baldwin interrupted, his voice more intense than she'd ever heard and his cadence double time from his normal meandering speech. "I've sent you an image of a house on Newport Avenue in Hyde Park here in Tampa."

She lowered her phone from her ear and swiped to the image.

"Got it," she said, putting her mobile on speaker.

"This image was one of the encrypted files sent through the third-party phone to the receiver here in Tampa," Baldwin said.

The house looked familiar, but she couldn't quite place why.

"Is this a surveillance pic?"

"Yes, yes," Baldwin said, his voice clipped with urgency. "Scroll through. There are more . . ."

As she swiped through the images, her stomach lurched. The second picture showed a backyard where a young woman was pushing a toddler in a swing—a towheaded little girl no more than two or three years old—while a slightly older boy was running with a toy rifle in his grip.

"Oh fuck," she gasped.

"What is it?" Yi asked beside her, no doubt hearing the fear and strain in her voice.

"I believe the family has been targeted," Baldwin said. "And I believe it is a team member of yours, is that correct?"

"Any other pics of team member residences or family members?" she snapped.

"So far this is it," he said.

"On it," she said and disconnected the call.

She turned the phone to Yi.

"Oh my God, no . . ." Yi said, all the blood draining from her face.

"Gold One, this is Mother," Whitney said, regaining her composure. "Gold, we have a secondary target and it's Saw's house."

It was a horrible breach of protocol, but she couldn't afford to waste a single second trying to clarify.

"What?" Chunk's voice came back immediately. "What are you talking about?"

"Image intercepts from our Tampa source. It's confirmed, Sawyer's family has been targeted."

"God is now Three," came Saw's unbelievably controlled voice in her headset. "One, I'm moving to the vehicles at the rear. Blue Four, you are now God."

"Blue Four is God," the Blue Squadron sniper said taking the handoff.

"Three, One, I'll meet you there," Chunk answered. "We'll go together."

Whitney felt Yi's eyes on her.

"How is this possible?"

She shook her head. "I have no idea, but Chunk and Saw will save them. I know they will. You keep managing primary comms, I'll support Chunk."

"Check," Yi said.

"Enemy heavy sniper is located in the Marriott hotel," came a report from one of the HRT sniper spotters on the shared comms channel. "Eleventh floor, sixth window from the—"

An explosion drowned out the transmission, causing the speakers in the TOC to boom and rattle from the excessive bass. On the center monitor streaming the live satellite feed, Whitney watched the lead Sprinter van explode in a giant fireball at the front of the convention center. The second van, which had maintained a standoff outside the blast radius, opened its rear cargo doors and several men clad in body armor and carrying assault rifles jumped out and started charging for the blown-out main entrance.

All hell was breaking loose, and she feared how many other tricks Hamza al-Saud might have up his sleeve for them . . .

CHAPTER 47

TWO-STORY HOME ON DELAWARE AVENUE
ONE BLOCK EAST OF SAWYER HOME
HYDE PARK NEIGHBORHOOD
TAMPA, FLORIDA

Al-Masri pressed his cheek into the stock of the Chukavin, the feel of the rifle familiar and comforting, and scanned the front of the Navy SEAL's house through the Afzar scope. He savored the moment, this "turning of the tables" he was experiencing for the first time in his professional career. He imagined an arrogant American operator, sitting confident and clueless in his Special Operations compound in al-Masri's homeland.

Meanwhile, I'm here in your homeland to slay your family . . . Not so invincible now, hmm?

The SEAL's wife had been smart—or perhaps trained by her husband—and avoided death by closing the garage door before exiting her SUV with the children. He would have taken them all right then and there, leaving a horror show for all to see on the garage floor. But, her methodical entry after returning from day care pickup had stayed her execution.

Not for long, he thought, silently taunting her in his mind. *Your death is inevitable.*

Now he would need to make his kill shots through the windows, or even through the walls using the thermal imagery feature of the Iranian-made sniper scope. He'd been hoping an unobstructed shot would present itself—a package delivered to the front stoop, the children wanting to color with chalk on the driveway, or even a family walk to the mailbox—but he'd not been so lucky. Since returning home, the woman and her children had remained maddeningly inside and out of view.

"This is incredible," his young apprentice said with a laugh, and al-Masri resisted the urge to hush him. The young tech-savvy jihadist was presently using a tablet computer to control the robotically configured fifty-caliber machine gun. "They have no idea what's going on. They're running around like children."

Al-Masri appreciated this young man's talent. He also appreciated the fact that the attack on the convention center was the distraction necessary for his piece of the operation to succeed. But he also just wanted the kid to shut up and be his spotter. A strange nostalgia for the old days washed over him and he found himself suddenly yearning for Ahmed.

Ahmed knows when to speak and when to be quiet. Ahmed knows what it means to be behind the sight of the gun.

He forced himself to find patience and gave the younger man a nod of acknowledgment. Then he switched his scope to thermal imagery mode. The Iranian-made optic was high tech but lacked the penetration of the new Western technology. The instrument detected no thermal images moving in the front rooms of the house, but that was as far as it could see.

"Where are they?" he murmured.

"This is taking a long time," his partner said. "You still don't see them?"

"No."

"Maybe she took the children to play in the backyard."

"I have lines on the swing set but not the entire backyard," he said. "If they are on the back deck, I cannot see this."

The young terrorist nodded, his own spotter scope lying useless on the floor, while he focused all his attention on the tablet in his hands. "I'm almost out of ammunition . . . I can't believe they haven't found the gun yet. I can't wait to blow them up when they do."

This little surprise had been his own, to rig the fifty-caliber robot shooter with an explosive charge in the base. Whatever unlucky SWAT team the Americans sent to breach the hotel room and stop the rain of death would be incinerated.

"When you're ready, I can use a spotter," he said, no longer hiding the irritation in his voice.

He was beginning to feel the crush of time. He needed to execute the mission and exfil. They had broken into this house, and if the operation was not completed soon, the owners would return at the end of the workday . . . forcing a risky and unwanted confrontation.

"Okay, it shouldn't be much longer," the young man said.

The challenge al-Masri faced was to get all the members of the SEAL's family together. He would have to be quick to get all three of them. If he could get a shot on the little boy first, the mother would run to his side . . . unless, because of her husband's training, she recognized what was happening.

Maybe, I should wound the boy on the first shot.

The cries of a wounded child would be beyond the ability of a mother to resist. This was true anywhere, he imagined. If he wounded the boy, the mother was guaranteed to come to his aid.

When she steps into view, I'll take the kill shot, finish off the boy, and then, when the little girl comes crying to her mother's side, I'll take her too.

Yes, that would do perfectly . . .

CHAPTER 48

Chunk glanced at Saw in the passenger seat of the up-armored Chevy Suburban. His brother SEAL stared straight ahead, his assault rifle and sniper rifle both in his lap, his finger tapping the trigger guard of the latter with a steady, rhythmic cadence.

Like a war drum.

Chunk jerked the wheel left, cutting off an Audi convertible coming the other way on Swann Avenue, and the tires squealed. The Audi blew its horn, but he paid no mind. Getting to Saw's house as fast as possible without crashing was all that mattered.

"Do you want to call her again?" he asked as they approached Inman Avenue, the last cross street.

"I've tried four times. If she had her phone on her, she would have picked up."

Chunk nodded.

"Turn right," Saw snapped, and Chunk obeyed, swerving the truck westbound onto Inman Avenue.

"You need to slow down now, otherwise you'll draw attention."

Chunk eased off of the gas and brought the big brute down to a reasonable speed.

"Stop a block west on Willow," Saw said. "I'll go in the back on foot while you clear the front and position for exfil. Getting them out in this armored bad boy is our best chance."

"You're thinking it's a sniper attack?"

"That's been their MO from the beginning. Sniper in Erbil, sniper in Dubai . . . It'll be the same here." Saw's voice remained flat, but his face rippled with tension.

"Listen to me, bro," Chunk said softly. "If you're right, then you need to be on the long gun."

He slowed the truck a bit more as they approached Willow Avenue. Over the comms circuit, Chunk heard Riker planning to take a small team—Trip and two Blue Squadron SEALs— to the Marriott to take out the heavy gunner on the eleventh floor.

Godspeed, brother.

"No, I'm going in to get my family, Keith," Saw said through gritted teeth. "You're going to drive us out."

Chunk pulled the truck to the curb a block west of Saw's house, then turned to his brother SEAL. "Look, man, I get it, but we've got to think tactically. We're the very best operators in the world, not because we're the best SEALs individually, but because we operate as a team. We're most lethal when we leverage our individual strengths and skills to the max."

Saw stared straight out the windshield, and a tear spilled from his eye and trickled down his cheek. He said nothing.

"I assume we're stopped on Willow Avenue because if you

were Juba, you'd set up east for shots into the house through the front windows?"

"Yes."

"Then you need to set up here, a block west, and find the fucking sniper, Saw. If the real Juba is here, then trying to get your family into this Suburban to exfil is a nonstarter. He'll pick you guys off one by one as you try to load. Our best chance is for me to secure the house and for you to duel it out with Juba and end that motherfucker once and for all. That's the skill set you bring that I don't have. I'm the door-kicker, you're God. Understand?"

Saw turned to him, his eyes fire and rain. "I understand," he said and pointed to the roof of the only two-story building on the block. "I'm going to set up on the roof."

"And I'll approach from the back and secure the house until Juba's dead and the rest of the cavalry arrives."

"Take care of my family, Chunk," Saw said and then slipped out of the truck, two rifles on his chest and determination on his face.

"I will," Chunk said.

Saw looked back at him, and for a moment Chunk felt what it must be like to have this lethal killer staring down at you through his gunsight.

"If the bastard is here," Saw said softly, "he's a dead man walking."

CHAPTER 49

Assault rifle on his chest and a Sig 716G2 slung over his shoulder, Saw jogged to the house where he would make his sniper nest. Any neighbor looking at him through a window, would be on the phone already calling 911 . . . a development that may or may not work to his advantage. He pushed the scenario from his mind, resigned to deal with it when it happened. In the meantime, it took every bit of self-control and discipline he had as a SEAL to *not* sprint to his house where Ellie, Connor, and Maggie were in imminent, mortal danger. But Chunk was right—the best chance to save the three people he loved most in this world was for him to kill the assassin hunting them.

A battle between lions only ends one way.

Only one sniper would walk away from the duel alive.

He moved two trash cans behind the fence and climbed on top to reach the roofline of the covered back porch of the craftsman-style home. Using the gutter as a handhold, he swung his hips up and rolled onto the porch roof. Then he scurried up the low slanted roof and hauled himself up onto the second-story roofline. Staying low, he crabbed his way over the Spanish tile, careful to place each foot on the seams so as not to crack the shingles, potentially giving away his position— or worse, causing him to slip and slide off the roof. A moment later he sprawled out on a rear elevation dormer section behind the main ridgeline that ran parallel to the facade of the house. With expert efficiency, he set up his Sig 716G2, snugged his cheek into the weld on the buttstock, and aligned his right eye with the optical scope.

From this elevation and by setting on the street behind his house, he could see both into the backyard of their single-story, South Tampa ranch, and over the roof to survey the homes across the street. He was instantly relieved to see that his kids were not in the backyard playing on the swing set or blowing bubbles on the deck. He scanned the rear patio slider door but saw no movement in the kitchen. The best view into the house was through the front, via two large picture windows that flanked the door and looked into Ellie's office and the formal dining room. He'd already done the math—if he were Juba targeting this house he'd position himself looking through those two well-lit windows.

"God is in position," he called, the words reflexive but for some reason sounding foreign in his ears. "Sitrep on the target house?" he added, simply unable to not.

"Contact made via landline," Watts said, the news taking him by surprise. "Subjects sheltering in place."

He let out a long breath through pursed lips. He'd been unable to reach Ellie on her mobile—not unusual because she only remembered her cell about half the time when making the short run to pick the kids up from preschool—but Watts had smartly thought to also try the landline Ellie had just activated with their new cable TV package . . . a number so new he hadn't even entered it into his phone yet.

"Where are they in the house?" he queried, forcing the question to be tactical and not emotional.

"Laundry room behind the kitchen," Watts said.

He shook his head. He knew where his own damn laundry room was. Emotions won, and he pictured Ellie, terrified and huddled on the floor of the laundry room, the kids crying in her lap. He chased the unproductive imagery away and focused on scanning the buildings on the other side of the street through his Tango6 scope.

"In position behind the fence in your backyard," Chunk said in his ear. "On your mark, I'll up and over."

"God," he said. "Hold . . ."

Everything inside him wanted to tell Chunk to go now, to hop the fence, bolt across the yard, breach the house, and secure his family, but he couldn't do that. The truth was, he had no idea where the sniper was located. What if he'd been wrong? He couldn't send Chunk with zero ISR and risk him getting dropped with a head shot.

No way . . .

Instead, he got to work scanning the houses across the street for sniper hides. One, in particular, stuck out as a perfect sniper roost. Like the house he was resting on top of, it was one of the rare two-story homes in the neighborhood. Saw made a slow scan of the roofline, but nothing caught his eye—no glint off an optics lens, no muzzle peeking out of some crack, no shadows behind windowpanes. He forced himself to be slow and meticulous in his scan, but he found nothing.

"Mother, I need thermal eyes from above," he said softly.

"We have a drone overhead engaged with the action at the convention center," Watts said. "Retask?"

"Yes," Chunk answered for him, and Saw sighed, squeezing his eyes shut tightly and then blinking them open again.

What he really needed was his thermal scope, but he'd opted for the better precision of the Sig Tango6 when he'd assembled the weapon for the convention center op. He didn't need thermal imagery there, but he sure as hell wished he had it now. Even in warm daylight, the highly classified thermal scope could penetrate structural walls and give detailed depth perception inside a building.

Even better here than downrange since everyone is running AC.

"I need imagery inside the houses along Delaware Avenue," he said. "I need you to clear the second story of the lone two-story house in the middle of the block across the street from my house."

"One minute, God," Watts said, her voice tense. He imagined she still had tasking on the other channel—his brothers still locked in combat with shooters attacking the convention center.

"Standing by to cross the backyard," Chunk said, a not-so-subtle prompt that time was ticking.

Saw pulled his eye from the scope and looked to where his boss was crouched behind the six-foot-tall privacy fence at the back of his property. Without the thermal scan, should he give Chunk the green light? He slid his eye back behind the scope to scan the front-facing second-story windows of the house on the other side of Delaware Avenue. For a moment he thought he saw something—a subtle shifting of a shadow.

It could be shadows cast from the tree branches swaying outside.

Or a man inside . . .

"God, One—I'm going," Chunk said, apparently no longer content to wait and ready to take his fate in his own hands.

Saw clicked up his magnification, but nothing came into view. He lifted his head and scanned the other rooftops.

Nothing.

He has to be in the two-story . . .

He pressed his cheek back into the butt-riser on the Sig, let out a long, slow breath, and took aim at the middle window.

CHAPTER 50

TWO-STORY HOME ON DELAWARE AVENUE

ONE BLOCK EAST OF SAWYER HOME

HYDE PARK NEIGHBORHOOD

TAMPA, FLORIDA

"The machine gun is out of ammunition," the spotter announced from where he sat cross-legged on the floor with his tablet. "It's finished until SWAT arrives at the room. Do you need my help spotting?"

Al-Masri, for his part, lay prone on a dresser they had centered in the room, eye pressed into the spotter scope, reticle fixed on the picture window to the left of the target house front door.

"Yes," he said simply, happy to finally have the help he needed.

The young man picked up his spotter scope and repositioned at his side, set back from the window to start his scan. "Where are you focused?"

"The left picture window," he said.

"Okay, I'll scan the backyard and the sides of the house,"

the young man said, and after a few seconds he said, "They're not in the backyard. I don't see them anywhere."

"Keep looking," he said, irritated that his apprentice seemed incapable of grasping the most fundamental tenet of what it meant to be a sniper—watching and waiting. A hunter without patience, without the capacity to scout his prey for hours before the kill, will fail every time.

The spotter suddenly cursed. "There's a man crossing the backyard—an operator—eighty-seven meters. Hurry."

Al-Masri swept his muzzle left, shifting his aim from the picture window to the backyard. His companion's report was true. A stout operator, clad in body armor and carrying an assault rifle, sprinted across the backyard. Anger flared in his chest as he repositioned his targeting arrow, put tension on the trigger, and . . .

CHAPTER 51

Saw wasn't sure if he squeezed the trigger before Watts's emergency broadcast or while the words flowed from her lips into his ears. Cause and effect sometimes swapped places in the most prescient and time-warped moments of combat.

"Shooter-spotter pair—second floor, center window, in the two-story house on Delaware!"

Saw's bullet punched a hole in the second-story window of the target house. A moment later light flashed behind the glass and a second hole appeared as the sniper returned fire . . . but the round wasn't meant for him.

Saw knew better than to take his eye off the scope in the middle of a sniper duel, but that was Chunk down there, damn it . . .

He looked away to his backyard where he spied Chunk sprinting for the back deck. The decorative top of the stair railing newel exploded in a cloud of wood and smoke right next to Chunk's ducked head as the SEAL officer bolted up the stairs.

"I'm clear," Chunk hollered in between heavy pants as he fell in behind the rear wall of the house, out of the line of fire.

Saw ducked below the tiled ridgeline, knowing that after taking his shot at Chunk, Juba would immediately scan for the sniper who'd fired on him. By taking his eye off the scope to check on Chunk, he'd ceded the advantage to his adversary and it would be nearly impossible to get it back. But he had to try.

"Mother, are you on the landline with Ellie?" Chunk said.

"Check," Watts said.

"Where is she?"

"Still inside the laundry room off the kitchen."

"Tell her I'm breaching the back door and not to shoot me," Chunk said.

"She knows," Watts said. "You're good."

The ridge tile directly above Saw's head exploded, sending shards of clay and red dust all over him.

"Sniper still in the middle room, God. Still show two thermals," Watts reported.

No shit, Saw thought, wiping clay dust from his eyebrows and lids.

Reengaging here was out of the question; he had to relocate. With a groan, he shuffled awkwardly east, the fragile roof tiles cracking and shifting underneath him as he did. *Please don't let this fucking roof slake off with me on it,* he prayed. He was about to pop his head up for a quick look over the ridgeline but stopped himself, deciding it would be the last dumb decision he ever made. Ten feet to his right, the second-story roof ended, but the first story continued.

"Mother, God—sitrep?" he said.

"Sniper and spotter haven't moved a muscle," she came back.

"Check."

"Package is secure, God," Chunk announced in his ear.

On the news that the SEAL he trusted more than any other had secured his family, Saw's heart rate instantly slowed and all the doubt and noise in his mind went quiet. Now that his wits and ability to concentrate had finally returned, he worked out a countersniper game plan in his mind.

"I hope this fucking works," he murmured and dropped onto the back side of the lower roof.

Roof tiles crunched on impact, but he did not go crashing through the ceiling into the room below or fall off the roof like he'd feared might happen. Pressing himself against the second-story wall for cover, he pictured the slight up angle to the window across the street. He would be firing around the corner and upward, and his fingers clicked an adjustment into the elevation on his Tango6 scope. With a calming exhale, he leaned into the wall, steadied himself, and brought his rifle up. Then, in one swift and fluid movement, he took aim around the corner from under the soffit. His alignment was spot on and the target window completely filled the scope. To his surprise, he saw the top of a man's head pop up above the windowsill in the darkened room, the orange reflective glass of a spotter scope pointing directly at him.

He squeezed the trigger and shifted back behind the corner before he could watch his bullet find its mark.

And just in time.

The corner beside him exploded in shards of stucco as the other sniper retaliated with his own shot, impossibly predicting where Saw would be. He felt something rip through his right cheek and something else cut the side of his neck, uncertain if the wound was created by a scything bullet, metal shrapnel, or stucco from the damage around him. He pressed tight against the wall and dropped to a knee so that he was below the line of the lower roof.

Holy shit.

Two more rounds tore through stucco and soffit material, high-velocity fire wrecking the wall beside him as the enemy sniper tried to flush him out with blind shots through the wall and fascia. He retreated, sliding down the lower roof and dropping to the ground behind the house in cover.

"One tango down, God," Watts reported. "Looks like you got the spotter."

"God, check," he whispered, his mind reeling with what to do next.

He could either breach this house and try and set up from a second-story window before this asshole squirted or . . .

He chewed the inside of his lip as the picture became clear to him.

Juba hadn't moved. His position was compromised, his spotter killed, and still, he hadn't moved. He was dug in like a tick and not going anywhere. Which could only mean one thing—the game was not over yet.

CHAPTER 52

Chunk spun in a slow circle, clearing the house of threats. He felt the warm trickle of blood on his face and the burning laceration on his forehead from broken glass where he'd crashed action-movie-style through the Sawyers' glass slider door. He felt no heavy aching pains that might suggest he'd been shot, and his head was clear, his pulse slow and strong.

Of course the last time he'd been shot, he'd barely noticed until well after the adrenaline had cleared his bloodstream . . . but he was confident this time that if the sniper had hit him he wouldn't be having this dialogue with himself.

"Ellie, stay put," he barked. "It's Chunk. I'll come to you."

"Sniper still in play, One," Watts said in his ear and Chunk understood. This was not his first visit to the Sawyer home, and he was familiar with the layout and architecture. The sniper was undoubtedly sighting through the large picture windows at the front of the house. He would have to cross a vulnerable lane to reach Ellie and the kids in the laundry room. He dropped low, belly-crawling across the kitchen floor until he was covered behind the butcher block island. From there, he scurried across the floor, pressed tightly against the cabinets beneath the sink, well below a sight line from the window in the dining room.

He was going to be fine, unless the bastard had thermal imaging . . .

He tensed as he crawled behind the pantry, but no bullet popped his head open. A moment later he was at the final challenge. He could see the laundry room door, but he'd have to cross a five-foot gap of hallway open to the foyer and a lane for the sniper.

"I'm coming, Ellie. Open up," he barked, and sure enough the door swung open a foot.

He shifted into a squat and, with a fatalistic exhale, dove across the gap like a swimmer from the blocks. He made it halfway, landing with a thud on his stomach on the hard tile floor. With a grunt, he slid past the corner. Unscathed but heart pounding, he crawled into the laundry room and kicked the door shut behind him with his boot. With a sigh of relief and his back against the washing machine, he scanned for Ellie and found her huddled in a little nook between the wall and the dryer, both kids crying in her lap.

"Oh my God, Chunk, you're bleeding," she said, her eyes wet and brow furrowed. "Are you . . . ?"

"I'm not shot," he said, flashing her the best smile he could muster under the circumstances. "Just a little cut from the glass." He was up on a knee now and held up a finger. "Mother, One—I have all three packages and they are undamaged."

"Copy. We have a QRF en route from the convention

center. ETA: ten minutes. Recommend you shelter in place," she said.

"Check," he said. He looked at Ellie, unable to imagine what to say to make the situation better or easier.

"Help is coming," he said. "We're going to shelter here until they arrive."

She nodded, pulling her kids in tighter on her lap. "What about Nick? Is he . . ."

"Saw's fine," Chunk said, praying that was still true. "He's the reason we're all still alive. He's out there, doing what he does—saving the day."

She nodded and wiped tears from her chin on her shoulder.

"One, Mother—we might have a problem. I hold an unmarked panel van driving down Delaware Avenue. It's not one of ours," Watts said in his ear.

Fresh adrenaline flooded his bloodstream, but he did his damnedest to keep his expression neutral as he looked at Ellie.

"What's happening?" she said, her mother's intuition apparently seeing through him instantly.

"Ellie, I can't stay in here with you. I need to set up a defensive position outside, just in case," he said.

"One, Mother—the van is stopping in front of the house," Watts said.

"Check," he said into his mike, then to Ellie added, "I'm going to leave you my pistol."

"Keep it. There's a gun safe in the corner," she said, directing Chunk's gaze to the low black safe in the opposite corner. "I know how to handle myself."

He suddenly remembered Saw telling him that he'd taught Ellie how to defend their home, since he was away deployed over 50 percent of the year.

"Perfect. So listen to me—even if you hear gunfire, I want

you to stay put. Do *not* come out of this room under any circumstances. Stay hidden behind the dryer like you are, but if anyone tries to come in that isn't me or Saw, shoot them."

"Don't worry," she said, fire in her eyes as she hugged her children tightly. "I will."

She kissed her young son who looked up at her and sniffled.

"Where's my daddy, Uncle Keith?" Connor said, tears streaming down his cheeks.

"He's coming, buddy," Chunk said.

"Is he going to kill the bad guys first?"

"Yes, son," Chunk said.

"Good," little Connor said, and Chunk saw a flash of something, something visceral and passionate, that made the boy look like a miniature version of his dad for just a moment. Ellie was already on her knees in front of the safe, punching a combination into the keypad.

"One, Mother—I hold four thermals inside the van, and they're armed. Get ready," Watts said, her voice as tense as he'd ever heard it.

"Copy," he said and locked eyes with Ellie. "This will all be over in a few minutes."

"Hurry back," she said, now clutching a weapon.

He nodded and closed the laundry room door behind him, ready to lay down his life for the wife and two children that he'd sworn to protect.

CHAPTER 53

Al-Masri glanced down at his dead spotter and resisted the urge to curse.

Even in this moment of tremendous stress, he refused to soil himself in the eyes of Allah. If he were to die today, he wanted his soul as clean as possible. Bad enough he'd missed the call to Asr Salat and his final *wudu*. He knew Allah and the Prophet understood the reason why, but he wanted to be clean when he entered paradise.

The Navy SEAL operator he'd missed in the backyard was now inside the house, undoubtedly protecting the family. The Navy SEAL sniper, who he'd also missed, was still out there, but where that man had gone was a mystery. Most likely, his opponent was repositioning, but without a spotter there was a chance he'd missed it during his scans.

I am Juba, al-Masri reminded himself, *the greatest Iraqi sniper to ever live and I will . . . not . . . lose.*

Movement outside caught his attention, and he swiveled his scope to watch an unmarked panel van with his jihadi brothers inside brake to a stop. This van was meant to be his exfil, or in the event things went badly, his backup.

His mobile phone rang. Grudgingly, he uncoupled himself from his rifle, slid off the dresser, and took the call.

"Juba," he said.

"Your instructions?" the voice on the line said.

"In one minute take the house," he said. "Kill everyone inside."

"It will be done. God is great," the voice said, and the line went dead.

Juba started to pocket his mobile phone, then thought a moment. The likelihood of surviving what remained of his personal jihad seemed low indeed, and his gaze flicked to the tablet computer lying on the ground next to the body of his dead apprentice. The screen was livestreaming video from multiple cameras on the remote-controlled fifty-caliber machine gun. The weapon, having expended all of its ammunition, was now inert but the Americans had not raided the hotel room yet and taken it offline. The bombers and shooters attacking the convention center in the cause of jihad were most certainly dead and martyred by now, overwhelmed by the security and FBI presence.

But the game is not over yet, he thought and picked up the tablet. The device linked to the robotic weapon but contained no other information or communication software that could be traced. But the phone . . .

He moved to the rear bedroom of the house, his eyes darting about, looking for the perfect place. Finding none, he dropped the phone to the wood tile floor, crushed it with his heel, grinding it into the floor. Then he cracked the window at the rear of the house and let the ruined phone slide down the Spanish tile, ending in the deep gutter where it disappeared into the leaves and dirt.

Satisfied he had hidden the only link to his command and control, he shouldered the Chuvakin and quickly relocated to the upstairs bathroom which, via the small window over the toilet, gave him another line on the house across the street. He set the tablet on top of the toilet's water tank and, grunting, stepped onto the rim of the bathtub. He dug his left foot into the corner of the tub, keeping himself steady with the back of his right shoulder pressed into the wall beneath the showerhead. Set back from the window, his view was somewhat limited, but he was not out of the game. He raised the sniper rifle, and using the slow, whistling breathing technique taught to him so many years ago by his Russian mentor, he scanned for the American sniper.

Through the scope, he saw nothing. No movement. No shadows marking the position of his foe. This American was good, but he had to be out there somewhere. He scanned a neighboring single-story house—a much less suitable hide, with its lack of elevation.

Which the American might trade for stealth . . . a trick he already tried once.

When two snipers battled, the winner would likely be determined by an advantage measured only in seconds, or even milliseconds. Now it was simply a matter of who got a scope on the other first.

Slowly, meticulously, he moved his reticle across the landscape of homes, anticipation building as he waited for a soft clue as to the location of his adversary. If he didn't find him in the next few seconds, the American sniper would cut down his assaulters in their tracks as they moved in for the breach.

And then the entire operation—my final jihad—will have been a failure.

He forced the negative thought away before it could sabotage his pulse rate and unsteady his respirations, knowing that would spoil his shot.

Still nothing.

Where are you?

Movement outside grabbed his attention, and he watched the team of assaulters exit the van and sprint toward the house. He observed carefully, waiting for the first of his brothers to fall from a head shot that he could use to deduce the firing angle and find the American shooter, but the shot never came.

Hmm . . . odd.

He watched the fighters split, two heading to the front door to breach and the other pair circling to the rear. Baffled, he pulled his eye off the scope and scanned the street with his naked eye. Movement on the tablet screen facing him caught his attention and he shifted his gaze. In the video feed window showing the inside of the hotel room, he saw four American operators clearing the suite, sighting over their assault rifles.

Maligned excitement surged in his chest as he remembered his dead acolyte's words: *I can't believe they haven't found the gun yet. I can't wait to blow them up when they do.*

He climbed down off the tub to grab the tablet, intent on sending the Americans straight to hell . . . if only he could figure out how to detonate the bomb remotely. Surely there was a simple button to press. Why did they make technology so difficult?

A floorboard creaked and his heart skipped a beat.

An American voice, speaking Arabic in a flat whisper

barely audible over al-Masri's pounding pulse, commanded him to set down the tablet.

He froze, his mind furiously searching for a solution to this new problem. How had he, the last Juba, the true Lion of Ramadi, allowed an enemy fighter to sneak up on him? How was it that with literally hundreds of kills to his credit and never a scratch from the enemy, it should end like this?

Forgive my failure, Allah, and allow me a place in paradise . . .

He did not lower the tablet, however, and instead turned to face the man standing in the bathroom doorway.

"You came to me," he said through a breath, staring at the American sniper who stood in the hallway, holding an assault-style rifle, muzzle pointed at his face. "A tactic I didn't see coming."

The bearded killer stared back at him—through him almost—fire burning in the man's eyes. "I said put down the tablet," the American said, this time in English.

Through the open window behind him, gunfire echoed outside, and he smiled at the sound of his fellow warriors attacking the target house. Soon, this man's family would be dead and, despite not firing the kill shots himself, Juba would be victorious today.

"Your family is going to die," he said and turned the tablet to show the American sniper. "And so are your brothers."

Time slowed as he turned the screen back around, certain that Allah would reveal the secret of the computer program—a button he could press to detonate the bomb.

But instead, light flashed from the muzzle of the American's assault rifle.

His head exploded with pain and his life ended . . .

The same way he'd ended the lives of so many others.

CHAPTER 54

SAWYER HOME

DELAWARE AVENUE

HYDE PARK NEIGHBORHOOD

TAMPA, FLORIDA

Chunk crouched in the short hallway outside the laundry room, debating how to best defend the precious people sheltering behind him. Until Saw dispatched the terrorist sniper across the street, he was in a real jam. Ideally, it would be best to be back in the kitchen, but he'd already played Russian roulette crossing the gap once.

Dare he try again?

"Two assaulters breaching the front—two more circling to the rear," said Watts in his ear.

Machine-gun fire drowned out whatever she said next, as an onslaught of bullets blew out the front picture windows. Chunk was overcome with dread that the indiscriminate fire would punch through the walls and hit Ellie or the kids, but he couldn't worry about that now. Based on Watts's last update and the timing of the gunfire, he deduced the front assaulters hadn't waited for their teammates to get set before breaching. With only seconds to work with, he surged forward, despite knowing that would take him across the field of crossfire. He leaned into his rifle as he came to the corner, swiveled, and blind strafed the front door. Over the next few milliseconds, his brain processed the tactical picture, and he went to work, systematically placing his holographic red dot onto the chest of the lead breacher.

He squeezed the trigger, dropped the terrorist with a head shot, and jinked right.

The second shooter behind the man he'd just shot let loose a burst of fully automatic machine-gun fire, which licked across the floor beside Chunk and up the wall behind him. Chunk held his ground, the wild, undisciplined look in the killer's eyes matching the wild, undisciplined volley. Chunk returned fire, his single bullet vaporizing the man's left ear. The man screamed, dropping his subcompact machine pistol, and raised both hands to cradle his ear, eyes wide in terror. Chunk's second 5.56 round hit the man center mass, dropping him with a thud.

With no time to spare, he whirled back toward the kitchen to engage the rear breachers. His instincts were accurate, as both shooters breached the floor-to-ceiling gap where the patio slider door had once been. The lead shooter moved left, clearing a like a pro; the second followed close behind, already targeting Chunk with his short barrel assault rifle.

Chunk, whose aim was already fixed on the lead assaulter, squeezed the trigger a split second after the throaty roar of the second shooter's rifle hit his ears. He felt the excruciating thud of a 7.62 round slamming into the ceramic SAPI plate in the front of his kit. The SAPI plate saved his life, but the impact caused Chunk's shot to pull down and to the right, hitting the first shooter in the hip instead of center mass. As he fell, Chunk moved his red dot onto the lead fighter's head and squeezed twice more. The top of the man's head erupted like a fountain, painting an oversize canvas photo of Saw and his family with a sick pattern of red and gray.

Chunk hit the ground hard and rolled right.

He tried to swing his rifle back toward the last breacher, but instead of completing the arc, his rifle sling hung up on something and the barrel stopped short. The surging assaulter pounced on top of him, his full weight knocking the air from Chunk's lungs. The back of Chunk's head hit the tile floor— hard—and his vision filled with stars. During that millisecond of disorientation, the burly jihadist clamped both hands around Chunk's throat and went to work, compressing his windpipe and instantly cutting off blood flow to the brain.

Chunk's head went swimmy, and his vision washed out and turned gray. Reflexively, he reached for the pistol holstered on his right hip, but the man's legs were locked around Chunk's lower chest, blocking access. Black shadows began to consume the light until all he could see was the man's snarling mouth above him.

Relying entirely on muscle memory, his right hand found the hilt of the combat knife in the leather scabbard on the front of his kit. He pulled the blade, grunted, and rammed the point upward between the man's arms into the V under the assailant's jaw. A carnal scream filled his muffled ears. Hot blood soaked the back of Chunk's hand and his arm as the jihadi's grip on his throat released.

The shadows in Chunk's vision receded, as blood surged into his oxygen-starved brain. He tucked his chin and reached up with his gloved left hand to grab the man's long hair. Clutching a fistful, he pulled down with all his might, wrenching the man's forehead to his own chest. With methodical precision, he swung the blade around the back of the man's head and plunged it into the notch at the base of the skull, puncturing the terrorist's brain stem and severing the connection between brain and body.

The burly assaulter instantly went limp and collapsed on top of him like a bag of wet cement. Chunk lay there, the dead man on his chest, while he sucked in desperate slurps of oxygen-rich air. As his foggy mind cleared and his senses returned, he heard a wheezy, rasping breath and the shuffling of feet.

And in that dread-filled moment, he realized his mistake.

CHAPTER 55

Chunk heaved the dead man off his chest and rolled to his right, spinning up into a kneeling position. He drew the compact Sig P365 SAS from the holster on his hip, but when he looked up, he found himself staring into the muzzle of a machine pistol held by a bearded assaulter with only one ear. A snarling smile twisted the terrorist's face. Time slowed, but he didn't need a calculator to do the math. His own pistol was still coming up . . . the assaulter needed only to squeeze the trigger.

I'm sorry, brother, Chunk thought in that final moment. He'd promised Saw that he would keep Ellie and the kids safe, but in the end, he'd failed.

He squeezed his eyes shut to the deafening roar of a rifle.

But no bullets tore through his chest. No burning pain went through his body. He didn't see a white light, nor was he transported away to wherever warriors went in the next life.

He opened his eyes.

The jihadist lay dead on the floor, facedown in a pool of his own blood and brains. Behind the dead terrorist, Ellie stood in a perfect combat crouch, knees bent, leaning forward into a short barrel MCX Rattler. Behind the rising tendril of blue smoke, he saw tears streaming down her face.

Her shoulders sagged and she began to sob. "Is he . . . is he . . ."

"Yes," Chunk said, getting to his feet. "You did good, Ellie. Real good."

Reflexively, he kicked the terrorist's submachine gun away from the dead man's hands, scanning over his pistol behind Elle as he did. Then he spun the other way, clearing behind him and sweeping the backyard just in case.

He heard the clatter of Ellie's Rattler hitting the floor.

"Mommy," Connor cried as the four-year-old wrapped his arms around her leg, his baby sister clutching his small waist. Ellie scooped them both up and backed into the kitchen. Chunk started to follow her, when a dark shape leaped into the living room through the blown-out picture window. He whirled on the intruder, aiming his pistol center mass at the armed figure breaching the house.

Saw locked eyes with Chunk over the sights of his assault rifle, then lowered the weapon as Chunk did the same. Tears spilled out of the SEAL sniper's eyes and onto his blood-smeared cheeks, streaming down to where the blood had caked in his beard. Chunk saw that Saw's shirt was soaked completely through with blood from a nasty laceration on his neck that would need some attention.

"Mother, One—target secured," Chunk radioed in.

"Ellie?" Saw said, fear and pain in his eyes. "The kids?"

Chunk smiled. "They're in the kitchen."

The SEAL sniper's shoulders dropped, then shook with

emotional release. He locked eyes with Chunk again. "I don't have the words, man."

Chunk nodded, his lips pressed together in a tight smile. "They're waiting for you," he said, tilting his head toward the kitchen. "Go."

He followed his brother into the kitchen and watched as Saw swept his entire family into his powerful arms, all of them sobbing as they clung to each other. Chunk stood beside them, hypervigilant, still scanning the X.

"Oh my God, Nick," Ellie sobbed as she pulled back and touched her husband's face. "Are you okay? You're wounded. You're really bleeding, baby."

"It's nothing, baby. It's just a scratch. I'm fine." He pulled her in again, tight to his chest. "I gotcha now."

It suddenly occurred to Chunk that Ellie had never seen the wounds her husband had borne over the years—at least not when they were fresh. Chunk was used to seeing his brother bruised and bloodied, but family members only saw clean, dressed, post-trauma battle scars. For Ellie, seeing the love of her life caked in blood and their family home transformed into a war zone . . . Chunk could only imagine the thoughts and emotions running through her head.

His own thoughts drifted to a conversation he'd had with Saw what felt like an eternity ago, but he knew was really measured in days. A conversation where he'd let his brother know that the team needed him, that the Navy and the nation needed him, that to stop the evil in the world he needed Saw on the long gun up in his perch. But in his heart, Chunk now recognized that he'd been selfish that day. He'd appealed to Saw's sense of higher purpose, but it had also been *him*, Chunk, who'd needed Senior Chief Special Operator Nicholas Sawyer. He'd needed him because how could he effectively lead Gold Squadron and execute Tier One level missions without his best shooter? He watched Saw's wife cling to him, his children wrapped around his legs, and Chunk closed his eyes in soul-wringing epiphany. Chunk, Gold, the Tier One, and the Navy were not, in fact, the people who needed his friend the most.

The children had stopped crying, and he heard only urgent whispers of love and comfort and healing.

How did Saw do it? How did he balance two families—the wife and kids he loved so desperately and the brotherhood he loved just as much, but oh so differently? How did he abandon one for the other, over and over and over again? And how powerful must be the calling he felt, that he could kit up and leave Ellie and the kids behind, knowing that *this time* might be the time he didn't come back?

Because Saw is stronger than me . . . I couldn't make that choice. That's why the brotherhood is my family. It's why I've made sure no romance ever advances past the fun stage. With commitment comes dependency . . .

He let out a slow, raspy breath and felt suddenly depleted.

"Blue One is up on channel two. Coming in the front," his counterpart, Commander Malkin of Blue Squadron, called in Chunk's ear.

"Gold One and Three are inside," Chunk said, snapping back into mission mode. "House is secure."

The front door opened, and the QRF operators poured in, weapons at the ready and boots pounding. Chunk greeted Malkin and the other SEALs with a raised hand. An instant later he was surrounded by brothers—a hand slapping his back, someone else bear-hugging him from behind—and he finally felt catharsis set in.

"We need to get Saw's family out of here," he said to Malkin. "I want them secure on base ASAP. And we need to mobilize a communications tree to the rest of the unit who live off base. We need one hundred percent accountability of everyone and all family members. Once we're secure on compound we'll decide what to do next."

"Agreed," Malkin said.

"We're on it already, Gold and Blue One," Watts replied in his ear, and Chunk relaxed ever so slightly.

"Sitrep?" he said, his mind going to the convention center.

"The convention center is secure. Gold Two and Four secured the heavy sniper at the Marriott hotel," Watts said, referring to Riker and Trip. "Turns out the room was empty. Juba set up a remote-controlled fifty-cal unit."

"A robo-shooter?"

"Yes, and the base of the unit is rigged to blow, so the hotel has been evacuated and EOD is en route to disarm the thing."

Chunk smiled and shook his head, hearing that Riker had narrowly escaped yet another brush with certain death. He looked into the kitchen, at the Sawyer family clinging desperately to one another, and wondered how anything could ever be the same for them. With this attack, al Qadar had changed the rules of the game and brought the fight home, targeting the beating heart of the SEAL team family.

What did that mean for Saw going forward?

What did that mean for the Tier One?

What did that mean for him?

Malkin clapped a hand on Chunk's shoulder. "C'mon, let's get out of here, bro."

Chunk nodded and told himself those were questions he'd have to reckon with, but not right now.

Tomorrow, he decided and bent to pick up the Rattler machine gun that Ellie had saved his life with. *I'll answer the hard questions tomorrow.*

CHAPTER 56

TOP SECRET JOINT SPECIAL OPERATIONS TASK FORCE
    COMPOUND
THIRTY-FIVE MILES NORTH OF THE AFGHANISTAN BORDER
QURGHONTEPPA, TAJIKISTAN
NINE DAYS LATER
0545 LOCAL TIME

Chunk pushed through the wooden door feeling more pensive than ever. It wasn't that Saw was still in Tampa with Ellie and the kids, it wasn't that JSOC had sequestered all the Tier One families, or that WARCOM was drafting new security protocols for all of Naval Special Warfare. It wasn't even that they were moving more slowly than he had hoped to hunt down what remained of the al Qadar network . . . No, his dysthymia was related to things inside him, the things that drove him and defined him at the most fundamental level.

Leadership, brotherhood, and the nature of his true calling.

He'd been thinking about fundamentals a lot lately.

He stopped and knocked on the door to Watts's Batcave, which stood partially opened and swung open farther in response.

"Watts, you in here?"

He hadn't been able to call her "Heels" since they'd returned for some reason. It was as if the joy he usually felt downrange working with his team was hiding from him. She didn't answer, and he stuck his head through the doorway, scanning the case wall beside her small desk which was still covered with pictures, maps, screenshots, and handwritten notes. In the center were two pictures of Asadi Bijan, under which she had recently written "Hamza," the more recent picture with a big red *X* across the face.

He pulled the door closed and headed to the tiny intel office one door down, but no one answered when he knocked there either.

Where's my N2 shop?

Feeling frustrated but without good reason, he clomped back down the hallway, intent on checking the TOC again and asking Riker if he knew where Watts had run off to. He plowed through the door and nearly bowled over Yi.

"Oh, shit. Sorry, Yi," he said, stepping right to keep from knocking her to the ground.

"No worries, boss," she said, smiling. "Looks like you're in a hurry. Something going on I should know about?"

"Nah," he said. "Just looking for Watts."

"She's at the range with Riker." Yi jerked a thumb over her shoulder.

Chunk's eyes widened. "The range? You're kidding me."

"No, she goes every day, since Tampa. Says it helps her think."

"Thanks, Chief," he said, acknowledging her recent promotion with a wink.

As he walked toward the back of the compound, he caught himself scowling. When did he lose touch with his team? A month ago, he would have known Watts was going to the range every day, would have understood why, and would have teased her mercilessly about it. Hell, a month ago, it would have been him training her.

Am I that jacked up because Saw's not here?

He walked out the back gate, past the gym, past the makeshift fire pit Riker had built, toward the *pop . . . pop . . . pop* of rifle fire. Adjusting the worn ball cap on his head, he rounded the corner of the simple wooden shack where the operators cleaned their weapons after using the range. Just beyond, Riker stood, hands on his hips, watching Watts plink targets. She was lying prone on the ground, of all things, firing her Sig MCX at the targets seventy-five yards beyond. Each pop was followed by a satisfying *clink* as her rounds impacted the steel targets Riker had set up.

"Hey, boss," Riker said as Chunk stepped beside him.

"Looks like you got her dialed in."

"Nah, she's got herself dialed," he said with a single shake of the head. "I'm just enjoying the show."

"Why don't you take a break. I got this," Chunk said.

Riker grinned, taking the hint, and wandered off toward the weapon cleaning tables behind them.

"Oh, hey, Chunk," Watts said after popping off another round. She moved to get up, but he held a hand up, stopping her.

"Finish your magazine," he said.

She smiled, pressed back into the stock of her rifle, and popped off seven more rounds, all but one followed by the lovely *clink* designed to give rookie shooters the instant feedback that they were at least hitting the target. As soon as her magazine was empty, she was on her feet beside him, weapon secure on her chest.

"Everything okay?" she asked, concern on her face. "Something going on I need to know about?"

"Nope," he said.

In fact, nothing was going on . . . too much nothing. Gold Squadron had been outside the wire exactly zero times since they'd returned from Tampa.

She nodded. "Well, quiet can be good too, I guess."

"It never stays quiet long," he said. "JSOC has some new tasking coming soon, or so Bowman hinted last time we spoke."

"Cool," she said, but watched him carefully—studying him he thought—as they walked to the cleaning shack. Riker already had his bag over his shoulder.

"See you guys back there," he said and gave Watts a nod. "Great job, Heels. Getting better every time."

"Thanks," she said, unable to suppress a grin. She took a seat at the wooden bench to clean her weapon while Chunk slid onto the bench across from her. "How are Saw and Ellie doing? Have you heard from him?"

"Yeah, I spoke with him early this morning," Chunk said, the question irritating him for some reason. "They're in base housing now and thinking about renting out the house now that repairs are finished. Connor and Maggie are going to preschool on MacDill, and Ellie's still on leave from her job. Saw is keeping busy, helping with Green Team training and the like."

"Yeah, but how are they doing?" she asked, looking at him like he had a horn growing out of his head.

"I don't know," he grumbled. "Good as can be expected, I guess."

"Is Saw coming back?"

Of course, he's coming back! he wanted to snap, but instead erred toward the more benign and said, "Once the family is settled into a routine, I told him he can join us for the remainder of the deployment if he wants, or he can hang back with his family. Whatever he needs to do."

"Sure," she said, wiping down her rifle and beginning to place a few drops of oil where needed. Her tone suggested they both knew that wasn't what she meant, but she'd become pretty good at reading his moods and seemed to understand he wasn't looking for her counseling or approval.

"So, what have you got cooking? Have you and Yi ferreted out anything new on the al Qadar front?"

She snapped the rear of the lower and upper receivers back together, pressed the locking pin into place, then cycled the weapon. Still not answering his question, she inserted a fresh magazine, advanced a round, and set the short rifle on the table.

"So, you know that everyone has basically cleared Qasim Nadar, right?" she finally said, leaning in on her forearms. "MI5—or the joint CT task force at least—will continue to 'monitor' him, whatever that means. But I think the task force chief, McLean, totally buys Nadar's story. In the aftermath, it's going to be harder for him to justify surveilling Nadar."

"What do you mean?"

"After Dubai, the British tabloids took his story and ran. They made him a hero for not getting shot. He's now a poster child for cultural diversity, a real immigration Cinderella story. On top of that, he got a big promotion at British Aero. Put those two things together, and Qasim Nadar has some sway now. People care what he has to say."

"What about the agent runner, Kim?" Chunk asked. "Is she buying it?"

"I think Lucy is in my camp on this one. Last time we talked, she was still bent on trying to recruit the wife. We'll see where it goes."

A comfortable silence lingered between them a moment, and Chunk decided to play devil's advocate. "We confirmed that Asadi Bijan was the real Hamza al-Saud. The Tampa attack was his last hoorah, executed with him in the grave. The Juba snipers are all either dead or incarcerated; the al Qadar network is defunct. Why not leave Nadar alone?"

She looked up from staring at the trefoil knot on her wrist, but she seemed to resist the urge to trace her finger over it as she often did.

"Counterterrorism is like a mathematical proof," she said. "We've got all these equations that we need to balance in order to solve the problem. As long as you still have variables you haven't solved for, the proof is incomplete. Nadar is the unknown variable in the al Qadar equations. I haven't been able to solve for him yet, but I will. Just because everyone else is giving up, doesn't mean I should."

"How do you do it?" he asked, intensely curious how she would answer.

"Do what?"

"Maintain your conviction that you're right even when all the evidence seems to point to the opposite? How do you defeat the self-doubt?"

"I remind myself that I chose this job, it didn't choose me. I think sometimes we try to tell ourselves that the opposite is true, but that is not a self-empowering paradigm. We're not slaves to fate. I'm here because I want to be here. I'm here because I want to catch guys like Hamza al-Saud. I want to outsmart them. I want to beat them. I know what I'm about to say might not fit your SEAL ethos of patriotism and brotherhood, but I'm here for me. Yes, I serve for my nation. Yes, I want to make you and my teammates proud. But make no mistake, I'm here because I want to be here."

"Spoken like a true millennial," he said before he could stop himself.

"And what's that supposed to mean?" she said, her expression hardening.

"You just said your service is all about you," he said with a defensive chuckle. "Me, me, me . . . That's the millennial battle cry, is it not?"

"As opposed to what, the boomer belief that for service to matter it has to be a sacrifice? That serving one's country is a cross to bear, and when that tour of service is over it's time to suffer in silence? Gimme a break. Why should my service be deemed any less important because I don't look at it as a penance? Why should my service be judged as less meaningful because it's a job I actually want to do? Leadership looks at my generation and thinks we're somehow less worthy because we don't drone on and on about all the sacrifices we're making in the name of God and country. Tell me, Chunk, why does service have to be a sacrifice?"

He stared at her, mesmerized. "That's a very good question . . ."

"I look at people with that mentality, and I think to myself, *Those poor fools. What a wasted life.* That's not the way I want to live my life. I want my passion and my purpose to be aligned. If they're not, what good am I to anybody—professionally, or even psychologically for that matter?" She pursed her lips and fixed her gaze on him. "I always thought you and I were cut from the same mold on this . . . Was I wrong?"

"No," he said simply. She wasn't wrong. He was a SEAL, first and foremost, because he loved being a SEAL. Nobody had forced him to join. He wasn't here out of guilt, or to please his parents, or because of some pathological sense of duty. Like her, he was here because he wanted to be here. And now that she'd spelled it out for him, he realized that there was a fundamental difference in the perception of service between her generation and the boomers, and he was stuck in the middle.

"Really, that's all you've got to say on the matter?"

"I think there's a lot to unpack in what you said. But more importantly, you reminded me of something I used to know about myself, but seemed to have forgotten recently." Then, suddenly starting to feel like his old self again, he flashed her a crooked grin. "And thank God too, because I was afraid you were going to lecture me about the universal fine constant or some math shit, in which case I'd be screwed."

She shook her head. "You can be such a dick, you know that?"

"So I've been told." He rose from the bench and folded his arms. "Thanks, Watts."

"For what?"

"For doing what you do." That was only half of what he wanted to tell her, but he wasn't quite there yet. "See you at the intel brief this afternoon."

When he was a few paces away, she called after him, "Hey, Chunk?"

He stopped and turned, aware his arms were still folded defensively on his chest. "Yeah?"

"It's going to be okay," she said looking deep into him. "Whether Saw comes back or not . . . it's all going to be okay."

"I know," he said with a tight smile and, for the first time in two months, decided that she just might be right.

EPILOGUE

Diba stuck the little white plastic stick between her thighs and peed on it. She'd gone over the First Response pregnancy test instructions three times and even typed them into Google translate so she could read them in Pashto, just to make sure she didn't mess it up. It was quite simple: urinate on the absorbent tip, wait three minutes, and then check the results window. One or two ink lines would tell her what the future held. After finishing, she shook the plastic wand dry over the toilet bowl and set it down on a piece of folded toilet paper she'd laid out on the counter next to the bathroom sink.

Then, she waited.

She paced nervously in the tiny bathroom, stopping every few seconds to look at the results window before flipping the test upside down so as not to torture herself.

You have to give it time, she told herself.

After what felt like an epoch of the Earth, the requisite three minutes had finally passed and she flipped the stick over. Inside the little oval window, she saw one bright-pink line and the shadow of a second pink line materializing. Her heart fluttered and her knees suddenly went to jelly, forcing her to sit cross-legged on the tile floor.

"I think I'm pregnant," she muttered, not sure whether to feel joyful or terrified.

Was it possible to feel two such contradictory reactions at the same time?

Trembling with emotion, she inhaled deeply through her nose and exhaled through her mouth—once, twice, three times—trying to get control of herself.

Maybe it is a false positive? The kit came with two sticks. *I should test again.*

Resigned to this idea, she got to her feet and opened the wrapper for the second test stick. She stepped toward the toilet and then realized that she'd completely voided her bladder and couldn't pee right now even if she wanted to. Frowning, she turned back to the vanity and looked at the used test again.

Is it my imagination or is the second pink line even a little darker now?

She blew air through pursed lips and looked at herself in the bathroom mirror. She was four days late, and she'd never missed a period before. Despite all the change and unpredictability in her life over the past ten years, the one reliable constant had always been her biological clock.

"I'll try again in a half an hour," she said and walked out of the bathroom.

She thought about going for a walk outside but decided to wander their flat instead. She didn't feel like changing clothes.

She didn't feel like being seen. In the kitchen, she poured herself a glass of water and sipped at it while she paced, contemplating Qasim's reaction to the news.

At first, he will be shocked. Then he will be happy. And finally, he will become angry . . .

This would be his reaction.

I know my husband well.

Tears threatening, she rushed back to the bathroom. In a frenzy, she hid both the used and unused test sticks and disposed of all evidence—the wrappers, cardboard box, and paper instructions going into a trash bag, which she buried at the bottom of the main rubbish bin on the back patio. No need to rush things. She still had plenty of time. Qasim didn't keep track of her cycle. He abhorred any and all talk of menstruation.

Besides, I need to take a second test. This could be a false positive. I'll wait two more days and try again.

The sound of the front door unlocking made her jump. She looked at the digital clock on the microwave in the kitchen which read: 4:18 p.m.

Why is he home so early? He never comes home early.

Today was his first day back to work since returning from the tragic events in Dubai. The terrorist attack had made the world news, and as one of the targeted companies who'd suffered casualties, British Aero was now at the center of a massive global counterterrorism investigation. Since his return, Qasim had been tight-lipped about the incident, sharing nothing with her other than insisting that he had absolutely nothing to do with it.

She wasn't so certain she believed him.

The front door swung open and her husband stepped into the little foyer. He looked haggard and grim and didn't even bother greeting her. He'd not been sleeping well since Dubai. She'd awoken many a night lately to find him missing from bed and either pacing the living room or reading the Quran at the kitchen table.

"You're home early today," she said, putting on a smile.

"It was not a productive day. People are still very upset," he said, kicking off his shoes and walking past her toward the bathroom.

"I'll make chai," she said to his back as he shut the door on her.

She set out the tea service and some biscuits on their modest dining table. He joined her a few minutes later, inhaling deeply when he entered the kitchen.

"Is that the chai I bought from the Afghan import shop?"

"Yes," she said, pouring him a cup and sweetening it with a pour of simple syrup.

"It is very good," he said, accepting the cup from her. "It tastes of home."

She nodded and fixed herself a cup. They drank in silence for several minutes, but she could tell that much weighed on his mind. Recently, she'd stopped pressing him to communicate as it seemed to have the opposite of the desired effect. Patiently, respectfully, demurely . . . she waited for him to address her when he was ready.

Abruptly, he stood and walked out of the kitchen, only to return a minute later with a pad of paper and a pencil. He sat back down in his seat and began to write in rapid, controlled strokes. After finishing a line, he turned the pad and pencil toward her. She looked at the top sheet and then up at him. He nodded at her—or maybe at the paper, she couldn't be sure which—but the meaning was clear: *read it.*

She scanned his meticulous Pashto, each character drawn

with an engineer's precision. What he'd written made her heart skip a beat.

ARE YOU COMMITTED TO ME, YOUR HUSBAND, ABOVE ALL ELSE?

She looked up at him and opened her mouth to answer but he cut her off with a raised hand, tapping the pad of paper, the message clear: *write it down . . .*

She nodded. With uncertain fingers, she picked up the pencil and wrote, *Yes, my love, above all others.*

She pushed the pad back to him and the back and forth note writing began:

CHALLENGING TIMES LIE AHEAD FOR ME. I NEED YOU, NOW MORE THAN EVER.

I will support you and all your needs.

IT COULD BECOME DANGEROUS HERE FOR US. WE MIGHT HAVE TO LEAVE ENGLAND AT A MOMENT'S NOTICE. I WANT YOU TO PREPARE A BACKPACK WITH A CHANGE OF CLOTHES, A BURQA, AND TOILETRY ITEMS. EVERYTHING YOU NEED TO TRAVEL AND WALK AWAY FROM THIS LIFE.

A lump formed in her throat as she read the instruction. She knew what she should write, what he *expected* her to write, but her fingers danced with disobedience.

I don't understand? I don't want to leave England. I like it here.

She pushed the pad back to him and watched her reply instantly redden his cheeks. He penciled his rebuke in fast, hard strokes. He showed her the pad, but did not pass it to her.

YOU WILL DO AS I COMMAND.

She lowered her gaze and nodded, accepting the rebuke, and then waited while he wrote more. What he handed her next shook her to the core.

IT IS ONLY A MATTER OF TIME UNTIL THEY COME FOR ME. I WILL NEED YOUR COUNSEL AND SUPPORT IN THE

COMING MONTHS. I HAVE NO ONE ELSE I CAN TRUST. NO ONE ELSE TO TALK TO, AND I CANNOT SHOULDER THIS BURDEN ALONE ANYMORE.

She looked up at him and saw that his lower lip quivered. She felt her heart soften for him, reached out a hand, and squeezed his arm. He smiled at her tightly. She picked up the pencil again.

What about Hamza?

This question prompted his gaze to go distant and a sad smile to curl his lips.

I AM HAMZA NOW, he wrote.

She took the pad. *I don't understand. What does that mean, Qasim?*

He breathed a heavy exhale and replied: HAMZA IS DEAD. I WILL SHOULDER HIS LEGACY AND CONTINUE HIS WORK.

She grabbed the pencil to write her response, but he ripped the top sheet off the pad and walked over to the stove. He lit one of the gas burners, lit the corner of the page on fire, and tossed it into an empty skillet where he watched it burn to ash. When he turned back to her, they locked eyes.

She bowed her head to him—understanding, assent, and subservience all rolled into one simple gesture. He nodded his acceptance and extended his hand to her. When she took it, he led her to their bedroom. As he stripped her of her clothes, her mind went to the nascent life that had just taken root inside her.

I'm carrying the child of a terrorist, she thought. *What kind of mother will that make me?*

And as he lay her down on their marriage bed and kissed her breasts, she began an inventory of what she would pack in the backpack he'd instructed her to prepare. For she now understood that she *would* be leaving this flat in great haste, with great urgency, and under circumstances in which her life, and the life of her unborn child, would most certainly depend on it.

But whether she would leave with Qasim clutching her hand or chasing her tail . . .

Only fate knew the answer to that question.

ACKNOWLEDGMENTS

There is no one in publishing more committed, more passionate, and more imaginative than our team at Blackstone. You helped bring this book to fruition—for your insights, hard work, and creativity we thank you from the bottom of our hearts! A special thanks goes out to Rick Bleiweiss, who patiently and thoughtfully cares for our work. And to Josh Stanton, who welcomed us into the Blackstone family of authors, and for his tireless genius which helped make him *The Strand Magazine*'s 2021 Publisher of the Year!

Thank you to our wonderful families who never stop loving and supporting us on this crazy adventure.

Thank you to *you*, our loyal readers who give us the gift of embracing all our series and empowering us to write new adventures with the characters we love.

And thank you to those still out there—working and serving at the pointy tip of the spear, who inspire all that we do—and their loving families who wait anxiously for them back home.

—Brian Andrews & Jeff Wilson

GLOSSARY

AAI Ansar al-Islam

AMR Anti-Material Rifle

AQ al-Qaeda

BDU Battle Dress Uniform

BUD/S Basic Underwater Demolition/SEAL training

CASEVAC Casualty Evacuation

CENTCOM United States Central Command

CIA Central Intelligence Agency

CO Commanding Officer

CONUS Continental United States

CSO Chief Staff Officer

CT Counterintelligence

DIA Defense Intelligence Agency

DNI Director of National Intelligence

DoD Department of Defense

DWTC Dubai World Trade Center

Eighteen Delta Special Operations Medic

EOD Explosion Ordnance Disposal

Exfil Exfiltrate

FARP Forward Area Refueling Point; a forward staging area

FOB Forward Operating Base

GCHQ Government Communications Headquarters (United Kingdom's Signals Intelligence organization)

GID General Intelligence Directorate (Jordanian Intelligence)

GRS Global Response Staff

GSW Gunshot wound

HALO high-altitude, low opening

HRT Hostage Rescue Team

HUMINT Human Intelligence

HVT High-Value Target

IC Intelligence Community

Infil Infiltrate

IR Infrared

ISAF International Security Assistance Force in Afghanistan

ISR Intelligence, surveillance, and reconnaissance

JO Junior Officer

JSOC Joint Special Operations Command

JSOTF Joint Special Operations Task Force

KBR A government support contractor

KIA Killed in Action

LCPO Leading Chief Petty Officer

MARSOC Marine Corps Special Operations Command

MEDEVAC Medical Evacuation

MI5 British Domestic Intelligence (FBI analog)

MI6 British Foreign Intelligence (CIA analog)

NCTC National Counterterrorism Center

NCO Noncommissioned Officer

NOC Nonofficial Cover

NSA National Security Agency

NSW Naval Special Warefare

NVGs Night-vision goggles

ODNI Office of the Director of National Intelligence

OGA Other Government Agency, frequently refers to CIA or other clandestine organizations

OIC Officer in Charge

ONI Office of Naval Intelligence

OPSEC Operational Security

PJ Parajumpers; Pararesucmen of the Air Force Special Operations Command

PsyOps Psychological Operations

PTT Push to Talk; a setting on a radio requiring a button to be pushed to transmit

QRF Quick Reaction Force

RPG Rocket-Propelled Grenade

RTS Relay Tracking Station

SAPI Small Arms Protective Insert

SAS Special Air Service; British Special Operations f\Forces equivalent to Green Berets

SCIF Sensitive Compartmented Information Facility

SDV SEAL Delivery Vehicle

SEAL Sea, Air, and Land Teams; Naval Special Warfare

SecDef Secretary of Defense

SF Special Forces; refers specifically to the Army Special Operations Green Berets

SIGINT Signals Intelligence

SITREP Situation Report

SOAR Special Operations Aviation Regiment

SOCOM Special Operations Command

SOF Special Operations Forces

SOPMOD Special Operations Modification

SPACECOM United States Space Command

SQT SEAL Qualification Training

SWCC Special Warfare Combatant-craft Crewman; Boat teams supporting SEAL operations

TAD Temporary Additional Duty

TS/SCI Top Secret/Sensitive Compartmented Information; The highest level security clearance

TOC Tactical Operations Center

UAE United Arab Emirates

UCAV Unmanned Combat Aerial Vehicle

UAV Unmanned Aerial Vehicle

USN United States Navy

VOX Military jargon for Voice Acutuation, allowing radio transmission hands free

WARCOM United States Special Warfare Command

PARTNER PAGES

Andrews & Wilson actively promote and partner with veteran-owned small businesses that demonstrate a mission of giving. The organizations featured here donate to and support the health and well-being of US service members as well as their families. We encourage you to learn about and support our partners and to spread the word about the important and uplifting work that they do.

BONEFROG

A premium, small-batch coffee roastery and vineyard, owned and operated by veterans, located in the Pacific Northwest.

After serving twenty-five years in the Navy, former SEAL Tim Cruickshank created Bonefrog Coffee and Cellars as a tribute to the brotherhood of US Navy SEALs, the Naval Special Warfare community, and to all Americans who bravely served, or who are currently serving, in our United States Armed Forces. Each label they create tells a story to remind us of battles fought and great American heroes who answered the call, and proceeds from every sale support the men and families of those who served in the Naval Special Warfare community.

www.bonefrog-coffee.com
www.bonefrogcellars.com

ALL SECURE

FOUNDATION

Founded by Army veteran and retired Delta Force Tier One operator Tom Satterly and award-winning filmmaker Jen Satterly, the All Secure Foundation provides resources, education, post-traumatic stress injury resiliency training for active duty units, warrior couples workshop retreats, and family counseling for Special Operations warriors and their warrior families. They believe that every family member deserves tools to heal from war trauma and that no one is left behind on the battlefield on the home front.

Web: AllSecureFoundation.org
Contact: information@allsecurefoundation.org

COMBAT FLAGS

Founded by US Army veteran Dan Berei, Combat Flags began as an idea to connect veterans and give back in a meaningful way. Combat Flags is dedicated to helping Stop Soldier Suicide and Dan's personal mission to leave the world a better place than we found it.

In addition to the store, Dan interviews veterans and talks leadership, life lessons, and service on the Combat Flags Podcast.

www.combatflags.com

ABOUT THE AUTHORS

Brian Andrews is a US Navy veteran, Park Leadership Fellow, and former submarine officer with a psychology degree from Vanderbilt and a master's in business from Cornell University. He is the author of three critically acclaimed high-tech thrillers: *Reset*, *The Infiltration Game*, and *The Calypso Directive*.

Jeffrey Wilson has worked as an actor, firefighter, paramedic, jet pilot, and diving instructor, as well as a vascular and trauma surgeon. He served in the US Navy for fourteen years and made multiple deployments as a combat surgeon. Wilson is the author of three award-winning supernatural thrillers: *The Traiteur's Ring*, *The Donors*, and *Fade to Black*. He and his wife live in Southwest Florida with their four children.